LYNN PHILIP HODGSON
ALAN PAUL LONGFIELD

WORD OF HONOUR
CAMP 30

**THE
INSIDE CAMP X
SERIES**

BOWMANVILLE

"In October 1941, Camp No. 30 at Bowmanville, Ontario, was opened to accommodate officers and was possibly among the best accommodation ever provided in any country for this purpose.

"Though we lacked the means for comparison we were convinced that Camp 30 must have been the finest prisoner-compound in the world on either side of the fighting lines.

"If it had not been for the barbed wire, Camp 30 could have been a combined officers' academy of the German armed forces.

"Jokingly, I have often said that the one mistake I did not make was, though involuntarily and unknowingly, to become a Prisoner of War on the wrong side. I am convinced that nowhere in the world did Prisoners of War have better housing, better food, better recreation facilities, better educational opportunities, and above all, fairer treatment, than in Canada."

Eckehart J. Priebe
German Luftwaffe Pilot
Camp 30, Bowmanville

Excerpt from: *'Thank You Canada'*

Lynn Philip Hodgson, Alan Paul Longfield

Copyright ©, Blake Books Distribution, 2003
Cover Design and Page Layout
© Peter A. Graziano Limited, 2003

Editor: Barbara Kerr

Distribution by:
Blake Books Distribution
467 Fralicks Beach Road
Port Perry, Ontario
Canada, L9L 1B6
905.985.6434

lynniso@idirect.com

National Library of Canada Cataloguing in Publication

Hodgson, Lynn Philip 1946

Bowmanville - Camp 30 : word of honour /
Lynn Philip Hodgson, Alan Paul Longfield

Includes bibliographical references and index
ISBN 0-9687062-9-0 (bound).—ISBN 0-9687062-8-2 (pbk.)

1. World War, 1939-1945--Concentration camps--Ontario--
   Bowmanville.
2. Prisoners of war--Germany. 3. Prisoners of war--Canada.
   I. Longfield, Alan
   II. Title.

D805.5.B69H64 2003   C813'.6   C2003-900480-5

Design and Production
Silvio Mattacchione and Co.

Peter A. Graziano Limited
pgraziano@sympatico.ca

Printed and bound in Canada
by Friesens, Manitoba

To Bruno and Volkmar
September 2003

Table of Contents

Quote: Eckehart J. Priebe   2

Signing Page   3

CIP Data   4

Dedication   5

Table of Contents   6

In Appreciation   7

Foreword   8

■ **Chapter 1**   *Beware the Hurricanes*   12

■ **Chapter 2**   *Hot over Afrika, the Desert Winds Blow*   22

■ **Chapter 3**   *This is Where I Will Die*   40

■ **Chapter 4**   *The War Ends for Some*   58

■ **Chapter 5**   *Willkommen in Kanada!*   80

■ **Chapter 6**   *Marlene*   98

■ **Chapter 7**   *Operation Anorak*   126

■ **Chapter 8**   *The Battle of Bowmanville*   166

■ **Chapter 9**   *Operation Kartoffel*   184

■ **Chapter 10** *Finally; success*   212

■ **Chapter 11** *Clever Canadians*   240

■ **Chapter 12** *War is Hell*   252

■ **Chapter 13** *D Day at Camp 30 and Other Breaking News*   260

■ **Chapter 14** *Coming Home*   274

Interview with Volkmar König   290

My Personal Thoughts - J. B. Petrenko   294

Camp 30 - Under Construction   298

Camp 30 - Today   302

The Officer's Mess   306

Drawings Made by PoW's   308

PoW Orchestra   318

Letter from Donitz   322

Officer's Camp 30   324

Stage Plays   328

History Worth Saving   338

Subject References   346

Authors' and Editor's CV's   348

www.camp-x.com

In Appreciation

Alan Longfield and Lynn Hodgson wish to acknowledge and thank our Production Team for their superb contributions to the production of ***Camp 30 Word of Honour.***

Barbara Kerr, **Editor**; Silvio Mattachione and Peter Graziano, **Design and Production**; Rik Davie, **Technical Consultant**.

Thanks also to: Leanne Barfoot, Colin Blakelock, Fred Blakelock, Darrel Brown, Roy Cowan, Mayor Nancy Diamond (City of Oshawa), Kiel Frederiksen, Caylie Gilmore, Elizabeth Ginn, Brian Gough, Marcel Goyette, Director of Economic Development and Promotions (City of Bathurst), Larry Grasby, Barbara Habib - née Eckert (translation), Nancy Hamer Strahl, the late Bill Hardcastle, Caitlin Henderson, Marlene Hodgson, John Longfield, Judi Longfield, Michael Longfield, Klaus Richter (translation), 'Mac' McDonald, Marisa Melas, Hamish Pelham Burn, the late Harry Smith, Peter Snaith, Mike Strahl, the late Robert Stuart (The Robert Stuart Aviation and Camp-X Museum), Charles Taws, Bowmanville Museum (archives and photographs), Jane Wilson, and Brian Winter, Archivist, Town of Whitby.

Very special appreciation also to Volkmar Kônig (King) and Bruno Petrenko, both of whom provided invaluable service in generously providing access to their personal archives. To Wolfgang Arnold, thank you for the many days spent researching and translating documents at the Bowmanville Museum with Lynn Hodgson.

(**Clarington/Bowmanville Museum**, 37 Silver Street, P. O. Box 188, Bowmanville, Ontario L1C 3K9. Telephone: 905-623-2734)

And to all those who have read the ***Inside Camp-X*** series of books: you have played an important part in bringing the story of the brave Canadians who were associated with Camp-X out of the shadows.

September 2003

Foreword

Welcome to **Camp 30 Word of Honour**, the fourth in the **Inside Camp X** Series. **Camp 30 Word of Honour** is an historically-accurate account of what went on during World War II behind the barbed wire fencing of **Prisoner of War Camp 30**. Situated on the site of the former Boy's Training School in the town of Bowmanville, Ontario, Canada, **Camp 30** housed hundreds of German officers of the Luftwaffe, Wehrmacht and Kriegsmarine. Names of the leading characters have been changed to safeguard their anonymity; however, details concerning the major events, as well as the descriptions of day-to-day life at the Camp, are accurate and authentic, in the minutest detail. Great care was taken in recounting the importance of the roles played by supporting characters in key events. All are faithful in principle to the facts as known to the authors. In some cases, secondary characters have been represented as composite personae where necessitated by insufficient detail to be found in personal records or official references.

Researching and writing **Camp 30 Word of Honour** was not only the most challenging, but also the most rewarding project in the series. Of the eight hundred and eighty PoWs held at Camp 30, those who are alive today in Germany or in Canada, can be counted upon two hands. Unfortunately few of the Canadian Veteran Guards who served at the Camp could be located.

As the official record is similarly sparse, the task of researching Camp 30 would have been insurmountable was it not for the generous and unstinting assistance of two remarkable persons: **Volkmar König** (King), in Germany, and **Bruno Petrenko**, in Toronto.

Volkmar König served as a midshipman aboard the famous U-99, under the command of Korvettenkapitän Otto Kretschmer.
Bruno Petrenko, a Luftwaffe fighter pilot during the Battle of Britain, was shot down over England on his first mission. Both of these men were subsequently interned at Camp 30. Together, Volkmar and Bruno have provided us a wealth of new, historically-invaluable information.

Their memoirs include scores of never-before-published photographs and documents, enriched by their still-vivid memories of daily life as detainees. As well, each man has contributed his personal reflections regarding 'The Battle of Bowmanville', in which Volkmar was an active participant, and Bruno, an observer. Using these first-hand sources, the authors have endeavoured to portray the underlying causes and actions preceding the uprising, as well as the hour-to-hour account of the episode with realism and impartiality, from the perspective of the German PoWs, as well as that of the Canadian authorities.

Historically-accurate, meticulous descriptions of the prisoners' tunnel construction projects, from preliminary design to completion, as well as documented escape exploits by PoWs, within sight of the Veteran Guards, as masterminded by Korvettenkapitän Otto Kretschmer, are recounted in gripping detail. We accompany one such fugitive on his flight to freedom from Bowmanville to New Brunswick, on Canada's Atlantic coast.

We are honoured and indebted to Bruno and Volkmar for granting unlimited access to, as well as permission to include their wealth of print and pictorial resources in this book. In the **Afterword**, Volkmar and Bruno offer their highly personal remembrances and reflections upon their imprisonment in Canada at Camp 30.

It should be noted that ***Camp 30 Word of Honour*** is neither intended to glorify war or to judge the combatants. Rather, it provides a richly-detailed and accurate account of life inside Camp 30, as recounted by the few remaining persons who truly know; they were there.

Thank you, Volkmar and Bruno, for making ***Camp 30 Word of Honour*** possible.

Lynn Philip Hodgson
Alan Paul Longfield
2003-03-30

Volkmar König

-Boot- Kommandanten u. Kommandanten-Schüler

Elbe   Heyda   Kretschmer   Schreiber v. Gopler   Lorenz
    Wentzel   Engel   Ey   Matz

CHAPTER 1
BEWARE THE HURRICANNES

October 1985
The Darch Farm
Bowmanville Ontario Canada

The autumn landscape had unveiled itself in its full splendour overnight, the old man reflected appreciatively. Seated on the front porch of his farmhouse, he could read the signature of each season's colours, smells, and sounds: a calendar marking the passage of the months in this idyllic setting. Just as the spectacular fall hues and the formations of Canada geese in flight overhead signalled the approaching end of Indian summer, the magnificent, flaming oak trees ringing the fields like sentries had marked the passage of his years.

Rising above the treetops in the distance, he could see the familiar flat-roofed buildings: Boy's Training School, Bowmanville, Ontario, once, and always in his mind, Camp 30. The Provincial Institute of Correction had been his place of detention and education for many years. 'Strange,' he thought. 'It was my prison and my school, neither hell nor heaven; I came against my will, and yet, I also came to love the place.' He closed his eyes, trying to recall the sights and sounds of another time.

The spring on the screen door creaked in protest as his wife interrupted his musing.

"Here's your tea, Karl."

"*Was?*" he started. "*Ach, wünderbar*, thank you, sweetheart. Sit here beside me, please." Karl Semmler settled back in his rocking chair, balancing his saucer and teacup. Tentatively, he sipped the piping hot drink. "Always exactly the way I like it, with a drop or two of our own honey. What would I have done without you all these years?"

"You would have been just fine, my dear, I'm sure," she replied, stroking his hair gently. "What have you been looking at, Karl?"

"The Canada geese. Have you ever seen such huge flocks? Here, take the binoculars! We humans can learn so much from nature. Our aircraft flew in V-formations just like that. Did you know why they do it? It really is extraordinary. Reduces drag, air resistance, and gives maximum protection...."

"Karl! You and I see them, and you lecture me, every day, often twice. Good heavens, by now I could teach a high school Physics course on aerodynamics. It's that dratted Camp again, isn't it?"

"That 'dratted Camp', as you call it, is the reason we're sitting here today," he replied gently.

"Yes, of course, Karl, but sometimes you do worry me, sitting here for hours on end, just staring at it. Must you dwell on it so? Can't you let it go? You know, I've been thinking. I'm going to have Mr. Grant build a nice veranda out back so you will have a new view, something different to look at. You're sixty-five years old, dear, and you've had a hard life. It's time to forget about what happened there. It was so long ago, Karl. Please," she pleaded, "live for the present!"

"I do try, but you know how it is. I see the Camp and can't help thinking that most of the folks around here see only a hodgepodge of old-fashioned buildings. There are stories to be told, important stories about Canada, my adopted homeland. Stories about the people, Canadians and Germans, most of them good, kind, honourable men, a few heroic, and a few not..." He paused to set down his teacup. "Most people wonder why anyone would want to leave those old buildings standing. Why we don't tear them down and put up something new and useful, a modern office building ... a shopping mall. Who knows, in twenty years, they may well have built grand homes on this very spot where we're sitting. This beautiful land could be turned into an asphalt parking lot. Do you know what I mean? Is that progress? Rubbish! Where is our country's sense of history?"

The Darch Farm
Bowmanville Archives

"Don't be silly, dear. Those buildings are beautiful, in perfect condition, and they would be fools to tear them down just for the sake of building something else. Sometimes when I'm out pruning the front bushes, a nice group of students will stop to chat on their way home. They tell me that they love it there; they wouldn't want to go to school anywhere else. They say it's like being at a real college, with all the different types of buildings, the swimming pool, the cafeteria, and, of course, the beautiful grounds. They're so proud of your Camp, Karl. They call it their 'campus school'.

"And, to answer your question, how could the town folk ever appreciate the stories those buildings tell? You're one of the few people in the world who can. Perhaps I should drive you over to see the Principal and inquire if you might speak to the students on Remembrance Day next month. The teacher in me says they'd be fascinated to hear about their beloved school's history, first hand.

"It's getting chilly and flu season's coming on. You know how much I worry since your heart attack. Come inside, Karl, and we'll telephone Mr. Grant about building that porch outback."

"Yes, in a moment!"

'Of course, they couldn't possibly know; how could they? If only they did. If only I could tell them.............................'

"Karl!"

1938
Leipzig, Germany

"Karl! Karl! Hurry up!"

"I'm coming, Wolfgang. Wait up, please! I have some great news!"

"I'm late for class! What is it?"

"Wolf, look! I have just received my promotion to Leutnant!" Karl shouted, waving a paper in the air.

"Wonderful, Karl! I'm delighted for you. Perhaps now I will have my chance as well," he added sardonically. Wolfgang von Heiden's fondness for his ambitious and clever middle-class friend Karl overcame his personal disappointment. "Know what, Karl? We'll celebrate tonight at the Academy's football team banquet. For now, you'd best get along and tell your mother! Do you think she'll be pleased?"

"I hope so, but I'm not so sure. She's never gotten over father's death. I wish he were alive today."

"Your father was a brave German who gave his life for the Fatherland in the Great War. You must never forget that, Karl. I'm sure that he knows."

"Thanks, Wolf. You truly are my best friend. Come over to pick me up at 0500h and, of course, the first round of beers this evening is on me!"

"That, I wouldn't miss for anything! 0500h it is then."

Karl raced up the steps of the old boarding house, threw open the front door, flung his book bag down on the boot bench and called out,

"Mother, where are you?"

"I'm right here, in the kitchen, Karl, and you don't have to shout, dear. Now what is so important?"

"Mother, I have been promoted at the air academy; I made Leutnant!"

Frau Semmler's silence spoke volumes as she meticulously dried her hands on her apron. Then, turning, she smiled faintly. "Karl, I'm happy for you; your father would have been so proud. But you'll forgive me if I can't share in your enthusiasm; I'm so fearful of where this will lead."

"Mother, please, we've had this conversation so many times. This is the career that I have chosen, and I beg you to accept my decision and be happy for me."

"But Karl, there is talk of war. In his speeches, Herr Hitler says bizarre things about the German *Volk* (people) fulfilling Germany's destiny and other nonsense that scares the daylights out of me. He is always talking about what rightfully belongs to the Third Reich, as he insists on calling it. I just don't trust the man. Perhaps he's crazy, as Frau Bendler next door says; perhaps it's all an act. Either way, he's bent on leading us on the road to ruin."

"Sssh! Mother, I am not a member of the National Socialist Party. I am in the military, like father, which is something completely different. You know that this has always been my dream."

"Your father..." she sighed. "Still Karl, if Chancellor Hitler decides to go to war, you will be involved. Mark my words!"

"Yes, that's likely true, but it's what I want to do. Flying has always been my dream, my passion, Mother. Just think, I started with five hours as a cadet glider pilot and now I am an officer in the Luftwaffe! I have three choices: a fighter pilot, a bomber pilot or an observer pilot."

"They all sound dangerous. Which one interests you the most?"

"Well, I think bombing is barbaric, not chivalrous at all, so that's definitely out and observer pilots have to stay in the air for hours; that would be unexciting, and besides, I couldn't sit still for that long, so, a fighter pilot it is!"

"Then so be it," she replied resignedly. "Here's a kiss for good luck. Now, Leutnant Semmler, please be good enough to peel these potatoes. And wash your hands first, young man!"

6 August, 1940

Pas de Calais, France
Jagdeschwader (Fighter Group) 62, Luftwaffe Base, The Briefing Room

"Gentlemen, today our mission will take us over London. We will be providing escort protection for twenty-eight Heinkel (He) 111's. The commander of the mission is Major Hans Moeller. Jagdeschwader (Fighter Group) 62 will, as usual, be flying Messerschmitt (Me) Bf 109's. Major Moeller?"

Aged forty-four, Major Hans Moeller, one of the Luftwaffe's senior flying officers, had done battle with the Air Ministry in Berlin in order to be assigned to active duty in France. Not surprisingly, he had won. Loathe to be perceived as dishonouring a celebrated and highly decorated hero of the Great War, as well as a fellow recipient of the coveted *Orden Pour le mérite* medal, nicknamed *Blauer Max*, 'Blue Max' by airmen, the Air Marshall himself had personally telephoned his congratulations to Moeller. A consummate pilot, he was as renowned throughout the service for his air combat virtuosity as for his ability to lead and inspire men many years his junior. His innate reserve and formal Prussian bearing had, as yet, prevented him from winning the hearts of his men in JG 62. Nevertheless, they knew they would follow him into hell and back.

Moeller, utterly at ease in his role as commanding officer, inclined his head slightly as he took the pointer that was offered and stepped up briskly to the wall chart. "Thank you, Oberleutnant. Gentlemen, as we cross the Channel and fly over the English coast, you can expect heavy concentrations of anti-aircraft fire at these locations: here, here, and here. And here. You can expect to be engaged by Hurricanes and Spitfires. Although the Spitfires will be concentrating on our 109's, the enemy's Hurricanes can do the Luftwaffe the most damage. The reason is straightforward: it is a preferred tactic, if not a religious practice of the RAF to dedicate the Hurricanes to targeting our bombers and only our bombers," he observed with a faint smile, then added emphatically, "We shall do everything within our means to prevent that! Any questions? No? Thank you. Good hunting, gentlemen! The weather report, Oberleutnant?"

Hawker Hurricane Mk I
Supermarine Spitfire F. Mk IX.
Bowmanville Archives

At the conclusion of the briefing, Karl Semmler and Wolfgang von Heiden remained seated as the other airmen filed out. Karl, barely five feet six inches tall (160 cm), with brown eyes and brown hair, was completely opposite in appearance to his best friend. Wolfgang, at six feet three inches (190 cm), was the blond haired, blue-eyed personification of the Führer's ideal German male.

"Wow, this is it," said Karl in quiet realisation. "We're really going. Our first mission over enemy territory! All those months of training and now we're going to be a part of the Battle of Britain."

"Yes! I heard that we suffered some terrible loses yesterday. I think that's why we were selected to go this time," Wolf replied.

"I hope to God we're ready!" Karl remarked quietly.

"We'll watch out for each other, my friend! Nothing, including hordes of Hurricanes and Spitfires will come between us!"

"It takes just one, Wolf..."

7 August, 1940
0623 h
Over The English Channel

Were he not attentive, he could easily become lost in the beauty of the scenery below and almost hypnotized by the finely pitched drone of the Messerschmitt's Daimler Benz engine. Breaks in the scattered clouds afforded glimpses of the sandy beaches of France below; then, as the white-capped, sparkling waters of the Dover Strait appeared under his wings, the breathtaking landscape was transformed from sable to aqua-marine. A quick glance upward into his rear-view cockpit mirror jarred Karl's focus back to their mission. The fighter squadron was spread out in echelons, stepped pairs, rising upon invisible stairs behind him. The splendid seascape and powder puff cumulous clouds notwithstanding, he reminded himself that he and his comrades in JG 62 were certainly not embarking upon a sightseeing tour to England, but were providing fighter escort for a daylight-bombing raid on the English capitol, London. Moeller's squadron was there to shepherd and safeguard the stolid He 111's bombers, the lumbering workhorses of Luftwaffe Bomber Group, flying below and just slightly ahead of the lead Me 109's. On his starboard wing, he could see Wolf; Karl wondered if his wingman was as transfixed by the scene. He recalled having read an article about deep-sea divers being overwhelmed by the experience of an almost mystic and sometimes deadly phenomenon called 'rapture of the deep,' actually nitrogen narcosis, and wondered if an aerial equivalent existed. 'Not likely, Wolfgang ... probably thinking about another kind of rapture with one of his adoring young *filles*', Karl mused. He couldn't ask anyway, as the armada had been ordered to observe strict radio silence until they engaged hostile aircraft.

Heinkel HE 219 UHU.
Bowmanville Archives

His blood turned abruptly to ice water; directly ahead, through the blur of the spinning triple bladed-propellers loomed the white chalk face of the Dover cliffs. 'Whether approaching, over, or departing enemy territory, always expect the unexpected,' the air combat tactics instructor had hammered into their heads.

"When will they come?" Karl wondered aloud. "And from where? From the rear and above, or from below, trying to pick off a bomber like a lioness searching out the weakest and slowest in the pack?" He had the greatest respect for the vaunted RAF Spitfires, but did not fear them as much as the Hawker Hurricanes; despite accounts of the Spitfire's superiority in speed over the older Me 109's, it was the slower, but more manoeuvrable Hurricanes that he dreaded.

"A Hurricane slips in behind you before you can react," an old hand had advised him over a beer at mess one evening. "The only thing for it is to go for the ground, or he'll chop you to pieces with his cannons. Remember this, if you want to survive: Fight Spitfires, flee Hurricanes. Against them, a *Gustav* (Messerschmitt 109) is nothing more than a flying tin coffin."

Beware the Hurricanes

'There was much truth in that, Otto, my friend,' Karl reflected, recalling the veteran fighter pilot's fiery demise in an explosion of flame, billowing smoke and metal fragments. Karl had watched from the ground in disbelief as Otto fell victim to his own prophecy in an uneven dogfight with two Hurricanes during an RAF raid on the airfield only the week before.

'Beware the Hurricanes,' Karl repeated to himself as he scanned the skies for signs of British defenders. 'They will come, soon, but from where?'

In reply, three hammer blows thudded against his back. The Messerschmitt shuddered violently as though the wings and tail section were being ripped from the body. Then, the overhead canopy exploded, spraying his goggles and facemask with flying shards. "Ambush! *Scheiss!* A Spitfire, which had come blazing out of the sun, bore directly at him, its eight .303 calibre machine guns raking the Bf-109, stitching the top of its fuselage. Narrowly avoiding a collision, the British pilot tipped the Mk II Spitfire's triple-bladed propeller upward only at the last moment, the fighter's RAF rondelles and registration starkly visible only centimetres above Karl's exposed head as it rocketed past the Me 109.

Spitfire over England.
Kim Chetwyn, Scramble Productions

A Messerschmitt on its mission.
Kim Chetwyn, Scramble Productions

His mirror now gone, Karl struggled to take command of the wildly oscillating control column while craning his head portside to see what had hit him from the rear. "Godammit! Hurricane!" Karl caught a glimpse of the British pilot's face as the Hurricane dipped nimbly below the 109's tail, in preparation for administering the *coup de grâce* into the Messerschmitt's vulnerable, robin's-egg blue underbelly. "Now what, Otto? You never mentioned a goddamn Spitfire and a Hurricane together!" The vibrations in the steering yoke rattled Karl through to his spine, although the Messerschmitt's heavy armour plate appeared to have stopped the slugs from ripping into his back.

"'Head for the ground!' Ground? Christ almighty, where's the water?" The aircraft bucked wildly as the Hurricane unleashed a torrent of fire into the 109's underside. Oil and hydraulic fluid had splattered the instrument panel and what remained of the lower canopy and gun sight as the plane began a slow roll to the right, which Karl knew was the start of a death spiral into the ground. As acrid smoke and fumes filled the cockpit, Karl prepared to bail out; it occurred to him that he hadn't fired a single round in self-defence. "Good luck, Wolf. Get one of the bastards for me! Jump, Semmler ... now!"

CHAPTER 2
HOT OVER AFRIKA, THE DESERT WINDS BLOW

"Kurt! Kurt Ludwig! Breakfast! Your train leaves in one hour, fifty-three minutes! You'll be court-martialled if you miss it!" Frau Ilse Löwen's usually solicitous tone had turned to one of motherly exasperation.

Kurt groaned as he rolled over. Opening his eyes, he smiled at his mother's use of military time. "I know, Mutti. I'm coming. Five minutes!" 'Late? No chance. Peter Faber and I'll be there with time to spare. Okay. One, two, three. Feet on the carpet, Kurt,' he muttered, swinging his legs from under the goose down comforter and over the edge of the bed. 'God, my head! How many litres did I put down last night in the braukeller? And that band! Pa boom boom squeak squeak ... Pa boom boom squeak ... Wonder what sadist invented the damn accordion! He should be shot at dawn! 'Whatever led Momma and Papa to choose 'Ludwig' as my middle name? 'What's in a name?' Who wrote that? Schiller? Goethe? Adolf Schickelgruber? Whoever it was, he sure as blazes wasn't saddled with 'Ludwig'; on that, I'd be willing to bet my life.

'God, what a mess! Is that lipstick in my ear? Definitely bad form: Not Regulation. Poor old Ludwig van Beethoven: didn't seem to have much effect on the maestro's music, although maybe it explains why he was such a cranky recluse. That, and the fact that he was deaf as a stone.

'Leutnant Kurt Löwen! Kurt the Lion! Kurt Löwen: the lion of the desert! Yes! Louis the lion. Ugh! For an up-and-coming junior officer in the Afrika Korps, Kurt Löwen has just the right ring: a lion-hearted German warrior of destiny.' Absorbed in his thoughts, he turned on the shower faucets while the toilet was still flushing. 'Dammit! This water's colder than the barracks', if that's possible!'

Kurt towelled off, shaved hurriedly, and scurried into his bedroom to put on the freshly pressed, stiffly starched dress shirt laid out on his bureau top. "Thanks, Mutti, splendid as always!" He inspected the knot in his necktie, and then brushed his closely cropped black hair, reflecting upon his good fortune to have been rejected by the Waffen (Fighting) SS, although it was the expected progression for the best and brightest members of the Jugend (Hitler Youth). As a patriotic German and a soldier,

Kurt had shared his recently deceased father's and his mother's nation-
alistic pride when their native Rhineland was reclaimed for Germany and
occupied by the army of the Reich. His joy soon turned to cynicism as
he witnessed the beginnings of a state-sanctioned campaign of oppres-
sion against the families of some of his school chums, representatives of
the so-called 'eastern aliens', the Jews. He had joined the Hitler Youth
because it was mandatory for boys between the ages of fifteen and twenty. Unlike his chum, Peter Faber, Kurt had quietly and steadfastly resis-
ted being taken in by the raving, calculating egomaniacs of the local
branch of National Socialists (Nazis) and their self-serving, flag-waving
fanaticism.

Thanks to the SS, he was soon going to be in the thick of the action,
under the command of modern Germany's greatest and most popular
General, Erwin Jürgen Rommel. Standing only 162 cm in his bare feet,
Kurt was six cm shy of the stringent SS recruitment standard of 168 cm,
(five feet, nine inches), which, by coincidence, was the exact height of the
Chief, SS-Reichsführer Heinrich Himmler. Kurt briefly feigned disappointment but then was genuinely ecstatic when he was accepted into
the 21st Panzer (Armoured) Division. One month earlier, in February of
1941, the 21st had been combined with the 15th Panzer Division to form
Germany's new elite force, the Deutsches Afrika Korps, or DAK. The brilliant tactics of the Korp's commander, General Rommel, had made
almost daily headlines, his lightning victories enthralling the nation during the battle for France.

The recruiting officer at the Prenzlau armouries had assured Kurt
that his physique would be an asset in the cramped interior of a Mark 11
or 111 'battlewagon'. Rapidly trained in the latest tactics of tank warfare, weaponry, gunnery, then inoculated against such exotic diseases as
malaria, typhus and cholera, and, finally, medically certified Fit for
Tropical Service, Kurt could hardly wait to wear the distinctive olive uniform and kit of the Deutsche Afrika Korps.

Now, in less than two weeks time, he, Leutnant Kurt Löwen, and his
best chum, Leutnant Peter Faber, along with their comrades-at-arms,
would be serving with General Rommel somewhere in the deserts of
either Libya or Cyrenaica. He would be manning the 50 mm cannon
inside the bowels of a formidable Mark 111 Panzer, 'brewing up' the
Englanders' puny sardine can Matildas (tanks). Kurt knew in his heart
that he would realize his dream of making tank commander. The
instructors at Prenzlau continually reminded his class that promotion

came most swiftly to those men who demonstrated their unswerving commitment to the German soldier's Führer Loyalty Oath through initiative, perseverance and unflinching courage under fire in the field.

"What's for breakfast, Mutti? I'm famished. Hmm, do I smell sausages, fresh rolls, and, could this be real coffee?"

"Good morning! It is real coffee, not *ersatz*; I ground the beans myself. How about a good morning kiss for your Mutti, who has been up washing, ironing and cooking since daybreak? That's better. Now sit, sit. So, tell me, how were things with Lisette?"

"Generally, or last night?" he asked cautiously.

"Last night, of course. Please don't talk with your mouth full, dear!"

"Last night? Fine, just fine. *Mmm, das schmeckt.* Very, very good."

"Did you ... pop the question?" she asked coyly.

"Mother!"

"Well, did you or did you not, Kurt?"

"No, not exactly, but we swore on our honour to wait for one another. Besides, she told me she'd be far, far too busy and worn out as an Operating Room nurse to even think about going out for an evening of merriment with another man. More sausages, if there are any, please?"

"That's good. Just like your Papa and me in 1914 before he went off to the Western Front. And we were true to our sacred oaths. Take my advice, Kurt ... write to her and to me. Often. It keeps the flame alive. I saved all of Papa's letters. Someday I'll show them to you, bundled up with coloured ribbons, by month and year..."

"There's someone at the door. It must be Peter. I'll get it. Where's my kit bag?" he said, thankful for the intrusion.

"Just where you asked me to put it, dear, on the bench by the entrance. It's packed and ready. There's a salami sandwich and an apple tucked in the right side, for the train trip.

"Good morning, Peter! Well, don't you two make a dashing pair of cavaliers!" Ilse Löwen exclaimed.

"Heil Hitler, Frau Löwen!"

"How's your mother keeping, Peter? I must drop by with some fruit preserves."

"Yes, please do, Frau Löwen. She's been a little under the weather these past few weeks with her sciatica, you know. That would definitely cheer her up.

"Are you ready, Leutnant Löwen?"

"Just about, Leutnant Faber.

"Well, Mother, this is it. Thanks for everything. Stay well and remember, at the first sound of an air raid siren, get down into the shelter. Promise?"

"I promise. I do hope the Air Raid Security Police will let me bring Kaiser Willy. I'll smuggle him under my coat if it comes to that," she added wistfully. "Go with God, my son."

"And with you. *Mach's gut, Mutti!* Be well, mother. I love you!" He kissed her tenderly.

"I love you, too. Be careful! Write often and remember to change your socks! I packed four extra pairs just so..."

"Farewell! Heil Hitler, Frau Löwen!" Peter proclaimed with an exaggerated straight-arm salute.

Reaching the sidewalk, Kurt and Peter turned for a final wave. "Kaiser Willy?" Peter queried.

"A stray tomcat that she took in. He's slightly cross-eyed, with big whiskers, and mangy-looking in general. Get the picture?"

"I get the picture. If we run fast, we can flag down the tram that's just rounding the corner."

When they were seated, Kurt smiled inwardly at the memory of his mother's resolve that the cat be named 'Ludendorf'. He only dissuaded her by insisting that they would both end up in prison for having the cheek to cast disrespect upon a famous general, a living hero of the Great War and ardent supporter of the Führer. Kaiser Wilhelm's stock, on the other hand, was non-existent under the Nazi government, for his having forsaken the Fatherland for refuge in Holland in 1918.

"Off to join Generalleutnant Erwin Rommel in North Africa, Kurt! Can you believe that it's finally happening? My God! Let's make a pact."

"What kind of a pact, Peter?"

"That no matter what happens, we'll be inseparable, through thick and thin, even to death!"

"Really. That might not be so easy, Peter. After all, we don't know that we'll even be assigned to the same tank corps or company. The chances are slim to none, I'll wager."

"No problem. It's already done."

"What do you mean, 'already done'?"

"Father has a friend at Armed Forces HQ in Berlin. Very well connected. Has the ear of the top brass."

"I don't think that's such a good idea, Peter. The Army doesn't like pushy...."

"Trust me in this, my friend," Faber interrupted. "It's no problem! Here's the train station. Look, there's Sergeant Major Krauss, pacing and fuming as usual. Hop to it before he chews us out and fines us for tardiness. So, together like brothers through thick and thin? *Ehrenwort* (Word of honour)?"

"Word of honour: through thick and thin!"

"Good, let's shake hands on it. Heil Hitler! Heil Hitler, damn it, Kurt!"

"If you insist, Peter. Heil Hitler! Now we'd best shake a leg!"

5 April, 1941
North Africa   Cyrenaica, Benghazi

An arc of sand streamed from the sidecar's tire like an ostrich feather as the motorcycle lurched hard to the right. Blipping the throttle momentarily in an attempt to regain traction, Kurt felt the bike skew in the opposite direction, then the front wheel dug in, sinking hopelessly through the thin crust of sand into the deep, dust-like powder, called in Arabic *feche-feche*, about which the troops had often been warned by the Bedouin. The Zündapp KS 750 motorcycle's engine roared, spluttered, and then quit altogether. Kurt cursed in frustration as he pushed up his sand goggles. He removed his right driving glove impatiently, then tucked it under his chin and unscrewed the fuel tank filler cap. He rocked the bike slightly back and forth between his knees while he peered into the tank.

"So, how much is there?" Peter shouted anxiously.

"Plenty, more than enough to make it back to base. Just pray there isn't sand in either the fuel line or the carburetor. God knows, it's everywhere else! If we're lucky, it's only vapour lock," he added under his breath as he dismounted. The fine powder flowed over until it almnost covered his boot tops.

"What? I can't hear you!"

"We have fuel, Peter. Get out of the sidecar and help me or we're going to be buried alive with our sand sled!" Kurt shouted to be heard above the rising wind. "We have to get it out of the sand and let it cool down! Problem is, it won't start, and we can't push its dead weight."

"How am I supposed to get out of this? I'm a metre off the bloody ground, like that ride at the Munich beer fest!"

Kurt was unable to resist laughing at his friend's predicament. The sidecar was canted awkwardly upward at a thirty-five degree angle. "Jump. Carefully, or you'll sink in up to your butt!"

"And I'll be eaten alive by sand fleas! The machine gun's stock is jammed in my ribs. I can't move!"

Zündapp KS 750 (inset) with Map of Cyrenaïca

"Can you not swing it sideways? Good, now climb over the edge, carefully, and lower yourself with your hands. That's it! Splendid!"

Darkness swept over the desert like a black curtain, completely obscuring the sun. By the time the two men had managed to dig out the machine from the fine powder, the sandstorm that had been brewing for the past hour suddenly struck with full force, stinging their exposed skin and eyes, blotting out all visibility.

"So, this must be what our Italian allies call the *Gibli*, Kurt," Peter yelled. "It's North Africa, and it is the season: April. Can't say we weren't warned in Tripoli, no? It causes massive, skull-popping migraines. What's more, the Bedouin say the *Gibli* can make a man go mad."

"*Gibli, Scirocco*, come off it, man! They're desert storms, not magic spells! Let's take stock and save our energy for getting through it. Cover your face ... and check that the water containers are secured. While you're at it, reach into the saddlebags and get me the flashlight, the map, and the compass, please, so I can take our bearings." Kurt stood up. Walking five metres from the motorcycle, he vanished into the swirling dust.

"Where are you going?" Peter shouted.

Kurt's reply was lost in the howling wind. To console himself, Peter reached into the breast pocket of his tunic and extracted a crumpled, damp, cello–covered package of stale Turkish cigarettes and a shiny metallic American lighter, both of which he had purchased at an exorbitant price from a dodgy fourteen year old Arab in the Agedabia marketplace. After six futile attempts to light a cigarette, Peter threw it into the wind in disgust and hunkered down to wait for Kurt's return.

Nothing had turned out as he had hoped. Shortly after landing in Tripoli in March, violently seasick, he and Kurt had been transferred without explanation to Motorized Company 580, later the 90th Light-Afrika Division, an independent reconnaissance unit, serving as support for the Afrika Korps, and they had not yet seen the inside of a Mark 111 Panzer.

'Thanks for your help, Father! No problem!' Peter grumbled. 'Kurt had been right: the Army is not an old boy's club, at least not for the junior ranks. And so far, we have accomplished none of our recon objectives, unless you call hauling the Zündapp out of four bloody great sand dunes in two hours an accomplishment. No sign of any British tank squadron, supposedly heading for Mechili. Wonder if the BMW R75 bikes get hung up as often? Both have sidecars with drive shafts for better grip.

'So,' Peter continued gloomily, 'fate has kicked us in our backsides with this windstorm from hell! All we need now is to drive over a landmine or stumble into a group of trigger-happy British Tommy's' "Kurt? Is that you?" he whispered, reaching for his Luger pistol.

"Of course it's me. Who did you expect, Rommel? I had to get away a distance. There must be an iron deposit underground, giving the compass false readings. Now move over, hold the flashlight, and listen closely. The best I can figure is we are here, fifty kilometres south west of Mechili. Over there," he explained, while indicating a dark patch with a stabbing motion at the map, "is a *wadi*, a dry depression, which may have a trickle of fresh water at the bottom."

"I know what a *wadi* is. So why go there? We have water."

"Listen, *Dummkopf*, we'll head there for cover, wait out the storm, and perhaps we can top up our water supplies. Now, pay attention; I need you to be the navigator. On this heading. Ready?" The two-cylinder engine roared to life on Kurt's first try. He gunned the motor and called over to Peter, "Hold the compass level and steady. Do you remember the bearing I told you? Do not take your eyes off it! Your goggles are crooked, Peter. Fix them, for God's sake, or you'll be sand blind and no good to anyone."

"Thanks. I'm ready!" Peter waved.

"Good. Hold on. And you can help me steer by sitting perfectly still. We're off."

"Heil Hitler!" As Peter thrust out his right arm, saluting, he was thrown backwards, cradling the compass in his left hand, as the motorcycle lurched into the fierce sandstorm at full throttle.

The ride into the deep depression was equally hair raising and exhilarating. Kurt's mastery of the motorbike in navigating the steep, treacherous walls of the *wadi*, slowing their rate of descent by alternately braking, accelerating, zigzagging, and generally finessing their way downward, was extraordinary, Peter thought. He later admitted to Kurt that his friend was a far superior cyclist and, had he been in control, they would have been thrown off and lying at the bottom of the gully, their necks snapped.

Kurt smiled in acknowledgement of Peter's unusual compliment. "You can thank my father, Horst Dieter Löwen for that. He was a dispatch rider in the war and caught the bug, I suppose. When he came home, he took up racing, semi-professionally, but he fractured his right leg on a dirt track somewhere in France. The French surgeons damn near left him a cripple. Anyway, he was forbidden to ride competitively again, but, from the time I was twelve, he and I would sneak out occasionally on Saturday mornings. He kept a beautiful second-hand British 250 cc twin cylinder BSA in a friend's shed. He'd put me through the paces on the back trails and sand hills.

"Did your mother know?"

"She had to; heavens, we came back reeking of castor oil and exhaust fumes, and our fingernails were black with grease, although she never once mentioned it. She knew that Poppa had it in his blood, I suppose. Glad you enjoyed the ride. Listen, Peter, can you hear that sound?" His voice was deadly earnest.

"I can't hear anything but the wind."

"No, this is different. Sssh. Listen... What do you make of it? You're the storm expert."

"It sounds like rain! Coming from the west!" Peter proclaimed. "Yes, it's rain, definitely!"

"That it is," Kurt replied grimly after a moment, his face turned upward. "And it's coming this way. At high velocity!"

"At least the rain should wash the sand out of our ..."

"We have to get out of here!"

"Why, Kurt?"

"Why? Because we'll be drowned down here if we don't!" he shouted over the rapidly intensifying downpour. "We're going to make a run for it. If we wait another minute, the sand will be turned into a quagmire and we'll be trapped like desert rats in the rising water. Get in the sidecar; pull that oilcloth cape over your head and be ready to lose your breakfast."

Kurt stood up to manoeuvre the motorcycle, choosing to take a diagonal path up the forty metre-high embankment. The intense beam of the headlight was reflected back by the driving raindrops, creating a dazzling, mesmerizing light show. "Zero visibility! I'm running blind! Can you see anything?"

Peter raised the oilcloth and peered intently ahead into the void. He shook his head in a futile effort to clear his goggles of raindrops and fiercely gripped the edges of the sidecar to steady himself. He leaned forward, doing his best to be vigilant and to remain motionless, a model passenger, to avoid a sudden shift of mass that would throw off Kurt's efforts to keep the machine on a steady course. The fury of the storm had lessened in the past minute or two, he thought. The Zündapp responded valiantly to Kurt's urgings, ploughing upward at a steady fifteen km per hour as he deftly applied throttle and brakes and slight steering corrections. "I think I can make out the ridge at the top!" Peter called. "There, thirty metres .... Oh, my God!" Kurt had disappeared, simply vanished as the front wheel of the motorcycle smashed into an outcropping, throwing the bike violently forward and upward in an arc. Peter felt himself lifted by a gigantic hand and hurled into the air. He landed face down, less than five metres from the motorcycle. His last sensations before sinking into unconsciousness were the feeling of sand mixed with a thick, warm, sweet-tasting liquid at the back of his throat while, close by, an engine screamed in protest at full throttle.

"You'll be as right as rain, old son!" Bit of a bump on the noggin, some friction burns on your chin, one or two loose choppers, that's all. Your mate over there's a little the worse for wear. Here, drink this!"

Kurt blinked; he looked around, mystified by his surroundings. He shut his eyes, dazzled by the light. The reek of disinfectant assaulted his nostrils. Perhaps he was in the Regimental infirmary at Prenzlau. 'What dialect is this?' He struggled to understand the male voice somewhere on his right. 'Not familiar, not German... English?' he puzzled.

"*Wie bitte? Ich verstehe kein Englisch.*"

"Sorry mate. No comprendo. Are you in pain?"

Kurt responded with a shrug of incomprehension.

"Pain? Hurt? Hur ten ze?"

"Thick as a proverbial plank, this one.

"Say, Captain, can you come over here for a tick and see if you can get anything out of this Jerry?

"Drink this, Fritz. It will help you to sit up. All of it; down the hatch. There's a good lad!   Righto, Sir, the blighter is all yours."

"*Leutnant Löwen: Sie befinden sich in einem englischen Krankenhaus...* Hello, Leutnant Löwen. You are in an English hospital, at least it is for the time being. You and your friend, Leutnant Faber, were found halfway down a wadi by one of our units, battered, and half-drowned. My name is Eamon Davies, Captain, Welsh Guards. I am a surgeon. At present, we have twenty or more of your fellow German officers here. The battle lines shift back and forth almost on an hourly basis."

"What happened, Captain? Do you know?"

"Yes, your motorbike had a sudden meeting with a rather large outcropping of granite, called a monad something-or-other. I'm not very knowledgeable about such things. The ferocious rainstorm likely exposed it. The chaps who brought you and Faber here said that you would have been goners if you had not been thrown sideways and landed in the sand. As it was, you were washed down the hillside several feet. Luckily, you weren't drowned; the *wadi* had become a good-sized lake."

"Thank you, Captain."

"You can thank your rescuers. We estimate that you and Leutnant Faber had been lying there for at least eight hours. We will take good care of you. Then, when you and your comrade are fit, you'll be released and shipped off to a prisoner-of-war camp, its whereabouts I can't say. Military intelligence will certainly want to interview you there. Don't worry. No rubber hoses. It's all quite civilised out here. Until then, try to rest. Your medication will make you feel drowsy. You should be on your feet by tomorrow. Leutnant Faber, unfortunately, has a concussion, a fractured right arm and some rather nasty abrasions, but, all said, he should recover well."

"And our motorcycle, Captain?"

"In the drink: six feet under water. You both are very fortunate...nasty great brutes, those goliaths. Road machines...never, never intended by their designers for bashing about the dunes. I've seen far too many of our own chaps with various bits of their manhood mangled beyond redemption by being vaulted over the handle bars because of the rider's inexperience, stupidity or bloody bravado. Oh yes, I am on duty every day, should you need my help. Good day, Leutnant."

Kurt's first impulse was to refute Captain Davies's low opinion of cyclists. Thinking better of it, he saluted the friendly British captain, and thanked him. Then Kurt sank back onto the hard pillow, gloomily contemplating their impending internment in a British prison camp until he fell asleep.

The next day, Kurt bounded out of bed, and was soon occupied in helping the hard-pressed Englanders care for the German and the few Italian patients. Although the heat in the old, converted school was stifling, none complained. The flies were much worse than the heat, the men said, but far better than the sand lice. When Peter regained consciousness and was resting somewhat comfortably, Kurt recounted the incidents leading to their capture, as Captain Davies had told them to him. After feeding Peter his lunch, Kurt asked Captain Davies for permission to take him outdoors in a wheelchair for half an hour to get some fresh air.

"Once around the daffodils, old man, and no funny business. Understand?"

"I understand. But what are 'the daffodils', Sir?"

"A figure of speech! Bloody hell, take him, and get along with you!" he replied, with a dismissive wave.

"I, that is, we will return, Captain Davies. *Ehrenwort.* Word of honour."

"Good then: see that you do, Leutnant Löwen!" he chuckled.

April, 1941

My Dearest Lisette,

Thank you for your lovely letter, darling. I miss you so very much, too! Peter and I are in a hospital, 'prisoners' of the British authorities. Don't worry; we're being treated well! Good food, what there is of it and excellent medical care. No, I'm not sick. I can't give any details except to say that we had an accident with our motorcycle and are in an army hospital in North Africa. Peter is recovering nicely and I am back on my feet with only a few bruises (that are somewhat painful) but otherwise, I am feeling fighting fit. The motorcycle did not fare as well.

Today the most amazing thing happened. I don't know if the authorities will allow this to pass, but I'll take a chance. I'll show it to my Doctor, a grand officer named Captain Davies, to get his approval before putting it into the post. Here's the story.

I took Peter outdoors for a bit of fresh air after lunch this afternoon and missed the drama. A top (and I do mean top!!!) German General dropped into the hospital (unannounced of course). Yes, truly, my love. If I were to tell you his name, you would seriously doubt my state of mind. Apparently, thinking it was a German Army infirmary he drove up to the front door in his newly captured, British-made command vehicle, dismounted and came inside, walked past the guards and straight along the corridor to our ward. Can you imagine the stunned surprise of the patients, many of whom are German? The story going around is that the British guards and medical staff thought that he was a Polish general. Can you believe it? And his picture is in their newspapers here almost daily! To continue, he spoke briefly with some of the wounded men; then, realising he was in a British sickbay, he made a hasty retreat. One of the Afrika Korps fellows swears he overheard the General say to his driver, "Ich glaube, ich habe einen Fehler begangen. Wir sollten hier schleunigst ver-schwinden!" "I think I've made a mistake. Let's get out of here quickly.")

Thank heavens for our side he got cleanly away! What an inspiration to have had this truly great man, here, in the flesh! I regret not seeing him standing here grandly in the ward, although I caught a glimpse of him in 'Moritz', his command vehicle, as he sped away. Amazingly, Lisette, not one of our men saluted or gave him away, but they knew damn well who he was. Maybe they were too shell-shocked by his sudden appearance. As you can imagine, our morale is sky high! Our British hosts' is not.

I feel a little tired with all of the excitement so I'll sign off for now, darling.

Kisses and love, always,

Kurt.

P.S. When Peter has recovered, we will be transferred to an Allied Prisoner of War camp somewhere here, and then after that? Captain Davies has no idea when, or where, but once we're settled in, I hope to be in touch. Please give Mother a kiss and hug for me and scratch Willy's ears. Tell Mutti I'll write very soon!

We're here on behalf of the Department of Defence
17 August, 1941
Bowmanville, Ontario, Canada

A black 1938 Buick Roadmaster entered the fieldstone gate of the Boy's Training School, and proceeded around the driveway that traversed the

well-kept gardens, and then drew up to the entrance of the Administration Building.

The Administration Building – 1942
Bowmanville Archives / DND - National Archives of Canada

Alerted by the scrunch of tires on the gravel, Principal Dr. Darren M. Cooper swivelled his oak chair to the left in time to view a uniformed man hastily exit the driver's side and hold open the left rear door from which two army officers emerged. The driver saluted as they strode toward the entrance. Each officer carried a black briefcase. "Miss Burns, it appears our visitors are here. I'm going out to greet them. Do you have the refreshments ready?"

"Yes, Dr. Cooper, the kettle's on the boil."

'I wonder what this is about?' Cooper muttered as he walked the short distance from the school office to the front stairs. 'The caller wouldn't give Miss Burns any details yesterday. Anyway, I'm too old to be conscripted, so it must be quite urgent. Thank goodness the boys are calm and quiet today'.

"Good morning, gentlemen, welcome to our school. My name is Cooper, Dr. Darren Cooper, I'm the Principal," he announced, holding out his hand.

"Good morning, Dr. Cooper. I'm Major Brighton; this is my Adjutant, Captain Murray. We're here on behalf of the Department of Defence. I apologize for the very short notice, but under the circumstances, it was unavoidable."

Camp inspection with the Darch farm behind
Bowmanville Archives / DND - National Archives of Canada

"Not at all! Anything I can do to assist..."

"Things do have habit of popping up unexpectedly these days, right Captain?" Brighton remarked rhetorically.

"Yes, well I know," Cooper interjected. "My Vice-Principal, Mr. Myers, was called away at the last moment to a meeting in Toronto, at the Ministry of Education ... for the third time this month," he added pointedly.

"Lovely grounds, Dr. Cooper. May we speak with you inside?"

"Of course, this way, please."

As they passed by her desk, Miss Burns' looked up and smiled. "Would you care for tea or coffee, gentlemen?"

"Now gentlemen, might I ask what brings you out to the countryside, and specifically to our school?" inquired Darren genially when Miss Burn's had finished dispensing the refreshments.

"Well, Doctor..."

"Darren, please, Major."

"Thank you; Darren. Captain Murray and I are here to inform you, officially, that the Dominion Government has an immediate, and I should say, pressing need for your school."

"My school, Major? Whatever for?"

"I'm sure that the reason will distress you, initially," Captain Murray added. Major Brighton nodded in acknowledgement, waiting for Murray to continue. "Darren, the Allies are capturing large numbers of German prisoners, particularly officers: Kriegsmarine, I mean navy, the Luftwaffe, air force, as well as Afrika Korps. At any rate, the reality is that they can't find suitable prison accommodations in Britain quickly enough. This presents a rather interesting dilemma. While the Allies are delighted to have these men out of the equation, so to speak, and we are bound by the Geneva Convention to house them according to its rules, it would be unbelievably short sighted, and foolhardy, to keep these high-ranking personnel in Great Britain. Imagine the consequences if England were to be occupied by Germany in the near future. These men constitute a core of talented and experienced leaders who, once released, would wreak havoc. The British Government has declared that it must begin shipping them overseas immediately. Major?"

"The present facilities in southern Ontario fall short of ideal, shall we say? After discussions during which several alternate sites were considered and rejected, it was obvious that your facilities clearly exceeded all of my Committee's criteria. It was our recommendation to the Deputy Minister that your establishment be appropriated to serve as a PoW internment camp."

Darren sat back in shocked silence. After a pause, he regained his composure. "Well, I must say, I am at a loss for words. I'm sorry, gentlemen, but this has set me back. My school...how in the world can this be? How can it be?"

"We understand, Darren," Brighton replied brightly. "I want to assure you that senior Federal and Provincial officials have been involved in drawing up the transfer protocol: the arrangements. As you are well aware, the Boy's Training School, that is this institution, falls under the authority of the Ontario Departments of Education and Corrections. Believe me, a considerable amount of detail, red tape if you like, has had to be ironed out with all and sundry and signed off before we came here today. I must say it all came together rather quickly, wouldn't you agree, Captain?"

"My students, Major, what about my students?" Darren asked, still incredulous. "And my staff: my teachers, counsellors, caretakers, kitchen...?"

"The Province has the primary responsibility for making those arrangements. It isn't my place to interfere in their bailiwick but I can assure you that the students will be transferred and housed locally, wherever judged appropriate. They will continue to be served by you and your staff in another facility, during the transition period. It's my understanding that Vice-Principal Myers will be bringing a letter of confirmation from the Minister today."

"Major Brighton, how much time do I have? A week, a month...?"

"Not that much, I'm afraid, Darren.

"The documents, please, Captain?"

"These papers give authorization to The Royal Canadian Corps of Engineers to start constructing barracks for the Canadian guards."

"Effective when, Major Brighton?" Darren asked anxiously.

"They will be here... at 0730 on Saturday."

"Saturday! Are you...? But today's Thursday! Great Caesar man, that's just over 24 hours from now! That's impossible! Forgive me..."

"Quite all right, Darren," Major Brighton responded reassuringly. "I assure you your boys and staff will be well taken care of."

An urgent rap on the Principal's office door preceded Miss Burns' softly soothing voice. "Please, excuse me, gentlemen. The Provincial Inspector of Schools, Dr. Hallman, is here, Dr. Cooper. He wishes to join you, if that would be convenient."

"Yes, of course. Please, have him come in!" Cooper replied with forced enthusiasm.

As soon as the three visitors had left, Cooper called through the open door, "Can you step in, please, Miss Burns?"

She materialized soundlessly, stenographer's pad and sharpened pencil poised. "Problem, Doctor Cooper?"

"Sit down please, Miss Burns. Miss Burns, I... I ... that is, our boys, the staff, you, me, everyone...we've been evicted to make way for German prisoners of war!"

"Evicted? For German prisoners?" She wanted to laugh, it was so incongruous, but she caught herself. It was true; Darren Cooper's eyes were overflowing with tears. She shifted uncomfortably in her chair as he shuffled slowly to the window, his hands thrust into his suit jacket pockets, lost in thought.

When at last he turned toward her, she witnessed the renewal of the old Cooperian fervour; Darren's deeply–ingrained Scots Presbyterian sense of duty and faith in a divine plan had triumphed over the demons of doubt and despair.

"'Thy will be done!' Miss Burns, this is an opportunity to make a silk purse out of a sow's ear."

"Sir?"

"It is my intention to meet every single expectation fully as an example to all Canadians. I am calling an emergency meeting of all teachers, instructors, and senior support staff this afternoon...in the auditorium, three-fifteen, sharp. No exceptions, no delays! Please see that they are notified immediately, and send Mr. Myers in here the moment he returns! Oh, and please call Town Hall, the Office of the Mayor. We're going to need all of the high-falutin' help we can muster!"

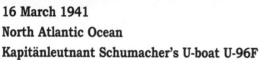

16 March 1941
North Atlantic Ocean
Kapitänleutnant Schumacher's U-boat U-96F

"Sonar reports hydrophone activity; multiple ships' propellers ten degrees starboard, range 1500 to 1700 metres, Herr Kaleu!"

"Bow up five degrees to periscope depth and hold steady. Continue to steer present heading. Switch on red lighting! *Periskop ausfahren!* Up periscope! Order all men to battle stations and standby!" As soon as the periscope pierced the ocean surface, Kapitänleutnant Frederick Schumacher commenced a scan of the grey North Atlantic horizon. He drew away from the eyepiece for a moment, to wait impatiently as the waves washing over the lens subsided, and then continued searching. Seconds later, Schumacher slapped the handgrips upward into the instrument's shaft. "Steady, steady...stop engines!"

"There is a target, Herr Kaleu?" ventured Oberleutnant Gerhard Hoffmann.

"British convoy, HO Category, small, twenty merchant freighters. Escorts: three destroyers, two frigates. Speed: fast. Exactly where the Wolfpack Leader predicted, Oberleutnant." Schumacher permitted himself a brief smile of satisfaction. "We have permission from Base to take a run at this one on our own, Hoffmann. Ready torpedoes one, two, and three!" He resumed probing the convoy searching for a likely target, a straggler.

"The identification manual, quickly please, Oberleutnant!" Schumacher ordered, while peering intently into the periscope's Zeiss optical viewer, inspecting the convoy. He sharpened the focus and selected a freighter, then glanced sideways at the silhouetted outlines of Allied vessels in the binder held out by Hoffmann. "Turn the pages, keep going, Oberleutnant. Stop! British manufacture! Yes, that's the one...Ocean Class." He paused to consider the table of specifications: tonnage, draught... "Set running depth: two metres," he ordered

Hoffmann. Making slight adjustments with his wrists while he locked in the cross hairs of the rangefinder, he stated, "Range 1,650 metres!

"Range 1,650 metres...depth two metres. Ready torpedoes one, two and three!" Hoffmann shouted. "Torpedo one ready, Sir."

"Fire torpedo one!"

"Fire torpedo one!" Hoffmann echoed Schumacher's command.

"Torpedo one fired, Sir." U-96F shuddered as the forward port tube released a seven metre, electrically propelled torpedo.

In rapid sequence, Captain Schumacher and First Officer Hoffmann repeated the sequence, firing torpedoes two and three from the starboard and port bow tubes. U-96F recoiled perceptibly twice from bow to stern. As soon as the third torpedo had been launched, Schumacher unfolded the periscope's handles. Hooking his underarms over the handle grips, he watched in silence as the trio of 'fish' sliced two metres below the water's surface, while praying that a sharp-eyed observer would not notice their nearly invisible wakes. To his satisfaction, each 'fish', a *Whitehead* type, of Italian-manufacture, and carrying an esoteric charge of high explosives: TNT, ammonium nitrate, and aluminium, mixed with a chemical 'enhancer', HND, appeared to be running dead true on target.

In the dim glow of the U-boat's Control Centre's low-level red lighting, Schumacher glanced at the sweep second hand of his wrist chronometer, while making a mental calculation. While he waited for the outcome, he thought about the critical importance of timing; it was everything in his trade. Each torpedo had to be fired at a precise, mathematical pinpoint, not where the ship was at the time of launch, but where the ship would be, so that quarry and 'fish' would intersect for maximum effect, annihilating the merchantman, *Rose of Tralee*, and her hapless crew.

Schumacher watched anxiously as the trio of torpedoes neared the end of their timed runs, sweeping outward like the points of the trident, Neptune's three-pronged spear. "Three seconds," he commented to Hoffmann. Hoffmann was about to consult his watch when U-96F shook as the sea erupted in a massive burst of water, flaming bunker crude oil, black smoke, and debris. "Dead centre hit!" Schumacher noted matter-of-factly. A second explosion followed as a torpedo penetrated the freighter's stern. "Down periscope! Dive," Schumacher shouted. "Gentlemen, our third kill," he commented to the men standing by.

"Congratulation, Herr Kapitänleutnant, you are the finest U-boat commander in the Kriegsmarine," exclaimed Hoffmann.

"Or the luckiest! Well done, all! Thank you, Oberleutnant, but no time for champagne, just yet," he smiled. "The Canadian escorts will be after us with everything they have. Signal the engine room. All engines full ahead; we're getting the hell out of here. Dive to one hundred metres and hold steady, Oberleutnant."

"Yes, Herr Kaleu!" Hoffmann replied, joyfully. "One hundred metres! All hands who are able will move forward, now, on the double!" Crewmembers ran madly from throughout the vessel, diving through open hatchways, threading their way amid fixed obstacles and shipmates at their diving stations to take positions at the U-boat's bow end, shifting the ship's centre of gravity, enabling it to submerge more rapidly.

The Type V11-B U-boat, seventy-three metres in length, began its descent to a depth of 100 m, its hull knifing through the water under the battery powered engines at its top speed of seven knots. The four men waited, listening, for twelve minutes. "Signals report?" Schumacher's query finally broke the silence.

"Nothing unusual, Herr Kaleu," replied Chief Petty Officer Helmut Bauer. "There was a flurry of faint ASDIC soundings detected, but they have died out, ten minutes ago."

"*Gut!*" he smiled. "We might be clear. Oberleutnant, I'll be in my quarters; alert the radio operators to continue listening for any unusual activity. Notify me immediately if there is any news from the Wolfpack. Otherwise, maintain radio silence. Absolutely no transmissions!"

"Yes, Herr Kaleu."

Frederick Schumacher walked the short distance to his cramped but snug quarters. Once there, he drew the curtains, which afforded him a measure of privacy. Removing his jacket, shirt and trousers, Schumacher lay down on his cot, reflecting on his ship's contributions to the Kriegsmarine's "Happy Time" which had begun in 1940 and still con-tinued. 'But for how much longer can it last?' He closed his eyes, and was asleep within seconds.

Most of the enlisted men worked shirtless, as the temperature on board could reach a stifling thirty-three degrees Celsius. The constant heat, in combination with *Mies*, the distinctive, pervasive, ever-present aroma of sweat mixed with diesel fumes, along with the odour of human waste from the heads, all blended with stale cooking odours, made the submarine's environment at times almost unbearable. The officers and crew of U-96F took it all in stride without complaint, as did their fellow submariners of every nation's 'silent service'.

Upon hearing CPO Bauer's 'Stand Down' order, those men who were not on duty returned to their quarters to follow Schumacher's example. Cots were at a premium, thus the men had to sleep in shifts. With the sub's hull a mere five metres wide, many seamen had to bunk in beside or literally on top of the nine remaining torpedoes.

17 March 1941
North Atlantic

"Herr Kaleu! Sir, respectfully, but it's urgent," Hoffmann announced through the curtain.

"Yes, what is it?" Schumacher called out sleepily. "Something wrong, Gerhard?"

"Herr Kaleu, we have received a signal, type: Secret Enciphered Radio Message: Officer Procedures, from the Admiralty. Urgency sign: 'Top Secret'," he confirmed eagerly.

"Very well, Oberleutnant. Give me the message. Bring the Book Groups and the machine with settings prepared for Officer Decoding!" Sliding open the curtain, Schumacher swung his legs over the side of his cot. Hoffman returned quickly carrying a Naval Enigma encoding/decoding machine. "Set it down carefully on the desk. Thank you. Dismiss, Oberleutnant!" Hoffmann saluted and retreated.

Taking a small ring of keys from his pocket, Schumacher unlocked the overhead cabinet. From it he took out a manual entitled, Enigma Officer and Staff Procedures 1940, and the logbook. Using the Book Group settings page, while consulting the manual, he began pecking out the coded message on the Enigma's keyboard. With each keystroke, a corresponding letter on the machine blinked on, which Schumacher recorded in the logbook. When the message was finally 'unbuttoned', Schumacher's eyes were drawn to the single 'D' at the end. It was a direct order from Admiral Karl Dönitz. 'This is a first,' Schumacher reflected, letting his breath out slowly.

Very important convoy headed your way. Intercept at coordinates, (sixty degrees north, ten degrees west); U-37, U74, U-100 and U-110 are joining you at this time. Expect rendezvous at 2100 hours. When you have radio confirmation of their arrival, attack immediately. Imperative that you effect maximum damage possible.
D.

He reread the signal word-for-word. It was unambiguous. He was to lead the attack.

Schumacher pressed the income button on his wall, barking, "Oberleutnant!"

An agitated Hoffmann reappeared. "Herr Kaleu?"

"A moment while I adjust the Enigma's settings. Now, take it back, on the double!" he commanded.

Minutes later, Oberleutnant Hoffman reappeared. "Herr Kaleu, we have received another signal from HQ in France. General Procedures; just unbuttoned, Sir!" he blurted. "Coffee, Sir?"

"Yes. Thanks, Gerhard. Wait...

'Confirmation, convoy consists of forty-one merchantmen and tankers guarded by five destroyers and two corvettes.'

Schumacher handed the message to Hoffman. "Oberleutnant, we have been given the honour to be designated as the lead ship by the Admiralty. The assignment involves a large convoy: speed unrated, likely

fast, outbound from Halifax. Heavily protected." While Schumacher dressed, he continued briefing his 2-I -C. "There can be no miscommunications and no technical foul-ups. We have approximately two hours until rendezvous with the Wolfpack. All officers are instructed to inform their section heads of the urgency and importance of this mission, immediately, after which I will give them a detailed briefing."

Taking his coffee mug, Frederick Schumacher sat bent over at his small desk, studying the navigation chart of the North Atlantic. With protractor and compass, he began plotting distances and possible points of attack. When he finished, the prospect that Admiral Karl Dönitz and his entire cadre of senior tacticians at HQ would dissect his performance in minute detail caused him a moment's hesitation. His thoughts turned back to Gretta at the Kiel Submarine Base, 18 January. They had been married for less than a month when they said farewell that day. After commending Schumacher's distinguished record, the Grand Admiral Erich Raeder and Admiral Dönitz had presented him with the coveted Swords emblem to embellish his Knight's Cross-with Oak Leaves. Following the award ceremony, Admiral Dönitz inspected the flotilla of U-boats; in his closing address, he challenged the departing crews, "You have three duties: to pursue, to attack, to destroy."

'Four, Gretta: Or die!' Schumacher reflected, while locking up the Procedures Manual, Logbook and decoded message in the cabinet.

17
March 1941
2135 h
North Atlantic

"Herr Kaleu, Sir!" Hoffmann's voice echoed over the intercom.

"Yes, Oberleutnant. No need to shout!" Schumacher realized that he must have dozed off. He put on his cap and replaced Gretta's framed picture in the drawer.

"Sorry, Sir. Radio contact established with all four U-boats in the pack. They are awaiting your orders."

"*Gut.* Have them come up to periscope depth and begin reconnaissance at sixty north, ten west. I'll be there straightaway." Schumacher tucked the rolled chart under his arm and hurried to the Control Room.

Engineer Ensign Konrad Eckert was central to the execution of Oberleutnant Hoffmann's order: "Engine room, surface to periscope depth. Stop all engines." Eckert's task was, by definition, straightforward: to maintain and manipulate the array of valves, which his mates nicknamed 'The Christmas Tree', that regulated the submarine's buoyancy by flushing and filling the ballast tanks. Yet, it was a highly specialized duty, a delicate balancing act, requiring consummate skill and a deft hand on the valves, a keen eye on the depth and pressure gauges, and an intimate understanding and appreciation for his U-boat's unique personality. Any of a number of misjudgements or mistakes on his part could render the submarine vulnerable either by a sudden, unwanted surfacing or by taking the vessel down to hull-crushing depth and certain death for all hands. He spun and closed the last stopcock, keeping an eye on the depth gauges, and then reported, "Periscope depth, Sir."

As the periscope broke the surface, Schumacher peered intently, slowly scanning from east to west. 'Nothing yet, be patient!"

"Signal Room reports a faint disturbance, Herr Kaleu. By its signature, it might be the convoy."

"Thank you, Chief Bauer. Range and bearing would be helpful," Schumacher remarked dryly.

"Yes, Sir," the Chief Petty Officer responded apologetically. "Sir, we have confirmation that U-100 has the convoy in sight, and is standing by. Coordinates are precisely as relayed in your signal."

"Send out word to get into position and commence attack at will. I have sighted them also. Liberty ships, mainly, American manufacture. Steer three degrees starboard and all ahead full," Schumacher snapped. "Oberleutnant, are all forward tubes charged?"

"Charged, Sir!"

"Ready torpedoes one to four."

Schumacher made the calculations required to enable the torpedo crews to adjust the *Whiteheads*' gyroscopic guidance settings.

"Torpedoes ready, Sir."

"Fire torpedo one!"

"Torpedo one *loss!*"

A hiss of escaping air could be heard as the starboard torpedo tube

door opened. The submarine rocked in reaction. Schumacher waited exactly fifteen seconds before giving the order, "Fire torpedo two!"

"Torpedo two *loss*!"

Fifteen seconds passed, "Fire torpedo three!" After the fourth had been discharged, all was silent. Schumacher looked into the eyepiece, searching the night's blackness for a sign of success. He examined his wristwatch. Torpedo one was well overdue; apparently, it had missed the Liberty ship's bow. He cursed silently, 'Damn, and I'm running low on fish! The Admiral won't be....' "Hello!" Two separate flashes followed seconds later by a double explosion that sent massive shockwaves rolling against the hull made Schumacher realize that they had scored two direct hits. Result: two merchantmen were aflame. Ten degrees to starboard, another flash erupted as one of the other hunters in the pack scored a decisive hit.

"Fifty percent. I'll accept it," he commented, dryly. "Oberleutnant, direct the others in the pack to expend their torpedoes and make a run for it. Admiral Dönitz wants us to throw everything we have at these poor bastards."

"Yes, Herr Kaleu."

The night was alight with explosions and fire. Schumacher counted at least eight ships ablaze in the convoy, two of which were their work. He turned away, as he could look no longer. "Take her to one hundred metres, turn to fifteen degrees south and all ahead full. Down periscope, dive!

"Oberleutnant Hoffmann, when this is over and we are safely ashore, we will break out the champagne, personally requisitioned from a charming little café on the Champs-Elysées by yours truly, when we acquired France! I will see to it that the Admiral is made aware of your sterling service and will personally recommend you for your own command."

"Really? Thank you, Herr Kaleu!"

"You're welcome. Now that's out of the way, I require your complete concentration on the tasks at hand. Status reports from all stations."

This Is Where I Will Die

17 March 1941
2200 h
North Atlantic

"Herr Kaleu, the radio room reports high-frequency pulses from a probable Canadian Tribal Class destroyer closing in at flank speed!"

"ASDIC! Damn! Dive to one hundred and eighty metres and run silent. Perhaps we can slip under its zone of silence." Schumacher knew the limits of ASDIC, the Allies' anti-submarine acoustical detection gear. If he could go deep enough while slipping inside the ASDIC's 'blind spot' then he might be home free.

"Yes, Sir. Dive to one hundred and eighty metres and run silent."

The incessant pinging grew more menacing.

17 March 1941
2315 h
North Atlantic
On board HMCS *Mohawk*

"Sir, ASDIC has picked up a German sub dead ahead, presently at two hundred eighty feet and sinking like a rock! It has to be one of the raiders, Sir!"

"Very good. Have the depth charge crews at the ready, then standby to wait for my order to fire, Lieutenant."

The Captain watched the water closely, as he wondered at what depth the U-boat's commander would level off. He had an accurate fix on the German's course and depth based on the duration and frequency of the ASDIC signals being bounced back to the *Mohawk* operators' headsets. "Our pinging's driving him down. I estimate that he's heading for maximum depth, at or very near the boat's structural limit. What do you think, Lieutenant?"

"I agree, Sir."

"Set the depth charges to five hundred feet and fire in alternating patterns, every thirty seconds."

An Allied destroyer depth charges a U-boat
Imperial War Museum

The large canisters, each containing six hundred pounds of TNT commenced rolling off their cradles at the Mohawk's stern and mid section. Captain Wilson waited, counting silently as the cylinders sank at ten feet per second. He knew that he had little or no hope of a direct hit. Even four or five near misses would not necessarily be catastrophic for the Krupp steel hulls of the most current U-boats models. The most effective depth charges could barely make a dint, unless, by sheer luck or accident, the charges exploded within a radius of ten feet of the vessel.

17 March 1941
2335 h
North Atlantic
Kapitänleutnant Schumacher's U-96F

"Herr Kaleu!"

"Quietly!" Schumacher hissed. "What is it, Gerhard?"

"We have received a status report from the Wolfpack," Hoffmann whispered. "U-37 has been rammed by a corvette and is seriously damaged, but is limping home. U-74 escaped and is heading home having expended all of her torpedoes. U-110 also made a clean getaway. U-100 was likely sunk with no word of survivors."

As Schumacher walked without comment to the wall chart, the vessel rocked and resonated with an explosion fifteen metres from its hull. "Oberleutnant! Counter-attack defensive measures! Turn off all electrical instruments. Total silence!" His command was barely audible, but Hoffmann understood fully what was meant.

With each deafening explosion, objects that were not battened down or firmly stowed were thrown about violently. Lighting flashed and flickered on and off. Even at such depth, the crewmembers could still make out the faint, but ominous sound of the destroyer's screws as it crisscrossed relentlessly overhead. They looked up; blinking involuntarily as ASDIC pulsations lashed the submarine's hull, gripping pipes, or anything else they could hold onto. Schumacher dispatched Chief Petty Officer Bauer to the engine room for a damage report.

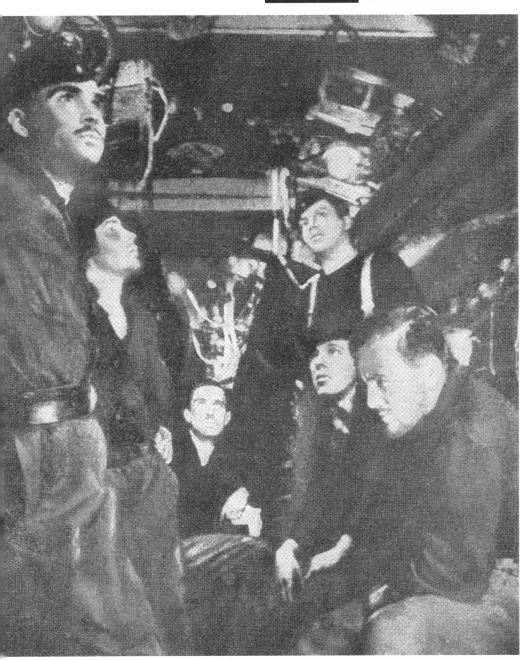

A U-boat crew awaits depth charges
Imperial War Museum

"Sir, a couple of water pipes are burst. They're repairing them now. Nothing more serious."

"Very well, keep me posted, Chief." Schumacher watched water drip from the overhead piping. Blood pounded in the back of his head, as explosion after explosion hammered the U-boat. He knew that his sub could withstand a severe thrashing, but this destroyer captain knew his business, carefully stalking them, following a grid pattern and concentrating the attack on a mathematical probability formula, which delivered the charges at an alarming rate, increasingly close in proximity.

Schumacher realized that if the barrage continued, at some point they were done for. In the meantime, there was nothing to do but run silently, praying that the captain of the Canadian destroyer would eventually give up. Two massive explosions, seeming to burst only centimetres from the port side, rendered Schumacher deaf. His head rang. He swallowed to clear his ears. Bauer stood directly in front of him, his lips moving soundlessly. Schumacher could hear nothing. He swallowed again, this time, hard.

"...reports that two major lines are split and they're taking on hundreds of litres of water," CPO Bauer whispered. "Ensign Eckert thinks they can be repaired, but the hull, Sir, port side, aft, is cracked. Critically. Leutnant Eckert estimates we'll start to lose buoyancy within forty-five minutes. It can't be repaired without surfacing then making a run to port. If we could surface Sir, we'd be able to pump out enough water to make it back. In the meantime, all hands are trying to stuff the cracks in the shell with cork and rags to hold back the water! Orders, Sir?"

"Oberleutnant, go to the Torpedo room. Have torpedo tubes numbers one and four filled with oilcans, clothing, rations, and life jackets, whatever might pass for flotsam and jetsam. Release when ready." Schumacher looked at his wrist chronometer, waiting for a reaction from his foe. "Let them think they got us!"

17 March 1941 2355 h
North Atlantic
On board HMCS Mohawk

"Captain! Over there; debris!"

"Yes, I see it, Lieutenant. Do you see any bodies floating, Lieutenant? Of course not! It's an old submariner's ploy. *Der Kapitän* wants us to believe that his vessel has been sunk in the hope that we'll call off the attack. We must be hammering him six ways from Sunday. He's desperate: not a wise command strategy. Sorry, Jerry, it didn't work. Continue," he ordered matter-of-factly. "Cigarette, Lieutenant?"

17 March 1941 2359 h
North Atlantic
Kapitänleutnant Schumacher's U-boat

"Sir," Hoffmann reported, "We've sustained another major breech of the hull, starboard side. Chief can't stop the water fast enough. No sooner he patches one crack than two more appear. Eckert estimates that we have, at the outside, only thirty minutes before we sink!"

"Oberleutnant, do the following immediately: turn on the electrics, break silence, and radio H.Q.:

We are sinking; we must surface and will have to surrender. Stop.

Then, signal the convoy in English as follows:

We are sinking. We are surfacing to surrender. Please save my men! Captain Schumacher. Stop.

Write it down! Now have them sent. Next, order Eckert to bring us to the surface. You heard me!"

"Yes, immediately, Herr Kaleu!"

"I'm going aft to assess the situation." Walking past the crew, he maintained an outward calm. "Well, Konrad, are we going up? It doesn't seem so to me..."

"Herr Kaleu, I'm trying to pressurize the ballast tanks but the damn things won't respond. We're sinking!" Eckert reported solemnly. "The pumps are useless! I'm now trying to empty the tanks manually. It's our only hope!"

"What's our depth, son?" Schumacher asked tersely.

"Sir, one hundred seventy metres, and still dropping," Eckert replied.

"Keep trying to blow the ballasts."

Eckert, frantically working the manual pumps shouted, "They won't respond, Sir. Two hundred metres and...!"

"You three men! Lend Ensign Eckert a hand here at the pumps.

"Be calm, Ensign; keep trying, it will come." Schumacher's voice was steady and reassuring, despite his personal reservations about the outcome.

The sailors' torsos glinted with sweat as they struggled to operate the pumps, knowing well that the fate of everyone on board U-96F rested upon Eckert's seamanship and the vessel's ability to withstand the extreme pressure. Without warning, a rivet suddenly burst from the metal plating, shooting across the engine room to shatter the glass face-plate of a gauge. It had missed Schumacher's head by a hair's breadth. "Jesus Christ, Herr Kaleu. Watch out!" Eckert shouted. "Sorry... Sir! You're right! Look at the gauges! We are rising!" he exclaimed, his face glowing with perspiration.

"Just as I told you; we'll be fine. Keep it going, men!"

Hoffmann appeared with a situation report from the engine room. "Both propellers are mangled, Sir. We couldn't make a run for it if we wanted to. Which we don't, do we, Sir?" he asked tentatively.

"Absolutely not, Gerhard," Schumacher stated with finality. "Your first consideration as Captain in any emergency is the safety of your men; you must never forget that! Only a damned incompetent fool or a medal-hungry idiot would risk exposing them to certain death. Do you understand?" he shouted.

"Yes, Herr Kaleu. I understand," an intimidated Hoffmann replied, cowed by the intensity of Schumacher's outburst.

The U-boat continued to slowly ascend. Before its bow broke the surface, Schumacher dispatched Hoffmann to ensure that all logs, manuals, and codebooks were being collected and destroyed.

"Including the two signals from the Admiral, Sir?"

"Yes, Hoffmann, them as well! Now get to it, lad! And instruct

Signals to ready the coding machine for jettisoning as soon as the hatch is opened..."

"Sir, Signals Room here," the intercom crackled. "We have received a signal from the destroyer, HMCS *Mohawk*. They say that they have received our distress signal and will hold off firing if we surrender and do not scuttle our boat."

"Tell them I surrender myself and my crew, but I cannot do that. Tell them:

We will scuttle and surrender. I implore you to save my men. Stop

"Open the hatch! All hands will don their lifejackets! Hand me the Enigma...hurry, damn it!"

"Hatch opening, Herr Kaleu."

"Hold this machine and give me the microphone...

"Ensign Eckert! Blow air from ballasts immediately. We are scuttling. All hands will put on their lifejackets, and will assemble on deck! I repeat! All hands on deck! No panic, gentlemen! Mr. Eckert, as soon as you are sure that the ballasts are filling, follow the others to the deck."

Schumacher scrambled up the conning tower ladder, Enigma cipher machine held tightly under his left arm, to emerge, expecting to be raked with machine gun fire. He turned and tossed the naval Enigma machine downward. It bounced noisily off the ballast chamber and then sank from sight beneath the waves.

"Damn it! The son of a bitch threw something overboard!" Captain Walker shouted angrily, striking the railing with his fist.

"What do you think it was, Captain?"

"How the hell would I know?" Walker retorted. "Sorry, Lieutenant. Maybe his radio, or logs, but I'm afraid we'll never know. He's scuttling her for sure." Walker did know. His tone reflected his frustration and anger that he had been outmanoeuvred by the German captain and would be unable to hand over the prized top-secret apparatus to the Admiralty.

Schumacher's little submarine was ringed with an intimidating phalanx of destroyers and corvettes flying Canadian and British naval ensigns. Slowly, he put up his hands and waited, before calling down the 'all clear'. The men filed up rapidly, clutching any handholds they could grasp on the deck as the waves threatened to wash them away.

Kapitänleutnant Schumacher stood impassively erect as a shell from a destroyer was fired over their heads, followed by a voice on a loudhailer.

"Attention U-96F! Surrender, but do not scuttle! Repeat, do not scuttle! We will consider it a hostile act!"

"Men, they're going to blow us out of the water, anyway." Schumacher saw the fear in the men's eyes. In another minute, he knew the water would rise to completely submerge the deck and all lives would be lost when the U-boat turned turtle. 'Gamble that they'll 'fish' us.' "Life vests secure! All hands overboard. Swim for the closest destroyer over there and we will meet up later. You will be fine, just keep swimming until you reach the ship," Schumacher shouted into the megaphone. "Good luck and May God Bless Germany!"

"Heil Hitler!" echoed Hoffmann.

"He won't save you, man, but the enemy might! Get swimming Mr. Hoffmann!"

As Ensign Eckert was about to release his grip on the ship's railing and slip into the cold North Atlantic water, he reflected with resignation, 'So, this is it. This is where I will die.'

A U-boat and her crew surrender
Imperial War Museum

CHAPTER 4
THE WAR ENDS FOR SOME

Late April, 1941
Egypt

"Cheer up you lot! I've spent a night or three in damn sight worse places meself!" The beefy Sergeant Major guffawed at his gesture of fellowship and good will. Maraschino cherry-red, his nose arose above his waxed regimental moustache like a beacon. Kurt wondered if it might be a symptom of terminally high blood pressure, an irascible temperament, or years of unstinting dedication to spiritual pursuits in the Non-Commissioned Officers' Mess: port wine and brandy. 'Possibly all three', he smiled. "What did he say?" Kurt whispered to his neighbour.

"*Sie sind guten mutes!*" translated the grizzled Afrika Korps lieutenant squatting beside him. "He's telling us to be cheerful! Sshhh. An officer's coming."

"*Aufstehen!* Be upstanding! *Achtung!* Atten...shun!" barked the Sergeant Major in passable German and parade ground English.

"He's damn well bilingual!" Kurt chortled as he struggled to unlock his knees, batting away a cloud of sand gnats that was encircling his head. "Oh, oh..."

"You there! Yes, you, the clod flailing his arms about like a bloody windmill! Did I say something funny?" the Sergeant Major demanded gruffly in Low German, pointing his swagger stick directly at Kurt. "Am I funny? Do I amuse you, Leutnant? Do I make you laugh?" As he spoke, he drew closer, as though stalking Kurt. Then, having flushed his quarry, he stopped dead and waited, before administering the *coup de grace*.

"*Nein*, Sergeant Major. *Es tut mir Leid*. I am sorry; no disrespect intended Sergeant Major," Kurt replied courteously, thinking, 'Fat pig English bastard!'

"*Ganz recht*. Very well," the non-com growled, seeming to relent, or so Kurt prayed. It was not to be. "State your name and rank!" he bellowed abruptly. Kurt had a fleeting vision of the Sergeant Major's head exploding like a grenade.

'You already know my rank, dunderhead! Very well, Kurt, you're a German officer. Show him!' "Löwen, Kurt...Ludwig, Leutnant, Sergeant Major!" he responded evenly.

The Sergeant Major, scribbling laboriously on a clipboard, paused, then demanded, "Which is it, then, eh? Ludwig or Löwen?"

"Sergeant Major?"

"*Der Familienname!*" he roared menacingly.

"Löwen.

"...Sergeant Major!"

"Löwen, Sergeant Major!" Kurt repeated. 'Damn that cursed 'Ludwig'!'

"Prisoners will remain at attention! Our commanding officer, Lieutenant Colonel Bedell-Hart!"

"Looks like you're off to a roaring start with His Worship, Löwen, Leutnant. Ludwig? Ludwig? Really? You never told me!" Peter commented, noisily scraping the remains from a tin of canned pork and beans with a deformed spoon. "Any particular reason why not? Sounds like he has it in for you! Better watch your back! Want some?"

"No thanks, finish it. Maybe I did set him off intentionally, but I think he was using me to play the hard-assed NCO to intimidate the hell out of us, to keep us in line. They're all cut from the same cloth ...bully-boys ...German Army, English... And to answer your question about my name, no. No reason to."

"Just wondering. Colonel Bedell-Hart seems all right, for an English 'long nose'. Think we can break out from here?" asked Peter cheerily.

"God almighty, we just arrived this afternoon, Peter! In case you've forgotten, we're in Egypt, the Sahara Desert, perhaps the Libyan, but North *verdammt* Africa!"

"So? I don't see any guards except *der alte Furz*, the old fart by the fence with the blunderbuss. He looks like he'd fall over at the first puff of air! I just don't want to go through an interrogation with these bastards."

"You and your winds, nature boy! Pay attention: this is a transit camp; that means it's a temporary stopover. If we did escape, we'd be captured in no time and, my friend, be put up in front of a firing squad. They don't play games out here. No, much too dangerous, for now. As for interrogation, neither do I, but Doctor Davies promised it would be fair. Geneva rules. If we play our cards right, we'll soon be shipped out to another facility, far away from the war. Maybe New Zealand, or Bora Bora…"

"Bora Bora?" Peter interjected excitedly. "Now you have my attention! Where's that? Are the girls luscious, pretty and…?"

"An atoll in the South Pacific, you dolt! And yes, I imagine they are. Just calm down a little, Peter. I know our chance will come, all in good time. Alright?" Privately, Kurt assumed that their destination would be far less exotic and warm.

"Well, if you say so. Say, maybe we could slip under the barbed wire at night, steal a fishing boat and sail back."

"Don't you listen to me at all?" Kurt retorted, his voice rising with impatience. "Back? Back to where?"

"Greece! Our forces are in Greece, no? Think baklava, retsina, mousaka, dark-eyed gypsy Adonia for me, fair-haired virginal Alexandra for you, dancing away the night under Orion…"

"And great hairy Communist partisans up in the hills, ready to pounce and gouge out our eyeballs with their thumbnails. You're incorrigible. I thought you were a believer, a *Führer treue* National Socialist! Sounds to me like you're counselling desertion."

"I am not! Just a well-deserved furlough!"

"Furlough my butt! Shut up and help me set up our cots. Can you see if you can scrounge a sheet to cover the window? The flies are worse here than in the hospital, if that's possible. What's the matter, are you feeling ill?"

Without warning, Peter gasped, his face ashen; he groaned, and doubled over in agony, clutching his mid-section. "It's my stomach! It… it feels…it's on fire! Must have been the canned pork!"

"Here, lie down! I'll call a guard."

Coincidental with Kurt's interrogation, a leading German neurosurgeon, who had previously served as medical officer on a U-boat, removed

Peter's appendix in a British Army operating theatre. Although Kurt was pre-occupied with Peter's condition, he had decided it would best serve their interests if he conducted himself civilly, as befitting an officer, by responding politely to the inquiry's grilling, without losing his temper, and with minimal detail.

As he walked the short distance from his quarters, Kurt was astonished to see what were clearly Afrika Korps PoW's wearing combat fatigues with pickaxe handles slung over their shoulders. He stopped to watch as they strolled in pairs, apparently patrolling the perimeter of the base within a two-metre wide tract flanked by an inner and an outer barbed wire fence. Italian PoWs, similarly equipped, sauntered nonchalantly behind, trailed by a smattering of Egyptians and Libyans. 'The PoW pecking order,' he noted. When Kurt opened the door of the Commandant's hut, his heart sank. The boisterous Sergeant Major was waiting for him at the reception desk.

"Löwen reporting, Sergeant Major," he stated with as much formality as he could muster.

"Good, Löwen. You're right on time. Well done. I'll let Colonel Bedell-Hart know you're here," he remarked, with icy pleasantry. After a moment, he reappeared. "The Colonel's ready to see you, Leutnant. This way, son." And that was it. No harangue, harassment, or hassle. After the Sergeant Major knocked on the Commandant's door, he leaned over and whispered in a chummy tone. "No need to worry, lad. The Colonel's a truly aristocratic gentleman. Just relax and be forthcoming, Leutnant Löwen. Sorry about yesterday. I was more than a little out of sorts, for a variety of reasons. The name is Jones, Sergeant Major Jones. Officers here call me 'S and M Freddy'," he added brightly. "Good luck, lad!"

Kurt was taken aback by the man's courtesy, whether put on or genuine. Self-consciously he apologized for laughing, offering *Danke schön* repeatedly, while shaking Freddy's extended ham-like hand.

The room was sweltering, austere, and dimly lit. Its furnishings consisted of a file cabinet, a wooden desk, and three chairs. A three–bladed electric ceiling fan only served to redistribute the heat evenly. As Kurt took his chair, a Royal Navy officer seated at Colonel Bedell-Hart's right removed his braided hat and placed it with anal precision on the desk in front of him as though covering a land mine. An aged, barefooted man, the name 'Mahamoud' stitched in blue on his steward's jacket breast pocket, entered with a tray of orange slices, sweet rolls and tea, then exited like a wraith. Without ado, Colonel Bedell-Hart arose, introduced his naval companion, poured three cups of tea, and then commenced questioning Kurt in flawless High German.

The opening salvo was courteous, probing his background: age, place of birth, highest education obtained, regiment, date of recruitment, and officer training college experience. Throughout, the serious naval man, appeared painstakingly disinterested, gazing out the window while absent-mindedly riffling a stack of index cards bound with a large rubber band that he occasionally snapped, causing Kurt to flinch involuntarily.

"And you were trained exactly where, Leutnant?" Colonel Bedell-Hart inquired, tapping a manicured index fingernail on the desktop.

"With respect, Colonel, I am not required to answer that question."

"No, you are not. Quite so, quite so," he sighed. "But did you not apply for membership in the Waffen-SS, in fact the Death's Head Division, first? You were rejected on physical grounds; it was your height I believe, and you ended up joining the 90th Light-Afrika Division, now the 380th?" he inquired, his voice spiked with irony.

"No comment, Sir!" Kurt felt his face flushing. '*Still, still,* be calm.'

"Are you now, or were you ever, a member of the National Socialist Party, Leutnant Löwen?" the naval man interrupted. "Are you not, in fact, a Nazi?" He spewed out the term with malice clearly aforethought.

"No, Sir, I am not!" Kurt retorted. "I am a patriotic German citizen, a member of my country's regular armed forces. That is all. Sir!"

The naval man pressed on, seemingly oblivious to Kurt's explanation. "Tell me then, Leutnant, exactly what were you and Leutnant Faber doing in the *wadi?* Where was your base and what was your assignment?" Hearing no response, he persisted. "You were obviously a part of an advance intelligence-gathering group, sniffing around Mechili, perhaps?" His voice had assumed the ring of cold-tempered steel.

Kurt did not reply. As if on cue, the Colonel and naval officer exchanged glances, then rose, and without comment left the room.

For ten minutes, Kurt sat reviewing his responses and trying to anticipate the next round. Distracted by the monotonous humming of the fan's lazy circling, he rose and went to the window. He watched the 'shitehawks' skim the sparkling surface of the Mediterranean, all the while sipping his tea and eating an almond-flavoured pastry, and then another. From time to time, the windowpanes vibrated while the floor shuddered perceptibly.

Feeling desperately in need of the washroom, he knocked on the

door. S and M Jones accompanied him down the hallway to an ancient porcelain fixture. "Hear that, Löwen? Guns, tanks...heavy artillery." He held his right hand aloft, as though invoking an avenging heavenly host. "Ours. Your General Rommel is getting the bejesus kicked out of him! Bloody hell on earth for your lot," he remarked with an obvious sense of self-justification.

When Kurt returned, Colonel Bedell-Hart was waiting. "Very well, Leutnant," he cleared his throat. "We're all but finished. You are dismissed, for the time being. Oh, one more thing. By any chance, was Warrant Officer Siegfried 'Siggy' Hertz your gunnery instructor at Prenzlow? Lovely fellow, Siggy; I shot against him in Berlin in '36. He trounced me thoroughly. We called him Siggy *der Scharfschütze*, the sharpshooter," he chuckled. "And not only for his prowess on the range, wicked little git! By the by, we resurrected your Zunndap motorbike. Fine piece of machinery it is. A bit of advice: you shouldn't carry your navigational charts in saddlebags. It would be smarter to... Ah, but that's giving away the game, isn't it? She should be running again, soon, if she isn't so already. Perhaps you'd like to see her?"

"Yes, I'd like that," Kurt muttered, staring at the floor. At length he asked, "May I go now, Sir?"

"You may, Leutnant. Wait.

The naval officer re-entered. "Any news from the surgeon, Commander?" Bedell-Hart inquired.

"Leutnant Faber's condition is stable. He is still under the anaesthetic. You may visit him tomorrow afternoon, Leutnant." Kurt thought he noted a tight-lipped smile, or a grimace.

"Thank you," Kurt replied. He stood up and saluted. As he reached for the door handle, he paused. "Can you tell me, Colonel Bedell-Hart, where Leutnant Faber and I are to be imprisoned?"

"The short answer? No, I cannot."

"All went well, I expect, son?" boomed Sergeant Major Jones as Kurt closed the door behind him.

"A piece of cake, as you English say, Sergeant Major."

"Glad your comrade has pulled through. And by the by, congratulations, Leutnant Löwen. You've pulled picket duty tonight, 2000 h. Be at the guardhouse for your kit and orders 1955 h."

"My kit? Do you mean my pick handle?"

"What did you expect, a flaming bloody Thompson sub-machinegun?" Jones shot back in English, with a twinkle. "Be there in a timely fashion, mind! Dismiss."

"'Be there in a timely fashion, mind!' Bloody stupid English!" Kurt muttered under his breath as he followed the rough-hewn stone pathway back to his tent. Cautiously, he pulled back the entrance flap, poked his head inside, and withdrew it instantly, his head reeling from the sudden scorching blast of fusty air. Looking around for relief from the high noon inferno, Kurt spied what appeared to be the hulk of a clapped-out army lorry in the distance and made a run for it. Flopping on the sand in the shade of the twisted wreck, he tried to compose his thoughts. 'How in the name of all that's holy did they know so much? SS, Prenzlow, W.O. Hertz; and especially Mechili...of course, *Dummkopf*, the damn maps!' Impatiently, he unscrewed the cap of his water container, took a mouthful, spit it out and replaced the cap. 'Peter's deathly sick. I've likely betrayed General Rommel, and Freddy's just waiting for an excuse to jump down my throat. What's next, wonder boy?' Leaning his shoulders against the disintegrating carcass of a tire, Kurt slept fitfully.

Guard duty, as Freddie explained, was not so much intended to keep in the PoW's, but to keep out the local 'entrepreneurs', meaning black marketeers, he said, who regularly attempted and often succeeded in penetrating the double barbed wire enclosure to raid the depots and pilfer any sort of sellable supplies, from flour to fishhooks. Kurt found himself in the company of five Afrika Korps PoW's, most of who spoke English coloured with a smattering of Arabic curse words. The patrol was rounded out with a ragtag collection of Egyptian irregulars. Duty consisted of two hours of walking the 'rounds' as the Korpsmen described it, keeping an eye out for 'bloody Wogs' and 'other assorted riff-raff', all-encompassing British and Australian Army terms of derision, which the Germans had adopted. A 'Wog', Kurt was informed, was a 'Worthy Oriental Gentleman'. 'If they are 'worthy and admirable" he wondered, 'then why insult them?' The irony of that and most British service slang eluded him. The pickets were expected to shout to the lone British sentry, Lance Corporal Alf, if they detected anything amiss or vaguely 'fishy'. To Kurt's disappointment, it never was.

To ward off the chilling desert night cold, the Egyptian 'fellahs' kept

small paraffin lamps under their robes. When they gathered to crouch in clusters, Kurt thought they resembled very short Christmas trees. Relieved at 2200 h, Kurt and his companions had four hours to sleep before resuming patrol duty at 0200. Then, the Afrika Korps Leutnant, who had translated Freddie's introductory comments, fell in step with Kurt. After introducing himself as Klaus Keppler, he confided that the likelihood of their remaining in North Africa much longer was slim to none.

"The English want to get us far away from the war zone here and from their 'doorstep', Europe, entirely. Things are going very badly for the Allies in Libya. Rommel's DAK is running circles around their lines. He can make the breakthrough into Egypt and then seize the Suez Canal in a month or less. If we escape, at the least, we're a costly distraction and, at most, a real threat."

"Where are we going, then?"

"First England; after which, we'll be shipped to Canada, I'm certain!" he whispered conspiratorially, as they stood and stamped their feet to restore the circulation.

"I'd prefer America! Chocolate bars and movie stars! But Canada!" Kurt exclaimed, "Eskimos, snow, rocks, more snow, and pine trees!"

"We're not at war with America, in case you hadn't noticed. Think Canada's cold? It's a damn sight warmer than Mother Russia; we're going in full force immediately after Britain collapses. At least that's my prediction."

"Not possible! The Führer and Stalin signed the Nazi-Soviet Pact in 1939. It guarantees no aggression between the two nations for ten years!" protested Kurt vehemently.

"Wake up, Kurt! The so-called Pact of Steel isn't worth the paper it's written on; Adolf Hitler and Joseph Stalin themselves did not sign it, their Foreign Minister flunkies Ribbentrop and Molotov did, so neither leader considers it binding personally. Remember Munich? Exactly! Then we waltzed into Prague in March 1939. Why? I'll tell you why, Kurt my boy: to protect Sudeten Germans in Bohemia and Moravia from the evil Czechs. Believe that lie? No, my friend, it was all about the superb Skoda Works, munitions factories, mines brimming with fabulous deposits of mineral ores...Slovakian iron, copper, tin, coal, and a technically sophisticated talent pool of slave labour to boot. We'd better get moving. We can walk and talk."

"Klaus, how do you know all this?"

"I am a political scientist by training and a cynic by upbringing. My Father was a pacifist and *Mutti* dear an anarchist. Father was jailed by the Kaiser in '15 for refusing to sign up."

"Why did you then? Join up?"

"Oh, let me see. First, a disastrous marriage...then I was cashiered from the Faculty for giving lectures spouting nationally subversive political diatribes. And finally, I saw the chance to pay off some of the mountainous debts run up by my mistress by serving my country, which I love dearly, under the great German *Führer* in the mould of Frederick the Great. *Fritz der Grosse* is long dead mind you, and his present incarnation is a cranky, dyspeptic and wildly delusional despot, an Austrian corporal into the bargain, but no matter. Both are geniuses. Read his book, *Mein Kampf,* if you don't believe me."

"You're saying things that could get you in hot water, maybe shot, Klaus. Even here."

"Listen, I'm a German first, and, you might say, an intellectual. My studies and my conscience tell me I can't support a regime that seems hell-bent on repeating the debacle of the First World War. Of course the *Führer* detests Slavs and distrusts Joe Stalin, and that feeling's mutual, but the real reason for breaking the treaty is our military's desperate appetite for the Soviet Union's immense resources: wheat, oil, minerals, their heavy industry and slave labour. Geopolitics..."

"Do you think Stalin suspects?"

"I don't think he's stupid, but Lord, who knows? By the way, you never heard any of this from me. You're correct. The hardcore Nazi fellows here would not be thrilled. Promise, Kurt?"

"I promise, Klaus. Word of honour."

"Good. Here. Take a swallow from my flask. Go ahead, it'll warm you up!"

"That's wonderful. What is it?"

"Cognac. French. The real thing. Do you like cigars?"

"Like Winston Churchill? I never tried one. Just a simple peasant boy, at heart."

"Peasant, maybe, but simple? I think not. Tomorrow night then."

During the final hour of their tour, Kurt and Klaus talked of nothing more serious than the terrible food and the rapacious flocks of screaming 'shitehawks', seagulls, that strutted and defecated, fouling everything, despite the PoWs' attempts to drive them away with hurled shouts and rocks. And they discovered a shared boyhood love for American cowboy movie serials.

Two days later, the twenty-five Afrika Korps officer PoW's from the internment camp were *en route* in a convoy of two army lorries destined for an undisclosed location near Alexandria, to board a Royal Navy troop transport. Peter Faber lay on a stretcher beside Kurt, his head protected with a sunshade held stoically by an Egyptian hospital orderly. The surgeon had reluctantly signed Colonel Bedell-Hart's discharge papers at the last moment on the condition that Peter be accompanied to the ship.

"So, how is the patient feeling now?" Kurt leaned over, inquiring quietly.

"Better, thanks." Peter smiled wanly, "Where are we going, Kurt?"

"England."

"England. Why? Why there?" His chalk-white face paled perceptibly. "Oh, oh, oh, *Gott im Himmel*! My stitches, Omar!" he shouted hoarsely at his escort as the truck rolled over a bone-jarring washboard.

"It's only a stopover. Don't worry; then, we'll be off to Bora Bora!" Kurt responded without conviction.

"You always were a rotten liar, Kurt," Peter replied. "I missed the interrogation, thanks to this. How was it?"

"I survived, but you know, we really should have been more careful. They found everything."

"Very good!"

Kurt didn't respond. He realised that Peter's attention was completely focussed on his own comfort and well-being. "Move the shade a bit this way, Omar; sorry, I meant Zahur. More, more, that's it. Perfect. You were saying you have a younger sister, Safiya, is it, in Cairo? By any chance you have a picture?"

Kurt leaned back, pondering their gaffe with the maps and the clever, crafty replies that he could and should have prepared for the likes of Bedell-Hart and the naval man. 'What if I have stupidly compromised General Rommel's battle plans?'

During the first day of gut wrenching, wretched nausea, Kurt decided that Mediterranean Sea travel was vastly overrated. Each of the PoW's aboard HMS *Hermione*, with the exception of Peter, it seemed, agreed. As a result, the ship's captain made an unscheduled one-hour stop at 'Gib', (Gibraltar), allowing the Medical Officer just enough time to requisition a fresh store of anti-seasickness pills. Peter, who, Lazarus-like, rebounded from his ordeal, was miraculously immune. Taking advantage of the boredom and natural instincts of the off-duty British sailors, he taught them the niceties of Skat, Germany's national card game. Soon, mixed trios and quartets of Cockney, Geordie, and Scouse voices were shouting variations of, '*Habe ich!*' 'I've had it!' '*Mischen!*' 'Shuffle!' and frequent, 'Bloody hells'!' To his credit, between hands, Peter tended to Kurt and Klaus, faithfully.

The *Hermione* docked at Liverpool under dark of night in a heavy drizzle. Immediately, the prisoners, many still suffering the effects of the voyage, were loaded onto canvas-covered Army lorries and carted off northward to be housed at a dreary sports arena in Preston. In the morning, after a hearty Lancashire breakfast of poached eggs, kippers and black pudding, Kurt threw up, and then scrambled to catch up with the others and boarded a London-bound train. Arriving at Enfield, the men were driven to Cockfosters interrogation centre.

Although Peter, Klaus, and the other men were intensively interrogated, the next five days were uneventful for Kurt. Following a brief session to process his PoW papers, he busied himself with regular exercise in the gymnasium, and reading, under the mentorship of an Anglican Chaplain, Father Ralph. Kurt was so pleased with his ability to conquer one 'Peter Rabbit' title a day that he felt ready to tackle Conan Doyle's 'The Hound of the Baskervilles,' which he had spied on the top shelf in Father Ralph's study. Despite the cleric's reservations, Kurt blithely assured him. "A piece of cake, Father!" before lapsing into German. "*Ein Deutsch-Englisch Wörterbuch, bitte?*" English-German dictionary in hand, he returned to his cot and read until suppertime.

The next stage of their journey took them north to the incomparable English Lake District, where they were housed in a grand forty-room manor home, Grizedale Hall, located between Windermere and Coniston Water. Grizedale Hall, Lager 1 (PoW Camp 01), Kurt learned, had

become known as 'U-boat Hotel', in recognition that scores of inmates were officers of that service. Despite Camp 01's barbed wire fencing and basic living conditions, a British politician of the day complained in Parliament that it might be less of a financial strain on the nation if the Germans were put up in London's Ritz Hotel. Numbered among its roster of temporary or permanent luminaries was the legendary Luftwaffe pilot and celebrity habitual 'escaper', Franz von Werra, as well as ace U-boat Fregattenkapitän Otto Kretschmer, and, from March 1945 until his release in July 1948, Field Marshall Gerd von Rundstedt, former Supreme Commander-in-Chief of the Western Front.

Subjected to intense questioning by British Intelligence, while existing on a diet of watery porridge and herrings with potatoes, there was little else to occupy the PoWs' time but to walk the exercise cage, concocting and discussing the latest rumours.

18 March 1941

0020 h

The North Atlantic

Konrad Eckert's head bobbed rhythmically in the rough seas. Salt water and diesel oil lapped at his mouth; he tried holding his breath in an effort to avoid gulping down the deadly soup. It was futile. In the darkness, he could not see the waves approaching. Konrad detected a faint voice.

"*Wer ist das?* Who is that? I can see the top of your head, but...I can't recognise you!"

"Eckert here! Captain, is that you?"

"Konrad? Yes, Schumacher here! Swim towards me, the others are over here. We must stay together." Captain Schumacher's voice grew louder.

"Sir, I'm freezing. I don't... don't think I can make it!"

"Nonsense, son. You'll be all right. Don't stop moving. It's important to keep your arms and legs moving constantly to keep warm. I can see the destroyer. Follow me. Keep swimming, son. Don't give up. Swim towards it."

Konrad stared in the direction Captain Schumacher indicated. He blinked; through the fog of water and oil, which moments earlier threatened to blind and swallow him up, he could make out the grey silhouette of a destroyer. It appeared that the crew were throwing something over the side. As he swam closer, he could see that sailors were climbing down nets towards the water, waving their hands to attract the men from the U-boat.

'Why are they doing that? They are the enemy... Too far, too far... Stay here. Safer...' Konrad was now drifting into unconsciousness. The water was a warmly seductive, comforting cocoon; soon, he would be at peace.

Something grabbed his collar, lifting his inert body out of the 4°C brine. The shock of the ice-cold air struck Konrad forcibly, shocking him into full consciousness. As he was being lowered onto the ship's deck, he caught sight of a figure dipping lifelessly in the slick, the oil-logged lifejacket barely keeping the upper body above water.

"The Captain! Save him, please!" Eckert screamed. On a shouted command from the boatswain, Schumacher's limp body was hauled out of the water and laid on the deck with the others. Konrad looked around anxiously, searching for familiar faces. He began counting the bowed, oil-streaked heads, as they huddled together, dazed, collectively shivering in the numbing sub-Arctic air.

The ship's Captain appeared, to announce in German, "All hands that could be found are safe.

"You men, take the prisoners below. Have them remove their clothing and shower. Then give them warm blankets and fresh clothes."

The forty-three surviving crewmen and officers of the U-boat began stumbling their way below deck.

"A moment, please. Kapitänleutnant Schumacher, I presume?" inquired Captain Wilson.

"Yes, Captain?"

"Captain Wilson. I have quarters set up for you. Come, let me show you the way."

"Thank you, Captain." As Schumacher followed Wilson along the

deck of HMCS *Mohawk*, he noticed a horseshoe fastened to the outside bridge. Unlike the one on Schumacher's U-boat, the tips were pointed upward instead of down.

"Captain, the horseshoe, why is it pointed up?" Schumacher asked.

"Oh, an old navy superstition, Kapitänleutnant; it's up to catch the luck!".

Schumacher didn't reply. Hoping to change and wrap himself in a woollen blanket, he followed Captain Wilson to the Captain's quarters.

"Please, sit down, Kapitänleutnant. Do you mind if I call you Captain? I'm sure you wouldn't turn down a glass of rum and a cigarette, would you?" inquired Wilson, unscrewing the cap of a new twenty-sixer. A package of Canadian navy cut cigarettes and a lighter lay temptingly close on the Captain's table.

"Yes, call me Captain. Rum? No, I wouldn't turn that down, Captain. I don't smoke, but could use one right now, for sure!" Taking the glass offered by Wilson, Schumacher's hand trembled violently, spilling some of the amber liquid on the floor. "Sorry, such a waste. I...I'm a little bit cold still. *Mein Gott*, that is so good! True Barbados rum! May I please have that cigarette now, Captain?"

"Not to worry, there's lots more where that came from, unless your chap Dönitz manages to cut that off, too! Here, let me light it for you. I'll leave in a minute so you can take off your wet uniform, have a shower, and put these on. Not fancy, but you'll be warm, or at least warmer. You're welcome to lie down on my bunk for a rest. When you wake, we'll have some food and a chat. I hope that there'll be no more excitement. Sleep well, Captain."

"Thank you, Captain Wilson. My men, are they all right? My first officer, Oberleutnant Hoffmann, did he make it?"

"Forty-three accounted for and snug as bugs... *Gemütlich*," he added for clarification then continued in German. "Getting cleaned up, fed, and likely ready to settle in for a nap."

An hour later, Schumacher awoke abruptly to sounds of cheering outside the Captain's cabin. When Captain Wilson returned, Schumacher was sitting on the edge of the bunk, smoking a cigarette. "Very bad habit, but pleasant enough. May I inquire, Captain? A little while ago, you were celebrating our capture, I think. No?"

The War Ends For Some

"Yes, the men are ecstatic. We just received word from Naval HQ England that I've been recommended for the DSO, Distinguished Service Order."

Schumacher looked dejectedly at the floor and then held out his hand. "Congratulations, Captain Wilson. It is well-deserved."

"Thank you, Captain. You know, it really was bad luck for you: wrong place, at the wrong time. We were actually expecting to see Schepke's U-boat surface. That's who we thought we were tracking. Quite a shock to find out that there were actually two subs in the same area. Do you happen to know of Korvettenkapitän Prien's whereabouts?" Wilson asked with studied casualness. Günther Prien was at the top of the Royal Navy's 'most wanted alive' list.

"No, I don't. He could be on holidays or at sea. I'm not really sure."

"Well, I'll take that under advisement. Fleet is fairly certain that we caught him flatfooted, too."

"Where will you be taking us?" Schumacher asked slowly, methodically butting out his cigarette.

"England, we're bound for England. We should be there tomorrow, Lord willing, unless one of your Wolfpacks gets our scent. Wouldn't that be ironic, Captain?" he chuckled ruefully. "Right about now, that would be a damn fitting conclusion to the day's events!"

In the evening, Schumacher was introduced to one of the merchant-man captains whose ship he had likely torpedoed and sunk the night before. They saluted. Awkwardly, Schumacher saluted and offered his condolences. To his surprise, the Captain, although reserved, inquired after the U-boat crews' well being. It was as though each man readily accepted the other's role in a deadly sport.

In the morning, Schumacher awoke to bright sunshine and a calm sea. 'We must be in port', he thought. Captain Wilson came to the door to say they would disembark in thirty-five minutes. As Schumacher, holding a coffee mug, stepped onto the main deck, he could see his men standing at attention on the pier, opposite the *Mohawk's* officers. Schumacher strode down the gangway to the pier; he realized that his life was about to become far less official. Noticeably missing was the shriek of the bo'sun's whistle to signal the departure of the ship's Captain.

On the pier, a British army captain took him by the arm. "Step this way, please, Captain. You're coming with me, Sir." Two military police-

men unceremoniously placed him in the back seat of a staff car. As they were about to drive away, Schumacher glanced back to see his crew and officers being loaded into army lorries. He caught a glimpse of Gerhard Hoffmann. Further back, Captain Wilson, and his officers were saluting the U-boat's crew. *'Unwirklich!'* It was surreal.

From Liverpool, blacked-out buses took the PoWs to Preston where they were to be housed in what appeared to be a racetrack or arena. As the buses pulled up to the building, a crowd was milling around. The military police opened the doors and began to march the men inside. The mood turned ugly as the crowd became more agitated and began shouting obscenities at the Germans. When the rock throwing started, additional soldiers had to be rushed in, for fear that the civilians would storm the building. Schumacher surmised that many of the women had likely lost husbands and sons on some of the ships that he or his comrades had sunk. 'Who could blame them after all?' he reflected as shattered glass flew around his head.

The arena in which Schumacher and his men were held was the first of many interrogation camps. During a session in the Lake District, the interrogator greeted him with a smile. "Please, sit down Captain. We are truly honoured today. While you have been a prisoner of His Majesty the King, your superiors have promoted you to the exalted rank of Korvettenkapitän. Congratulations."

"Thank you, Sir, but it is not much to celebrate under these circumstances," he commented gamely.

"Better for us this way than the other," the Englishman grinned.

The interrogator went on to list in minute detail the dates, times and locations when Schumacher had played a role in specific attacks on convoys. Schumacher was disheartened to learn how much the British knew about him and his U-boat's supposedly secret missions. 'How did they know?' would haunt his nights. He was grilled daily about the whereabouts of the notorious Korvettenkapitän Günther Prien: "*Wo ist Prien?* Where is Prien?" Schumacher rapidly concluded that they desperately wanted U-47 Korvettenkapitän Prien, the toast of Germany and the Kriegsmarine taken alive, to avenge the 1939 Scapa Flow Naval Base disaster. With great skill and daring, Prien had surfaced at night, threading the shallow Orkney's channels and eluding the Royal Navy's flimsy defences. Sighting what he believed to be HMS *Repulse*, U-47 fired two torpedoes. Both were harmless 'duds', a not-uncommon occurrence that had robbed Prien and his fellow commanders of numerous 'kills'. Undaunted, Prien turned the boat to aim her three bow tubes at what was, in fact, the pride of the Royal Navy, HMS *Royal Oak*, lying at anchor. Hit by all three 'fish' in her aft magazine, the blazing vessel capsized and sank within fifteen minutes with the loss of some 834 naval ratings and officers, including a visiting admiral. Winston Churchill, the then First Sea Lord of the Admiralty, magnanimously cited Prien's attack as, "a magnificent feat of arms." Decorated with the Knight's Cross by Adolf Hitler, the first U-boat skipper recipient of the high honour, Günther Prien, returned to duty. On or about 7 March 1941, all hands aboard U-47 were lost in the Atlantic Ocean. The German Ministry of Propaganda suppressed this information.

7 August 1940
0730 h
On Dover Beach

Dazed, Karl Semmler blinked rapidly, his head spinning. There was something strange about the figure coming toward him; was it upside down? Through the haze of oil and grime, he could make out the inverted silhouette of a man running along the beach. 'Maybe I've cracked my head!' he thought. Gradually, it occurred to Karl that he was hanging head down, suspended in a tangle of harness straps.

John Harning, a Veteran of World War I, was now a member of the Home Guard. He ran toward the downed aircraft; halting, breathless, he carefully affixed his bayonet to his old Enfield rifle then continued to scamper along the pebbled beach until he stood only three feet away from the helpless airman, bayonet at the ready.

"Don't make a move or I'll put my bayonet straight through your heart. And don't think that I won't do it, mate, 'cause I bloody well will!"

Getting no response, the Home Guard soldier stared at the man, wondering if he was unconscious, dead, or playing dead. He could see that the pilot was bleeding profusely from a nasty gash on his forehead. As he knelt down to take a closer look, he could see that the 'man' was a mere boy, likely only nineteen or twenty years old.

"Son? Son, are you alright?" John asked.

Karl moaned, making a few movements in response. John, no longer harbouring thoughts of thrusting his bayonet through the young man's body, now considered how he might save the life of the young pilot.

"Here, let me get you out of that thing." John placed his rifle on the beach. Having no reason to fear this helpless young man, he removed the bayonet and used it to cut the harness. John rested the pilot's head on a heap of sand and pebbles. By now, a group of people had gathered around, all talking and pointing at the young German pilot.

"You with the bicycle, young Eddie, go fetch the local coppers. Hurry!" Shortly, two constables drove up to the scene in an immaculate black Wolseley.

"Hello, John. What do you have here?" one of them shouted.

"A Nazi, is it then?" called his companion, seeing the markings on the wreckage.

"Hello, lads. This fellow was shot down by our boys and almost landed at my feet," John stated proudly.

"We'll take over now, John. Thank you for guarding the bloke until we could get here. The ambulance should arrive in two shakes to take him to the military hospital. You've done the country a great service. Run along now, John, and keep up the bloody good work."

"Right-oh, boys. We'll be seeing you then." John stayed long enough to watch the ambulance arrive and, with the aid of the constables, to see Karl placed on a stretcher, loaded into the back, and taken away.

9 August 1940 1436 h
An English Military Hospital, London

"Son, wake up," the bright-eyed angel chirped in German.

"Where...am...I?"

"You're in hospital, in London. You've had a nasty bump on the head but you'll be feeling better soon. A slight concussion: you've been out for two days, Karl."

"I have? Thank you, sister. Next question. Can you tell me what happened?"

"Well, I don't know for sure; only that you were shot down over the cliffs of Dover and you were brought here. We've given you the best care and you should be up and around in a couple of days. The military is anxious to talk with you, but I have asked them to wait until the doctor checks you over again. Right now, I don't think that you could give us your full name," she laughed.

"Karl Semmler," he stated.

"My, my, aren't we making headway, ducks!" she responded in English. 'And so handsome.' "It's time to take your temperature, Karl Semmler. *Verlängern!* Roll over!"

11 August 1940
1000 h
An English Military Hospital, London

"Are you ready to go, young fellow?"

"*Was?*" Karl found the man's German nearly incomprehensible because of his peculiar English accent.

"Ready... *fertig?*"

"*Ja.* Yes, ready as ever, I suppose, Sergeant. Where are you taking me?"

"We're going to the train station. There you will be taken with a number of other PoWs to an undisclosed place. Don't worry, you'll be in good hands."

Karl bade an emotional farewell to the doctors and the nurses who had taken such good care of him. "I will miss all of you. Thank you. Thank you all for your kindness!" He clambered into the rear of the paddy wagon.

As the Sergeant drove away, he reached back to slide open the small glass window which separated him from Karl.

"What's the name, son?"

"Karl, Sergeant. Karl Semmler."

"'arvey. Have you ever been to London before, Karl?"

"No, 'arvey, I haven't," Karl answered. "Why do you ask, please?"

"Just curious." As the two men conversed, Karl looked at the streets of London in awe. He was amazed to see so little damage to the buildings, contrary to the German press reports and photos, which boasted of the ravages rained on London by the Luftwaffe in night after night of

heavy bombings.

"What are you looking at, Karl?"

"I'm surprised at how little damage there is. I mean, I can see build-ings that have been damaged but there is no debris."

"Us Londoners have our lovely ladies to thank for that. Each mornin' after an air raid, they come out with their brooms, and coal shovels and carts and, within hours, you wouldn't know that we had been attacked. Bloody spotless! Right marvellous, they are. Say, 'ave you ever seen Buckingham Palace, Karl?"

"No, never. I've heard of it, but I haven't even seen pictures of it."

"Well, Karl, you're in for a treat. My ticktock tells me that it's 11:30, which means they're changin' the guard right now. Would you like to have a look?"

"Oh, yes! That's very kind of you, 'arvey!"

Harvey backed up the paddy wagon as close to the main gates of Buckingham Palace as he could and opened the rear doors.

"There, take a gander at that. Isn't that a sight, lad? Not even old 'itler himself has seen that firsthand!" Harvey exclaimed, his face beam-ing with pride. "And he never will!" he added emphatically. "Sorry, lad, no offence."

"None taken, 'arvey." Karl sat on the back of the wagon mesmerized by the majesty of the Grenadier Guards in full dress scarlet uniforms, with black bearskin headpieces, executing their manoeuvres to the accompaniment of splendid military marches. Karl was spellbound by the spectacle. Up to that moment, he had thought such breathtaking precision existed only in German regiments.

"Right, Karl. We'd best get goin'. We 'ave a train to catch," Harvey announced cheerfully. "'ere, 'op in the front. No sense sittin' back there like a common criminal. Get in, lad!"

The wagon pulled into King's Cross Station where Karl could see hundreds of PoWs on the platform, waiting to be loaded onto the train. He found it difficult to believe that Germany could be winning the war when so many of her soldiers were plainly here, in custody.

"Right lad; well, chin up!" Harvey offered his hand. "Cheery bye!"

"Thank you, 'arvey. I'll always remember your kindness, and espe-cially our visit to Buckingham Palace!"

As soon as all were boarded and settled in for what they were told would be a long journey, Karl curled up in a corner seat and closed his eyes in an attempt to get some sleep. Before dozing off, he thought about the fate of his best friend, Wolfgang von Heiden, and wondered about his mother; by now, his poor, dear mother must surely have been informed that her son Karl was missing in action. Or had she? 'Perhaps she has been told that I'm missing, and presumed dead. I must write...and let her know I am alive.'

August, 1940

0700 h

PoW Camp Glasgow, Scotland

Karl, along with the other men, was herded into one of the makeshift huts in an interrogation camp on the outskirts of Glasgow. Fortunate in that he was a Luftwaffe officer, he had much more comfortable quarters than the other ranks. The days were long, damp, and boring, but Karl kept himself occupied by looking at English picture magazines and writing home to his mother. In his first letter, after telling his mother that he was in good condition, he asked for news about his friend and flying comrade, Wolf. For days, there was no response, but at last, a letter arrived from his mother.

Dearest Karl,

I was so excited to get your letter and to learn that you are not only safe, but also well away from the fighting. I know that you are anxious to find out what happened to Wolfgang. The sad news is that we don't know. He went missing the same day as you did, but no one here has heard from him. Letters to the squadron simply say that they will advise us at the first opportunity.

I hope you received the chocolates. Do let me know either yes or no. If you did receive them, I will continue to send more.

Love,
Mother

Dearest Momma,

Thank you for your letter. All is well here. It rains almost every day and it is very cool, but I'm surviving and practising my English.

My theories concerning Wolfgang are as follows:

1. He was shot down, seriously wounded, and taken to another hospital to recover.

2. Then again, he might not have been injured so he's already in prison elsewhere.

Hoping for the best! Please give my love to his family.

P.S. No chocolates. Perhaps they'll show up yet. Try again?

Love,

Your Karl

'3. Perhaps he didn't make it, God forbid.'

CHAPTER 5
WILLKOMMEN IN KANADA!

9 April 1942

Bowmanville

The roar of steam billowing from the locomotive's boilers jolted Karl awake as the train drew up to a level crossing and shuddered to a stand-still. He turned to retrieve the jacket that had served as a pillow and looked out the coach window: farm fields, unending forests, and sky. Endless sky.

'So, this is our new home. Very primitive and rugged, but it does have a natural beauty, nonetheless. Resign yourself, Leutnant Semmler, your flying days are over. There will be no escape from this backwater.'

He had found the journey from Halifax long, tiresome, and monoto-nous. The PoWs had been loaded on board regular day coaches without bunks. His back ached from sitting upright, though he was resigned to the discomfort, deciding that it was to be expected. After all, he thought, they were prisoners, enemies of their host country, not visiting bigwigs. 'At least we aren't wearing leg irons,' he chuckled. While the majority of his coach mates had passed the hours in quiet banter, with occasional outbursts of cursing and laughter, a handful of Afrika Korpsmen had made several unsuccessful attempts to organize the coach into a two-part choir. Their efforts to sing a rousing drinking chorus were firmly quashed by the guards, who mistakenly thought the song to be the noto-rious Nazi Storm Troopers' marching song, *Horst Wessel*, which, to some Germans, had become the unofficial national anthem. The Canadians were not entirely mistaken. The melodies were identical.

Karl thought it not only childish but also bad mannered of his com-panions to bait their captors so brazenly and so had elected to remain apart, absorbed in his thoughts. He glanced down at the crumpled ball of waxed paper on the floor and smiled, remembering when he and the others had boarded the train in Halifax and were each issued a brown paper bag, the top folded down twice. The men began muttering and cursing the guards when, upon opening the bags, they found one slice of bologna on a doughy, white substance that vaguely resembled bread, and an apple. In the belief that the food had to be rationed until they

arrived at their destination, each man ate sparingly, taking small, cautious bites, and then carefully returning the remnants to the paper bags. Four hours later, despite a chorus of protests, the guards had come by to collect the remains, which they casually tossed out of the train windows. In Germany, Karl realized, people would be lining the tracks, awaiting the scraps. Then, to the PoWs' astonishment, the guards re-entered the coach at 1700 hours, pushing metal carts stacked high with trays of hot meals.

Crossing into Ontario, as the train sped by the towns and villages, Karl's curiosity had been piqued by the similarity of the names in bold lettering posted near the stations' platform walls: 'Bovril, Hawes, Bovril, Bovril, Hawes... Very peculiar folk, these Canadians,' he concluded. He also noticed the towns' young couples walking hand in hand, typically dressed in service olive drab or blue, or others, with fresh, beautiful faces in automobiles, all smiling, laughing and even waving, waiting for the train to pass the crossings. He felt a pang of envy. It was as though these Bovril and Hawes natives were a race of naïve and innocent inhabitants of another planet, one in peaceful harmony with the universe, and very unlike the Germany that he had left behind.

Two cars back, Korvettenkapitän Frederick Schumacher stretched as he looked out the window of the converted rail car. He, too, had made a note of the signs along the way. Now, all he could see were vast landscapes of fields, trees, and a small stream winding its way along. 'But where does it go? That's the question'. Observing the extra guards at both ends of the car, he decided that it was not the right time to attempt an escape. 'Not just yet.'

"Frederick?"

Schumacher looked up. "Wilhelm?"

"So good to see you, Frederick," Wilhelm Klein stated warmly. "May I sit with you? The fellows in my section are too rowdy for my tastes."

"Yes, please do, Wilhelm. It's a pity we didn't meet up until now. How have you been?"

"Well, very well, thank you. I heard that you were at Grizedale Hall, when I was at Camp 198, Brigend. Congratulations on your promotion to Korvettekapitän! I was thrilled when the news reached us."

Kapitänleutnant Wilhelm Klein and Korvettekapitän Schumacher were, by U-boat standards at least, old comrades-in-arms, dating from their training together in 1937 at the Neustadt U-boat School.

"Thank you, Wilhelm," Schumacher replied. Frederick had a high regard for the young commander, whose clear-eyed, unemotional approach to emergency procedures simulations had won him Second Standing Overall in their class, behind himself. Schumacher knew that Klein's well-merited promotion to Korvettenkapitän had been short-circuited by bureaucratic bungling within the Admiralty, as a cover for hostility to his suffer-no-fools-gladly manner with his superiors.

Their conversation was interrupted by brusquely shouted commands. "Okay you fellows, come along. Let's move. Single file out the door; line up outside. No funny business; armed guards will be watching you. Okay, let's move it out, gentlemen. *Raus, schnell, schnell!*"

As Schumacher stepped down from the train, he shaded his eyes against the sudden brightness of the April sunshine. The air was brisk but refreshing, and wonderful to breath, after the cigarette smoke-filled coach.

"Alright, fall in. Line up, single file facing that way!" the sergeant announced, inclining his head southward. "Now, let's start marching smartly, we haven't got all day."

Frederick strode along the dirt road, dodging puddles from the spring runoff. He looked to his left toward a field where a farmer was driving his tractor, ploughing neat furrows in the rich black earth. 'We must be a merry sight. I wonder if the old boy thinks this is an invasion?' He chuckled inwardly, and then reconsidered. 'He's not even so much as glancing in our direction. How many PoWs have trudged this road so far?' he reflected grimly.

In single file, the men marched through the gates of what was evidently to be their new home. Schumacher glanced around, sizing up the layout. There were two fences, enclosing a strip of open ground roughly six metres (twenty feet) wide. He estimated the inner and outer fences to be approximately five and one-half metres (eighteen feet) high, topped with barbed wire. Guard towers were situated at thirty metre (one hundred foot) intervals. The gate closed behind them: Schumacher and the long line of PoWs were now inside Camp 30.

"Okay men, straight line along this pathway, by the right...dress...and halt! Eyes front!" the Adjutant barked.

"Sir, all prisoners present and accounted for, Sir!

"Prisoners, attention. Our Commanding Officer, Lieutenant-Colonel Armstrong."

An imposing man in a Canadian military uniform stepped forward to receive the Adjutant's salute. Schumacher judged that this was a hardcore professional soldier, all spit and polish and no-nonsense, in all likelihood a veteran who had seen at first-hand too much of the horrific carnage during The Great War. 'I wonder what he thinks of us?' mused Schumacher. 'Military failures? The blood-thirsty Hun?'

"Gentlemen, I am your commanding officer at Camp 30, your new home for what will be the duration of the war. You will enjoy your life here, as I know those who have arrived before you do. If you behave as model prisoners, and adhere to the Code of Conduct, which is posted, you will be well looked after. If you do not, it will mean a minimum twenty-eight day sentence to be served in solitary confinement. It is up to you, gentlemen," Lieutenant-Colonel J. L. Armstrong announced, matter-of-factly.

John Linton Armstrong, known to fellow officers and friends as Jack, was indeed a distinguished Canadian veteran of the First World War, one who had seen extensive action as an Artillery Officer with the Canadian Corps in France and Flanders. Highly decorated, he was wounded twice at St. Julien, promoted to Captain in the field at Ypres, and in 1917, was made Lieutenant-Colonel, in recognition of his dashing leadership at Vimy Ridge. Jack Armstrong was fluent in German, a principal reason he was selected for this assignment, as well as Flemish and French.

"Who is the ranking officer among you?" demanded Armstrong.

"Korvettenkapitän Frederick Schumacher, the ranking officer of this party, Colonel," he replied, saluting.

Armstrong returned the salute. "Very good. Korvettenkapitän Schumacher, let me introduce you to Oberstleutnant Werner Eberhart, the ranking prisoner officer in the Camp."

"Herr Kapitän, it is an honour, Sir!" Eberhart replied deferentially, saluting the celebrated U-boat commander.

"Oberstleutnant, I assure you the honour is mine," Schumacher responded gallantly.

"Herr Kapitän Schumacher, you are now officially in charge of our ranks as of this moment. If I can be of any assistance, please do not hesitate to ask."

"Thank you, Oberstleutnant.

"I would like a briefing later," Schumacher whispered as the two men shook hands.

"Korvettenkapitän Schumacher, let me show you around. I'll take you to your office first and then we'll go to my office for a bit of a chat. Oberstleutnant Eberhart, would you care to join us?" asked Colonel Armstrong.

"Yes, Colonel, I would, indeed!"

The three men headed down the pathway which cut through the centre of the Camp, while the other prisoners dispersed for their new homes, under the vigilant eye and supervision of Staff Sergeant Robert Murray.

"The building on our right is the Mess, where we feed six hundred men three times a day in six sittings. I'm sure you'll find the food quite satisfactory," Armstrong remarked with pride. "Most of the buildings were donated by local service clubs such as Rotary and Kiwanis and each building has a proper name. That's Ferguson Hall to our left, Jury house over there, and Victoria Hall is the building we just looked at. Your fellows have renamed them Haus I, II, III, IV, and so on. Quite simple and practical that way, I must say.

The Hospital – 1942
Bowmanville Archives

"The one straight ahead is the Administration building, we call it Admin, Haus II to your fellows, where your office and a number of Adjutants and staff are located. We also have several classrooms but they're quickly filling up with prisoners. Until recently, Korvettenkapitän, the Camp was a correctional institution for delinquent boys."

One of the Haus' – 1942
Bowmanville Archives

Camp 30 – As seen from Haus IV – 1942
Bowmanville Archives

"I understand the irony in that, Colonel," Schumacher smiled. "It certainly is unlike anything of a similar nature at home."

"Well now, there's more, including a full-size theatre, and very well-equipped at that. The theatrical company has started casting a play by Shakespeare."

"Really?" replied Schumacher. "I studied several of Shakespeare's plays at university. Which one are they producing?"

"*A Midsummer's Night Dream*, I believe. Am I right, Werner?"

"You are, Colonel. Try-outs are already well underway. I'm in

The auditorium of the Administration Building – 1942
Bowmanville Archives

A play on stage performed by the PoWs
Bowmanville Archives

charge of the lighting. Opening night is 21 June. It promises to be a gala event."

"Wise choice. *Romeo and Juliet* might present some casting problems here," remarked Schumacher.

"You'd be surprised. Last year they produced *Macbeth*. Oh, sorry Werner, that's bad luck. Let me say, *The Scottish Play*. Anyway, the fellows were absolutely scrambling to win the part of Lady Mac, for the juicy bits like the bloody dagger speech, I imagine.

Perhaps you'd be interested in an audition, Korvettenkapitän?" Armstrong suggested with an innocent smile.

"Possibly, although I suspect that reading and actually performing Shakespeare on stage are worlds apart. Perhaps I could contribute something behind the scenes, Werner?"

"I'm sure that can be arranged. Can you guess what is in the building on our left, Korvettenkapitän?" Armstrong continued.

"Britain's gold reserves?"

"Very amusing: a comedian in uniform, that's what I like. You and I will get along famously, Korvettenkapitän," laughed Armstrong. "No, nothing as clandestine as that. Nevertheless, it's something which you and your men will enjoy. Come, let's take a look."

The three men walked up a few steps and entered the building, which was sectioned off, with two sides. As they walked through the first door, Schumacher's jaw dropped in astonishment.

"*Was ist das?*" Schumacher stared in disbelief as he watched a group of about twenty men playing water volleyball in a large swimming pool. Upon seeing Schumacher, those who were former submariners attempted to come to attention and salute, which resulted in a comical display of bobbing heads and bare bottoms in the deep end that fell far short of Kriegsmarine regulations. Schumacher returned their soggy salutes, then, suppressing an impulse to laugh at the unintentional slapstick, quickly turned and began to walk to the door.

"Well, Korvettenkapitän Schumacher, those naval lads certainly recognized you! Head over heels with delight, it seems!"

"Or what is more probable, disbelief!" Schumacher rejoined.

"But tell me, Korvettenkapitän, do you approve of such recreational activities?"

"I do Colonel. It's truly a wonderful way to keep mind and body fresh and fit."

"We're not done yet! Just take a peek through that window on the other side."

Schumacher looked through the window indicated. He could see another group of PoWs playing basketball on a full - sized court. "I am doubly impressed Colonel Armstrong, but I think that I've seen enough for one day. Frankly, I don't know if my heart can take anymore, thank you," he laughed.

"Well Korvettenkapitän, that calls for a refreshing cup of tea and a bit of a chat in my office.

"We'll just take a peek in the Admin building or the PoWs' Haus II first," Armstrong continued. As they entered the Administration Building, Schumacher was impressed by the quality of wood that had been used to finish the interior. The banisters that led upstairs were made of solid wood at least fifteen centimetres (six inches) thick. Looking straight ahead, Schumacher could see the large proscenium stage where a troupe of PoWs, some standing, others lounging on chairs, all with scripts in hand, were auditioning. One man, wearing a large set of donkey's ears, was earnestly attempting to make braying sounds, to accompanying hoots of laughter from the others.

"That's the spirit of this place, Korvettenkapitän. As you can see, we each make every effort to work and play together in harmony. Very well, that's enough for now. There will be ample time for a thorough tour later.

"Werner, would you please excuse us?"

"Certainly, Colonel.

"Until later, Herr Kapitän!" Eberhart stiffly saluted each officer in turn, and then quickly walked away.

"Korvettenkapitän," Armstrong continued, "follow me please, and we'll head back up to my office."

"Here we are, have a seat. Miss Burns, might I prevail upon you to bring us a pot of tea and some cookies, please. Does that sound alright to you, Korvettenkapitän?"

Schumacher laughed, shaking his head. "Yes, Colonel, tea would be fine."

"May I ask what's so funny?"

"The names... the names, Hawes, Bovril, Lieutenant-Colonel Armstrong," Schumacher chortled. "I thought they were towns. On the way over, Werner informed me that they're advertisements for floor wax and a liquid beef extract!"

"Oh, I see. That is amusing!

"Now tell me, what were the circumstances that brought you here, Korvettenkapitän Schumacher?"

"Colonel, with all respect, you must realise that I cannot discuss these matters. Let's just say that your Captain Wilson got the upper hand on us, shall we? He is a very shrewd and skilled commanding officer, and a gentleman. Besides, I am certain that you have more intelligence on me than even I am aware of, after so many interrogations in England. Is this not so?"

"I accept your position, under the articles of the Geneva Convention. I do have your file here, Korvettenkapitän, which I have read thoroughly. I must say, it's a damn good thing that Captain Wilson snatched you out of the Atlantic when he did. You are quite a catch! Highest Decoration Awarded: Knight's Cross, with Oak Leaves and Swords, at only twenty-nine years of age. Quite an achievement! 'One torpedo, one ship' was your motto, I read. Your tally of forty-seven confirmed sinkings, including a British destroyer and seven armed merchant cruisers is altogether remarkable...and blood chilling. So many lives..."

For a moment, Schumacher was mute. Clearing his throat, he

replied, his voice quavering slightly. "Colonel, I must say that the drift of this discussion is making me very uncomfortable. For me, as a sailor, it is a very emotional subject. Our submariners' code of honour requires that we do whatever we can to rescue and assist survivors. That is not always possible, or practical, unfortunately. Perhaps some other time? Can we talk about the Camp? You said, I think, that until the outbreak of the war, it served as a training school for incorrigible youngsters."

"Yes, that's so. Thank you Miss Burns. Korvettenkapitän?"

"Yes, milk please, no sugar. May I assume that these dessert biscuits are 'cookies'?"

"They are. Please help yourself. Well then, shall we begin with the remarkable Miss Muriel Burns? Miss Burns was a legal clerk with the Office of the Crown Attorney of the Ontario Government in Toronto and was seconded as a temporary secretary to the Boy's Training School. She has been here since the school's opening day.

"You see, Korvettenkapitän, these grounds, and of course, the buildings were intended as a reformatory school for young boys found guilty of one or more misdemeanours by the courts and sentenced to correctional custody under the Provincial Statutes. Some, unfortunately, were repeat delinquents. However, as juvenile offenders, the Government of Ontario chose to house them separately from adult offenders, the thinking being that they were likely more capable of mending their ways here than by putting them in with the worst elements of society in a conventional prison.

"Back to Muriel Burns. As a member of the civil service, with considerable seniority, she was entitled to return to her position at Queen's Park. However, she chose to remain as a civilian member of staff, at a reduced rate of compensation, mind you, and we have retained a first-rate person, one who knows the Camp and the community exceedingly well."

"How fortunate for you, Colonel. An employee of that calibre and experience is to be prized."

"Indeed, and what's more, the men here absolutely adore her. Perhaps she's a mother figure, perhaps a big sister, or something else. They write her long letters, confiding their personal problems, pouring out their most private confidences, she tells me. Only last week she came to me, rather hesitantly, to say that she had received a letter from a PoWs' Committee complaining that the toilets and urinals are too close to the floor."

"Must be flyboys," Schumacher laughed. "Standard operating procedure for a submariner, however, I will take that as an official warning!"

"Now Korvettenkapitän, down to some serious business. Some of your fellows have been, shall I say, *verschmitzt*, quite crafty, mischievous."

"How so, Colonel?"

"Well, let me see. Let's look at these clippings from the local newspapers. Oh, by the way, it was very thoughtful of Air Marshall Hermann Goering to send the men $25.00 each for Christmas. It boosted our sales at the canteen to a new monthly record, and no doubt aided the local economy no end. However, I digress. Where was I? Oh yes, here's the item:

"January 1st, 1942

Two More Nazis Escape

One Caught in XXX, blacked out by censors, After Hiding in Laundry.

"Let me apologise, Korvettenkapitän Schumacher. It seems that the bright lights guiding our local press do not know, or care to know, the difference between a Nazi and a German serviceman. Military District HQ informed them that there aren't any Nazis in this Camp. But nevertheless, most people just take for granted that all Germans are card-carrying National Socialist Party members."

"It is to be understood, I suppose, Colonel, given the times."

"Now, I'll read on.

"Frederick Oeser, escaped by hiding in a laundry truck. He jumped in just as the truck was leaving the Camp. And one Walter Manheardt who had been confined in the detention barracks managed to make a break for freedom. Both men of course were quickly caught.

"My point is Korvettenkapitän; it is fruitless for your men to even attempt such tomfoolery. No one has ever successfully escaped from Camp 30 and I intend to keep this record intact."

"Colonel Armstrong, surely as an Officer you appreciate that it is one's duty to attempt to escape. I cannot fault these men for trying," retorted Schumacher.

"I do understand Korvettenkapitän, but I'm only trying to save your men from wasting twenty-eight days in solitary confinement, the mandatory punishment for attempted escapes, particularly in the summertime when temperatures can reach one hundred degrees Fahrenheit.

"Let me read you more.

"Two German Officers Who Made Mysterious Escape Captured at XXX.

"This fellow Steinhilper had attempted three previous escapes! Hello, this reporter has done his homework! **Hun**, sorry for that, **Trouble-Makers No longer Enjoy Palatial Quarters**

What has been recommended locally among citizens who have felt that too much leniency has been accorded German prisoners repeatedly making attempted breaks for freedom from Internment Camp 30, has apparently come to pass. From observations of our local reporter, without in any way seeking confirmation from officers in charge who are prohibited from giving out information, the fact seems to be that six or seven of the ring leaders among Hun prisoners who caused much trouble and expense have been removed to more secure quarters, presumably at XXX.

"Now please understand, Korvettenkapitän. Not only will your men serve twenty-eight days in solitary confinement, but the Steinhilpers and his ilk are now subject to the new Camp policy of 'three strikes and you're out'!"

"Three strikes...? Do you mean, beatings, Colonel?"

"Oh, no, worse. Much worse. 'Three strikes' is a term borrowed from the American game of baseball. Simply put, the batter gets three swings at a pitched ball; if he doesn't hit it, he has three strikes, then retires, and lets a teammate try. In our case, three escape attempts at Camp 30 and he is sent to a prison from which escape is impossible and where his stay will be lengthy and not at all pleasant."

"I'll certainly take that under advisement, Colonel," Schumacher replied sharply.

Armstrong's body contracted, as if it had received a jolt of electrical current. "Consider this an official warning, Korvettenkapitän. I intend to enforce this policy without reservation," he countered icily, and then his tone moderated. "You know, Korvettenkapitän Schumacher, Oberstleutnant Eberhart and I respect one another. We enjoy a very good working relationship; there is an understanding between us, as senior officers. I sincerely hope and expect that the tradition can contin-

PoW Officers of Camp 30
Bowmanville Archives

ue. By your record, and your reputation, I know you to be a gallant and honourable officer. I ask for your co-operation and guarantee of good conduct by you and your men. In return, I will ensure that the privileges and just treatment that the men presently enjoy, continue, along with firm but fair administration of the camp's rules. Now, let me show you to your quarters. I think you will find them quite comfortable."

Camp 30 – Bowmanville
Bowmanville Archives / DND- National Archive of Canada

They made their way around the driveway to the 'Triple Dorm' building or Haus IV, as the PoWs had named it. Schumacher marvelled at the size of the campgrounds. Colonel Armstrong remarked that it was all of one hundred and ten acres. Mentally, Schumacher converted the acreage to hectares. As they continued walking, Armstrong pointed out that they had an exercise field where the men could do callisthenics or play football. Recently, tennis courts had also been installed nearby, which would be flooded in the wintertime to provide a skating rink where the guards would teach the PoWs the game of Canadian ice hockey.

"Here we are Korvettenkapitän, in this door and to your left.

The now famous 'Otto Kretschmer's' Haus IV
Bowmanville Archives

"There, these are your quarters. Living room, library over here and in that room is your bedroom which I'm sure you will find snug but accommodating."

Schumacher surveyed each room, saying nothing. Inwardly he was dumbfounded by the lavishness of the suite. It was far more luxurious than he, a prisoner of war, deserved at the same time as his colleagues sweated and toiled, risking their lives in the claustrophobic confines of their vessels undersea.

"What do you think?"

"*Ausreichend.* It will do, quite satisfactory, Colonel, thank you."

"Rest, take a walk. Get to know the place, the men; enjoy your new home, Korvettenkapitän! I hope you don't mind my asking, but, may I address you as 'Captain'?"

"Yes, of course, Colonel! I am quite sure that I'll find my way around. I do hope that we will meet again, soon," Schumacher replied quietly.

"Yes, we will. Did I mention that we do have some daily necessities? Three roll calls, regular mess hours, that sort of thing. Well, I'll be off now. Please remember, my door is always open. Any impending sign of trouble and I want to know about it immediately. Cheerio for now, Captain Schumacher."

PoW Officers with their dog
Bowmanville Archives

As soon as Colonel Armstrong was out of sight, Schumacher leaned his head out the front door. "Oberstleutnant Eberhart, a moment please."

"Yes, Herr Kapitän?"

"Come inside. I would like to have a word with you." Schumacher was still feeling extremely ill at ease as he sank down in the well-upholstered couch.

"Oberstleutnant Eberhart, you are my 2IC. Given that, when we are together, just we two, you may call me Frederick or Sir, if you prefer, and I will address you as Werner. At all other times we will recognize one another by rank. Do you agree?"

"Yes certainly, Herr Kapitän. Frederick."

"Good, now fill me in on everything that has been going on here."

As Werner was one of the first PoWs to enter the Camp, he was able to give Schumacher a detailed account of all of the events that had taken place since its earliest days.

"The Colonel told me about a couple of attempted escapes but was careful to leave out specific details. Can you fill me in?" inquired Schumacher.

"I assume that one of them was Steinhilper?"

"Yes, I remember that name. He's tried four times, apparently."

"That's correct. He was recently shipped off to a high security prison somewhere. I'm not sure where as we haven't heard from him. One fellow sneaked out in a laundry truck but was quickly apprehended and another guy crawled under the fence but he too was captured soon after."

"Damn disheartening. Much too amateurish."

"We've had several other attempts but nothing really organized, Sir. Each man sort of doing things on his own, in his own way."

"Well, we must rectify that, mustn't we, Werner? Henceforth I want daily reports on everything, and I do mean everything, that comes to your attention, which relates to the morale or concerns of the men. Moreover, be especially on guard for plots and escape schemes. From now on, all planning will be assessed, approved or rejected, and co-ordinated through me. And you. Is that understood, Werner?"

"Perfectly, Herr Kapitän. This is the start of a new chapter for Camp 30's PoWs!" he remarked, standing and saluting. "I'll put the word around, quietly, Sir."

Schumacher frowned. "See that you do, and please Werner, no more of that. His expression softened. "Now, before you leave, tell me, where in the name of Saint Nicholas are we?"

"Bowmanville, Sir, Bowmanville," beamed Eberhart.

"Bow-man-ville?" Schumacher hesitated. "Is that French, as in B-e-a-u?"

"B-o-w", Sir."

"Well, it's better than floor wax, I suppose."

One week later, Kurt, Klaus and Peter headed by rail to Glasgow/Greenock to board another RN troop transport, bound for an

'unknown eastern port', Halifax, Nova Scotia. Constantly aware of the possibility of being torpedoed by a lone U-boat or Wolfpack, the Afrika Korps PoWs couldn't resist needling their Kriegsmarine brethren.

Thirteen days and many motion-sickness pills later, the CN train, which they had boarded in Halifax, arrived at their destination in south central Ontario. The sign at the train station was covered to hide their location.

The three managed to regroup as the Canadian Veterans' Guards lined them up, single file, to begin the march to camp. A handful of young boys and girls and a scattering of their big sisters stood well back, behind the guards, gawking, laughing, and pointing.

"Do you think they're getting ready to attack us, Kurt?" Klaus whispered.

"They're just kids! Not that the guards look capable of preventing it, though."

"She's welcome to try, anytime!" Peter remarked, blowing a kiss to a local belle. She blushed, smiled, and averted her eyes, her hand demurely covering her mouth.

"See that beauty with the blonde hair! She loves me, already!"

"*Verschliessen*! Lock it up! And stand at attention, Faber! You'll have us all in serious trouble!" Kurt hissed.

"My God, Klaus, to think we'll have to put up with this cheesy Don Juan show until the war is over!" Kurt muttered.

"You three fellows there! Eyes front! Silence! By the right, quick...march!"

CHAPTER 6
A GIRL NAMED MARLENE

Camp 30 April 9 1942

Oberstleutnant Eberhart led Karl and his fellow PoWs down the pathway to their new residence. Passing Haus VII, they slowed down to watch a group of PoWs in a field, their gym clothing spattered with mud, playing a strange form of football. Karl thought it involved a great deal of running and chasing after certain players with fierce charging at one another. He was fascinated by the fact that some individuals were apparently permitted to catch, hold onto and even throw the brown, oval ball.

The 'Sportplatz' Camp 30
Bowmanville Archives / DND-National Archives of Canada

As they continued walking, Karl realized that he must resign himself to the reality of his new life by resolving to make the best of it by meeting new friends and joining in some of the activities. Slowing his pace, he shaded his eyes from the brilliant sunshine to watch as one man threw the ball toward another player. He stopped. "Wolf? Wolfgang von Heiden!"

Eberhart turned to look at Karl who was now shouting and waving his arms frantically. "Who do you think you see, Leutnant?"

PoWs enjoy summertime at Bowmanville
Bowmanville Archives

"It's my best friend! I'm fairly certain, Sir!

"Wolf! Wolfie! Wolfgang! Over here!" Karl yelled.

"That is Wolfgang von Heiden quarterbacking," Eberhart confirmed.

Wolf paused and turned to look at the source of the commotion. Then, tossing the football to a teammate, he trotted toward the cluster of new PoWs. "What? It can't be! Karl? Karl, is that you?"

"Oberstleutnant, a moment please?" Karl asked excitedly.

"Sure, Leutnant. Go ahead."

"Wolf! It's me, Karl!" Shouting, the two men ran toward one another, and then collided, falling to the ground together.

"Wolf, I thought you were dead," Karl sputtered, laughing.

"I thought the same, Karl," Wolf answered, laughing and choking, "that is, until I got a letter from home saying you were in a PoW camp in England. I can't believe you're here!"

The two friends helped one another stand up. "You're a mess!" Karl pointed out, brushing off his friend's sweatshirt.

"All part of the game!" Wolf replied grinning, "Canadian football!"

"Leutnant Semmler!" Eberhart appealed. "Come! We're waiting!"

"You had best go. Find your quarters. After I've cleaned up, I'll come looking for you. Give me fifteen minutes. Do you know which building you are in, Karl?"

"Oberstleutnant?" Karl queried, shrugging.

"This one, Haus I," Eberhart replied.

"Okay, Karl. Fifteen minutes. Be ready! I'll take you on the grand tour."

Karl walked into his new quarters and was immediately taken aback by its roominess, as well as by the quality and quantity of the furnishings: arm chairs, coffee tables and couches throughout.

"Oberstleutnant, this is for the Generalleutnant when he arrives, yes?" Karl ventured.

"No, Leutnant. Gentlemen, this is your barracks. I know you will be comfortable here. We might be here for a while, so please try to make yourselves at home."

"But Oberstleutnant, where do we sleep?" asked another prisoner.

"See those benches along the walls? Take off the couch pad like this, lift this board and, watch me please, insert the support beam here. Gentlemen, we have bunk beds!"

"That's very clever, Oberstleutnant."

"Yes, isn't it, Leutnant? Your mealtimes are posted over here. There will be a general meeting this afternoon at 1500 hours in the auditorium; it is mandatory that every one of you attend, so be there promptly, gentlemen. In the meantime, enjoy yourselves. Until 1500 then, good day."

Karl looked around, quickly deciding that a corner bunk would be his best option. Precisely why, he wasn't sure. He took immediate ownership of the bottom bed, remembering how often, as a young boy he had rolled out in the dark, landing painfully on the hardwood floor, to endure the further humiliation of his older brother's inane cackling from the lower bunk.

"Karl, aren't you unpacked yet? C'mon, *Kamerad!*"

"A minute, Wolf!"

"Hurry!"

"Go soak your head, *Kamerad!* I have to take a piss! Back in a minute."

"So, tell me Wolf, what have you been doing here? I'm curious to know how you pass the time, besides playing this Canadian football."

"Karl, my friend, there are so many things to do here you can't believe it. The days go by so quickly."

"Things to do? Like what, Wolf?"

"Okay, let me tell you. Cigarette?" offered Wolf.

"No, thank you, and when did you start smoking?"

"I have to spend my money on something, you can only buy so many toiletries at the canteen."

"What money? What canteen? Anyway, I don't care; it's not good for your health, Wolf. Buy chewing gum, or something!"

"Yes, little mother. Never mind. First, there are tennis courts. And if tennis is not your game you might want to try playing football. You saw me doing that," he announced grandly. "It's great fun, but damnably rough, the way these guys play it. How about swimming? You used to like to swim Karl!"

"Yes, I love to swim, but where? I didn't see a pool."

"No, you didn't, because it is indoors. And heated!" Wolf stated proudly, as though he had constructed it with his own labours.

"Oh, come off it, Wolf. I'm going to write your mother and tell her that you are still a pathological liar. And a smoker."

Wolf raised his hands in protest. "I'm not lying, Karl. Trust me, old man! Later on, I'll take you over to Haus III and I'll prove it. What's more, there's a gym on the other side of the building where we play basketball, volleyball and other sports."

"I can't believe it. We're prisoners of war, not Olympic athletes in training. Aren't we?"

"You have to wonder, but just wait. We do that too! Now, as for the meals Karl, the meals are *wunderbar*! Soon we will have a complete farm with pigs, goats, cows, and chickens even for fresh eggs. We'll grow all of our own fresh vegetables. Isn't that something? Believe me, being sent to Canada was the best thing that could have happened to you."

"It sounds too good to be true; I wonder what the hitch is?"

"*Gar nichts*, nothing at all. Come on Karl, I can't wait to show you around."

The two men got up from the leather couch and walked to the front entrance of Haus I, opened the door and stepped out into the sunshine.

"Ouch, that's bright!" Karl exclaimed, shading his eyes.

"No problem, Karl, you can purchase good sunglasses like these at the canteen for less than a buck!"

"Buck?"

"Buck! It's Canadian for their currency. They use dollars, bucks, not Reich Marks. No big surprise, eh? Wait till you get your first allowance, then you can go crazy!"

"Sunglasses at the canteen, dollars, bucks: it's overwhelming! How much is a buck in our..."

"You'll figure it out, don't worry. Let's walk this way, to the right," Wolfgang continued. "Just to get your bearings straight, this direction is south. We've learned a lot about this place in the little time that we've been here. For instance, we're only a couple of kilometres away from a small town called Bowmanville. I'm not sure of the population but it's not very many."

"What's this building, Wolf?"

"Haus II, the theatre. The next building is Haus III, the Gym. Now, look over there; the tennis courts! I'll teach you to play like a professional! Way over there is a huge field where someday we will hold our Camp Olympics. And finally, the farthest building, Haus IV, that's Korvettenkapitän Schumacher's place."

"*The* Korvettenkapitän Schumacher is a prisoner? Here?"

"Uh huh, the very same. And then, back we come to our Haus. See? Simple. So, how do you think that you would like to spend your days, Karl?"

"I don't know, Wolf, but your speech about farming made me really interested. It's something I have always wondered about: what is it like to be a farmer? Yes, I think that's what I want to try."

"Really? Suit yourself. By the way, after you were attacked, as your plane was hurtling down, what ran through your mind?"

"Lots of things..."

"Such as?"

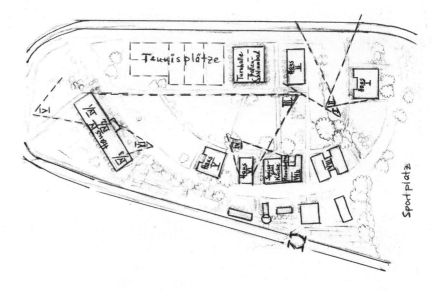

Sketch of Camp 30 showing the location of the different Haus'
Volkmar König

"Such as: Why me? Where were you? And I prayed, a lot!"

"Me too! It worked, didn't it? That and destiny, that's why we are reunited!"

Karl kept busy during the next several weeks familiarizing himself with his surroundings, meeting his new comrades, and reading anything he could find about farming. The days were becoming longer and it would soon be time to plant the crops. Karl spent hours in the Camp library absorbing everything he could find about agriculture. He couldn't wait to sow the first seeds, which he purchased through the canteen with his allowance. Although the canteen didn't routinely carry seeds, Wolf had convinced the manager of the benefits for everyone if he were to place a special order for Karl.

Karl's long-standing practice of running two kilometres before breakfast paid off shortly after he decided to resume the habit. One morning, sighting Eberhart ahead of him, he sped up, calling, "Oberstleutnant! Pardon me, Sir. May I have a minute?"

Eberhart looked back, slowing his pace to a walk. "Yes, Leutnant Semmler, what is it?"

Karl caught up and fell in step. "Sir, I'm eager to start working in the garden. According to the *Farmer's Almanac*, we can sow seed on May fifteenth in this growing zone of Ontario."

"You're becoming quite an expert! Good for you, Karl. May fifteenth sounds close, although all danger of frost at nighttime isn't past until after the May twenty-fourth holiday weekend. Besides, it's academic, Karl; you won't be working the crops. Commissioned officers do not do manual work."

"I realise that, Sir, but this would not be work for me. This would be a hobby, a passion, something I really want to do."

"Listen, Karl, there are no exceptions to this rule. It's not done, period," Eberhart declared, dabbing his forehead with the corner of a terry cloth towel wrapped around his neck.

"Sir, with respect, could you please ask the Korvettenkapitän if I could just ready the garden and plant the seeds? I've been reading up on it and I know that I can help produce a bumper crop. Then I'll back off and let the NCOs take over."

"You're really quite serious about this aren't you? Very well, Karl, I'll risk it and ask him, but just this once!" he shouted, resuming his run.

Sunday 17 May 1942
Camp 30

"Frederick, may I have a word with you?" asked Eberhart. "It's about young Semmler."

"The moment I return, Werner. The Colonel wanted to see me a half hour ago. You know how testy he can be if you keep him waiting. I'll be back shortly," replied Schumacher.

At Colonel Armstrong's office, Miss Muriel Burns welcomed Schumacher.

"He's expecting you, Korvettenkapitän. Please go right in."

"Colonel, you wanted to see me?"

"Captain, come in and sit down, please. I would like to read you a

report which I have just received from the FBI relative to the events of 17 April," stated Colonel Armstrong.

"Whatever for, Colonel? Surely that is old news now," Schumacher replied, edgily.

"Quite so, however, I cannot stress too strongly how important it is for you to keep your men advised of these events to ensure that they don't follow in the footsteps of men such as Krug and Boehle."

"Very well Colonel, I'm listening."

"On 17 April 1942, two men, began to walk toward the double barbed wire fences. The pair were being guarded by one of your own men, wearing a Canadian army uniform, which, I might emphasize, was provided by the theatrical group, who also donated the supplies they would need. As well, a soccer game had been arranged specifically to create a distraction at the very moment that the men planned to make their escape.

"Pretending to be repairing the barbed wire fence, and marking the spots with paint, the men climbed the fence using a ladder and went over the top. Now, there was the problem presented by the outer fence about fifteen feet away. The men simply walked toward the outer fence and once again, put the ladder into position. After successfully climbing over the second fence, they sat down for a rest and a few minutes later, stood up again and proceeded to walk away.

"The men made it successfully to Union Station in Toronto where they apparently decided it would be best if they were to split up and did so, going on their separate ways. Leutnant Erich Boehle was captured on Lewiston Road only a mile from potential freedom. Peter Krug however had a much more exciting time of it.

"While Boehle was being returned to Camp 30 to serve his regulation twenty-eight days in solitary confinement, Oberleutnant Krug, still at large, was now a wanted man. He was the subject of a massive search conducted by law enforcement agencies. Krug's cover story was so convincing that he managed to convince a priest to buy him a bus ticket to Windsor, Ontario, where there was a job purportedly awaiting him.

"Arriving at Windsor on the evening of 17 April, Krug lay low until the next day when he would attempt to get across the St. Clair River to Detroit. The morning of the eighteenth, Krug walked along the shoreline of the river searching for some means of getting across. Finally, he found a rowboat and after manufacturing some makeshift oars; he succeeded in rowing across the river. Captain, did you know that Peter Krug celebrated his twenty-second birthday in the United States?"

"No, Colonel, I really have no recollection of the facts," replied Schumacher.

PoWs stand in front of one of the Camp 30 buildings
Bowmanville Archives

"Very well, I'll proceed. Somehow, Abwehr agents in Germany, we assume, had provided Krug with names and addresses of safe houses, which he was to contact if he were to make it safely to Detroit. His first contact was a Mrs. Bertelmann, who, in turn, introduced him to restaurant owner Max Stephan. Given food and lodging and money for his trip, Krug headed out for his final destination, Mexico, a neutral country.

"Krug's luck changed from good to bad when he arrived in San Antonio, Texas. Here he checked into a hotel where a keen eyed manager had recognized Krug from an FBI photo, which had been distributed the previous day. The manager contacted the FBI who quickly arrested the surprised Oberleutnant Krug. After two hours of interrogation, Krug finally admitted to who he was and when questioned further as to how he had planned to cross the border into Mexico, Krug replied that he intended to, 'swim across the Rio Grand.'

"A very energetic young fellow as I recall, Krug was. Do continue," interjected Schumacher with a faint smile.

"Items found in Krug's bag by the FBI, among other things: a military map of his escape route, which FBI agents were able to trace back to Mrs. Bertelmann, Mr. Stephan and a man named Theodore Donway.

Also found in his hotel room was a .32 calibre handgun which he had purchased for $13.00 from a pawnshop.

"Back in Detroit, Max Stephan was arrested and charged with 'Harbouring an Alien'. Mrs. Bertelmann has been interned as an 'Enemy Alien'. Theodore Donway has been imprisoned for his involvement.

"Peter Krug is being returned to Camp 30 but not for long. I will immediately begin the necessary paperwork to have him transferred to a more secure camp. Elsewhere. Any comments Captain?" asked Colonel Armstrong.

"None whatsoever, Colonel. Thank you for the fascinating story. May I now return to my Haus? Oberstleutnant Eberhart and I have a long-overdue appointment with a deck of cards and some fine old Barbados rum."

Happily, Karl bit the hoe into the ground, pulling the rich earth toward him. The Veteran Guard who had accompanied him, Private First Class Maynard, had watched Karl in bored silence for the first half-hour and then retreated tactically to the shade of a distant elm. Propping his rifle against the tree trunk, he then proceeded to fall sound asleep. Karl looked up at the noonday sun, took off his hat, and wiped his brow with his handkerchief. 'I must be crazy being out here at this hour. It's only mid-May, but it sure gets hot by high noon. Summer time must be unbearable. I wonder if I did the right thing in asking the Korvettenkapitän for permission to prepare the fields? Oh, well, why worry? It's good exercise, no one's getting hurt, and it's sure safer than flying cover for Heinkels 111's over England in an Me109.'

As he paused, he looked around the Darch farm. In the near distance, he could see a young woman with long brown hair reaching up, pegging bed sheets onto a clothesline. 'Nice figure! She's obviously from that farmhouse.'

"Hallo, hallo!" he called softly.

The woman stared in his direction then bent down to continue her chores. Karl called again, but louder.

"Hallo, miss, may I speak with you?"

"No, you may not!" she shouted back indignantly.

Karl now realized that 'she' was quite young, probably in her early twenties. He watched her stride back into the farmhouse, shutting the screen door with a resounding slam.

'Not a good beginning, Karl; not good at all! You idiot.

"Private Maynard! It's time to go back! Hallo, Private Maynard!"

In the mess at lunchtime, Karl went on and on extolling the young lady to Wolf. "...and her hair, you should have seen her long flowing hair, Wolf. Like silk I tell you!" Karl enthused.

"Look, Karl, take it easy already, you're going to have a heart attack. Take my advice and forget about her. It's nice, lovely, enchanting and all that claptrap that you saw this pretty young *fraulein* on the farm, but the stark facts are: one, you are a prisoner of war and two, you likely scared the daylights out of Miss Bowmanville with your craziness! You don't jump up suddenly to shout at a girl when you look and sound like a *verrückt* madman. Didn't I teach you anything?"

"I know, I know; I could have kicked myself! But Wolf, there was something there, a kind of electric charge."

"I'll give you a charge, Karl. Come over here and stick your finger in this electric socket," Wolf joked.

"Alright Wolfgang, you can laugh all you damn well like. I'm going to get that girl to talk with me. You just wait and see, *kamerad!*" Karl muttered, pushing aside his plate angrily, while getting up from his seat then steaming away.

"What did you say to your friend Karl to upset him? He didn't even finish his lunch. May I?" asked Peter, seated across the table.

"Ya sure. Here, take it," Wolf replied, sliding Karl's dessert plate across. "He'll be okay. He gets moody like that every once in awhile, probably homesickness, or you know... You and your two friends, Afrika Korps, am I right?

"In a manner of speaking, yes. The cream of the cream," Peter replied laughing. "At least I thought so until... but some other time. I'm Peter Faber, Leutnant, on detached service, you might say," he quipped, offering his hand. "My wild-looking friends over there are Kurt Löwen and Klaus Keppler. Both quite civilized actually, although sometimes I'm afraid the desert sun might have addled their brains."

PoW Officers in their Haus
Bowmanville Archives

"Nice to meet you, I'm Wolfgang von Heiden, Luftwaffe, Leutnant," he replied with a friendly smile. "Wolf is good enough. We should get together sometime. Do you and your friends play cards?"

"Ya, I do, a bit, Wolf!"

"Okay, see you in the Rec centre at 1900 hours tonight. Bring money. Must go and calm down Karl. See you later!"

As Wolf walked toward the side door of the Mess Hall, he saluted as he passed Korvettenkapitän Schumacher.

"Leutnant," acknowledged Schumacher while carrying his tray to Werner Eberhart's table.

"Sir, would you like to know what is on the menu for this week?" Eberhart inquired.

"I would Werner. Please, tell me that it is roast pork again. I tell you the pork in this country is the finest tasting in the world," Schumacher commented with enthusiasm. "Better even than our home-grown variety."

"Sorry, Sir, you'll have to wait until tomorrow for that."

"So be it. Then what else is there?"

"Well let's see, starting with today's menu:

Lunch: soup, beef hash, potatoes, carrots

Dinner: fish and mayonnaise, bacon, butter, milk, and 1 apple

Tuesday:

Breakfast: as each day, jam, butter, toast, coffee and porridge

Lunch: pork roast, gravy, potatoes, cabbage

Dinner: macaroni, slice of ham, cheese, butter, tea

Wednesday:

Lunch: soup, rice goulash

Dinner: liver sausage, tomato salad, 1 egg, butter, tea

Thursday:

Lunch: roast beef, gravy, potatoes, carrots, stewed prunes

Dinner: bread soup, cheese, bacon, butter, tea

Friday:

Lunch soup, 2 fishcakes, onion sauce, and potatoes

Dinner: beef tartar, cheese, butter, milk

Saturday:

Lunch: homemade pea soup, 1 apple

Dinner: potato salad, ham, butter, tea

Sunday:

Lunch: roast of pork, gravy, potatoes, sauerkraut, pudding

Dinner: liver sausage, tomato salad, butter cocoa

"Well then, what do you think of that Sir?"

"Sounds like I'm looking forward to every day this week. But seriously, Werner, please caution the men again about writing home and telling their relatives about how good things are here. We don't need another episode like Ensign Eckert writing home, telling his family about how absolutely wonderful life is here. I thought that the men were going to kill him," laughed Schumacher. "Including me!"

"Will do. Permission to confine to barracks with stale bread and water rations to the first one who tries it, Sir?"

"Permission granted!"

The next morning, Karl bounded out of bed feeling refreshed and invigorated. He couldn't wait to get back to the Darch farm in the hope of seeing the lovely young woman again. The guard at the gate challenged him courteously. Karl explained that he was on his way to the Darch farm to tend his garden.

"That sounds innocent enough, Lieutenant Semmler. Wait here. Private Maynard will accompany you." Karl paced back and forth impatiently while Maynard was tracked down and ordered to the gate.

Pleased to have been relieved of his morning inspection rounds, Private First Class John Maynard grinned, "It's you again, Semmler. Off to the vegetable patch are we?"

"Yes, Private Maynard, if you don't mind."

"Damn sight better than trudging around here, checking for violations of the Pure Food Act, or whatever the Colonel has in mind," he guffawed. "Now listen, lad, you won't pull a fast one on me and run? *Ehrenwort?* Word of honour?"

"Yes, of course, *Ehrenwort,*" Karl replied cheerily. As they approached the farm field, Karl began searching anxiously for a glimpse of the young lady of the clothesline; she was nowhere to be seen. Private Maynard retired to the shade of his elm tree retreat. Karl worked all morning, forgetting to eat the light lunch, which he had packed. He continued well into the afternoon until the position of the sun told him that it was time to get back for dinner and evening roll call.

Feeling worn out and dehydrated, he decided to walk up the hill for a drink of cold water from the well. "Going for water!" he called to Maynard, who waved his approval.

Karl pumped the handle until a stream of deliciously fresh, cold, spring water gushed from the spigot. Cupping his right hand, he continued pumping with his left, gulping the water as if it were to be his last drink on earth. Suddenly, a sound caught his attention. He turned slowly, water dripping from his face.

"Hey, you're not supposed to be here!"

"I'm sorry, miss. I was feeling a little dizzy from the heat. I needed to have a drink before going back to Camp."

"I thought so; you're one of *them* aren't you?"

He bristled, but quickly regained his composure. "Miss, if by one of 'them', you really mean, am I a PoW, well then, yes, I am. My name is Karl Semmler. May I ask yours?" he inquired.

"Sorry, mister, but I'm not supposed to talk with you or any of the prisoners. You'll have to leave. And what are you doing out here, all by yourself, without a guard? Did you escape?" she asked nervously.

"Oh, no, don't worry, miss. I'm a flying officer in the *Luft*...German Air Force. I'm harmless, not a Nazi. My plane was shot down over.... shot down. We are permitted some freedom to leave the camp, on an honour system; I assure you I am not out illegally. Private Maynard's just over the hill."

"So, you bombed helpless civilians in Poland, or was it France?" she inquired. "Did you blow up Madrid, too?

"No miss, I did not. I was a fighter pilot. I flew one sortie over the English Channel and boom! That was it. I was hit and crash landed."

"Tough luck for you, mister." 'Good luck for us!' I only came out to fill this pitcher with cold drinking water for the kitchen, so, if you'll please excuse me..."

"I'll pump for you, please...there, it's brimming over. I cannot leave until you tell me your name," Karl stated gently.

"All right, if that's what it takes. My name is Marlene."

"Mar-le-ne. I like that," he echoed, using the German pronunciation. "I went to school with a girl named Marlene, back home," Karl reminisced. "Marlene Dietrich was my father's favourite actress."

Marlene smiled momentarily, knowing that her father, despite his limited exposure to filmdom, would have agreed. "Listen, it's because of people like you that we have to leave our farm." Privately, she was becoming intrigued by this good-looking pilot's chivalrous manners.

"Whatever do you mean, Marlene?" asked Karl.

"The Camp Commandant, Colonel Armstrong, has informed my father that we have to leave because the Camp is being expanded to take in the Darch property. I probably shouldn't be telling you this, but you'll find out soon enough. That's where my dad is now, at a farm on the other side of the Camp, to see if it will do for us. The Commandant will make it available if Dad likes it."

"I'm so sorry. I had no idea."

"Well now you do, and you'd best be on your way before my father gets back."

"Yes, I wouldn't want to get you into trouble. I hope that I might see you again some day, Marlene."

"I doubt it Karl, we're moving next week, one way or the other."

"I'm truly sorry Marlene, and I do hope to see you again. *Auf Wiedersehen.* Sorry, I meant goodbye, for now. One last question if I may. What is your family name?"

"Clark. *Auf Wiedersehen,* Semmler."

When Karl was halfway back down the hill, he was met by a perspiring Private Maynard. "So, Semmler, what did the young lady have to say?"

"Nothing, Private; I think I frightened her."

"Quite likely. Well, let's shake a leg. If you miss roll call, we'll both be in for it!"

The summer weeks flew by and Karl's garden flourished into one of the best crops that farmers in the surrounding area had ever seen. There was little for Karl to do except ensure that his beloved plants were free of blight and bugs, take a daily walk, swim, read, or play volleyball.

Marlene and her family had been gone for several weeks now. Karl often wondered about them, her, to be precise. He barely knew her, and yet, he missed her. He hoped that one day they would renew acquaintances.

Karl had become acquainted with one of the Veteran Guardsmen, a Corporal, Brian Steers. Twice weekly, Karl gave Brian lessons in conversational German and often brought tomatoes for Mrs. Steers.

"*Guten Morgen,* Karl, *was is los?* What's up?"

"Very good! *Guten Morgen,* Brian. Not very much... beautiful day!"
"Sure is! I brought something for you, Karl," Brian stated in halting German.

"What is it?"

"Here, catch!"

Karl tried to catch the object but it sailed past. It hit the ground. When he tried to pick it up, it bounced in a completely different direction. 'What the hell?' thought Karl.

"What kind of crazy thing is this?"

"A football, Karl!"

"Ya, sure, a football. It's not round! I've asked Wolf to show me how to throw the damn thing, but he always says he's too busy."

"It's not supposed to be round! This one's American, but Canadian ones are the same. Here, hand it back to me, I'll show you how to catch and throw it. "Step back, back, back some more... good, and stop. Now watch and learn! When it comes at you, don't hold out your arms like you're trying to snag a beautiful blonde for a kiss, just let it come into your arms, then pull it fast and snug into your chest, like a baby. Ready! Here goes!"

Brian threw the ball with a perfect spiral. Of course, Karl missed. It struck the ground on one end, and bounced in the opposite direction to which Karl was running.

"Four hands for beginners!" Brian joked.

"It was the sun! Once more please!" Karl pleaded after retrieving the ball and throwing it back awkwardly.

"Hup, hup, here it comes! You got it! Good catch, *Leutnant*!" With a leap, Karl caught it, and then landed on his back, cradling the ball tightly in his arms. "Wow, thanks Brian, this is *wunderbar*!" he shouted, jumping back up.

"Good! One or two more, and then I'll have to get back. By the time we're finished, you'll be showing Herr von Heiden how to play like a pro!"

Karl couldn't get enough of this new sport, Canadian football. He followed all of the professional teams in the daily papers although The Hamilton Flying Wildcats were his favourites, if only for the reason that some of the players were pilots. Each day he would force Wolf out to play with him, teaching him how to hold the ball and throw it properly. Karl had found a secluded spot behind the maintenance building where he could practice with Wolf without being ridiculed by the others.

"Come on, Karl! What's the problem, man? I've taught you how to hold it a hundred times for a punt," Wolf shouted in frustration, as the ball flew over his head and bounced into heavy brush. "Sometimes I think that you are doing that on purpose!"

"I'm not, Wolf. I'm trying to drop kick it properly. My fault. Stay there, I'll get it!"

Karl walked over to the approximate spot where the ball had disappeared, stopped, and looked up at the guard tower.

"Permission to get my ball? It bounced into the brush."

"Try letting it roll off your shoe laces, don't just hoof it with your toe. No control that way. Okay, go ahead, Karl!" replied the guard encouragingly.

"Thank you, Tom, I'll try to remember that!" Waving in acknowledgement, Karl walked into the bush with his arms outstretched to part the branches that threatened to tear his clothes.

"How are you doing in there? Do you see it yet, lover boy?" Wolf shouted after thirty seconds.

"Shut up, Wolf! It's thick, like a bloody jungle in here! Everything's tangled, and these damn wasps are vicious!" As he lifted branches and scraped around, he stepped into a hole. Hitting the ground with a thud, he struggled to free his leg, catching it on something in the hole.

"Wolfgang, come and help me!" Karl yelled.

Wolf looked up at the guard. "Permission to go in after him?"

"Go ahead."

Wolf fought his way through the now partly bent and trampled vegetation until he reached Karl, who was sprawled on the ground, his left leg buried almost up to the knee. "Those were big wasps, man eaters! Are you hurt?"

"Wolf, for God's sake help me, my leg is caught; it might be broken!" Karl pleaded.

"Stuck? What is it stuck in?"

"A hole, you idiot! It's caught in some kind of wood covering. I tried to lift it, but I can't."

"Hold on!" Swiftly, Wolf knelt and scraped away the topsoil and brush, then using a thick branch which was lying nearby, levered the heavy wood plank aside.

"Help pull me up. Owww! Okay I'm free, thanks! My God, look, it's a tunnel!" whispered Karl, rubbing his shin.

"Where do think it leads? Do you think it's one of ours?" whispered Wolf.

"I don't know, but I'm going to find out. Help me cover it back up. Good, rough up the earth and throw on some debris, a bit more, perfect. There's the football, over there. Grab it and let's get out of here. Give me a hand; my leg is throbbing from this gash on my shin."

"Are you men coming out of there?" The guard's voice seemed a world away.

"Coming, Tom! Right now!" Karl replied.

Karl put his arm around Wolf's neck and together they made their way back into the clearing.

Camp 30 The Mess The next morning

Karl and Wolf sat having breakfast.

"More toast, Karl?" asked Wolf.

"No thanks, I'm full," replied Karl.

"How is your leg today?"

"The throbbing kept me awake last night, but it will be okay. Hey, there's Korvettenkapitän Schumacher. I want to ask him a question. I'll be back in a minute, Wolf."

Karl walked over to the table where Schumacher sat.

"Good morning, Herr Kapitän. Sir, may I have a word with you?"

"Good morning, Leutnant. Yes. Please, sit down. Something wrong with your leg, son?"

"Just a bruise, Sir, football!" Karl replied glibly.

"Well, take care of it. By the way, Karl, I've been meaning to tell you, that's a fine garden you have cultivated. Damned fine. Say, I've wanted to thank you for the container of excellent Dutch pipe tobacco. A wonderful blend, indeed!"

"You're most welcome, Herr Kapitän. And thank you, Sir. Without your permission, the garden would not have been possible."

"Well, you'll be in charge next year, as well. If we're still here, that is. Why must I include that phrase in almost every sentence I say? Anyway, that's not why you are here. What is it, son?"

"Sir, have there been any new tunnels started lately, or, any tunnels in progress left unfinished?"

"No, if there were I would know about it or them. Why do you ask, Karl?"

"Oh, no particular reason, Sir. I was just wondering when we would be starting a tunnel as it seems such a practical thing to do."

"Well Leutnant, it will be starting soon enough. And I'll make sure that when that time comes, you'll be involved."

"Thank you, Herr Kapitän."

"Any time, Leutnant."

Turning to Oberstleutnant Eberhart, Schumacher muttered, "Werner, did you hear the latest news?"

"No, I haven't."

"It's not good, mind you. It comes from the local papers so we're not one hundred percent sure, but so far, they've been bang on. Admiral Dönitz has withdrawn all U-boats from the North Atlantic."

"My God! When did this happen?" asked Eberhart incredulously.

PoW Officers of Camp 30
Bowmanville Archives

"Recently, after two U-boats were sunk by convoy HX-239, which just so happened to bring that month's losses to a total of thirty-three U-boats. Not long after that, a pack of thirty-three U-boats attacked SC-130 and failed to sink a single vessel. Five of the Wolfpack were sunk. It's grim. And it gets worse," Schumacher stated.

"How could it, Sir?"

"One of the U-boats, U-954, was sunk with all hands on board including, Grand Admiral Dönitz's nineteen year old son, Peter. The Admiral must be beside himself, grief-stricken."

"This is dreadful news, Sir."

"Werner, we have to find a way for me to get out of here. I must get back into the fight!"

"We'll find a way, Sir, I promise."

Karl walked back to the table where Wolf was chatting with Kurt, Klaus, and Peter, the three 'sons of the desert' as Wolf called them behind their backs.

"So what did you ask the big man, Karl?" Kurt asked.

"Whether or not he likes my vegetables. Who wants to go to the canteen? A fresh shipment of candy bars is due today. Some U-boat type always beats me to it and grabs the whole box of my favourites!"

"Candy bars? How bourgeois! And right after breakfast!" Klaus commented with a stage shudder.

"So I have a sweet tooth; blame my mother, already. Football at 1330! See you there," Karl answered, picking up his tray. Then he set out for the Camp library.

1415 h

"That's it guys, let's take a break. It's getting too goddamn hot out here. I'm drier than a camel with a leaky hump. Could someone get some water?"

"So, all of a sudden, our Luftwaffe ace thinks he's a desert expert, Peter," Kurt remarked.

"That's what comes of hanging around with you three desert rats!" Karl laughed.

"Okay, Peter, Klaus, let's go."

"Thanks, Kurt, guys.

"I wanted to talk with you alone, Wolf," Karl began, his hands leaning back on the grass.

"What is it Karl? Oh, I know, it's that girl, Miss Bowmanville, isn't

it? You've been thinking about her night and day, haven't you?" Wolf began crooning a popular tune that had been playing on the local radio station, hourly.

"His career's not in jeopardy. I always told you that you're tone deaf. Just listen, Wolf. I have a plan."

"Oh oh. I don't like the sound of this."

"Look, I need your help. Nothing you can say is going to change my mind, so you might as well back me."

"Okay, what is it? Just don't tell me you're going to elope!"

"Will you please cut the sarcasm and listen? The bushes by our Haus lead directly into the heavy brush where the tunnel is. Tonight, right after roll call, I'll take a flashlight and see where it goes, and then I'll come straight back. I'm going to need something to protect myself with so that I'm not covered with mud. Now, I haven't told anyone about it, including Schumacher, so don't you dare, either! Understood?" Karl looked at Wolf sternly.

"Understood. *Ehrenwort*, I swear!" Wolf replied.

"One more thing I need from you: a sturdy knife with a long handle."

"Do you know what you're doing, Karl? If it turns out that it's an old forgotten tunnel, it can collapse if you sneeze and you'll be suffocated. And why tonight?"

"I know, but that's a chance I'll take. As for my decision to go tonight, I checked the *Farmer's Almanac* in the library this morning. New moon," he responded emphatically.

"Okay, I'll get coveralls from my friend Horst in the maintenance shop. The flashlight and kitchen knife are easy. Where do I leave everything?"

"I'll explain that. It's crucial that you cover for me, with the guards and the PoWs. I don't want anyone, anyone at all, knowing what I'm up to."

"*Hu*, whew! Don't you worry about what Schumacher will do to us if he finds out?"

"Us? No, because up to now he hasn't set down any rules about escapes. He told me he's still assessing the situation. So, until he puts the clamps on, it's fair game."

"Okay, Karl. I'll help."

"Thanks for the water, guys!" Karl reached up, taking the container.

That night, after the 2215 hour roll call, the men disbursed in all directions. Karl walked quickly toward Haus I. Melting into the shadows, he dropped to his knees and crawled along, hugging the foundation until he reached the brush just fifteen metres away. The coveralls were lying neatly bundled exactly where he had instructed Wolf to leave them. He quickly checked the pockets. Wolf had placed a four-cell flashlight in one and a wooden handled knife in the other. Sitting on the ground, he pulled the mechanic's coveralls over his clothes and waited for the guard tower's searchlights to sweep by, and then darted into the heavy thicket. Following his well-travelled route along the embankment, he reached the wooden plank covering the tunnel opening. The thick branch lay beside it. After a quick glance around, Karl wedged the end of the stick under the side of the plank and pried it up, exposing the opening. The slightly sweet, familiar odour of damp soil and decaying vegetation greeted his nostrils.

Lying on his stomach, he shone the flashlight's powerful beam into the entrance. Leaning against the opposite wall, he could see a crude ladder of thick branches lashed to two sturdy uprights. He estimated the ladder to be three metres long. 'Who dug it? Of course, the kids! I'll be damned! The little beggars must have been excavating it when the school was taken over to make way for us.

'Here goes nothing!' he thought, as he tucked the flashlight into the back pocket of the coveralls, and stepped cautiously onto the top rung. "*Sehr langsam*, slowly, very slowly, Karl," he muttered, descending one step at a time. Upon reaching the bottom, he retrieved the flashlight and shone it down the narrow passageway, revealing walls and ceilings that appeared to be properly shored with wooden slats. As he began crawling on his hands and knees, he recalled his early days around Eisenach, Thuringia, when he, Wolfgang, and their friends played 'explorers,' in the caves that honeycombed the riverbank. Karl remembered how angrily they had plotted revenge the following day to find that someone had come along and ruined their hours of laborious digging by throwing the piles of earth back into the passageways. He now understood that their tunnels hadn't been destroyed by other boys, but had simply caved in under the weight of the unshored earth above. He shuddered with the realisation that it might just as easily have happened when he and his

chums were three or four metres inside.

Fortunately, Karl reflected, he had never suffered from claustrophobia, then as now. The tunnel in some places was barely wide enough to accommodate his shoulders without a determined effort to force his way through. When he reached the end, he stood up, panting, unable to resist shouting, "Fine work, lads, very fine work indeed. And there's another ladder!" his voice echoing dully. He tested the ladder's placement on the tunnel floor and climbed warily until his head touched the roof. Using the kitchen knife as a probe, he poked gently at the earth until the blade pierced the surface. Tentatively, he teased and chopped at the soil, unmindful of the clods of dirt falling in his face, until the sky was visible. "Look at that! The Big Dipper!" Dropping the knife, he clawed at the earth with his fingers to enlarge the opening until he was just able to poke his head through. Eagerly, he took the final step up, pushed hard, and scrambled out, collapsing on the ground, gulping the cool night air.

'Freedom,' he whispered like a prayer. Looking back toward the Camp's distant watchtower beacons, he sighed, 'How long has it been, almost two years?'

The hole was close to the roots of a large poplar tree, explaining why the farmer's tractor had never caved it in. He looked back once more to check the range of the Camp's searchlights. The arc of their beams fell well short. 'Perfekt! Now, to get back before all hell breaks loose!'

The next morning at breakfast, Wolf signalled Karl to join him at an empty table. "Pass the marmalade, please. So, tell me Karl, how was it? Did you find everything where I left it? How long were you gone? I was asleep by 2330. Did anyone catch you when you came in?"

"You did everything I asked, thanks. No, no one Wolf, it all went perfectly. Now I can slip out of Camp at any time without being detected. All I have to do is come and go between roll calls, it's that simple. I was gone for about an hour and a half, at most. Just enough time to get out, look around, and return. My timing will get better. The tunnel is very well constructed; it must have been built by some of the older boys. They used slats from crates, or something like that, for shoring. Remember our cave-ins? We didn't know how to do that, but these kids did!

PoW Officers at Bowmanville – 1942
Bowmanville Archives

"It comes out in the farmer's field, right beside a tree that you can see from the gate. I say it's perfect because the opening is hidden behind the tree so any activity there is blocked from the guards' view. What's more, it's in the middle of a cornfield, so, it will be easy to walk around without being seen. When the time is right, I'll take you out with me."

"That's amazing Karl! What luck! Are you going to tell Schumacher?" asked Wolf excitedly.

"No, not yet; all in good time. For now, I'm going to use it for my own purpose."

"Which is? The young woman, *Natürlich*! How dim-witted of me!" Wolf replied, striking his forehead in self-disgust. "Listen, Karl, I hope she's worth all the risk and bother. You know...!" he grinned, meaning-fully.

Karl cut him short. "If you're getting up, Wolf, more coffee, please?"

That afternoon Karl, slipped out of the Camp, and made his way through the tunnel, out into the warm sunshine in the farmer's field. He lay back, congratulating himself on his good fortune. There were no officers to tell him what to do, nor any guards, including Brian, watching his every move. Here he could relax and enjoy the solitude. After a while, Karl decided to have a closer look at the farmhouse, visible off in the distance. After all, this was the one that Marlene had said that her father was looking at the day he had met her. He wondered, hoped even, that her father had found it satisfactory. Perhaps not. It appeared deserted. After watching the farmhouse for about an hour, Karl, disappointed by the lack of any activity, decided to return to Camp.

At supper that evening, Peter, Kurt, and Klaus came to sit with Karl and Wolf. "Move over; thank you very much!" Peter stated civilly as they placed their trays on the table. "So, where were you today, Karl? We missed you; we wanted to have that game of football."

"I wasn't feeling well, so I stayed close to bed and the washroom."

"Oh, that's why everyone from your Haus kept coming into ours to use our can," Peter laughed.

"Yes, something like that."

"Tell me, Peter, have you heard from your family back home?" Karl asked.

"Yes, I have as a matter of fact. Everyone is fine. I haven't had the nerve to tell them about our *Lager*, Camp. They think that I am being ill treated."

"Yes, we're all in the same boat on that one. Excuse me, no pun intended," interrupted Konrad Eckert, from across the table. "Suffering, deprivation, and those are the good parts."

"Apparently it's a touchy subject with Korvettenkapitän Schumacher. He doesn't want the brass in the homeland finding out either. It doesn't sit well for possible promotions," replied Wolf.

"Promotions, *ja*, for sure," Klaus replied, with mock seriousness. "You are hereby promoted to *Lager* Latrine *Obermeister*, soldier! Heil Hitler!"

"Shut up, Klaus!" Kurt snarled. "Do you want to get us all shipped out of here?"

"Sorry! It was just a little joke."

"The Commandant's on the lookout for Nazi sympathizers and troublemakers. They'll get a trip to some godforsaken, hard labour camp in the north woods.

"I've managed to break you of that bad habit, haven't I, Peter," Kurt stated.

"*Jawohl, Mein Führer.* No, really, lads, he has!" Peter responded, flashing an innocent smile. "I am a reformed man!"

"So, Peter, tomorrow! We'll have that game of football you are so looking forward to, foolish as you are. It'll be Wolf, Klaus, and I against you and Kurt. A beer a touchdown. Deal?"

"You're on, Karl!"

CHAPTER 7
OPERATION ANORAK

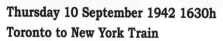

Thursday 10 September 1942 1630h
Toronto to New York Train

"The usual? Two fingers, two ice, Mr. Brooker?" the bartender called.

"Yes, please, Augie!"

Robert Brooks snapped shut and locked his briefcase then slid it carefully out of sight between the legs of his lounge chair. Selecting a Pall Mall Regular from a slimly elegant, gold-plated case, he lit the cigarette with the chromium Ronson lighter, which Roger Stedman, Commandant of Camp X, had presented him. Brooks' support in managing a hostage crisis at St. John's Anglican Church in Whitby had resulted in the release of the three captives as well as the killing of one German agent and the capture of another.

As the bartender set down the drink, Robert nodded his thanks, drawing the smoke deeply into his lungs. "Thanks, Augie. How are you?"

"Just fine, like the weather, and getting better, Mr. Brooker! You?"

"Tip top. Kind of quiet in here today, although I see Chuck and Howie are up to their old tricks. Say, she's new!"

"Yes, Sir. Adds a little class to our surroundings, wouldn't you say?"

Brooks nodded in agreement, inhaled, and then settled back to savour his first scotch in more than a week, or was it two? He always enjoyed watching the Club Car dramatics. Most of the regular late afternoon Toronto-to-New-York-express-run habitués were missing in action except for the two conspicuously tipsy middle-aged supporting players currently attempting, with a singular lack of success, to spark the interest of an unaccompanied ingénue. Robert noted approvingly that the slim, strikingly attractive blonde wore an exceptionally well-fitted Canadian Navy WREN uniform. She concentrated on her knitting with single-minded resolve. She was definitely a 'looker' but appeared to have the situation well in hand. 'No need to play Sir Galahad,' Robert noted approvingly as he stirred the amber liquid lazily with a straw.

Robert Brooks, or 'Brooker', his public alter ego, glanced down at the

crumpled, wafer-thin white paper tube lying beside the coaster. The bar-man, Augustus, Augie to the club car's regulars, always supplied one straw per drink, regardless of his patrons' choice of cocktail. While set-tling his tab, Robert never tired of nagging Augie, good-naturedly. "A bit of a luxury in wartime, these drinking straws, don't you think, Augie?"

"You used two, Mr. Brooker, now didn't you, Sir?" he would reply, smiling, as he polished the immaculate mahogany counter for the hun-dredth time. When Augie rang up 'Mr. Brooker's' total, Robert would invariably proffer a Canadian ten-dollar bill.

"Now, let me see. Are we in the US of A yet? Well, no matter, here's your change, Mr. Brooker. Canadian! Why, thank you kindly, Sir! Very generous of you, yes, indeed! The baby will be getting new booties this Christmas after all." The cadence and warmth of his baritone drawl, and his broad smile were tonics to the souls of the chronically over-stressed business-class clientele in his care. "Be seein' you on your return, I expect, Sir?"

"You can count on it, Augie! Best to Harriet and little Clarissa," Robert automatically replied. The drama rarely varied, he smiled.

Robert relished this time to sit quietly and unwind. He knew that the head of British Security Operation, his old friend Erik Williamson, would not have ordered him to New York HQ on short notice for any rea-son other than a 'most urgent and exceptionally sensitive matter'. 'Then again,' Robert reflected, 'in this job, isn't everything?'

When Robert arrived at 0720 on that morning at the Canadian HQ of British Security Operation, King Street West, he found the red mes-sage light flashing insistently on his red scrambler telephone. Erik Williamson's message was unusually cryptic and concise: "Arrive soon-est. *Anorak* 3600, 11 09 42, 0715." All else was clear: Friday, September 11, at 0715, in Room 3600, Rockefeller Centre. 'But what in hell is *Anorak*?'

Robert shrugged, picking up the complementary copy of the Toronto Evening Telegram. The headline trumpeted: RCAF PLANES OF EASTERN AIR COMMAND DESTROY TWO GERMAN U-BOATS IN ONE DAY. As he scanned the article, he noted approvingly that it was lacking in specific detail; as well, the story was one week stale-dated. In fact, Robert knew that all of the ship's crew and officers had been rescued. As soon as Ted Reynolds' RCMP Security Service sorted them out, they would be on board CN or CP trains from Halifax, destined to be 'Guests of His Majesty' in Canadian PoW camps for the duration of the war.

The WREN looked up, as though searching for a thought mid-air. Her eye caught Robert's; she smiled briefly, and resumed knitting. He smiled and nodded, in tribute, as the two well-lubricated Lotharios, resigned to defeat, settled into a game of Down The River, for drinks. She re-crossed her knees, primly pulling down the hem of her skirt, and unwound a length of azure blue wool, exactly the colour of her eyes. Despite an effort not to stare, Robert was fascinated by her manual dexterity and speed. 'She'd make an outstanding wireless operator. Should I order her a drink? Milk? She's barely twenty, if she's a day. She's likely making socks for her fiancé overseas.' He sipped thoughtfully on his drink. 'It has been almost eleven months since Nancy passed away…Stop it Brooks, you don't have time for a romantic interlude!

"Say, Augie, could you pop over for a moment, please?"

The gamblers studiously ignored her reaction when Augie delivered the rye and ginger ale highball, with a straw, setting down the silver tray with a flourish and a discrete tilt of his head toward Robert. Augie sidled over to quietly inform Robert that the lady had invited him join her.

She said her name was Rita, from Toronto. She was on a seventy-two hour leave, and bound for New York City to meet her fiancé, Alistair. He was Canadian, a junior military attaché. He had been given a pair of tickets for one of two Brooklyn Dodgers vs. St. Louis Cardinals games either on the 11th or the 12th at Brooklyn's Ebbets Field, she couldn't recall exactly. She smiled, confessing that she was not remotely interested in baseball, but had solemnly pledged to accompany Alistair, in return for, "A lie in, with breakfast in bed, window-shopping, and perhaps more, on Sunday morning." She lowered her eyes, and smiled self-consciously.

By the time the train pulled up at the platform in Grand Central Station, Rita had invited Robert to join Alistair and her at a swank restaurant in lower Manhattan for drinks and dinner at eight o'clock that evening. Robert graciously accepted, noting that the eatery was located on Fifth Avenue, close by his hotel and Rockefeller Centre.

Friday 11 September 1942 0705h
BSO HQ, Committee Room 3600, Rockefeller Centre, New York City

The small, burnished brass plate on the hallway entrance door discretely announced the office of **British American Overseas Importing Ltd.** Robert inserted his passkey and entered. The door closed silently behind him. To his left, through the open door of the Committee Room, he could see Erik Williamson seated at the large, dark oak conference table, absorbed in the *Times*, a stout Havana cigar clenched in his mouth. No one else was to be seen in the British Security Operation headquarters.

"Good morning, Erik! I thought you gave up those infernal things at Casa Loma!"

Williamson set down the morning paper, and smiled cordially as he rose, extending his hand. "Good morning, Rob. When Mr. Churchill does, then so will I, and there's little chance of that!" he rejoined, laughing. "I'm so pleased that you could make it, ahead of time, at that. I wouldn't have asked you to come, if I felt that we could have discussed this rather sensitive matter by the usual methods. How was the trip?" inquired Erik, carefully tamping the end of his cigar in a very large, cut glass ashtray. "Any excitement along the way?"

"Relaxing, as always, thanks, and fortunately, no, nothing exciting," Robert replied casually, sitting across from Erik at the table. 'Damn, why do I feel guilty?' "So, a 'sensitive matter', Erik?" 'Sounds ominous.' Glancing out the expanse of plate glass, he could see the morning traffic already clogging the streets below.

"I've ordered breakfast to be delivered at 0715. Perhaps we can begin now with a cup of my caustic brew and work through."

"Of course, Erik, that'll be fine." Robert sipped cautiously from the steaming cup. "Oh, my Lord, that is strong! I'm glad to see that your coffee-making skills haven't been corrupted here. Any sugar in New York?"

"Try this. It's artificial, saccharin, very sweet without the calories. Now, Rob, Bowmanville, Camp 30, CO Colonel Jack Armstrong," Erik began, articulating slowly and precisely.

"Yes?"

"Jack Armstrong has asked General Constantine's assistance in carrying out a complete security audit of the Camp, on the 'q.t.', of course.

Apparently, the General polled Ted Reynolds who recommended that we be approached. Armstrong reported to me that he has no reason to suspect that anything untoward is going on, or to believe that it isn't, but he's not content to leave it at that. His reasoning is sound. Given that several of the PoW's represent the best and brightest of Germany's officer cadre, and here I'm referring specifically to Korvettenkapitän Frederick Schumacher and General Albrecht Schröder; men of this calibre are, without question, sorely missed at home. It shouldn't come as a revelation if the inmates are working a fiddle with the intention of organizing a series of breakouts to get these gentlemen back to Germany. The outcome would be a triumphant coup for the Nazi propaganda machine at best. At worst, well, we can only imagine."

"Yes, of course, they not only possess the brains and will..."

Interrupted by a knock on the door, Erik rose. Placing his index finger to his lips, he walked to the door, calling, "One moment, please!" While the white-jacketed busboy arranged the steaming buffet trays, Erik carried on a spirited, and to Robert, informed analysis of the Brooklyn Dodgers' chances against the St. Louis Cardinals' powerhouse in the upcoming two-game series.

"I am truly deeply impressed, Erik," Robert stated when they were alone. "I had no idea! Mind you, if I had known, I would have pegged you as a Yankees' fan, but that's the only team I've ever remotely paid any attention to. I'd like to see a baseball game some day!"

"That's the correct response, old man! We're going, tomorrow," Erik declared, withdrawing a white envelope from his vest pocket.

"Going? Going where?"

"To tomorrow's game, dear boy! Hope you didn't make any plans for Saturday afternoon." He paused, "It would be a shame to miss it, providing we complete our assignment, of course."

"No, nothing for Saturday."

"Good, then it's settled. Oh, yes; you'll be returning to Toronto first thing Sunday, 0910, non-stop. Do try the Eggs Benedict, Rob. They're superb: Chef André's specialty. As I was saying, the possibility of an escape by one or more of these fellows would not only be a political and diplomatic embarrassment to Canada, but a major security gaffe with potentially disastrous military consequences."

"Sure. But how to find out: who, when and where?"

"I'm coming to that. At the outset, I eliminated what won't work.

First: the guards are an unreliable factor. Not that they are unreliable as guards per se, but they have limited contact with the prisoners, under Armstrong's organization. Moreover, the prisoners tend not to have any dealings with them, for whatever reasons. Second: it would be difficult or well nigh impossible to 'turn' a prisoner into an informer, without an extremely sophisticated scheme in place, which we haven't. Third: external monitoring is out of the question. We lack the means and technical staff to mount a large-scale operation, and, even if we had them, Rob, the Camp is simply too large and complex a facility in which to establish concealed listening posts. No, we must insert a fluently bilingual agent into the camp: someone fully immersed in and current with German military culture who can carry it off without arousing the slightest hint of suspicion. Ideas?" He cocked his head, waiting, and then continued. "Rob, we do have a pool of superb intelligence talent that could provide what we're looking for."

"The Farm, Erik?"

"Precisely. The Farm, STS 103."

"Who, Erik?" Robert asked quizzically.

"The Commandant, Roger Stedman. More coffee? No? Can't say I blame you. Heaven knows Leah's tried for many years to curb my enthusiasm with the scoop, but to no avail," he remarked, smiling wryly. "Roger Stedman's profile exactly fits our needs. Look, why don't you read over his dossier to refresh your memory; take as much time as you need. Consider how we can slip him in, and have him be accepted immediately by the inmates. I'll go now and tend to some business. Drop into my office when you're finished. Keep in mind such things as personal flaws and weaknesses, operational shortcomings, drawbacks, and the like. Also, Rob, be thinking about Stedman's replacement. I want Operation Anorak to be running within two weeks this coming Monday. No later. This afternoon, we'll write it up in detail."

After Williamson left the room, Robert poured his second cup of Erik's coffee, which, although industrial strength, he found more flavourful than the anaemic brew in the restaurant's silver carafe. He settled back to review the contents of the Stedman, Roger Douglas file. 'Erik's already made up his mind, so why does he want me to vet Stedman's credentials? *Theirs is not to question why...* Finding a replacement on short notice might be a test of our ingenuity, though. Operation *Anorak*? What in the world does that mean?' he grumbled.

Friday 11 September 1942 0825h
Erik Williamson's Office

"Good morning, Mr. Brooks. So good to see you again, Sir! Please go right in. Mr. Williamson is expecting you." Erik's Special Assistant, Miss Helen Stapleton, was a Canadian citizen, as were all of the female support staff at BSO HQ, Manhattan. Robert had recruited each one through discrete Toronto newspaper want ads followed by exhaustive background assessments and one or more selection interviews.

Robert noted a passing similarity in Helen's manner to that of Erik's first Special Assistant, Miss Mary Ward. Mary had risen quickly through the organization to become Erik's dedicated and superbly gifted administrative anchor and confidante. Robert and Erik, and her long-time admirer Major Samson of Camp X, still grieved Mary's brutal murder in central Toronto at the hands of one Colonel Max Schneider, counterintelligence agent of Germany's Abwehr, Military Intelligence Service. 'But you paid in full, Schneider, you swine!'

Robert closed the folder and walked over to Miss Stapleton's desk. "Would you happen to have a dictionary on hand, Miss Stapleton?"

"Robert? Are you coming in?" Erik called from his office.

"On my way, Erik!"

"Here, Sir!" Miss Stapleton smiled, producing a standard American reference.

"Oh, the dictionary! Thanks, perhaps later, Miss Stapleton," Robert commented graciously before closing Erik's office door.

Erik looked up. "Well, that certainly didn't take you long to digest. Please, sit down. Now, give me your candid appraisal. Is Roger Stedman our man?"

Robert blinked involuntarily at the brilliant sunlight streaming through the windows of Erik's spacious corner office. "Without any doubt, Erik. If he were any more qualified, he'd be sitting here instead of me," Robert replied.

"Thank you for the suggestion, Mr. Brooks. I'll file it for future reference," Erik answered with mock seriousness. "Now, get on with it, please."

"Right. Stedman, Roger Douglas: Born: 1906, Jaipur India, the first of two offspring, sister Margaret, born 1913. Father: Nelson Douglas, Scottish-born Presbyterian minister-missionary. I can relate, the impoverished clergyman's son and all that," Robert commented, smiling. He continued with a rapid-fire delivery. "Mother: Katrina, 'Kate': German and Irish, Roman Catholic, missionary-teacher. Lord, that must have made for some interesting Sunday table talk! Carrying on. Primary education: Jesuit academy in Madras, thence to England and Scotland. He has all of the academic prerequisites: German: native-like fluency based on his mother's influence, also French, Spanish, Italian as well as Hindi, Punjabi, and...."

"Yes, yes, we know he's an accomplished linguist, Robert," Erik remarked, his voice rising with his mounting impatience.

"Yes, Sir. Sorry, let me see. Ah yes, undergraduate studies at Universität Karlesruhe, Germany, where he read Comparative Linguistics, and Political Science, with distinction. That was followed by postgraduate studies in nineteenth and twentieth century European military history at the Sorbonne. Enlisted 1928, Royal Scottish Fusiliers, Second Lieutenant. Gazetted 1930, Captain. Background verification comes up spotless, credentials flawless. Let me see, specialized intelligence instruction, and advanced Commando training at sundry SOE stations, appointed to staff at Beaulieu, promoted to rank of Chief Instructor. Not to mention time spent as recently as 1938 in Berlin and Vienna attached with the British Foreign Office. Status: single; parents: mother deceased, father retired from the clergy, resides near Stornaway in the wild and enchanting Scottish Outer Hebrides. There's more, but that should suffice. In conclusion, Erik, I agree. Stedman is our man!"

"Very good. And a pro tem replacement?"

"Hamish? Yes, Erik, definitely Hamish."

"Agreed, a first-rate choice, our Major Findlay. We'll chew that over in due course to be sure. First, concerning Colonel Stedman, I want you to consider one or two aspects that could come a cropper. You'll recall that among his many accomplishments, Roger's service in the diplomatic corps, although relatively brief, was one of the determining factors in our requesting his transfer from Beaulieu to replace Colonel Graham as Commandant of Camp X. However, that in itself may well pose a liability in these circumstances."

"How so?"

"Perhaps I should explain. You were in the domestic diplomatic service where I'm sure you brushed shoulders, and were on more than nodding terms with, hundreds of embassy, political, military and diplomatic types. As a mid to high-level attaché in foreign embassy circles, it's logical to assume that Roger encountered one or more of these officers as a matter of course. I'll give one example: General Albrecht Schröder was a senior staff functionary with the OKW, High Command of the Wehrmacht, before the war. It's not a stretch of the imagination to speculate that Herr General and our man Stedman traded chitchat over canapés and champagne at one or more embassy soirées. And there, as they say here in America, goes the whole ball game."

"Saints, that would be a stopper! We can verify that possibility with Colonel Stedman, no?"

"That we must. Miss Stapleton will forward him wire photos of the top men at Camp 30, courtesy of Armstrong and Reynolds, as soon as she receives them. No explanation given; simply a request to look them over and jot a notation upon any that looks even vaguely familiar, with the instruction, Complete and Return Soonest."

"Brilliant. However, let's suppose that one or more of these mug shots registers a positive. Then what's our course of action? Surely we can't abandon Stedman, given all other factors in his favour."

"I think that would call for an immediate administrative transfer," Erik replied. "Several options are available, with eighteen internment centres operating to date in Ontario, Alberta, and Quebec, and eight more being developed. Any relocation action would have to be carried out swiftly and cleanly. That already happens for any number of security and personnel considerations, I'm told, and should not present any difficulties."

"It would be to our advantage though, if none were necessary, I assume."

"Oh, definitely. The less turmoil and potential for awkward questions, the better."

"Well then, what needs to be done? Two weeks is an exceptionally short timeline, even for you, Erik!"

Erik leaned forward, "I know, and naturally, I do share your concerns, Rob. We have two major tasks facing us today. First, Stedman will require an identity that is credible, virtually untraceable, and impermeable. In other words, airtight. Second, he will require an extensive

briefing as well as a 'crash' course on current German service jargon, strategy, and the state of the armed services jungle telegraph. What do field officers think about the war: the complaints, grousing about the senior OKW staff officer cadre and the high command in Berlin: who's in, who's out, who they think should be out. In other words, the usual rumblings and rumours they discuss quietly over a late night schnapps.

"Consider this: although Roger is ideally suited to take on the persona of a German intelligence officer, and not just the garden variety Abwehr sort that could easily be cracked, I was stumped to think of a way in. Slowly it became clear that he could best pull it off if he were an officer in a little-known, elite unit. But I had no idea how, in short order, you and I might transform Lieutenant Colonel Roger Stedman SOE, into Major Theodore Brückner.

"Major Theodore Brückner? Any particular reason, Erik?"

"A bit of a joke, really, no other significance. Anton Brückner is Hitler's favourite composer.

"You are deadly serious; all this within two weeks?"

"Yes, two weeks, Robert. Obviously, given the makeup of the prisoners in Bowmanville, we can't risk any direct connection with the Afrika Korps, Luftwaffe or the Kriegsmarine U-boat Command. Stedman would be well out of his depth, so to speak, and it's not worth the risk. Something major is likely brewing at Camp 30 and it is essential we have Stedman in place to uncover the when, the what, and, most importantly, who's involved. We'll need your Toronto staff on this watch twenty-four hours, seven days a week."

"Unquestionably. How can we get the latest goods on the state of things from within a German officer's head, as it were?"

"Ask a German officer," Erik replied. "That will be your assignment, Robert."

"Erik, I know this will sound as though I'm asking that you lead me by the hand, but exactly where will we find such an animal, on short notice, who's willing to tell all?"

Erik pushed a file across his desk, and opened it to display the identity papers with a photograph of a German officer, aged thirty-one. "Say 'Guten Tag' to Leutnant Ulrich. The Leutnant is currently locked up in a maximum-security prison in British Columbia. In protective custody, I might add."

"Protection for whom? And why is he there?"

"For his own protection. The Leutnant was, and is, a thoroughly disgruntled intelligence officer of the Reich's elite *Brandenburger Tropenkom*panie, Brandenburg Company, a more or less autonomous combination intelligence/reconnaissance and commando-type force, which operates independent of regular forces. He was relegated to remain behind as liaison with what's left of the Italian forces in Cyrenaica. More importantly, he harbours a deep dislike for the high command, including his Brandenburger CO and even the godlike General Rommel. He truly believes that he was unfairly and arbitrarily passed over for promotion, not once, but twice, before his capture by British special forces on a street corner in a village somewhere in Cyrenaica, a fate, incidentally, which he squarely blames on his superior officer's bias and incompetence. All of this, and more came to light when he became involved in a brouhaha on board the transport ship from England. He actually attempted to stab the major in question using a length of steel welding rod, likely left lying about by careless workmen dockside. He was charged with a litany of offences under British maritime law and tossed into the ship's brig. The captain, a Belfast man like you, incidentally, wanted to hang him from the yardarm as an example, after a fair and impartial drum head court martial, of course. Our General Charles Constantine got wind of it somehow." He paused, smiled, and then continued. "When he realized the man's potential intelligence value, Charles became embroiled in a hot jurisdictional battle with Whitehall. Fortunately, for us, he prevailed, for which the Leutnant is exceedingly grateful.

"Naturally, Ted Reynolds' Security people culled him from the crop destined for Bowmanville."

"What if it's all an elaborate ruse?" Robert queried.

"Ottawa checked out his story thoroughly and it holds up to scrutiny. Furthermore, I believe he can be persuaded to do us a service, as a quid pro quo for keeping him beyond the scope of swift justice under British assizes. To keep his expected cooperation hushed, he will be transferred to His Majesty's Department of Prisons in Bermuda, where our BSO Station people can keep an eye and an ear on developments. He will be informed that any breach of confidence will result in extremely harsh penalties, subject to the full range of corporal punishment remedies available under Bermuda law, up to and including execution."

"That should concentrate his mind," Robert commented.

"It should indeed. Rob, would you object if I were to forward Ulrich's

file immediately via special courier to your chum Derek Wainscott on King Street? Somewhat of an odd duck, Derek, as you've said yourself, but a thoroughgoing professional with an inquiring mind. High marks from Sir Willson Cunnington, his former chief at SIS, and from you, as well, I might add, based upon your experience together in the consulate. He acquitted himself worthily with the 'Clipper' file, in my estimation. Your opinion, Robert?"

"I agree with you on that point, Erik. Derek's nobody's fool and he's razor sharp. He absorbs information about everything and everybody through his pores, and stores it. Better yet, he can retrieve it when required. If anything, he tends towards being obsessive in the details department. But you know, he's deceptive. You'd never guess the intellectual depth and canniness for reading people from his outward manner. Somewhat of a lone wolf, Derek. He's a bohemian by choice, but capable of wittiness, warmth and charm. And there's certainly no pretence, that is, when he's in the right mind frame. Abrasive and caustic when he's not."

"Good. Helen will call Toronto to ensure that Wainscott's cleared and ticketed to fly out to Vancouver, early Monday, returning to Toronto with Ulrich on Tuesday. I suggest that you get together with Derek Sunday afternoon, at your office. Helen will call Toronto to arrange it for 1500 hours. She'll prepare your briefing notes today in order that you'll have them to study on the train. I want Derek to get a sense of Ulrich's willingness to co-operate, using the carrot and stick approach, if necessary, and to explain the rules of the game. You'll find it all laid out clearly in the briefing notes."

"'Need-to-know' for Wainscott, I assume, Erik?"

"Wainscott will not be privy to *Anorak*, the operation per se, at this time," Erik confirmed. "Care for a bite of lunch downstairs and some fresh Manhattan air? Afterward, we can finalize Major Findlay and get on with devising Stedman's cover."

As the elevator descended, Robert recollected the unusual circumstances and coincidences which had led to his association with this extraordinary Canadian, Erik Williamson, code-named *Stalwart* by the British Prime Minister despite Erik's objections. Robert recalled Erik's stunning telephone call in the fall of 1939, following fifteen years of infrequent contact, the upshot of which was Robert's appointment as Deputy Director, British Security Operation, Canadian Headquarters.

Their friendship dated almost from the moment they had met while enrolling as fledgling pilot trainees in 1915 with the Royal Flying Corps, both recent transferees from the trenches. Prior to being mistakenly shot down by Allied artillery and badly wounded, Erik had achieved ace status, was four times decorated, and credited with twenty-three enemy aircraft destroyed while Robert tallied eight destroyed, along with four probables. Their friendship was cemented firmly in 1919 when, after abandoning plans to establish a viable flying school business in Regina, they scraped together their life savings and returned to England, somehow managing to talk their way past the Foreign Office recruitment bureaucracy to enter the British Secret Service, SIS.

Both men went on to serve honourably and with distinction in Northern Ireland, despite the constant threat of betrayal and summary execution by any number of factions of every political stripe and religious persuasion. Robert had been astonished at his comrade's unique flair for absorbing and mimicking the local Dublin street dialects and accents, a talent that had saved their lives on two occasions.

"We're here, restaurant level; after you, old man," Erik announced.

"Oh, sorry, Erik, I was wool-gathering. I do have one question, but it will have to wait."

By 7:20 p.m., it was already dark. Robert stood up to stretch and glanced out Erik's windows. The early evening Manhattan traffic seemed much lighter than he remembered. "Is gasoline rationed here yet?" he wondered aloud.

"Yes, since May. Motorists are permitted just eight gallons per month. Rubber production for automobile tires was cut drastically last January, following Pearl Harbour, in the fear that the Japanese would quickly seize the Far-Eastern plantations. Surprisingly, there appears to be no lack of either gas or tires for enterprising New Yorkers," Erik commented wryly.

"Well, that was a good day's worth of work. Continue and conclude tomorrow morning, starting time the same? The sun's well over the yardarm; time for a drink, don't you think, my friend?"

"Perhaps a short one, thanks. Actually, Erik, I have a dinner engagement at eight. I should get away to catch a cab, by," he paused to

consult his wristwatch, "seven thirty, latest."

"I see. I had booked us into the club for dinner at that same time. Positive I can't dissuade you?"

"Sorry, Erik, but this is a very charming couple that I met on the train."

"Oh, not to worry. We can do it tomorrow night. I must admit that I'm exhausted, but I think that I'll pop in for a bite and a nightcap, just the same. Why don't we forego the drinks here, head downstairs, and catch a cab together? They're devilishly hard to flag down at night. During the day, they're lined up three deep at the entrance. Which way are you going?"

"Fifth Avenue."

"Couldn't be better. The club, you'll recall, is on Park Avenue. I'll see you downstairs in five minutes, after I lock up!"

'It was the second Spanish coffee,' Robert decided as the elevator glided silently to an abrupt stop. 'That and the half bottle of Chateau Neuf.' Erik was already at work, Dictaphone in one hand, cigar in the other, stacks of papers placed strategically within his reach, forming a perfect semi-circle on the conference table.

"Hullo! Sorry I'm late!"

"Good morning. I got here a little earlier than planned," Erik answered cheerily. "Come, see what we accomplished yesterday! Speaking of which, how was your dinner engagement?"

"Oh, very nice. Good people, Canadians, young, in love, career-minded, articulate, and bright-eyed, the sort one would give one's eye-teeth to have in BSO. I confess that I overdid it in the drinks department somewhat: no, in truth, more than somewhat. Still a touch fogged in, but I should recover, thanks. What's all this? **Operation Anorak. Most Secret**. Ye gods, man, when did you possibly have time to put this together?" Robert sat down and began to read aloud from the forty typewritten page, grey, soft–cover report, beginning with the index.

"Section 1.0.0. Background and Rationale

The agency, British Security Operation, henceforth known as BSO, having been apprised of unspecified threats to the integrity and security of the facility known as Prisoner of

War Internment Camp 30, located within or near the town of Bowmanville, Province of Ontario, in the County of..."

He continued reading silently, until Erik tapped his shoulder.

"Breakfast, old man. Can your constitution manage a poached egg and toast?"

"Give me another minute, please."

Erik set down a cup of coffee beside Robert. "This morning, you might finally appreciate my handiwork at last," he chuckled.

Thirty minutes later, Robert turned to **Section 5.0.0. Anorak: Executive Summary, then 5.0.1 Actions, Responsibilities, 5.0.2 Location, 5.0.3. Timelines, and finally Section 6.0.0 Statistical Probability of Accomplishment of The Four Main Objective: ~45-55%. End**

"Did I miss anything, Mr. Brooker? Best eat up, the eggs are nearly rock hard, and the toast is getting as soggy as an Irish peat bog."

"Thanks, I will," Robert laughed. "You left out nothing. There's more here than we ever discussed. It's brilliant, Erik, absolutely first rate. A question: When is Roger Stedman to be briefed? And Hamish? Oh, I see it all here in **5.0.3.**"

"Both will require the blessing and approval of Colonel CG at SOE. We'll be calling Baker Street, London for his verbal authorization at 10:00 a.m., New York time. Following that, the final paperwork will have to be wired back and forth. However, I don't expect any hold-ups, unless the Executive Head of SOE has had a change of mind since we last spoke on Thursday," Erik explained.

"Then this has been in the works for what, two days? Three? A week?"

"Two weeks is closer," Erik replied. You've read that you've been designated the messenger for Stedman, once all the ducks are properly lined up. Baker Street politely insists upon carrying the ball in bringing Hamish up to speed. 'By all means! Done!' was my comeback.

"The next step is dodgy," Erik continued. "We have to arrange a series of face-to-face meetings with Roger, Derek, you and Ulrich, and perhaps others, well away from ferreting eyes, obviously in a secret and secure location. The question, and it's hinted at nowhere in the proposal, is, where?"

"Why not STS 109, 'The Citadel'? It's close, in British Columbia, the

Okanagan," Robert offered.

"Yes, that is close to Ulrich's location in B. C., however, distance, travel time, for our chaps are negating factors. Think critical timelines, as in **5.0.3**. Any other thoughts, or suggestions?"

"STS 103, then, Camp X," Robert offered.

"That's a possibility. Now, consider how to whisk him in, board, feed, interrogate, and convince him to cooperate, without ever giving him the slightest hint of where he is."

"Wait, I think I have it! As a matter of fact, I'm absolutely sure of it!"

"And...?" Erik asked, fountain pen poised.

"The Blue Swallow Inn," Robert exclaimed excitedly. "Fact: It's only moments away from Camp X, for the convenience of Roger *et al.* Fact: We can put up Derek and anyone else there, and use it as the base of our operation. There are always two rooms ready at our disposal. Fact: we know that the owners, Wilma and Wesley Curtin, are solid, trustworthy and completely on side, as you're well aware from my, or Derek's *Clipper* murder investigation report at the Swallow, and Wilma's rescue from the clutches of the two Abwehr agents in the Anglican church. In a pinch, and to be one hundred percent assured, we can swear them in. Fact: When I was digging around on my own during the *Clipper* investigation, I discovered a small but adequate, furnished three-room suite complete with shower, wash basin, and toilet in the basement. No windows, hot water heating ergo no air ducts to connect with the upstairs, ventilation via a baffled intake/exhaust two-stage reversible blower in the ceiling that is vented via a four-inch pipe externally, and, six-inch thick concrete walls. Not your typical granny suite. It's ruddy near hermetically sealed and escape-proof, with Camp guards posted round the clock for good measure. Oh, I made sketches, by the by, for future reference. It also has a separate entrance at the rear. Herr Ulrich would be comfortable, secure, and completely isolated, and utterly soundproof. How does that fit?"

"Keep talking, Rob, I'm interested."

"Or, as an alternative, there's the Sinclair farmhouse at Camp X. Your opinion, Sir?" Robert asked expectantly.

"My opinion, Sir, is to mull over your options at the ball game. You're still up for that, I hope?"

Robert followed Erik into the already crowded stadium. A gum-chewing youth at a turnstile ripped their tickets in half, then shouted the gate number of their seating section in what was to Robert an incomprehensible dialect. Erik nodded. They proceeded amidst the shouts and cries of vendors hawking knickknacks, novelties, and programs. They jostled and pushed, eventually making their way through the wildly raucous crowds across the majestic, marble-tiled rotunda. Erik located their seats without the help of a frazzled, elderly usher. After they sat down, Robert examined his ticket stub: $1.50. Together, the two seats had cost Erik $3.00, American.

"My Lord, is that a flagpole in the centre of the playing area?" Robert asked, incredulous.

"It is. The playing area is known as the diamond, or field. Wait until they run up the Stars and Stripes and the fans all stand like a tidal wave to sing the national anthem! Thrilling, almost bone chilling!" Erik stated solemnly. "Robert? Robert?"

"Oh sorry, Erik, I was daydreaming again."

Erik leaned over to Robert and confided, "This little gem from *Tasker*, our BSO operative in the Canary islands, was received by the Hydra boys at The Farm at 1156 this morning and forwarded to HQ, just before we left for the stadium. It confirms that, at approximately 2200 hours last night, one of Admiral Dönitz's boys, U-156 Korvettenkapitän Werner Hartenstein, torpedoed and sank the White Star liner *Laconia*."

"Oh, no! Bloody hell! Where?"

"In the South Atlantic, off the Liberian coast."

"Any survivors?"

"Just wait. As a result, Dönitz has found himself in a pickle."

"How so? Why would Dönitz be upset with that?" inquired Robert. "With unrestricted submarine warfare the order of the day, anything that floats is considered a legitimate target."

"Well, nonetheless, this Hartenstein is apparently a man of principle. The problem is, the ship had been converted to a troop carrier. And here's the rub. *Tasker* reported that *Laconia* was bringing 1,500 Italian prisoners to a PoW camp, as well as British women and children, and several hundred Free Polish and British soldiers. That and an additional one hundred thirty or more crewmen."

"Oh, I see," Robert commented under his breath.

"Before attacking, Hartenstein was under the mistaken impression that the *Laconia* was an armed Royal Navy or Allied target vessel, carrying a regulation-sized crew. When Hartenstein surfaced, he signalled the Admiralty in Hamburg to report that he was horrified to find the sea full of survivors." Erik paused, looking about casually, to ensure that their conversation could not be overheard. "When he approached the scene, he could make out voices coming from the lifeboats and the water shouting and screaming for help in Italian. He immediately undertook a rescue effort, fishing survivors from the ocean until U-156 was literally jammed to the gunwales: decks, and below. He radioed Dönitz requesting backup. Dönitz diverted two subs to the area.

"Then, being the good fellow that he is, Korvettenkapitän Hartenstein sent out a message in plain English, in essence promising not to attack any ships that would or could come to the rescue. No response to that as yet, from Allied Naval Command."

"So, as I see it, Erik, the three U-boats are sitting ducks, doing the humanitarian thing. What do you think will happen?" Robert asked.

"Personally? I hope they're left unmolested and make it safely to port."

"Of course. But what are the chances of that?"

"I wouldn't count on it," Erik replied. "That's all for now. Back to the game."

"What do you call this location, Erik? It's sure close to the field. My god, what is that infernal clanging noise?" Robert put his hands to his ears.

"For a country bred boy, it's cowbells, my lad, all part of the home crowd atmosphere. We're seated in the midst of the madness; this is the famous left field grandstand. Close enough for you?"

"I think I could reach out and touch that fellow," Robert exclaimed.

"That's the beauty of this place. No other ballpark comes anywhere close to it for many reasons, though I can't wait to visit Boston's Fenway Park. Number 1, yes, that's Pee Wee Reese, the Dodger's brilliant shortstop, currently batting .255. Oh, we have company," Erik announced, rising slightly to allow a couple to pass.

Robert continued to thumb through the program, wondering if it would tell him exactly what Erik's statistics meant.

"Good afternoon, Sir! Why, Robert Brooker!" a female's voice exclaimed.

Robert looked up. " Rita? Alistair?"

"Isn't it wonderful! Mr. Albertson had four tickets for today, and gave Alistair two!"

Robert was dumbstruck momentarily, and then commented sarcastically, "That's awfully generous of you, Mr. Albertson!"

Erik smiled, nodding. The tempo and intensity of the crowd's jeering increased and bedlam ensued as players of the St. Louis Cardinals team took to the field for batting practice. "Number 6, Enos Slaughter, .318 and Number 9, Stan Musial, .315. Watch them closely, Rob. Every 'at bat' counts now!" Erik confided knowledgeably.

Robert took advantage of the pandemonium to lean over and whisper in Erik's ear. "Why didn't you say something?"

"I spotted them as potentials here. She was visiting her father, an associate in the building, who you haven't yet had the opportunity to meet. She'll be a superb asset in wireless ops and he's off to the Farm, shortly. If he makes it through, which I have no reason to doubt, he'll be attached to your domestic operation. I might send her to you."

"Well, I'll be damned!" Robert exclaimed, shaking his head. "Good lord, it is insane here. I can't wait until the match...game begins! So all of this was a set-up, then, was it?"

Erik leaned over closely. "Yes, and no. She, they, had no idea. I simply took the opportunity to put you two together in the same place and then my man helped to move things along a touch."

"Your man?" Brooks reacted incredulously. "'Augie! Of course! The straw man'! That explains a lot. Carry on. Oh, my lord, do you see that?" Two seats to Robert's left a wizened man wearing a stained and faded Dodgers uniform was holding in his hands what appeared to be a miniature doll, in a white and red uniform. A very large hatpin was sticking sideways through the doll's head.

"A kewpie doll. Voodoo. Anything to defeat the hated Redbirds, at this stage, I suppose! It's 'do or die' time," Erik confided.

"As I was saying, from thereon, I was counting upon your natural Irish charm, wit, and dashing good looks to clinch it. I wanted your independent opinion, to assure me that I was correct in my assessments. Now, let's enjoy the afternoon, shall we? Stand up, lad, it's the National Anthem!"

"I am, dammit! Well," Robert muttered, quickly regaining his composure, "this only confirms what I have suspected since God knows when,

that you, without a doubt, possess the most devious, cunning, and Machiavellian mind that I have ever had the fortune or misfortune to know!"

"You don't manage so badly in the deception department yourself, old man!" Erik whispered, with a chuckle. "The Swallow."

"Pardon? I didn't hear you! What did you say?"

"The Swallow; and by the way, "Anorak" means a heavy jacket with a hood, from the Greenland Eskimo language. Sing, or you'll be thrown over the stadium wall! *Oh, say, can you see, by the dawn's early light, What so proudly we hailed at the twilight's last gleaming?*"

10 September 1942
Camp 30   The Mess Hall

"Wolf, I'll be out this afternoon for a while. Cover for me, please?" Karl asked.

"Sure, but be careful. May I ask what you're up to?"

"Just feeling the itch to wander a little," Karl replied, non-committally. "Don't worry, I'm always careful; besides, you can't believe how easy it is," he whispered. "I can come and go as I please. Well, I'll be off now. See you soon."

Stealthily, Karl made his way along his now very familiar escape route. He couldn't wait to tell the Korvettenkapitän about it, but for now, he was on his own mission.

Karl crept closer to the farmhouse than he had ever been before, in the hope that he would finally be able to see some sign of activity at the house. As he crouched, watching, the screen door opened. Marlene stepped out, carrying a full laundry basket. He watched as she walked to the clothesline and stepped up onto a wooden platform. As she reached down to pick up a bed sheet and clothes pegs, Karl called out softly.

"Psst, Marlene, over here."

There was no response.

"Marlene, over here!"

She looked around; seeing nothing, she bent down to retrieve another clothes peg.

"Over here!" he persisted.

"Karl? Stay down, wait a minute," she stated softly, as she continued pinning the sheet to the line. She turned, smiling quizzically. "There, no one can see us from the house. What are you doing here?"

"You told me that you thought that you might be moving to this farm, remember? I took a chance on finding you here."

"How did you get out?"

"It's a long story, I'll explain it to you later. Here, catch!" he shouted, tossing something to her.

"Sssh! Wow! A Macintosh apple! Why thank you, Karl! From the Darch Farm, eh? I've missed these beauties. We don't have an orchard on this farm. Thank you so much!"

Encouraged by her response, Karl continued enthusiastically. "It's my pleasure; next time I'll bring you a whole bag full. Listen, if I were to come back tomorrow morning, could you get away for a picnic?"

"A picnic, eh? I suppose I could; I often go for walks down along the back end of the farm. There's a nice stream there. It's lovely, really peaceful."

"*Wondervoll!* Then it's *ein Begleiter!*"

"A what?"

"*Ein Begleiter*, a date!"

"A date? Not so darn fast, mister. It is not a date; I only agreed to join you for a picnic, okay? Now, what time? It's safer if I meet you down at the creek. I'll bring something nice," she added with a smile.

"That would be perfect. Ten hundred hours. My apologies, ten o'clock in the morning, right in between roll calls," he added with a grin. "See you then," Karl called back as he walked into the cornfield.

Wolf waited impatiently for Karl to return and took him aside the moment he entered the building. "Karl, something's up! It's a damn good thing you're back. Eberhart is searching for you everywhere. I had to make up a feeble excuse to buy us some time, but you had better go and see him right now!"

"Thanks, Wolfie. I owe you again," Karl replied with a wink as he set out for the Oberstleutnant's barracks.

"Sir, you wanted to see me?"

"About time, Leutnant. There will be an emergency meeting tomorrow morning at 1030 hours at the sports field. You are expected to be there."

"Sir, with respect, may I ask what this is about?"

"No, the Korvettenkapitän himself has called this meeting. You should feel honoured that you have been hand picked to attend, Semmler!" Eberhart declared sternly.

"Yes, Sir, I will be there!" Karl saluted, turned, and walked out.

'Dammit! I can't get out of this and Marlene will be waiting for me!'

11 September 1942
The Farm adjacent to Camp 30

Marlene had been up an hour earlier than usual tackling her chores. She did not want her mother to have reason to keep her from meeting Karl. "The dishes are finished, Mom. Fresh tea towels in the drawer; the kitchen floor is mopped and nearly dry! The vegetable soup is on low, ready for dinner," Marlene called out, mentally checking off her morning duties, adding 'Picnic lunch packed.' "You know, I think that I'll go for a walk down by the creek. It's so lovely there at this time of year." She waited expectantly for her mother's reply.

"You go ahead dear, have a nice walk. Will you be back in time when your father comes in from the fields?" her mother queried from the sewing room.

"Probably not. I'm going to take a sandwich and an apple with me!"

"Alright dear. Have a good time and be careful. The creek's higher than usual for this time of year."

"I will, Mom, see you later," Marlene chirped as she skipped out the side door of the old farmhouse.

It was a beautiful fall day, the colours were out in all their splendour, and Marlene couldn't help but think that she was going to enjoy her 'non-date' with the dreamy young German flier. When she reached the creek, she found a tree that had recently fallen over, lying partially submerged in the stream. 'This would be a good place to wait, Marlene,' she told herself, sitting on the horizontal trunk. She looked at her watch, 'Nine-fifty.' Karl should be here soon, I sure hope.'

Operation Anorak

11 September 1942 1035h
Camp 30

Out of respect to the illustrious Korvettenkapitän Schumacher, Karl changed into his Luftwaffe dress uniform and then hurried to the sports field where he found the two senior officers seated on the grass, deep in conversation. He stood, waiting, just beyond earshot.

At length, Oberstleutnant Eberhart looked up. "Be seated please, Leutnant."

Karl complied. Eberhart said nothing while Korvettenkapitän Schumacher smoked a meerschaum pipe, seemingly deep in thought.

Karl dared not glance at his wristwatch. It was *verboten* that a junior Leutnant would ever betray the slightest sign of impatience or irritation in the presence of a superior officer, regardless of one's service affiliation. 'Not only is it impolite, impolitic, and likely insubordinate, it simply isn't done,' Karl reminded himself.

By Karl's estimate, five minutes passed in silence until suddenly, the Korvettenkapitän removed the pipe from his mouth to address him. "Leutnant Semmler, Generalleutnant Schröder has asked us to oversee the committee in charge of escapes. It will be our job to develop plans, organize work details and most importantly, determine who should go," Schumacher stated.

Karl did not feel it was his place to comment.

"You, Leutnant, will play an important role in our communications plan."

"Communications, Sir?" Karl asked, hesitantly.

"Oberstleutnant, would you explain?" Karl had fully expected that a Knight's Cross Commander of Korvettenkapitän Schumacher's stature would be overbearing and disdainful of a mere Leutnant, and Luftwaffe at that. Instead, this man was soft–spoken and pleasant, so far.

"Certainly, Sir. You see Leutnant, the Korvettenkapitän and I have been writing letters home on a regular basis, as you have been to your mother."

"Yes, Sir?" 'My God, what did I say to her?'

"What I am about to tell you is absolutely confidential, top secret; it goes nowhere else. *Ehrenwort?*"

"Yes, of course, *Ehrenwort*, word of honour, Oberstleutnant," Karl replied.

"Very well, we have developed a coding system to which we have assigned the name, *Ireland*."

"*Ireland*, Sir?"

"Yes, *Ireland* is a simple code which permits the user to spell out messages using letters within words. Each designated word, let us say, the second will contain one designated letter, perhaps the first, so that when strung together the letters form the message. Are you with me so far, Leutnant?" Eberhart queried.

"I, I, think so, Sir," Karl responded. "It's a cipher, if I'm correct, I would think."

"Very good, son," Schumacher added, smiling.

"Carry on, Oberstleutnant, please."

"This is where you come in. Up to this point, the Korvettenkapitän and I have been sending all of the messages. However, we're concerned that the censors might soon catch on. We are going to continue to write home, *natürlich*," he chuckled, "but will be sending no more messages. You have been chosen as the principal communicator for *Ireland*. Your mother has already been briefed by Admiral Dönitz and..."

"My mother...The Admiral...Do you mean, *Grand Admiral* Dönitz, Sir?" asked Karl in disbelief.

"Yes, Leutnant, the Grand Admiral himself. I was about to say that your mother knows what to do when she receives a letter from you."

"Can we count on you, Leutnant?" Schumacher asked.

"Yes, Sir, absolutely. But could you tell me a little more about how it works?".

"It is very simple. Let's say that you are writing a letter home which might go like this." Eberhart took a slip of paper from his tunic's breast pocket. "Here, look,

It is **S**o good to **E**xchange letters and **N**ot have to **D**epend on other **R**esources we know **A**bout. You're a **D**ear mother that **I** miss so **O**ften. Could you **P**lease give old **A**nton my best **R**egards the next **T**ime that you **S**ee him.

"The first letter of every third word makes up the secret message that we want to transmit. In this case, it reads, SEND RADIO PARTS. The code can be changed to every second word or fourth, and so on."

"So long as the pattern is consistent, the intended recipient, in this case the Admiralty, will decode the message," Schumacher added reassuringly.

"Very clever, Sir. Is this an actual message which you want me to send, that is, SEND RADIO PARTS?"

"It is Leutnant. Please go back to your barracks and get started. The code is: word three, letter one. Let us know when you have it composed. And remember, son, not a word to anyone, and that goes for your chum, Leutnant von Heiden as well," Eberhart cautioned. "*Ehrenwort?*"

"Yes, Sir. You have my word of honour."

"Good luck. Dismissed, Leutnant."

"Yes, thank you, Oberstleutnant, Herr Kapitän!"

Karl stood up, saluted and then turned and walked away. As he did, he glanced at his wristwatch, 'Eleven hundred!' He rushed back to his barracks to change out of his uniform into his casual clothes. When he had changed, he made his way quickly to the tunnel.

Karl ran through the cornfield toward the creek. He had never been this close to it before. Cautiously, he scanned the banks; he could see no one. 'Up the stream,' he thought, 'away from the Camp, this is where she would go!' He walked closer to the edge, and searched in both directions again. Marlene was nowhere to be found. Karl looked at his watch again. 'Damn! 1135. Damn!'

Reluctantly, he started back to Camp. 'What must she think of me? She'll never want to see me again, and I deserve it, but it was unavoidable...and I can't explain!' he concluded bitterly.

Tuesday 15 September 1942 0815h

STS 103 Camp X The Parlour of the Commandant's Residence

"Thanks for your excellent hospitality, as always, Roger. I promise not to take very much of your time, gentlemen. I do hope you'll each agree when I say that for once, I'm the bearer of good news." Robert paused long enough to arrange the papers he held in his hand, then continued. "First, Lieutenant Colonel Stedman, Roger: I have been instructed by BSO HQ to inform you that effective 2400h today, you will be posted to detached service, on special assignment, Temporary. Please read carefully and sign this memorandum of understanding.

Camp X
Hamish Pelham Burn

"Next, Major Findlay, Hamish: I am delighted to inform you that in Colonel Stedman's absence, effective today, 2400h, you will be appointed Commanding Officer, STS 103, Acting, with the rank of Lieutenant Colonel, Permanent, effective 0800 today. My apologies, Hamish, I was delayed by fifteen minutes. These are the papers of authorization and the confirmation of your rank from SOE London and BSO. Congratulations. Well-deserved. Please read them carefully and sign each page.

"Thank you," Robert commented as each man silently returned the signed documents. "Duplicates will be returned to each of your dossiers at the earliest opportunity. I know that you must both be quite taken aback by these developments, gentlemen, and on Erik's behalf, I thank you for your co-operation and compliance.

"A few final words: Hamish, you can expect to receive further information and directives from SOE HQ London and BSO, New York," Robert added for clarity.

"Roger, we count upon your fullest co-operation over the course of the day to help Hamish assume his duties. Erik will be forwarding an official communiqué at some point today, for announcement to staff at 2100h. Please ensure that it is read only, not reproduced, and stated exactly as it is taken down. No questions, and, no explanations, of course," he concluded, fastening his briefcase.

"Very well, then, I shall be on my way. Best wishes, Lieutenant Colonel Findlay! Lieutenant Colonel Stedman, would you please accompany me to the car?"

Wednesday 16 September 1942 1400h
British Security Operation Headquarters 25 King Street West, Toronto

"Excuse me, Mr. Brooks. This wire just came upstairs from the Signals Intercept Group."

"Thank you. That will be all, Charles." Robert tore open the sealed envelope, extracted a folded Teletype sheet, and scanned the message. It was Enigma traffic, specifically, a top-secret communiqué from Admiral Dönitz to his most senior commanders.

At 1125h, this date, an American B-24 Liberator bomber attacked a flotilla of three U-boats, consisting of U-156, U-506, U-507, and the Italian submarine Cappellini, which were lawfully engaged in the transportation of survivors of the Laconia incident to safety. Each vessel was clearly displaying the Red Cross flag.

Number of survivors is unknown at this time.

This unprovoked aggression will result in an immediate review of policy directives governing rescue operations at sea by all vessels under my command.

D   (Dönitz)

Wednesday 16 September 1942 1535h
British Security Operation Headquarters 25 King Street West,
Toronto

Roger Stedman's transition in persona from Commandant to that of one Major Theodore Brückner was progressing more quickly and easily than either he or Erik had anticipated, Robert informed Williamson on the scrambled line. "Yes, first rate, really. A few bumps, but no major road-blocks. Yes, he's very eager to complete the foundation and get on with the rest. His mind's a sponge. Yes, and the alias you supplied is proving a nearly perfect fit. We're working on that, yes. Sorry, please say again? The packages arrived late last night.... both were travel worn, but in good shape. Oh, yes, two sit-downs so far. The first, at 0900 today, as you might guess, was a bit chancy, a sparring match: the subject was very uncommunicative, and then by stages irritable, obnoxious, and becoming quite nasty, and abusive. It wasn't shaping up well at all from the out-set, however his 'minder' intervened and restored peace and order, firmly, but tactfully, I must add. No, no rubber hoses, I swear!" Robert laughed. "A carrot or two tossed into the cage worked wonders, but he's no fool.

"Now? Well, as of 1500, he is focussed, well on the road to full com-pliance, and soon I expect, will be singing like the proverbial canary. Sweet revenge, the promise of better things to come in this lifetime and all that, I gather," Robert remarked, jovially. "Yes, I will. Tomorrow. Same time? Yes, the replacement is installed on the Farm. No worries on that front.

"By the by, how's my fellow traveller making out there? Surviving? She is? Excellent. Give her my regards. The World Series, Cardinals versus the Yankees, you think? That's a shame. Better luck next year, Brooklyn! And thank you again. It was quite an experience. Indeed, you'll make a fan out of me yet. I enjoyed it all hugely. Right, you too. Cheerio!"

Operation Anorak

Thursday 17 September 1942 0835h
The Blue Swallow Inn Whitby Ontario

As Robert entered the lobby of the Blue Swallow Inn, he looked up to see the proprietor, Wesley Curtin, high on a stepladder, polishing the globes of the ornate overhead light fixtures.

Blue Swallow Inn
Al O'Donnell

"Morning, Sir!" Wes called down.

"Good morning, Wes. Need a hand to steady the ladder?" Robert asked

"Oh, no thanks. If it starts to wobble, Sir, I'll just grab on to this here light, then swing and sway, like Sammy Kaye," he laughed.

"Well, be careful. Where's Wilma?"

"Oh, out gallivanting, more as likely. She finally got up the nerve to take her driver's licence test. Passed on the first try. Now I can't keep her at home!"

"Give her my regards."

"I will, thanks, Sir!"

Robert ascended the broad, central staircase to the second level, turned left at the landing, and walked quickly to Derek Wainscott's room. He stopped and knocked twice recognizing the distinctive odour of smoke from Derek's Buckingham cigarettes wafting under the door.
Withdrawing a key from his vest pocket, he unlocked the door and entered. The air was blue.

Derek arose from the desk, wiping his hands on a huge white linen napkin that was fastened around his neck. "Morning, Mr. Brooks," Derek uttered, his words garbled. "Excuse...me...have you had breakfast, Sir? I can order you something!"

"Whew, try opening the window, man! No, thanks, Derek, go ahead and finish while we talk," Robert remarked. He remained standing, studiously examining his nails. "Any developments?" he asked, casually.

"Yes, Sir! I dropped down last night to see how Leutnant Ulrich was getting along. He agreed to provide written answers in full, to all of your questions, Sir. He says he feels much better, rested, relaxed, likes his digs, the food. No surprise, compared with the poky, and he's ready and primed to spill his guts. Sorry, Sir."

"Well done, Derek. The question is: to what extent can we be assured of his sincerity? Could he be trying to have us on?" Robert queried.

"Well, Sir, there is that risk, but I'd say it's minimal to nil. Our informal chinwags in the privacy of his cell convinced me of that. As you pointed out on Sunday, he's a royally pissed soldier, I mean, a man with a massive chip on his shoulder. No reason to suspect we have an *agent provocateur* on our hands. He may be a rogue and scoundrel, but he realizes the consequences: that he has everything to lose and nothing to gain by playing silly bugger with us."

"Well, I do trust your judgment, Derek, be assured. However, to be sure beyond a reasonable doubt, the questionnaire contains certain items, which, if he fudges, will give his game away."

"'Plants', quite elegant, subtle, Sir. I like that approach. As likely to produce good data as a needle of Scopalamine, sodium amytol or thiopental sodium!" Derek stated knowingly. "I never had much of a head for organic chem., so more than likely, I've fouled up the names," he added. "These compounds, Sir, they interfere with the neuro-receptors and ..."

"Interesting," Brookes interjected. " And where exactly did you hear about these exotic 'sodiums' and the like, Mr. Wainscott, if I may be so bold."

"Oh, I read about some work involving a new class of powerful psychiatric drugs, so-called truth serums. It was in an article from a journal of experimental psychiatric medicine, a pre-war German research paper. I also read a Canadian study that was more recent. I can't recall the name of the doctor from Montreal, English, no, a Scots' name, like Mc, McDougal, no, MacDonald. Yes, Doctor Allan MacDonald! Anyway, it came from the university's medical library. You know how I like to dig up weird books about unusual things. I have a friend who works there, in the library, that is. It was marked restricted, so I just kept it overnight. Why, Sir? Cigarette?"

"Not right now, thanks. I really wouldn't put much credence in that kind of science fantasy, Derek," Robert stated dismissively. "There are far more important things to keep you occupied."

"Yes, Sir, I believe I understand," Derek replied, quietly.

"Nothing to understand, just do as you are asked," Brooks responded firmly. "Well, let's get on with it then, shall we? Bring reams of paper and sharp pencils; here's the questionnaire," he commented, withdrawing two folded papers from his inside breast pocket. "Lead the way to the dungeon."

"Morning, Mac! And how is our 'guest' this morning?"

"Morning, Sirs!" The guard, Private 'Mac' snapped to attention, saluting smartly. "No complaints, Sir. Quiet as a church mouse."

"This is good news, Private. Unlock the door, please," Robert ordered softly.

Robert was unprepared for the reception. Instead of a sullen and obstinate prisoner, a clean-shaven, well groomed, and courteous Leutnant Ulrich was standing at attention, saluting him.

"I am very grateful to you, Sir, and want to demonstrate my thanks by co-operating to your fullest satisfaction."

"At ease. Very well, Leutnant," Robert replied affably. "We're certainly pleased to hear that. I must caution you, however. You do understand that any future consideration for leniency on our part will depend entirely on the completeness and truthfulness of your answers? Every detail in your responses will be thoroughly studied for accuracy, by our

experts. It will not go well for you if we find the slightest attempt to mislead or misinform us or be less than forthcoming in any detail whatsoever."

"I do understand, Sir," Ulrich replied earnestly. "I have no greater wish than to regain my self-respect, and earn your complete confidence. As an officer, I swear and pledge that upon my honour."

"I accept your pledge, Leutnant. My assistant, Mr. Derek will remain with you to lend whatever help or explanation you might require. There is no time limit, per se, but I do expect your responses no later than 1430h, today.

"Mr. Derek, take over, please. Private Mac will be on hand at all times. He will be informed where I can be reached in the event of a problem. Carry on, gentlemen!"

Thursday 17 September 1942 0800h
Camp 30 The Mess Hall

Karl leaned across the table. "Wolfgang! Wolfgang! Put down the paper and listen. It's important."

"So's this: According to our newspaper, *Die Bruecke* (*The Bridge*) Germany's only months away from winning the war! Very interesting, considering the number of fresh new PoW faces showing up at roll call every week."

"Wolf, I have something important to tell you."

"What?"

"Quietly! Listen, I'm going out this morning!" Karl whispered.

"When?"

"Right now. Cover for me?"

"Not a problem, my friend. Besides, there's not much else to do any-way but read this crap. Did you know or care that Leutnant so-and-so's wife had their third baby, a boy? I wouldn't advertise the fact: he's been here now for at least a year. Oh, and Major so and so is convalescing in an unnamed hospital, after having his prostate snipped. Let's hope Herr Doktor knew where to stop. Poor devil."

"Wolf!" Karl stamped his boot on the linoleum impatiently.

"Get going, Karl. I'll hold the fort!"

"Thanks, Wolfie. I knew that I could count on you. I have to change. See you!"

As Karl loped along his escape route, he was sure that he could find his way blindfolded. Upon reaching the tunnel, he knelt and examined the ground. Satisfied that it was undisturbed, he removed the cover. After a painstakingly thorough inspection of the entrance with his flashlight, he descended the ladder and began to make his way to the cornfield. As he neared the halfway point, the ground trembled slightly. He stopped, holding his breath, listening. "What the hell was that? Please God, do not let it be an earthquake!" He counted to ten, shining his light up and down the walls and over the earthen floor for any signs of a cave in, then shrugged and resumed crawling, now faster.

An abrupt, deafening clap and shock wave shook the ground. He flinched, recalling the shock and horror when he realized that the Hurricane's cannon shells had hit his *Gustav*. The air inside the tunnel was rank, as though a pot of potatoes had boiled dry. He covered his head while chunks of dirt and rocks showered down. "My flashlight!" It was lying sideways, a metre ahead. His ears rang. "Am I deaf?" He swallowed and called Marlene's name. Nothing. "This is your fault...you've been looking for trouble and now you've found it! Do not panic! Now save yourself, Semmler!" he wheezed. Gingerly he crept forward until he could feel the cold metal cylinder. Grasping the flashlight in his right fist, he propelled himself on his knees and elbows, scrambling crablike to the end, certain that the tunnel was caving in behind him. He clawed at the ladder's rungs, climbing blindly until his head broke through the sod. He lay panting, his heart pounding, as he gulped in volumes of fresh air.

When Karl opened his eyes, the sky was leaden. A bolt of lightning flashed, briefly illuminating the cornfield, followed by a rolling peal of thunder. Then, the sky opened up. It was a deluge. 'Get away from this tree!' As Karl stood up, another flickering discharge revealed an irregular swatch of charred cornstalks ten metres away. "I'll be damned! It was a lighting strike! It could have been disastrous!" he muttered.

As he ran pell-mell through the downpour, he laughed uncontrollably. "I must have snapped down there! What in hell am I doing, running soaking wet in a thunderstorm through an open cornfield? How the hell do I get back?" Then his heart stopped. There was Marlene, wearing a raincoat, removing the washing from the line. 'Is that all she does, *die Wäsche*?' he wondered briefly then his scientific side took command. 'She'll be electrocuted if that line is metallic.' "Marlene, Marlene! Over here! Listen, I have something to tell you."

Marlene glanced in his direction while continuing to pull pegs off the line.

"Marlene, I'm sorry that I couldn't meet you!" he yelled. "And you should stop doing that. It's dangerous...the lightning!"

"What do you mean you couldn't be there?" she shouted back. "And since when did you care?"

"I was called to a meeting at the very last minute which I couldn't get out of. And I swear, I do care!"

"Thank you, but I didn't appreciate being stood up, mister!" she replied, clearing the rain from her eyes. "Prisoners of war have meetings, do they? What did you talk about? Your big escape plans?"

"Ah, so you admit it was a date!" he teased, ignoring her allegation.

"I thought no such thing!" she retorted, suppressing a smile. "You look like a scarecrow!"

"I was nearly stricken by lightning!"

"Stricken! Struck, hit, zinged maybe, but not stricken," she giggled.

"Thank you. Are you a teacher?"

"Marlene, what's taking you so long out there? Don't you know enough to come in when there is lightning?" shouted her mother from the door.

"I'm going as fast as I can Mother. Stay inside, you'll be getting wet; I'll be right there."

"Can I meet you tomorrow; I promise that I'll be there, no matter what."

"Okay Karl. But if you're not there, don't bother coming back. Ever!" Marlene replied as she turned and carried the clothesbasket up the steps.

"I'll bring the lunch, same place, same time, 10:00 a.m."

Marlene waved in acknowledgement as she entered the house. Karl turned and dashed back through the cornfield. Without a thought of possible storm damage, he re-entered the tunnel. He emerged at the other end, checked that he was alone, then set out on his pathway, keeping low until he reached the hiding place where he removed and covered over his coveralls, and then crept toward the opening in the brush. The rain was beating down fiercely. 'No one in his right mind would be outside, but me. And that's doubtful. All clear, Karl, go, slowly!' Walking nonchalantly toward Haus I, only fifteen or twenty metres away, his worst fear materialized out of the shadows in the person of Veteran Guard Captain Jimmy Blair.

"Hey you! Semmler! Halt!"

"Me?" replied Karl. "Are you talking to me, Captain?"

"Of course I'm talking to you. You're the only one out here. Where are you coming from?"

"I was walking on the other side of the sports field when the storm started. I thought I could wait it out but it seems that it's not going to stop anytime soon, so I'm returning to my Haus," replied Karl earnestly.

"Hurry up about it, then," Blair grunted. "I'll be keepin' an eye on you, fellow. Be careful, very careful, Lieutenant Semmler."

"Yes, Sir," Karl shot back as he scurried toward his Haus. "Lefff-ten-ant Simmler reporting in!" Karl announced as he shut the door.

Thursday 17 September 1942 1930h
STS 103 Camp X

"Well, Roger, here is your reading, all twelve pages. Cramped, but, at least he gets an A plus for penmanship," Robert announced. "Erik's sources here and overseas have examined it, cursorily of course, and find it contains nothing to raise the alarm bells. A final evaluation from London has been promised no later than 1200 tomorrow. I think it's a safe bet to say that our Leutnant hasn't willingly played fast and loose with the facts, as far as he knows them. One thing I did notice, as you will, is that there are some gaps, which Erik assured me, are to be expected. 'It's improbable, if not imprudent, were we to assume that a junior lieutenant should be all knowing,' is how Erik rationalized it to me."

"Indeed, Robert, I'd be extremely concerned if the chap had reckless-

ly forged ahead, filling in all the blanks, to make us happy. To my mind, uncertainty shows an honest intellectual effort," agreed Stedman.

"Questions 2, 14, and one other, yes, 21, are as Wainscott would say, 'plants,'" explained Robert. "He passes with flying colours on all counts. I'm going to leave it with you to read and digest tonight and then we'll see how Herr Ulrich bears up under cross-examination tomorrow.

"Anything I can do or get for you in Toronto, Roger? That reminds me: good news; your uniform will be delivered tomorrow. Listen, old man; have a drink, put up your feet, relax, and happy reading."

"Robert, you mentioned a cross-examination. Will I have an opportunity to meet this Ulrich fellow? I'd very much like to hear directly from him some, should I say, minutiae, about the Brandenburgers. As it turns out, SOE had a decent-sized base of information compiled at Beaulieu on these lads. Ostensibly controlled by the Abwehr. Special ops, highly-trained in guerrilla tactics including subversion, sabotage, small arms and unarmed combat; specialists in assassination; many tend to the non-conformist end of the scale who found regular duty stultifying and boring, their code of honour is unusually chivalrous, but in the final analysis, they are not to be taken lightly. The Brandenburg Division is currently wreaking havoc behind the Soviet lines."

"Sounds familiar!!" Robert remarked. "That's Erik's decision, Roger. Leave it with me. See you here 0700. Cheers!"

Friday 18 September 1942 0930h
The Blue Swallow Inn Whitby Ontario

"Leutnant Ulrich, this gentleman is Mr. Douglas," Robert began. "He has some questions regarding the answers you gave. No need to salute, Leutnant, Mr. Douglas is a civilian."

"You're not going to take me back to that prison, are you, Sir?"

"That shouldn't be necessary, Leutnant, if you cooperate."

Friday 18 September 1942 1315h
The Blue Swallow Inn Whitby Ontario

"Oh, the fellow is genuine all right, Robert," Roger declared, "I'll bet my life on that!"

"We may well have done just that, Roger. Let's hope for all our sakes that we're not sucking air on this one!"

Friday 18 September 1942 0835h
Camp 30

"Did you get it, Wolf?"

"Of course I got it; what do you think?"

"Good, where is it?"

Putting his hand under his sweater, Wolf pulled out a bag and placed it on the table. "Just as you asked, butter, hard boiled eggs and bread. Am I a friend or not?"

"You are, thanks; I knew I could count on you. And I have the apples, Macs, from the orchard."

After Karl had made the sandwiches, Wolf announced, "Well you're all set, so off you go and fill me in on the details when you get back."

"Thanks, Wolf and I owe you, again."

"*Ja, Ja,* that's what you always say. I'll take you up on it when we get home."

Karl set out on his familiar trip. It still amazed him that he could come and go as he pleased and no one other than Wolf knew that he was gone. He realized that the six hundred and fifty PoWs in the Camp certainly helped make him invisible in the crowd. At the end of his ten-minute journey, he sprinted through the cornfield until he reached to summit. Lying below the ridge, the creek wound its way along the bottom of the valley.

"Marlene, you made it!" Karl called loudly as he ran down the hill.

"No you made it, remember?" she answered. "Some wildflowers; I picked them for you. Aren't they pretty?"

"Beautiful, thank you! Yes, this time things went without a problem," he replied panting. "So glad you're here. Our CO called a meeting that morning I could not get out of; you don't say no to the CO."

"So you said, remember? I really didn't think that you would be back, Karl."

"Did that bother you, Marlene?"

"Yes, it sure did. I've had boyfriends before who made dates and then didn't show up."

"Ah, so again you admit it was a date!" Karl asserted teasingly.

"Yes, it was a date," she laughed, "and you stood me up."

"It will never happen again, I promise; not intentionally, that is. However, if it does, it's only because something has happened and I can't get out of the Camp. You'll understand won't you?"

"I suppose so. I guess it's a lot easier for me than it is for you."

"So then, let's pick a day of the week and we'll try to meet on that day, the same time. What's a good day for you, Marlene?"

"Actually, Saturday would be. That's my day off to do anything I like," she replied, flinging her hands upward.

"Saturday it is then. Here, look what I've brought: a picnic."

"Karl, did you make these sandwiches?"

"Yes, with the help of my friend, Wolf. I promised to bring him along one day."

"Wolf? What a strange name. Is he a werewolf?" She hunched her shoulders and made grasping motions with her fingers. "Like the one in the movie...all hairy and scary," she growled, coughed, and then giggled.

"Only when there's a full moon, then I lock him in the closet until it passes!"

"You are kidding. Seriously?"

"Kidding, what is that, please?"

"*Scherzend!*" she laughed.

"*Scherzend.* Ah, joking!" Karl exclaimed. "Kidding is joking!"

"J, J, joking, not yoking!" she corrected him, waving her index finger. Karl stared at her transfixed. "Marlene, may I kiss you?" he ventured.

"Jes!"

Saturday 19 September 1942 1912h
STS 103 Camp X

"This just in from Erik, Roger. Here, read it yourself!" Robert announced gravely.

Most Secret

Commence Anorak II 20 09 Stop

-30-

"Commence Anorak II, 20 09," Roger repeated. "But that means I'm leaving tomorrow! I had hoped to spend more time with Ulrich..."

"That is precisely what it means," Robert confirmed. "My task now is to get you there. Get your things packed, Major Brückner. You and I are off to Halifax tomorrow morning, courtesy of Air Transport Command. I'll be back shortly with our flight information."

Thursday 24 September 1942 1334h

Camp 30: Residence of Generalleutnant Albrecht Schröder

"Brückner, Theodore, Major, Sir," Roger responded, saluting the senior PoW officer.

"Welcome to Camp 30, Major Brückner. My name is Albrecht Schröder, Generalleutnant, Wehrmacht. I understand that you are a one of a kind, here that is! Tell me a little about your background. Take your time. That's about all we have in this place. But please, be seated."

"Thank you, General. I was with the Brandenburg First Company, deployed in Cyrenaica, where I served as liaison officer with Italian ground forces. That is, Sir, until I was captured by a British Commando unit."

"How unfortunate. But I'd say that you're lucky to be alive. Those devils have a 'take-no-prisoners' reputation, if you get my meaning. Were you subjected to interrogation?

"Twice, Sir. This ear," he gestured, pointing to the right side of his head," it buzzes and rings constantly as a result."

"And tell me, Major, what were your duties?"

"Basically, I was ordered to gather, co-ordinate and relay any intelligence which our senior command might find useful."

"And did they, Major?"

"I'd like to think so, General," Roger stated with pride.

"Well, I've enjoyed our brief *tête à tête*, Major. Now, you must be exhausted from the journey, as we all were; anxious to see your quarters, no doubt.

"Yes, I'm all in, Generalleutnant. Thank you, Sir. I believe I can find my way."

Generalleutnant Schmitt at Bowmanville
Volkmar König

CHAPTER 8

THE BATTLE OF BOWMANVILLE

Camp 30
12 December 1942

"Want to go for a walk, Karl? Now what are you doing?" asked Wolf impatiently.

"I'm writing. Don't bother me, Wolfgang. Besides it's too damn cold!" Karl called from his bunk.

"What, writing again? Wake up! Catch!" Wolfgang laughed as he fired an underhand spiral, narrowly missing Karl's head.

"Yes, again. And next time you throw that ball at me, I'll drill it right at your royal Thuringian jewels!"

"Okay, sorry; good catch! What about? Your *Fraulein*, Lili Marlene?"

"It's Marlene; no 'Lili', idiot. And no; guess again."

"The riot?"

Karl paused, trying to ignore Wolf, then murmured absently, "Uh huh."

"I hope you're not planning to mail it. You'll do twenty-eight plus a century in solitary!" Wolf observed flippantly, chucking the football at his pillow. "Pass complete!"

"No, it's not a letter. I'm just jotting things down as best as I can recall. I'll type it out and then tuck it away when I'm finished. Then perhaps some day my children and grandchildren will know the true story of our fight against arbitrary authority."

"Just what we need: a Camp historian with a social conscience. I thought it was fun! I got to smash a few things and decked a guy twice my size!"

"Go soak your head, *kamerad*, and leave me alone," Karl responded with a grin as he settled back against his pillow. "And take that damn cigarette outside!"

Dearest Children,

I am writing this for you. It is not my intention to unfairly portray individuals or parties as either villains or heroes, but rather, to tell the truth. What follows is my personal day-by-day reconstruction of some momentous events in October of 1942, at our internment Lager, Camp 30, Bowmanville, Ontario, Canada.

The sequence of the most important goings-on is accurate. Conversations are either verbatim or are close approximations based upon anecdotal accounts related to me during or shortly after the conclusion of the affair. I fully trust the integrity of my sources regardless of whether or not they were first-hand witnesses to the original conversation.

Saturday 10 October 1942

This day started like any other day but soon proved to be exceptional. In fact, the next three days would be unlike any others during the entire history of Camp 30.

In the officers' mess on the morning of October 10, Generalleutnant Albrecht Schröder was having breakfast with the senior officers when an orderly interrupted. "What is it son? Can't you see I'm in the middle of a conversation here?"

"Begging your pardon, Sir, the Camp Commandant wishes to see you, Herr Kapitän and Oberstleutnant Eberhart in his office. Immediately."

"Yes, yes," Schröder replied peevishly. "You can tell the Colonel that we'll be there as soon as I'm finished telling my story. Right gentlemen?"

The officers laughed in approval. "Certainly, Generalleutnant."

"Anyway, where was I? Damn, I've lost my train of thought now. We'd better go and see what the old man wants. Very unusual that he would ask for all of us at the same time."

The three men exited the steel door of the mess and walked the short distance to the gate. Fall was settling in with a brisk, chill wind.

"Here comes that Canadian winter, gentlemen. Summer is too short," Schumacher reflected.

"Yes, soon it will be time to lace up the skates. That and cross-country skiing are the only things I think I'll miss about the Canadian winter. I've set a goal: our boys will beat the Canadian guards at ice hockey by 1944, assuming that we're still here," laughed Eberhart.

Team Germany prepares to play the Camp 30 Guards
Bowmanville Archives

Schumacher and Eberhart waited at the Camp's entrance while Schröder informed the guards that they had been called to a meeting in the Commandant's office. The gate opened and they walked through. Upon entering the office, Miss Muriel Burns greeted them. "Good morning, gentlemen. I'll inform Colonel Armstrong that you're here."

"Generalleutnant, Captain, Oberstleutnant, welcome; please, sit down!" Armstrong began cordially. "May I get you something?" As a dyed-in-the-wool army man, respect for the hierarchical system of perks and privileges accompanying military rank were deeply etched in the soul of Lieutenant Colonel Jack Armstrong. Whenever in the company of Schröder and Schumacher, both men senior to himself, he became acutely conscious of his junior status, even though, as prisoners and according to the rules of war, they were his subordinates. The sensitivity of the matter at hand only heightened his sense of uneasiness.

"Thank you, no, Colonel. We just came from breakfast. May I ask what matter might be of such importance that you called us here, and, I might add, with such urgency?" Schröder inquired coldly.

'Goddamn arrogant Prussian!' Aloud, Armstrong replied in German, "Gentlemen, this is a difficult and sensitive matter, which will directly affect us all. It seems that the Allies and Germany are playing a kind of

tit-for-tat game involving the treatment of PoWs. Apparently, the majority of the Canadian troops who were taken prisoner following the 19 August attack on Dieppe were shackled, by order of Adolf Hitler, in direct contravention of the articles of the Geneva Convention. Now, unfortunately, I have received the following dispatch from our Dominion Government in Ottawa." He held up the communiqué to underscore his predicament. "In short, I am directed to shackle one hundred of the Camp's officers. I deeply regret this decision gentlemen, but I have no choice but to carry it out."

"Colonel, you said, and I quote, 'Apparently, the majority of the Canadian troops who were taken prisoner after the attack on Dieppe were shackled'. *Apparently...* where is the evidence, Sir?" demanded Schröder.

"The German Ministry of Propaganda's newsreels for one. Here, see for yourselves. These are still photographs that we have obtained. They are authenticated, as you can see, by the Reich Minister's stamp on the each, Generalleutnant." Armstrong waited for an angry denial. Schröder examined the grim pictures, passing them without comment to Schumacher and Eberhart.

"I cannot condone my government's actions. However, with respect, I must condemn your government's reckless and dishonourable act of reprisal; frankly, Colonel, we, that is the officers of the Kriegsmarine, will oppose force with force, if circumstances so dictate!" declared Schumacher icily.

"Colonel, that applies to my men as well," echoed Eberhart. "Also the Wehrmacht," added Schröder soberly. Schröder saluted, and turned to his colleagues, "Gentlemen?" They followed him to the door. "Good day, Colonel."

"Gentlemen, I understand your position, but as officers, please try to understand mine. I am duty bound to obey these orders, and, I *will* execute them. My Adjutant will be by to see you shortly. At that time, you will be given the opportunity to select the officers for treatment. Good day!"

The Battle of Bowmanville

Saturday 10 October 1230 hours

The Mess Hall

"Quiet, please, gentlemen. Generalleutnant Albrecht Schröder has an important announcement!" intoned Oberstleutnant Eberhart. "Generalleutnant Schröder."

"Gentlemen, I have called you here to this emergency meeting to let you know that this morning Lieutenant Colonel Armstrong informed us that he has received orders from his government to shackle one hundred of our officers, for political reasons. As you would expect, I let him know that officers of the German Wehrmacht, Luftwaffe and Kriegsmarine will not be intimidated or humiliated by threats and will never submit to being shackled, at least not without a damned good fight!" he shouted to cries of "*Niemals*! Never! Bastards!" amid raucous jeering and clapping.

"That includes the proud soldiers of the glorious Afrika Korps!" shouted Leutnant Kurt Löwen, generating a wild outburst of cheers and foot stamping. He and his colleagues rose spontaneously and began singing their Panzer song.

"*The treads are rattling, the motor is droning, Tanks are rolling forwards in Africa. Tanks are rolling forwards in Africa, Heat over Africa's ground, the sun is burning, Our tank motors sing their song...*"

When they finished, an eerie silence filled the room. Then, as if on cue, the Mess Hall broke into thunderous applause.

"Thank you! Thank you! Furthermore...furthermore...gentlemen please! Thank you for your enthusiastic condemnation of this illegal and shameful measure. Our battle plan is very clear. Korvettenkapitän Schumacher will take command of Haus IV. Oberstleutnant Eberhart, you will be in charge of the Mess Hall. I will personally be in command of Haus VI. The next highest-ranking officers will man the other buildings. Officers, you know who you are, take your posts. The rest of you will return to your own barracks to prepare. Now, when the siege begins, gentlemen, let's give them one hell of a fight!"

As Schumacher, Schröder, Eberhart, and the senior officers were about to leave the Mess Hall, the assemblage rose in acknowledgement; following a moment's silence, the hall echoed with a robust rendition of the German national anthem, *Deutschland, Deutschland über Alles*.

Saturday 10 October 1942

It was obvious that the atmosphere of the Camp had changed dramatically. Missing was the good-humoured banter and the climate of genuine civility between the Veteran Guards and the PoWs. The guards patrolled their beats with a newfound sombre determination while the PoWs kept their distance. Guards reported that few if any inmates were seen walking the circumference of the Camp.

Staff Sergeant Robert Murray strode out of his office, located just inside the Camp entrance, to hurry toward the Commanding Officer's office.

"Muriel, may I see the Colonel? It's important," he added tensely.

"Yes, Bob, I'll tell him you're here."

"Sir, Staff Sergeant Murray to see you."

"Oh, Bob, come in! I was just about to call you. Any developments?"

"Nothing you can nail down, Sir, but I'll bet my life they're definitely up to something. They've taken to their barracks. What's next, Sir?" asked Murray, his face ashen.

"We're little more than an hour away from roll call. Let's wait and see. In the meantime, stay alert. I'll expect you to keep me apprised of any and all incidents. That's all for now, Staff. Dismissed."

Saturday 10 October 1942 1400h

A sudden pounding at the window overlooking the Camp broke the quiet inside Haus I.

"Careful, it could be a trick," yelled the Haus commander. "Approach with caution!"

"Sir, it's okay. It's Karl Semmler."

"Semmler? What in hell is he doing outside? Well, just don't stand there! Let him in!"

With the help of another, Wolf removed the barrier as quickly as he could. Opening the door, Wolf whispered, "Karl, you had better have a bloody good excuse for this."

"Well, Semmler, what is the meaning of this?" demanded the officer. "Word passed around Camp an hour and a half ago that all ranks were to return to their Haus'. What do you have to say for yourself?"

"Sir, I was in the library reading a book and fell asleep. When I woke up and saw that there was no one around I thought I should head back here to find out what was going on."

"You mean to say that no one knew you were in there?"

"Apparently not, Sir. I was in the quiet room."

"Alright then. You can do something useful. Help put these barricades back in place."

Turning to Wolf, Karl whispered, "What the hell has been going on while I've been gone?"

"I'll tell you all about it. You're just damn lucky that you didn't get caught this time."

Saturday 10 October 1942

When not one PoW appeared for roll call on the sports field, Staff Sergeant Murray picked up the receiver and dialled the CO's local. "Sir, we have a situation. The prisoners didn't come out of their quarters for roll call. That's correct. No, Sir, none. Not any. What now, Sir?"

"Well, we'll have to smoke them out. Now listen, Bob, don't do a thing; I'm going to call Toronto HQ for reinforcements. I don't want any of the VG's (Veteran Guards) attempting to make contact with the PoWs. Is that understood?"

"Yes, Sir, understood. I'll wait for your orders." Robert Murray set down the receiver, reflecting that, had he paid attention to Gloria's urgings to pack up and move to Vancouver Island, they could be taking high tea at the Empress in Victoria, or attending the Rhododendrons and Azalea Growers' Society meeting this very moment. He shrugged and resolved to write her. "As soon as this war's over, Glor, it's a nice comfy bungalow in Vic for us, I solemnly promise."

Saturday 10 October 1942

To a visitor, the Camp that evening would have appeared calm and peaceful. But to Bob Murray, the utter lack of activity was unnatural,

deceptive, masking an underlying tension waiting to detonate. The phone in his office rang shrilly. He flinched, then answered gruffly, "Murray!"

"The troops are here, Staff Sergeant! Shall I open the gate?" requested the duty guard.

"Yes, have them enter and then stand down. They go no further until you hear otherwise, Corporal!" Murray barked into the receiver, pressing the hook repeatedly until he had broken the connection. He dialled the C.O.'s office.

"Well, go out and meet the C.O. and bring him to my office, man. Chop chop!"

Murray was astonished at the number of military transports idling in the column, their exhaust vapours gushing bluish-grey into the chilled night air under the intense glare of the guard towers' searchlights. "Who's in command?" he demanded.

"Major Hicks, Royal Canadian Ordinance Training Centre," replied the young, moustachioed officer in full battle dress stepping down smartly from the cab of the lead vehicle.

"Welcome to Camp 30, Major Hicks; Staff Sergeant Murray, Sir! Would you be good enough to accompany me to the C.O.'s office? This way, Sir."

Jack Armstrong waited for them at his entrance.

"Sir, presenting Major Hicks of the Royal Canadian Ordinance Training Centre," Murray announced brusquely, saluting.

"Lieutenant Colonel Armstrong, Jack, pleased to meet you, Major. How are things at Barriefield?"

"Fine, Sir. Colonel Armstrong, accompanying me are two captains and fifty men, and, confidentially, Colonel, all of them are itching to knock some German heads together."

"Major, on that subject, I have been ordered not to employ deadly force."

"Well, Sir, exactly what are we to fight with if we can't use our weapons?" asked the Major after a pause.

"My orders specify that you may employ anything you feel appropriate, with the exception of military ordnance, weaponry, Major. Do you understand?"

"Yes, Colonel. Message received and understood," Hicks replied unemotionally.

"Captain, the men will disarm and leave their weapons in the trucks," Hicks ordered.

"Major Hicks, in that Staff Sergeant Murray knows the prisoners well, I have asked him what you should arm yourselves with. He has recommended baseball bats."

"Baseball bats, Sir?" Hicks repeated incredulously, looking from Armstrong to Murray and back. "But surely, Colonel, my men can't be expected to beat the poor bastards..."

"Baseball bats, Major," repeated Armstrong. "Your men can pick them up over there, beside the guard house. Staff Sergeant Murray will take charge of the distribution."

"Very good, Sir.

"Captain Snell, the men will arm themselves with baseball bats and await my orders in the trucks. Sergeant Poole will supervise. See to it now, Captain.

"Sir, is there a current SITREP [situation report]?" asked Hicks.

"Come inside. Your Captains may join us as well."

The four men entered Jack Armstrong's quarters. A large sketch map of the Camp and surroundings was laid out on a table, illuminated by an overhead light. With a wooden classroom pointer to highlight significant locations, Armstrong launched into his lecture. "Gentlemen, as you already know, Camp 30 is situated here, approximately three miles from the town of Bowmanville. We do not want to have any shooting in order that we do not alarm the townspeople: shots out here in the country can be heard for some distance. And there are other reasons, as you might well imagine," he added in a conspiratorial tone. "As you can see by the sketch, there are several buildings scattered throughout the grounds, making it difficult to round up all of the PoWs in one operation. Questions?"

"How many buildings, Sir? I count eight."

"Precisely: eight in total. My plan is as follows. The Mess Hall was the first building occupied and, in all likelihood, it holds the greatest number of prisoners. If we can secure it at the outset, I am confident that we will be able to take over the others with relative ease."

"Sounds like a solid plan to me, Sir. When is zero hour? When does the operation begin?" asked the Major eagerly.

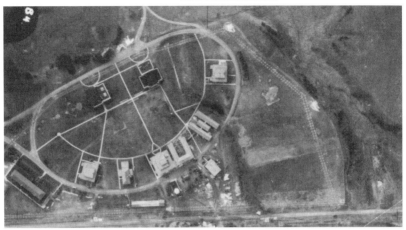

Aerial photo of Camp 30 – Bowmanville
DND - National Archives of Canada

"Immediately, gentlemen; I shall leave the tactical aspects to you and your Captains, Major. And good luck."

Saturday 10 October 1942

At 2000, Major Hicks ordered the two Captains to have their men on the ground immediately, in battle formation, then walked out of the C.O.'s office. "Men, here is the situation. Hundreds of German prisoners of war have unlawfully taken over and have occupied this base. Presently, they are barricaded inside several of its buildings." Hicks' phrases were clipped, his hands clasped behind his back as he strode in front of the soldiers. "To the best of our knowledge, they are unarmed. Our task is to take back and secure the Camp with the least number of casualties, including minor injuries, I might add. This is the reason you will not be taking weapons inside other than the baseball bats that you have been issued. Is there anyone who has difficulty understanding any part of what I have just said?" demanded Hicks.

"No, Sir!" the soldiers roared.

"Very good! Are we ready to proceed?"

"Yes, Sir!"

"Fine, then let's get on with the job. Captains will proceed as ordered!"

The Battle of Bowmanville

The soldiers quick marched to the Mess. Upon Captain Snell's command, they broke ranks and rushed forward, storming the front door, swinging their bats ferociously. The PoWs, who had barricaded the door with furniture, fought back determinedly with hockey sticks and makeshift clubs. Although the pitched battle raged for more than two hours, the Canadians troops were unable to take possession of the building. Both sides received injuries. The PoWs had thrown everything available at the Canadians: canned goods, beer bottles, bricks, even jam jars, and the soldiers withdrew.

"Major Hicks, Colonel Armstrong, Sir!" interjected the signalman, handing Hicks the portable 58 set's microphone and spare earpiece.

"Hicks, here, Colonel. It's been a sticky show, Sir. I have had to withdraw my men. That's correct, Sir, withdraw," he winced, "temporarily. Over."

"Major, a fifty-man detachment from your training school has just arrived. Over."

"Thank you, that is certainly very good news, Colonel," Hicks replied calmly. "We will hit them again after midnight, on all fronts! Out."

Jack Garnett, one of the soldiers brought in from Barriefield
Jack Garnett

Late in the evening, the battle for control of the Mess Hall flared again as Hicks' force, now reinforced with the fifty fresh but untested troops threw themselves at the German-held stronghold.

Simultaneously, Captain Snell's group converged on Haus V where the PoWs had retreated to the basement. "You men, bring that hose over here and connect it to that outlet," Captain Snell ordered. "Now, break that window and feed the hose through. Turn on the water, full! We'll bloody well flood them out, unless the buggers opt to drown!"

At the Mess, the hand-to-hand fighting continued fiercely. At last,

the Canadian troops broke down the outer entrance door and started to force their way through the fortified inner doors. Two of the first soldiers through fell face-first into the crush and were quickly seized by the Germans.

"Oberstleutnant, we have two prisoners!" Hauptmann Reiter called excitedly.

"Excellent! Advise the Canadian's Major Hicks that we have taken two of his men as prisoners of war. And tell him they are to be shackled immediately!" exclaimed Eberhart triumphantly.

"Yes, Oberstleutnant! But, Sir, how do I advise him?"

"How the hell would I know? Use some initiative, Hauptmann, as all German soldiers are trained to do! Get on with it!"

The two Canadians were hauled inside and tied to the tables while the battle raged, unabated. Finally, at approximately 2350 hours, a reserve contingent of Canadians charged the Mess and in the resulting *mêlée*, all of the PoWs were quickly subdued and taken into custody.

At 2352h, Hicks radioed Armstrong. "Colonel, Hicks here. We've taken the Mess. What should we do with the prisoners? Over."

"Breaker. Say again, Major," Armstrong shouted into the 19 set's microphone, tapping his radio operator's shoulder.

"Can't you clear up this goddamn static, Lance Corporal?"

"Repeat. We have taken the Mess. What should we do with the prisoners? Over," Hicks restated.

"Superb work, Bill. Have them shackled and moved to the Darch Farm for safekeeping. Any casualties? Over."

"Yes, Sir, minor: a broken arm, multiple contusions, bruises, etcetera. We've set up a first aid station outside the gates. I'm off to see if things are winding down at Haus V. Out."

Sunday 11 October 1942 0100

Indeed, he found things were winding down at Haus V. "Major, our men are soaking wet and cold; we wish to come out now," shouted the ranking PoW officer from the basement.

"Agreed: you may come out, *Hände hoch*! One at a time with your hands straight up in the air," ordered Hicks.

As the PoWs looked up the stairs, they could see a line of soldiers on each side of the staircase. On the top landing stood Veteran Guard Captain James Blair, whom they called 'Jimmy'. Jimmy' Blair was easily the most despised Canadian in the Camp. Jimmy's hatred for the Germans led him to constantly invent crude tactics to bait and humiliate them. Typically, when doing barracks inspection, Jimmy could be counted upon to use his swagger stick to flip over, or 'accidentally' knock onto the floor and step on one of the small photographs of Adolf Hitler, Admiral Dönitz or Erwin Rommel, hung above some of the prisoners' bunks.

"Okay you men, you may come up now," Jimmy shouted encouragingly. "Let's go, move, move, atta boy, *schnell*!"

Singly, the men ran up the stairs as ordered. They bolted into the darkness only to be met by the dazzling glare from the guard tower searchlights, now trained on the exit and a swift, sharp rap on the head or the rear end from 'Jimmy's' swagger stick. The PoWs, much too exhausted and dazed to react, swore silently to retaliate, another time.

"Get me Colonel Armstrong!"

Major Hick's signals man handed him the 58 set's mike. "Colonel? Hicks here, we've taken Haus V. What now, Sir? Over."

"Wonderful, Major! That's enough for one night. Tell your men to get some rest. We'll see what tomorrow brings. Oh, and Major, job well done! Congratulations to your fine officers and men, and thank you. Over."

"Thanks, appreciate it, Colonel. Wilco [will comply with]. Out."

Sunday 11 October 1942 0600

"Hey, Corporal Steers, come with me," Captain Jimmy Blair called to Corporal Brian Steers. "We're going to go and see what the krauts are up to."

"Yes, Sir!" The well-liked elder member of the Camp's Veteran Guard knew it was useless to protest. 'What is this crazy bugger Jimmy up to now?' Brian pondered as he picked up his pace to catch up with Blair.

The two men walked past Haus VI. They could see the Germans inside, their faces up to the glass, watching their every move. Next they

passed Haus V. All was quiet there after 'Snell's baptism,' as the Canadians were now referring to the flooding action that had forced the Germans' surrender.

"Here we are. Haus IV. Korvetten-bloody-kapitän Schumacher's barracks. Huh, Schumacher the big shot. Let's walk slowly, very slowly, around the building, Corporal; I want to let them know who's the boss!"

Steers bit his tongue. As the two men walked around the north corner, the door suddenly opened, revealing Korvettenkapitän Schumacher, Hauptmann Reiter, and Ensign Konrad Eckert.

"Jimmy! What in blazes do you think you're doing here?" asked Schumacher calmly.

"Steers and I are doing our rounds and you're coming with us."

"I think not. You see; we're in charge now. This is our Camp, Jimmy," Schumacher stated, meerschaum pipe in hand. "I'd leave, now, Brian. Jimmy's a touch more out of sorts than usual."

"Bloody hell, you wish, Captain!"

"Korvettenkapitän, if you please, Captain. I am placing you under arrest. Step in here, please," Schumacher continued speaking as he approached the two guards.

"Arrest us? Not bloody likely, Mr. U-boat hero! Let's go Corporal, we'll round up reinforcements," Blair shouted in Schumacher's face.

As Jimmy was about to turn away, Schumacher hit him with a sucker punch.

"Hey, Cap, you can't do that!" yelled Corporal Steers. Hauptmann Reiter struck Steers on the back of his neck. He dropped to the ground, "Like a sack of hammers," as the two men in tower 'B' joked later in the Guards' Mess.

"Leave Steers, he's stunned, but he'll be alright; it's little king Jimmy I want. Stand him up so that we can parade him like a zombie in front of the other guards," laughed Schumacher.

As Schumacher and the others raised the dazed and barely functioning Jimmy to his feet, a searchlight from guard tower 'B' shone directly on them. Then, rifle shots rang out; a bullet whined past, striking the door jam directly behind them.

The second shot ricocheted, then struck Konrad Eckert. "Oh, God!" he cried, taking the bullet and fragments of the concrete wall in his left thigh. The third shot hit Eckert in the abdomen. He clutched his mid-section and collapsed to the ground, screaming, writhing in agony.

"Help Eckert, Reiter! Leave Jimmy and Steers!" ordered Schumacher. Hauptman Reiter had already knelt to half-lift Eckert, dragging him backward into the Haus.

Schumacher cupped his hands and shouted up at the two soldiers, now training their rifles on him. "Hold your fire! No more! He's wounded! Get a doctor, we need a doctor!"

"There now, you'll be as good as new soon, Ensign Eckert. However, I'm afraid that the fun is over for you. You'll have to sit the rest of this battle out, Konrad," Doctor Gibson, Major, Royal Canadian Army Medical Corps, stated reassuringly as he turned to Colonel Armstrong.

"Hello, Jack. It's been a while."

"How is he, Gib? Is he going to make it?"

"He'll be just fine, Jack. He's woozy and nauseous from the anaesthetic. There's no evidence of shock, which surprised me. Ensign Eckert took two bullets; the one above his left knee had a smaller entry than the exit wound, telling me it was a ricochet. There were small bits of stone embedded, probably caused when the bullet grazed some concrete; fortunately, I was able to pull out all of the cement and the bullet fragments. The second round entered his lower left abdomen but miraculously, it went straight through, leaving a splinter of rifle bullet, which I easily removed. Fortunately, it was a clean exit wound. All of his wounds have been cleansed and dressed with sulpha to prevent infection. I'll keep him under observation for the next few days until any risk of that is past. Very lucky this lad is; the second bullet missed his appendix and bowels by a whisker. It could have been a far different story. I'd say that Ensign Eckert should be up and around in four or five days, Jack."

"Thanks, Gib. Apparently he survived floating around in the North Atlantic until he was rescued...quite the war stories to tell his grandkids, eh? You know, I told the lads 'No weapons.' When I questioned the shooter and his partner separately, their stories jibed. They thought the three PoWs were hell bent on killing our two men; that's why the one fellow fired. What can I do, Gib? Their stories are more or less the same, but not so close as to have been cooked up."

"Well, no permanent damage done, so far, Jack!"

"Not yet, thank God. Okay Gib, thanks again," replied Armstrong. "Now, I'm off to put an end to this nonsense, once and for all!"

"Be careful, old man. Remember what happened when you got carried away at St. Julien!"

Monday 12 October 1942 0635

Dawn had not yet broken over the Camp on Monday morning as the troops, arrayed in battle group formation, awaited Hicks' final orders. "Men, this is it. We will commence a charge on all of the remaining barracks simultaneously and we will continue that charge until all of the prisoners are under our control. Officers know which barracks your units have been assigned. Men, you also know your hard targets. Do not deviate from the plan. Clear?" Major Hicks demanded curtly.

"Yes, Sir!"

"Rout them out!"

With that, the troops advanced rapidly, each unit fanning out flawlessly on its predetermined course. Schumacher and his men heard and then saw them coming. They noted that the four hundred Canadians were manoeuvring in tightly disciplined groups, but the Germans were well prepared with pillows tied to their heads, armed with hockey sticks, bricks, axes, garden tools and anything else they could find at hand. Fifty yards away, the Canadians suddenly became transformed into the Dominion of Canada shock troops of the Great War, whose fearless lack of restraint in battle had horrified their foe. With blood curdling cries, they attacked. Nonetheless, the Germans rose to the challenge. The battle raged all morning and all that afternoon with casualties consisting of scrapes and bruises on both sides. One PoW lost an eye while another suffered a head injury. Finally, that evening, the PoWs sent out word that they wanted to parley. They had had enough and agreed to throw in the towel. Armstrong oversaw the shackling of the one hundred preselected PoWs who were then escorted to their barracks.

Over the next few days, the Veteran Guards led by Corporal Steers conveniently dropped the keys to the shackles on the floor as they were leaving after barracks inspection, enabling the PoWs to remove the handcuffs during the day and replace them for roll calls. Each side had fulfilled its obligations; face was saved; honour had been restored.

The Battle of Bowmanville

Actual shackles used on German PoWs, which incited the 'Battle of Bowmanville'
Rik Davie

12 December 1942

Yesterday, December 11th 1942, Colonel Armstrong ordered that the one hundred officers be unshackled as a goodwill gesture to usher in the festive Christmas season!

This is my record of the story of the Battle of Bowmanville. In the years ahead, you may read accounts by others who will profess to be experts. Indeed, theirs may contradict mine. *A wise American once wrote, To know history is to know what people did and why, that is to know their heart.*

This is from my heart; I was there.

Affectionately,

Karl Semmler (Leutnant, Luftwaffe).

P.S. My dear friend, Corporal Brian Steers recovered fully. Konrad 'The Cat' Eckert is now a living legend, for obvious reasons.

CHAPTER 9
OPERATION KARTOFFEL

Haus IV Camp 30 20th December 1942 0915

"Thank you for attending this morning. Please, be seated, gentlemen. Herr Kapitän?"

"Thank you, Oberstleutnant Eberhart. Would you begin by reading the list of names?"

"Certainly, Sir. Raise your hand, please, when I call your name: Major Brückner, Leutnant Faber, Leutnant von Heiden, Oberleutnant Hoffman, Hauptmann Kappel, Kapitänleutnant Klein, Leutnant Löwen, Leutnant Semmler."

"Gentlemen, I'm delighted to inform you that Berlin has accepted the proposal for a tunnel that Oberstleutnant Eberhart, Generalleutnant Schröder and I submitted," Schumacher began cordially. "What that means gentlemen, is that construction is to begin almost immediately and will continue around the clock if we are to meet our schedule," explained Schumacher. "Although I am unable to share with you many details at this time, suffice to say it is a complex undertaking. Timing and coordination of the various tasks and responsibilities is critical. If we are to be successful, we will need your support. Please, gather around the table.

"We have selected this location, here," Schumacher noted, pointing at a map with the stem of his pipe. "Haus IV, at the northeast corner is the closest point to the outside fence of any building. Even so, the tunnel must be 100 metres in length in order to extend beyond the towers. Questions so far?"

"Sir, if I may, do we have any tunnel experts amongst us?" asked Leutnant Löwen.

"Good question, Kurt. Hauptmann Kappel here is a civil engineer and has prepared a preliminary report for us, although, until this moment, he was not aware of the location of the tunnel. Am I correct, Hauptmann Kappel?" asked Schumacher with a mischievous smile.

"Rest assured, you are correct, Herr Kapitän. Gentlemen, each of

you will be assigned to supervise a major element of the construction. The categories are as follows: digging, shoring, earth removal, lighting, ventilation, earth disposal, and clothes cleaning (laundry). I will determine and direct the depth, width, height and the length of the tunnel as we go along," he explained.

"Is everyone clear on that?" Schumacher asked, and paused. "Very well. Hauptmann Kappel is the head supervisor and construction engineer."

"Yes, Sir."

"Herr Kapitän, if it is not out of order, what is the projected completion date?" inquired Major Brückner. "Of course I realize that may be classified."

"This August," replied Schumacher, curtly. "I might add that our theatrical group is making civilian clothes and forged documents. Leutnant Semmler is taking care of currency through other means. In future, men, we will meet as a group very rarely; need I explain why? Normally, you will channel your daily reports and receive updates through the Oberstleutnant. Nothing is to be written down, nothing at all.

"One more thing, gentlemen. I have received an urgent communiqué from the Admiralty, ordering that all PoW U-boat officers redouble their efforts to escape. The recent unveiling of a radically new prototype, which will require the most highly skilled and experienced personnel, has created a critical shortage of crews. The reason that I am taking you into my confidence is to emphasize that we must succeed with the break-out, at all costs," Schumacher stated.

"That is all. Dismissed. Oh, Gerhard, you have my permission to volunteer anything we Kriegsmarine types can do to assist the Christmas Committee. You'd best get a move on!

"Oberstleutnant, one minute please." Schumacher stared out the window until Hoffman shut the door. "Werner, what do we know about this fellow Brückner who you chose for the Committee?"

"He's been here three months, give or take. Solid, reliable, dedicated, enthusiastic, very bright. A Brandenburger. He was deployed as our intelligence liaison with the Italian SIM Secret Service in Cyrenaica, when the British nabbed him. He's genuine, Frederick. May I ask why?"

"Just keep an eye on him; I have a peculiar sense about the man, as though he's trying too hard to impress us. It may be his natural enthusiasm, as you've said. On orders from Berlin, the information that was just disclosed to the team is in fact a ruse, designed to flush out a potential traitor or spy. Keep that yourself. Oh, yes. We need a short wave radio receiver to pick up reports directly from Germany. Lord knows whether to put more credence in the CBC and newspaper reports here, or in the Reich's official line. Perhaps none is to be believed. At any rate, the truth likely lies somewhere in between." Schumacher paused "Any thoughts, Werner?"

"Yes! Leutnant Hans Neumann is a first-rate signals man, an amateur radio enthusiast before the war. Typical tinkerer, Neumann; he can build almost anything of that sort if you put him in a room with a pile of junk, a soldering iron and a beer or three!"

"You recall that we had Semmler write home for components?"

"Using the *Ireland* code. Was he successful, Frederick?"

"*Völlig!* Absolutely! Karl received the parts in the false bottoms of biscuit containers. Get them from him and then instruct your man Neumann that we need it in time to be able to listen to Propaganda Minister Goebbels' inspirational Christmas broadcasts from the Fatherland ...homesickness, etcetera, you know what to say. And tell him we'll increase his beer rations tenfold if it's ready in fewer than two days!" enthused Schumacher.

"I'll go now."

The Auditorium 20th December 1942 1000h

"Gentlemen, as the chairman, I am speaking on behalf of your Christmas Celebrations Committee. I must be frank and tell you that the members and I are quite concerned. With Christmas Eve only four days away, hardly anyone has signed up to volunteer for festive decorations, music, food, the pageant, and most importantly, to be Father Christmas. Perhaps the events in October have dampened your enthusiasm and we should stand down this year. If this is so, please tell me, here and now. Yes, Oberleutnant Hoffman?"

"Klaus, the Kriegsmarine have appointed me as their spokesman and direct me to apologize for not coming forward sooner. We feel as a group that this year, even more than last, we must show leadership and will do anything required to make this year's celebration even more splendid

and memorable for the sake of the Camp's morale, and in a spirit of goodwill to the Commandant and the VG's. Just tell us what you need and the Kriegsmarine will see it's done, with panache, as always!" declared Oberleutnant Gerhard Hoffmann.

His words were met with a chorus of cheers, punctuated with shouts of "Here, Here!" and "Give the navy the tools and we will do the job!"

"The Army takes a back seat to no one! You can count on us!"

"The Luftwaffe proudly joins with our brethren in offering its unreserved support!"

"Thank you. Thank you gentleman!" Klaus responded when the hall had settled down. 'Better late than never,' he reflected. "However, this is not an inter-service contest," he commented with a smile. "Secretary Schubert has posted new duty lists in the Mess. Please make sure that you encourage your Haus mates to sign up at suppertime today. Deadline is 1900. I am scheduled to meet with Colonel Armstrong at 2000 tonight in order to finalize the preparations and order food and supplies.

"One other thing before you dismiss; it would be helpful if I could tell the Colonel that we have selected our Father Christmas. Any volunteers?" The occupants shifted uncomfortably in their chairs. "Very well, would someone care to make a nomination? Yes, Gerhard, again?"

"Mr. Chairman, the Kriegsmarine unanimously nominates Korvettenkapitän Frederick Schumacher!"

"Konrad Eckert; I second the nomination!"

"Any further nominations, gentlemen? Further nominations? No? Before we declare the Korvettenkapitän acclaimed, may I ask if you had asked for his permission, Gerhard?"

"Ah, not in so many words, no, not exactly, Klaus," Hoffman responded awkwardly. "But who better is there?"

"Perhaps so, but the Korvettenkapitän is a very busy man. Don't you think it would be a good idea to obtain his approval?"

The room erupted with cries of, "Let's do it now," "No contest," "The Luftwaffe endorses Korvettenkapitän Schumacher," "The Army backs the Korvettenkapitän's nomination," "Let's get it over with now, Gerhard!"

"Four days to Christmas Eve, let's do it!"

"Frederick's our man!"

"So be it. But if he declines, we should have a second nominee

ready to step in. Anyone? No one? Very well, those in favour?
Opposed? Secretary Schubert will note in the minutes that
Korvettenkapitän Schumacher was acclaimed as Father Christmas,
1942. I suppose as Chairman it's now my responsibility to bring him the
glad tidings," Keppler remarked dryly. "Thank you all and please
remember that the signup lists will be taken down at 1915 sharp, this
evening. Spread the news. If they are filled, then Christmas at Camp 30
is definitely on. Have a good day, gentlemen."

Klaus Keppler pulled up his collar and leaned into the biting northwest
wind, as he made his way cautiously to Haus IV across the gleaming,
freshly crusted surface. The gentle snowfall, which had greeted the men
at 0730 roll call, had developed into lashing sleet and freezing rain,
depositing a treacherously thick build up of ice which coated everything.
Grasping the ice-sheathed railing, he climbed the steps slowly and
knocked on the door.

"Who is there?"

"Leutnant Keppler, Sir," Klaus responded, thrusting his bare hands
into the pockets of his greatcoat while he waited.

"One moment...come!" Klaus stepped into the welcome warmth to
see Oberstleutnant Eberhart and Korvettenkapitän Schumacher seated
at a large dining table. "Welcome, Klaus! Decidedly nasty out there!"
Schumacher remarked jovially. "Too miserable for the big hockey match
with the VG's that I was so looking forward to. Pity, but another time.
Take off your coat. Can I get you tea with honey, lemon, and a drop of
Barbados rum? The Oberstleutnant and I are having a little game of
Skat to pass the time."

"Oh, that would be fine, yes, Sir," Keppler replied, noting the eight
vacant chairs scattered around the perimeter of the table.

"What brings you here in such terrible weather, Keppler?" Eberhart
inquired offhandedly, studying his cards.

"The Christmas Celebrations Committee, Sir. We just finished the
meeting with representatives from all houses and I wanted to make my
report, time becoming critical, if you don't have any objection, that is."

"Ah, yes, the Christmas Committee. So, tell me, what was decided?"
Eberhart continued, "Are we going ahead, or not?"

"Yes, full steam ahead, Sir!"

"Well, I'm delighted to hear that, aren't you Werner?" Schumacher interjected. "Your tea, Klaus; now what, if anything, do you require of the Oberstleutnant or me?"

"At this point, not much, Sir. I'm meeting with Colonel Armstrong this evening to work out the final details. It will be touch and go, but I think we'll manage it!"

"Excellent. The men could use a morale booster about now. Are you quite certain I can't do anything? Money to help with gifts perhaps? St. Nicholas Night on the sixth has come and gone, but still, there should be presents for our fellows."

"That's a very generous offer, Herr Kapitän. I may have to take you up on it. I must be going. The tea was wonderful, thank you."

"Ready to brave the elements then, are you, Klaus?"

"Yes, thanks, gentlemen."

"Don't forget now, Leutnant Keppler, anything we can do," Eberhart stated, with forced congeniality.

Klaus bit his lip. "As a matter of fact, there is one thing." He paused, skipping a beat, then forged on. "The men, that is, their representatives, want you to be Father Christmas...Sir!"

"Who, me?" asked Eberhart, taken aback. "I'd be..."

"Actually, Sir, Herr Kapitän. It was unanimous."

Schumacher withdrew his pipe from his tobacco tin and methodically packed the bowl in silence. He finished, then carefully replaced the lid, stood up, and began to rummage through his dresser drawers. Finding a box of matches on his night table, he sat down and methodically lit up. "Who nominated me?" he asked between puffs, and then settled back, after shaking out the fourth match, his head enveloped with greyish-white swirls.

"Oberleutnant Hoffman, seconded by Ensign Eckert."

"Gerhard and Konrad. I should have guessed it," Schumacher acknowledged, shaking his head. "Unanimous, you say?"

"*Alle.* Everyone, Herr Kapitän."

"Hmm. Then I will do it, but with one stipulation."

"Sir?"

"That both Oberstleutnant Eberhart, and Generalleutnant Schröder volunteer to be my assistants! And, they must agree to kick into the pot equally for the presents. Agreed, Werner?"

"What can I say? I'm honoured Frederick!" Eberhart gushed, blushing.

"Good. Werner, now you convince Albrecht. When do you need this finalized, Klaus?"

"Tonight, Sir, before 2000h when I meet with the Colonel!"

"*Kein problem.*" Look after it, Werner, and inform Klaus directly it's done.

"And Klaus, see if Colonel Armstrong might be inclined to contribute to the kitty."

"I will, Sir! Excellent idea! Well, good day."

"Good day and good luck, young man," Schumacher remarked, returning Keppler's salute. "You have no idea how much I'm looking forward to this Christmas!" remarked Schumacher, his eyes twinkling.

"Did you pack the lunches and the pieces of kindling, Wolf?"

"Yes, Karl, in the bag."

"And the matches? I know, in the bag."

"*Richtig!* And you're quite certain that those few sticks will keep you two warm enough? Or shouldn't I ask?"

"Wipe that grin! Of course, once I get the fire going, there are all kinds of broken branches I can break up and burn," replied Karl confidently.

"Well, keep the fire low, just in case," Wolf cautioned. "Are you sure you want to go? It's terrible out there! Your episode with the lighting bolt really scared me."

"We'll be fine, thanks. We're dressing warmly. The wind has died down and the sun's out. It's far enough away so that the smoke won't attract anyone. It's about a kilometre and a half east of Marlene's house."

"And does the lady have a family name, Karl?"

"Why do you have to know?"

"Don't get all testy on me, just curious," Wolf remarked evenly. "I solemnly promise to say nothing to Peter Faber," he added grinning.

"Mr. Lady Killer, just ask him. Yes, it's Clark."

"What do you and *Fraulein* Clark do down in the valley?"

"We mainly talk about things: Canada, Germany, what we want to do after the war. Did you know that she used to be a teacher here at the training school before the war?"

"Seeing that I've never met her, how would I? Anyway, I don't recall you mentioning it to me before."

"Yes, she lost her job when the Army took over. Just about the time I first met her, the Camp was expanding and her family was forced to move out of their farm. That's why we didn't hit it off so well at the beginning. I was one of the bad guys!" Karl remarked, buttoning his jacket.

"Understandable, but you're certainly making up for it now, lad. Have a good time and tell her that your old comrade, Wolfgang, says hello. I'll continue to give the run around to anyone dumb enough to be looking for you," Wolf laughed as Karl picked up the bundle.

"What are you going to do while I'm out, Wolfie?"

"Prepare yourself, I'm reading this...a real book!" Wolf announced proudly, holding up a thick hard-covered volume.

"Oh my God! I'm in shock. What is it?"

"*Gone With The Wind*! I'm using your dictionary and making real progress. By the way, did you know that the American Sherman tank is named after the Civil War General, William Tecumseh Sherman who burned down Atlanta, Georgia?"

"That's news to me! The Afrika Korps guys call them 'Ronsons', for good reasons. They're deathtraps, they say. I'm proud of you, Wolf! Better than our *bekloppt* fruitcake Leader's *Mein Kampf*. Klaus is dead right about that. What colossal drivel!" he commented disparagingly. "Okay, I'm off...like the wind..."

"Karl, wait! Aren't you forgetting something?"

"I don't think so..."

"What about this! I even wrapped it for you!"

"Whew, thanks Wolf. If I had forgotten that, she wouldn't have had it for Christmas Eve," Karl replied, tucking the small package into his inner pocket. "See you."

"Wear your toque! And be back here for 1500 roll call!"

"Yes, Mother!"

"And have a good time!" Wolf called as Karl slipped out the door.

Mess Hall Camp 30
22 December 1942 815

Major Theodore Brückner walked quickly towards Haus V. The weather was bitterly cold. He had left his greatcoat in his closet, in his haste to accomplish his mission. He picked up his step to catch up with the man walking in front of him.

"Leutnant, wait up, please. This will take only a minute!"

"Yes, Sir?" The young lieutenant's cheeks were bright red.

"Damn cold, eh?"

"Positively frigid, Sir."

"Oh, I'm Theodore Brückner, Major. I have a question for you, Leutnant...?"

"Löwen, Sir, Kurt."

"Leutnant Löwen, can you tell me in which building the laundry is stored while it's waiting to be sent out?"

"Yes, Sir, this building. Just go around to the back door. May I help you with something, Sir?" asked Kurt, his teeth beginning to chatter.

"No, thanks, Lieutenant. You go ahead and get inside. I forgot to put my favourite shirt in for laundering and I want to make sure that I have it in time for the Christmas concert. Thank you again, Löwen," replied Major Brückner as he walked towards the building.

Camp X Office of the Commandant, Lieutenant Colonel Hamish Findlay
22nd December 1942 1120h

"Miss Robertson, has the laundry delivery truck arrived yet?"

"I'll find out for you, Colonel Findlay. One moment, I'll ring the gate," Betty replied. "Not yet, Sir. But it's due anytime."

"Who's on the gate? Private MacDonald?"

"Yes, it's Mac, Sir."

"Ring him back, please. Have him direct the driver to pull up in front of the office."

"Yes, Sir. Right away," she replied. Betty Robertson, Executive Secretary to every CO of Camp X, had now endured two commandants, both of whose personal foibles and eccentricities made them interesting, even, at times, charmingly roguish, particularly, dear Roger. 'Gordon Graham, Roger Stedman,' she reflected. 'Undeniably brilliant, demanding, and oh, yes, did I say handsome? Courageous, scheming, ruthless, cunning, and utterly cold-blooded.' Betty considered that she was well on her way to understanding and taming her latest, and most fascinating subject, Colonel Hamish Findlay, until this moment. Nothing had prepared her for what happened next.

As soon as the delivery truck pulled up, and taking a flashlight with him, Commandant Findlay rushed out the door and ordered the driver to open the vehicle's back doors. Findlay vaulted up and into the back of the truck and closed the doors. A moment later, he reopened the left rear door, to instruct the driver to stand down until he was finished. Forty-three seconds later, the door re opened. Hamish Findlay appeared, empty-handed. "Help me down will you, driver? That's a good fellow."

"Yes, Sir. Did you find what you were looking for?"

"Yes, thank you, I did. You can carry on to the laundry room."

Betty looked up as Findlay re-entered the office. "Everything alright, Sir?"

"Smashing! Have Blake Grey come here right away, Betty, please."

"Of course, Colonel." Dialling Grey's local, she inspected her nails waiting for a response.

"What, Betty?" Findlay queried.

"Nothing, Sir. Nothing at all."

"You think I've finally lost it, don't you?"

One moment," she interjected. She gave Major Grey the message. "Not at all, Sir. Mine not to reason why," she replied pleasantly. Miss Robertson replaced the handset and returned to her typing.

"Sir, you wanted to see me. Something up?" asked Major Grey.

"Yes, Blake. Sit down, please. It's time to let you in on some confidential information.

"I'm shutting the door now, Miss Robertson."

There was no reply.

"Yes, Sir?"

"You know, of course, that we have Colonel Stedman operating inside Camp 30 as a German PoW, one Major Theodore Brückner?"

"Yes, Sir. I was briefed on that."

"Well, Blake, what you're not aware of is that we have a means of two-way communication with him. I'm holding the first such message."

"Is that a laundry tag, Sir?"

"Correct; an everyday laundry tag. Now watch what happens when I..."

"Add the liquid which exposes the writing on the tag, Sir?"

"Bravo, Dr. Watson! As you see, Blake, Roger Stedman is writing secret messages on the tags of the shirts' bag. Now, what do we have here? It says: PoWs under Schumacher commencing work on tunnel in House 4 expecting major break out more ASAP end S."

"Brilliant! Obviously, it's working, Sir. They've bought his story."

"Yes indeed, Blake, it is working."

27 December 1942

Dearest Momma:

Yet another Christmastime away from home, and how I miss you all! I do hope that big brother, Anton, is well. Although his outfit's location is, of course, classified, perhaps you can forward him my Red Cross mailing address through his Regimental HQ. His little Katie must be quite the sophisticated young lady. Four, is she now? Kisses and hugs to her from der Onkel Karl, and a hug for her momma, Krista.

With the stories that we are hearing at the Lager about how scarce food, clothing and most other necessities are becoming in Germany, I hesitate to tell you that Christmas here was quite pleasant and suitably festive. It began with a candlelight carol service on Christmas Eve. The

Christmas tree was enormous and beautifully decorated with hand made ornaments by our Christmas Committee.

On Christmas Day, one of our top officers dressed up as very cheery Father Christmas, and, with the help of two of his colleagues, distributed gifts to every PoW. (I received the fountain pen and this stationery, which I am using to write this letter). Christmas dinner was a memorable feast. I fear that the local Canadian people fared far worse than we; all the potatoes and other vegetables that were served, I grew, harvested, and stored over the fall, supported with the hard work of some of the enlisted ranks. Yes, truly! Are you not surprised that your Karl, the aviator and hopeless town mouse, would find himself so keenly attracted to farming? I really can't explain it myself! Despite Wolfgang's frequent 'kidding' (a new English word for me), I do love working the soil and can't wait for the spring. That is, if I am still here. If so, I am promised a larger plot of land and more 'farm hands'.

Well, Momma, it's almost time for afternoon roll call and I mustn't be tardy. Wolfgang sends his love.

Please write soon. Chocolates and biscuits are always welcome, although I fear if I indulge much more I may become the size of a house with the wintertime inactivity!

Much love,

Your Karl

6 February 1943 2030

"Hauptmann Kappel!" Schumacher called as he emerged from the shower, wrapped in a towel. "Did you have an enjoyable swim?"

"Yes, very good, thank you, Herr Kapitän," Kappel replied adjusting his tie with some difficulty in the dressing room's fogged mirror.

"When you're finished, join us for a drink in The Red Ox. Ten minutes?"

Helmut Kappel was speechless. He could count on the fingers of one hand the number of times he had actually visited, much less been invited to, the officers' semi-exclusive watering hole, *Zum Roten Ochsen*, The

Red Ox, in the far corner of the Mess Hall. Socializing was not Helmut's strong suit. Brilliant, scholarly, and solitary by choice, he preferred studying Roman aqueduct construction methods and was an expert on the work of an obscure, German-born civil engineer of the Imperial Period, Lucillus Germanicus. "Why, I …yes! Thank you, Herr Kapitän!" Kappel replied, redoubling his effort to ensure that his tie was perfectly knotted and straight.

Drawing near the entrance, Hauptmann Kappel braced himself for a blast of ear-splitting accordion music and boisterous carryings-on; to his surprise, the atmosphere of The Red Ox was subdued. Standing at the door, he anxiously searched the tables for Schumacher and Eberhart.

"Helmut! Over here!" Schumacher called from the farthest corner. "Glad you decided to join us. Sit down, please! Here, this is for you!" Schumacher smiled, pushing a frothy stein across the table. "Oberstleutnant Eberhart tells me that he's been waiting for an update on your progress with Kartoffel," Schumacher continued.

"Thank you, Herr Kapitän. I do apologize if I've been remiss in keeping you in the picture, Oberstleutnant," Helmut responded, blinking rapidly. "To begin, the planning is completed and we've been excavating for a little more than three weeks! To get underway, we had to break through the concrete floor of the closet room in the northeast corner of Haus IV."

"How did you dispose of the waste, Hauptmann Kappel?" asked Eberhart.

"By breaking up the concrete into small pieces and removing them to various locations throughout the Camp. Then, we began excavating the hole, fifty centimetres by fifty centimetres (twenty inches by twenty inches)."

"I'm curious to know how are you able to keep the tunnel that exact size, Hauptmann," Eberhart continued.

"It's quite straightforward, Sir. I borrowed a technique used by our sappers (military engineers) during the Great War, and designed a wooden template measuring exactly fifty centimetres by fifty centimetres. As the men burrow through the ground, they use the template as a gauge," he explained, polishing his thick eyeglasses with a serviette. "Admittedly, it is primitive. But nonetheless, it works," Kappel added with an air of self-satisfaction.

"Quite clever! Do go on, Hauptmann," Eberhart replied, eagerly warming to the subject. "Drink your beer before it goes flat!"

A German tunnel
Bowmanville Archives

"Oh, yes! Yes, Sir," Kappel replied distractedly. "The biggest problem we've encountered is how to dry the earth before storing it in the ceiling of Haus IV. This is essential. I have installed additional vertical supports. However, by my calculations, the ceiling must inevitably collapse. It will be unable to withstand the pressure of so many tonnes of fill. I'm working to find another way to dry the mud, to prevent that. But as you know, engineering is ninety-percent analysis, problem solving and guesswork; the remaining ten-percent is the application... and guesswork," he added, smiling, self-consciously.

"I have chosen to cross underneath the heating duct tunnel instead of through it," he continued. "One can see where the guards have been drilling into the concrete walls at one-metre intervals, which permits them to drive rods into the ground, probing for signs of tunnelling. We've excavated between two of the holes, Sir. In this fashion." He took out of his breast pocket a small, spiral bound notepad and a pencil stub and quickly sketched a rectangle with two small circles, between which he drew two parallel lines, representing the tunnel's breadth.

"Ingenious!" Schumacher interjected. "Do you see this, Oberstleutnant?"

"I'm impressed, Sir. Brilliant!"

"We have also sloped the tunnel three degrees starting at two metres (seven feet) so that it will end with a depth of one and one-half metres (five feet)...in this manner. This will allow us optimum accessibility, as well as allowing the water to drain toward the Haus IV opening. I do hope I'm not boring you with these trivia, gentlemen?"

"Not at all Helmut, but you've hardly touched your beer! Would you prefer something else: rye whiskey, gin, rum, wine, a liqueur perhaps?" Eberhart inquired.

"Coffee, black, with three sugars, if you don't mind. I'm very sensitive to alcohol in any form."

"Very well. Frederick, another rum with cola? No?

"Let me get you that coffee, Hauptmann; in the meantime, hold off on your report, please."

Helmut stirred the coffee absently, and then took a sip from the steaming mug. "Thank you very much, Oberstleutnant. Of course, for obvious reasons, the tunnel is wired to provide the necessary lighting. We were able to patch into, rather, to connect to the Camp's 110-volt electrical mains without great difficulty. Thanks to our Committee, some expert scroungers went to work and frankly, I am astounded at what they were able to come up with so quickly: cable, bulbs, sockets, tools, even adhesive tape from the infirmary. Unfortunately, the adhesive proved unreliable in the dampness; however, with the cooperation of the theatrical company, that is now resolved," he smiled.

"Now, as to ventilation. We have rigged an airline constructed of tin cans, taped together, and suspended from the ceiling. There is always one man, and a spare for safety, pumping a bellows while the tunnel is occupied. The tin cans come from our men in the kitchen and, as I mentioned, the tape is supplied in quantity by the theatrical group."

"What about shoring, Hauptmann?"

"Reinforcement or bracing, if you will, is always a most important matter, Sir. The shop manufactures wooden supports, twenty by twenty centimetres square, using boards taken from the attics of the buildings.

These are positioned every one to two metres (three to seven feet) at the start of the tunnel. As we progress, we decrease that distance. For example, when we get to the road, they will be fitted closer together, every thirty centimetres (twelve inches). My calculations err on the conservative side, but a catastrophic cave-in must be avoided at all costs.

"As I said at the outset, drying the soil as well as locating new disposal sites are ongoing challenges."

"Just how does it get from the tunnel into storage?"

"That part was quite straightforward, Oberstleutnant. We opened a hole in the ceiling of Haus IV; using buckets, the dirt is passed from man to man until it reaches the ceiling, then it is carefully deposited between the joists."

"Refresh my memory, Helmut. How many men are working the tunnel in total?" asked Schumacher.

"Thirty-nine, not including logistical support: scroungers, mechanical, and of course, trainees; then, it's closer to forty-five, no, forty-six to be precise. We have three shifts consisting of teams of thirteen men: one man at the front end digging, three men transporting the dirt on a trolley system, one man hauling it up to pass it up to another man in the ceiling. Another three are needed there to disburse the soil, as well as two on the ventilation system, and two men on watch."

"And if an emergency arises, Hauptmann?" Eberhart asked.

"If the alarm is sounded, everything is thrown into the hole, the lights in the tunnel are switched off to warn the men to be silent, and a piece of the wooden flooring is put in place over the opening. For the finishing touch, a large wardrobe cabinet is moved to cover it up."

"Very impressive work, Hauptmann. *Nein*, Werner? Now, I think that it's time for a little nighttime snack, wouldn't you agree? The knackwurst with sauerkraut is usually quite reliable, and no heartburn at 3:00 a.m., or almost none," Schumacher laughed. "Allow me, gentlemen."

16 April 1943 0900
Camp 30
"Wolf..."

"I know, Karl 'Cover for me'," Wolfgang commented unenthusiastically. "I'm glad that one of us, undeserving as you are, is enjoying the company of a member of the fair sex. Listen, my love-struck friend, exactly when do you intend to tell the old man about your tunnel?"

"Sorry, tell who?"

"The Korvettenkapitän. Schumacher! You really are in pathetic shape!" Wolf commented, shaking his head. "Look, now that he has started the official tunnel, don't you think that you should let him in on your secret? Better sooner than later. He'll be mighty peeved if and when he finds out after the fact, don't you think?" Wolf declared.

"I had already planned to tell him today, as soon as I'd let Marlene know that I can't come out that way anymore. Must go...I'll tell you about it later," Karl replied. "Maybe she has a girlfriend!"

The frost was still coming out of the ground, making the downhill trek tricky. Karl travelled slowly, clutching at tree limbs to avoid sliding into the creek.

"Hallo, Marlene!"

"Karl! Watch your step; I nearly fell twice," she laughed sitting on her now-familiar downed tree. "*Kommen,*" she beckoned with her index finger. "*Kuss?*" She rose and they embraced eagerly.

"Wonderful, the creek has opened up, the ice is finally moving out!"

"Yes, isn't it wonderful? Summer is right around the corner."

"I'm glad you said that, Marlene." He took her hands in his. "It reminded me of something I have to tell you."

"You sound so serious. What is it, Karl?" she asked, drawing back. "Have I done something wrong?"

"No, of course you haven't, love! Listen, Marlene, I have to stop using my tunnel. I cannot keep it a secret from my CO any longer. The old man will string me up by my heels. The only honourable thing is to abandon it. No one else knows about it; correct?"

"Of course not. No one knows anything about it, or us. Why? What happened?"

"I can't tell you the reason. Just trust me. That's all I ask is that you trust me."

"I see," said Marlene. "And what of us?"

"I have another plan which will take us through the summer."

"I'm all ears..."

"Actually you're all soft brown eyes and lovely silken hair!"

"Oh, stop it, you jive talking... Where were we?" she reponded, flustered.

"*Ehrenwort...*"

"We have a code of honour in the Camp, *Ehrenwort.* If we give our word, *Ehrenwort,* that we will not try to escape, we are permitted to leave the Camp for an afternoon trip. In the wintertime, it could be for cross-country skiing. In the summertime, to go down to the lake and go swimming,

"How extraordinary. Does it work?"

"Yes, so far not one man has taken advantage. We want to keep it that way, obviously. It allows us extra freedom, which is very much appreciated when you are staring at barbed wire fences and guard towers all day long," Karl replied sombrely.

"You do alright on the outside, big boy!" she commented, fluttering her eyelashes in amusement. "So, what's your plan?"

"Two days before the first day of summer, on Saturday, June nineteenth, a few select PoWs plan to go to the lake for an afternoon of sun and swimming. We'll leave the Camp about 1100h, I mean 11:00 a.m. Wolf and I walked down there once last year; it took close to an hour to make it. Do you think that you could get away?"

"Sure! Saturday is my day to play and do as I please. Do you mind if I bring a girlfriend, Karen, Karen Livingston?"

"No, not at all. You've never told me about her before. That should make the boys happy."

"How many 'boys' are we talking about?"

"Including me, five. Is that okay?"

"In that case, maybe I should drag along another friend or two."

"Good, see if you can."

"We won't be able to go swimming; the water is far too frigid at that time of year. You can hardly go in Lake Ontario in August!"

"Yes, I know. Wolf and I just like to lie in the sun, walk the beach and throw flat rocks into the water and see how many times they'll skip. So, are we on?"

"Yes, sounds good. I'll check my social calendar," she teased. "Don't look at me like that. I'm kidding, for goodness sake. What route do you take?"

"Straight down Liberty Street to the lake."

"Okay, Karen and I will be there for sure. Karl?"

"Yes, Marlene?"

"You won't forget? It's going to be two months that we won't be seeing each other..."

"I promise, *Ehrenwort. I love you.*"

"Ditto."

"How was it, Karl?" asked Wolf, breathing heavily. "I just ran five kilometres and I think I'm going to throw up!"

"Jesus, not all over me!" Karl exclaimed, backing away. "We had a
good talk."

"Did you get things straightened out with her...about the tunnel?"
Wolf asked, kicking his running shoes into his closet.

"We've made a date for Saturday, June nineteenth at 1100h to go to
the lake for the afternoon, and you're invited."

"Me?"

"Yes you. She's bringing a girlfriend, Karen."

"Kar-en? Thanks for thinking of me, Karl. I bet she's a hound, I
mean a dog, as the guards say."

"Well, Casanova, you've got two months to decide. Anyway, it's the
least I can do, for all the times you've covered for me. I'll even make the
picnic," laughed Karl.

"Deal! I'm going, dog or dish, don't you worry!"

"Wolf, I've decided not to tell the old man about the tunnel."

"What? Earlier, you said that you must."

"I can't!"

"Why not, Karl?"

"Because I won't be able to lie to his face. God knows it's intimidating enough just to meet him on the pathway! He will want to know how
long I have known of its existence; that, and a hundred more questions.
I could be in deep shit, possibly even court-martialled."

"I see. You're right of course. So what will you do?"

"Nothing, absolutely nothing. We won't go near it. If someone finds it, so be it. Otherwise, it never existed. Right?"

"Right."

"*Ehrenwort?*"

"Okay, *Ehrenwort* already, Karl. I would never squeal on you; don't you know that yet?"

5 June 1943

Camp 30

"Hey Fritz! Over here." Jimmy Blair, the Camp pariah who had been transferred to Gravenhurst, had used his surprisingly persuasive political influence to worm his way back into Camp 30.

"Jimmy, what is it now?"

"I need some more 'juice'."

"How much?"

"A case. I'll give you a pack of smokes for each bottle."

"Two!"

"One; that's the deal, take it or leave it. Remember, I can shut you down any time I like, Herr friggin' Fritz."

"The name's Ulrich, not Fritz. Okay. Deal," he shrugged. "Where do you want me to drop it?"

"Behind my office, up against the building. When will you have it?"

"In the morning. And don't forget to leave the smokes!"

"Christ, doesn't anyone around here trust me?" Jimmy turned and started toward Haus I on his inspection tour.

'Trust you? You weasel!' muttered the PoW.

Upon entering the back door of Haus V, Ulrich walked directly to the room that doubled as a mudroom and a distillery.

"Ulrich, how are you doing?"

"I'm fine, Dieter. How's the operation going?"

"Slow, but steady."

"How many cases ahead are you?"

"Six, why?" asked Dieter.

Summertime Camp 30
Bowmanville Archives

"Jimmy wants a case for tomorrow morning."

"Blair? That bastard! I thought we got rid of him! Did you tell him to shove it?"

"No, he can cause too much trouble for us. We'll just have to put up with him. But I tried to get as much out of him as possible."

"Okay, you can take one of those." Dieter pointed reluctantly to a sizeable stack of corrugated cardboard cartons.

"What kind is it?"

"Damned if I know."

"Well, what's it made out of?"

"We're still working off the pear juice from last fall's harvest. Want to try some?"

Taking a small glass from the cupboard, Ulrich poured himself a drink. "*Toll,* amazing, that stuff is really smooth. You sure figured out how to get the bugs out of it, literally!" laughed Ulrich.

"Yes, it's really not too bad. Better than that first batch that we concocted. The poor sods that drank it are lucky they aren't blind. I don't even want to think about that mess," chuckled Dieter.

"Okay, thanks Dieter. I'll bring the smokes in tomorrow after I pick them up."

"You know, Ulrich, if I had some of that swill lying around, I'd be tempted to put a couple of shots into every one of these bottles for Jimmy, just for old time's sake."

"Vengeance is ours, brother Dieter. All in good time."

19 June 1943 1045

Camp 30

"Hurry up Wolf, what's taking you so long?" shouted Karl.

"I'm moving as fast as I can. What's your rush anyway?" Wolf shouted from the bathroom.

"I want to leave early; I'm not sure how long it is going to take to get down to the lake."

"It was an hour last time. Has it moved? Okay, okay. Ready? Let's go. Did you pack your swimsuit?" laughed Wolf.

"Two large towels, our swimsuits, lunch, all in my bag. Start engines!"

"Who else is coming with us?" asked Wolf.

"Kurt Löwen, Peter Faber and Klaus Keppler; they'll meet us at the gate."

"Race you there!' Wolf shouted and ran off.

Turning and looking straight up at the guard tower, Karl called, "Permission to leave the Camp?"

"For what purpose?"

"We are going down to the lake for the afternoon."

"*Ehrenwort?*"

"Yes, of course, *Ehrenwort.*"

"Okay, open the gate. You men are to be back by 1800 hours, understand?" demanded the guard.

"1800 hours, understood," replied Karl. "Thanks!"

The five men proceeded to walk along Concession Street toward Liberty Street, a few miles west of the Camp.

19 June 1943 1750

"Well what did you think of them, lads?" asked Karl as they turned north onto Liberty Street.

"Karen's a real dish!" Wolf enthused. "Your Marlene's very nice, too!"

"Good thing you said that!" Karl stated. "And no more 'dog' comments?"

"*Ehrenwort!*"

"Knock it off, okay, von Heiden? I'm hearing that enough in the camp, already! *Ehrenwort* this, Ehrenwort that...Listen guys, they're women, so they're all lovely, but Sheila's the sort I could take a run at!" Peter enthused.

"If that fence post had a pulse, you'd take a run at it!" cackled Klaus.

"Hey, I have my standards you know, Keppler. Besides, it's not blonde..." retorted Peter, laughing. "Mark my words, that Sheila's a winner! And she looks so...so, Aryan!"

"Get off it, Faber. She's Ukrainian, you dumb sod!

"Just before I said goodbye to Marlene a minute ago, she told me that all three of them want to go again, next Saturday. Maybe another two will be coming along. Well done, boys! Marlene was impressed, and so naturally, I'm impressed. Oh, oh! It's 1753, we'd better pick up the pace! Let's go!" Karl shouted.

29 August 1943
Camp 30 Haus IV
Crack!

"What the hell was that?" Ensign Konrad Eckert sat bolt upright. "Was I dreaming? It sounded like a rifle shot! It's always some damn thing when all I want to do is get some sleep," he muttered. "What time is it anyway? It's only 0310h. There it is again!"

With that, the entire ceiling of the northeast corner of Haus IV collapsed with a deafening thud. A mountain of soil and rubble lay in the centre of the room.

Schumacher raced out of his room in his shorts. "What the hell is going on, Ensign?" he thundered. "I can't see a god damn thing!"

"It's the ceiling Sir! It couldn't take the weight I...I guess!" exclaimed Eckert. "What should we do now, Sir?"

"What you can do is get Kappel that engineer who assured me that the ceiling could hold the weight of the dirt. That's what you can do, Ensign!"

"Immediately, Herr Kapitän!" Eckert replied, slipping on a shirt and trousers.

Konrad Eckert returned, moments later, along with an extremely agitated and dazed Hauptmann Kappel, in his housecoat. A crowd of PoWs, in skivvies, from the other end of the building was gathering at the scene, either out of curiosity about the cause of the pandemonium or to witness Kappel's impending fall from grace, or both.

"Well, do you have an explanation for this, Hauptmann?" demanded Schumacher balefully. All eyes turned to the diminutive, bespectacled engineer.

"Sir," he gulped, blinking rapidly, "I don't know what could have gone wrong. I introduced a new procedure, u-u-using a low heat kiln, to d-d-dry the soil. Perhaps, they did not follow p-p-procedures properly."

"We'll discuss this privately; Hauptmann; let's get started cleaning up. Eckert, rouse the crew and get them in here. Now!

"How in bloody hell are we going to keep this from the guards?" asked Schumacher to no one in particular as he stalked into his bedroom. "Hauptmann! In here! Now!" He slammed the door viciously, resulting in a fresh cascade of falling dirt and a whirlwind of dust.

30 August 1943

The next day, as the Guard was about to enter Haus IV for daily inspection, Captain Schumacher intercepted him outside the door, which he shut firmly behind him. "Good day, Corporal. There's something I've been meaning to ask you for the longest time. Would you happen to have a minute?"

"Shoot, I mean, sure, go ahead, Captain Schumacher. Something wrong?"

"Not in the strictest sense of 'wrong', Corporal, however, I wonder if you'd mind taking a short walk with me. This will only take a moment." Schumacher led the Corporal to one of the large elm trees which lined the playing field. "If you look at this poor fellow as I do every day, I'm sure you can see that it's finished, *kaput*, and likely to topple over in the next storm. So, I was wondering, if it's taken down before that happens, could the men have the wood?"

"The wood, Sir? But, what for?"

"Carving," Schumacher smiled patiently.

"Ah, yes, I see. You Germans are very good at that sort of thing, I've heard."

"Well, be that as it may, Corporal, and I wouldn't want to be seen as bragging, a number of the men are quite skilled in woodcraft. I'm sure we could arrange to have a fine hardwood table, naturally hand-carved, made out of a piece of that trunk! I'm sure it would make quite a useful and attractive addition to your Mess, no?"

"That would be great, Captain. Yes, indeed. Let me see what Staff Sergeant Murray thinks of your idea. I'm sure he'll be receptive!"

"Please, do, Corporal! " Schumacher glanced at his wrist chronometer. " I'll be awaiting your answer with bated breath, as you say," he smiled.

"What time is it, Captain?"

Schumacher extended his left arm toward the Corporal.

"Oh, I'm late. Must get on with the duties. I'll let you know tomorrow when I come by for inspection. Got to run!"

"Splendid, Corporal, just splendid," Schumacher remarked as the Corporal trudged off toward Haus V.

"Hope to hell he forgets," Schumacher muttered to himself, as he strolled back to Haus IV. "Schumacher here. All clear!"

13 September 1943

Camp 30 Haus IV

"What's all the commotion outside, Ensign?" asked Captain Schumacher, irritated.

"The guards, Sir. They want to go into the attic," replied Konrad Eckert.

"We'll see about that. You there, Brian, what is the meaning of this?"

"Orders, Cap," replied Corporal Steers.

"Orders! Whose orders?" bellowed Schumacher.

"Captain Blair's!"

"Huh? Jimmy! Where is that *Schweinhund*, swine? Is he not man enough to come himself?"

"I'm not sure where he is. Just following orders, Captain.

"Okay, boys. Up into the attic. Let me know when you've found it," ordered Corporal Steers.

"What are you looking for? No one has been up there."

"Just a routine check, Captain."

After a half an hour of stomping around, one of the men yelled down, "Corporal, you'd better get the CO!"

Within minutes, Lieutenant Colonel Jack Armstrong, Staff Sergeant Robert Murray, and Captain James Blair arrived and strode directly to the northeast corner of Haus IV.

"Colonel, who is going to repair this damage to our Haus?" demanded Schumacher.

"No worry, Captain, we'll repair the roof as good as new," replied Colonel Armstrong.

"What did you find, Private?"

"Sir, I pulled up the boards, as you asked, at several different spots. It's there alright."

"What's there, Colonel? Do you mind telling me what's going on?" implored Schumacher.

"Is there anything that you would like to tell me, Captain?"

"No. But perhaps you could tell me."

"Okay, we'll play your game. The tunnel, Captain. Where is it?"

"What tunnel? I don't know anything about a tunnel!" replied Schumacher staunchly.

"Captain Blair, have the men start the augers," ordered Colonel Armstrong. Several younger members of the Veterans' Guard trotted in, carrying augers with pipe extensions.

After an hour of rigorous digging, a guard shouted, "Sir, found it!"
"Bingo! Same here," shouted another. "It looks as if it goes straight out this way towards the road, Sir!"

"Well, Captain. This certainly is interesting. You say you don't know anything about a tunnel? Would you care to reconsider that remark before I lock up your ass in solitary?" snarled Blair.

"You little *Schweinhund*; just try it...!" spat Schumacher, stepping forward, threateningly.

"Captain, Captain," Armstrong interjected. "Gentlemen calm down, please. Let's try to approach this rationally, in my office.

"Staff Sergeant, stay here with the men.

"Gentlemen, follow me, if you will, please."

CHAPTER 10

FINALLY, SUCCESS

15 September 1943

Camp 30 *Zum Roten Ochsen* **The Officers' Club**

"Frederick, I'm glad I found you!" announced Oberstleutnant Eberhart. "May I join you?"

"Werner, of course, sit down; can I get you a beer? The usual?"

"Yes, a King Beer, please, Herr Kapitän.

"Thanks, I have..."

"It has been driving me crazy; Werner," Schumacher interrupted. "I can't stop asking myself, how in blazes did the Canadians know about that tunnel? I am convinced that it was not accidental! Jimmy Blair and the others knew exactly where to look. Any thoughts?" Schumacher asked tersely.

"It did seem more than mere coincidence, Frederick, but no rational explanation came to mind. That is, not until young Leutnant Kurt Löwen told me of something suspicious."

"Go on..."

'Kriegsmariners'
Bowmanville Museum

"It occurred just before Christmas. Brückner came out of nowhere, asking for directions to the laundry holding area, of all places. Löwen thought it somewhat peculiar at the time, although Brückner's explanation seemed logical: something about needing his best shirt for the concert."

"Why didn't Löwen report this incident until now? That was ten months ago!" Schumacher retorted angrily.

"He said that it had slipped his mind until this morning, when he and his Afrika Korps chums saw Brückner skulking around the back of the building. Frederick, can we step outside?" asked Eberhart. They walked around the building to the back of the Mess.

"Here." Eberhart handed Schumacher a manila laundry tag.

"What's this?" asked Schumacher.

"Proof," replied Eberhart. "Written in invisible ink. Our man Kaufman says it's definitely British. I'd be willing to lay odds that Brückner is an SIS agent. (Secret Intelligence Service)."

"I knew that it couldn't be one of ours! Brückner, you bastard!" Schumacher muttered. "I knew there was something odd about him. Remember, Werner?" As Schumacher read the message, his colour rose to a deep red. "Werner," he ordered. "Find a manila 'shirt tag'. Have Kaufman make up invisible ink, the same formula as this. I'll need a pen. And bring them to me directly Kaufman is done."

16 September 1943

Camp X Commandant Findlay's Office

"Miss Robertson, I need Major Grey here. Immediately!" shouted Hamish Findlay.

"Very well, Sir. I'll ring the Mess.

"Andy, get Major Grey to Colonel Findlay's office, pronto. No, it can't wait! The Colonel's... He's on his way? Good. Thanks, Andy."

Nearly out of breath from running, Major Grey burst into Colonel Findlay's office. "That's it Hamish, I'm going to quit smoking!" he laughed.

"Hello, Betty." An ashen–faced Betty Robertson sat facing Hamish' desk.

"Sit down, Blake. This is deadly serious," Hamish directed.

"What's up, Sir? The second front?"

"Read this." Hamish handed a laundry tag to Blake Grey.

"We're on to you. The PoWs, Colonel?"

"I'm afraid so, Blake. They've found him out! His life is in jeopardy: we must get him out of the Camp immediately. God knows what they're going to do to him, if they haven't already. There's no time to waste.

"Have my car sent here straight away, Betty. Call Colonel Armstrong. Tell him we're on our way to see him about... Just say, it's most urgent and to meet us at the gate. And he's to tell no one!"

"Immediately, Sir. God help Roger," she added softly, as she stood up.

Hamish opened the bottom right-hand drawer of his desk and took out his prized Browning High-Power pistol. Manufactured on an assembly line in Toronto by women who, before the war, had built washing machines, the John Inglis Browning High-Power was one of the most effective hand-guns produced during the Second World War. In comparison with the Colt .45, to which it bore a resemblance, the Browning High-Power pistol was light and highly-accurate; its 9mm slug carried stupefying stopping power at close range. Hamish, having changed into his dress red tunic and regimental tartan kilt, checked the safety before tucking the HP-35 into his waistband.

16 September 1943

Camp 30 Haus IV

"Sir, you wanted me?" Eberhart had rarely seen the Korvettenkapitän so agitated.

"Yes, Werner, do you know where Brückner is at this moment? I've had several men looking for him for an hour."

"I saw him walking toward the mess, Frederick."

"How the hell did they miss him? Werner, get out there, round up Gerhard Hoffman and some others and let's catch the bastard! Well, what are you waiting for? Get going! Now!" snarled Schumacher.

As Schumacher, Eberhart, Hoffman, and their squad turned the corner of the building, Schumacher sighted Brückner in the distance, close to the Mess Hall.

"Major Brückner! Theodore, a moment!" Schumacher called.

"Let's go, Gerhard! Take him down, men!" Schumacher commanded as they broke into a run.

Hearing Schumacher's voice, Roger Stedman realized that he was finished. His eyes darted to the approaching men, and then to the gate, about one hundred metres distant. 'Should I make a run for it?' Casting one more glance at the advancing PoW's, he opted to run. A spit second later, the gate opened. Through it walked Colonel Armstrong accompanied by two soldiers and a tall man in a regimental red dress tunic, and a kilt. 'It's Hamish, God bless him! The tunic's the signal that the game is up! As if I don't bloody well already know it!' Running furiously, with Schumacher's gang on his tail, Stedman began shouting, "I defect. I defect!"

One of the PoWs lunged and tackled Stedman, wrestling him to the ground. "Hold him down! Quickly, get him into the Mess Hall," Schumacher ordered.

"Hold on there!" shouted Armstrong, reaching the site of the scuffle. "Let him go!"

"Colonel, this is no business of yours. We would like to talk with the Major. He hasn't been himself lately."

"I strongly suggest that you do as Colonel Armstrong directed," Hamish announced.

"Who the hell are you?" exclaimed Schumacher.

"That's none of your bloody business," retorted Hamish. "Now, do calm down if you would, Captain. I believe the Major was trying to say something. Do you have something to say, Major?"

"Yes. I want to defect. I've had enough of these people, the war, this bloody prison camp, everything," snapped Stedman.

"Captain, that seems plain enough to me," Hamish replied.

"What do you think, Colonel Armstrong?" Findlay continued.

"Clearly this man wishes political asylum," commented Armstrong.

"This man, Colonel Armstrong, is a member of the German Armed Forces and, as such, is considered a fugitive. By my authority, he will be brought up on charges of desertion. Therefore, he stays with us," proclaimed Schumacher.

"I'm afraid not. Take the prisoner to my office, immediately, Staff Sergeant Murray!"

Armstrong's calm but resolute manner only served to further enrage Schumacher. Seething, he approached Colonel Armstrong. "Colonel, you won't get away with this! I will be lodging a complaint with the Red Cross immediately. Major Brückner will be back in the Camp within the week. And, he will be court-martialled! Mark my words!"

"Really? We'll see about that, Captain. Take him away, Staff."

"I am giving a direct order, Captain. You and you men will disperse immediately!" Jack Armstrong looked up at the guard tower, where, to emphasize his order, two guards aimed their rifles directly at Schumacher and Eberhart.

"You haven't heard the last of this, Colonel!" Schumacher thundered, allowing himself a brief glance upward.

Conceding temporary defeat, Schumacher turned his back and addressed Eberhart. "Oberstleutnant!"

"Squad will fall in. By the right, quick march!"

Jack Armstrong watched until the detachment had retreated into the Mess hall. Then, with a wave of acknowledgement to the guard tower, he walked back to his office with Hamish and Roger.

16 September 1943

Camp 30 Commandant's Office

"Lord, that was a near run thing, Jack! They were about to kill me!" said a still-shaken Roger Stedman.

"Yes, I'm sure of that," Armstrong responded. "It's a damn good thing that Hamish came to the rescue when he did."

"How did you find out that the game was up?" asked Stedman.

"The Germans told us," replied Findlay.

"They told you?"

"Yes, they just couldn't resist letting us know that they were onto our game with a little 'we-know-what- you're-up-to' valentine. Here, have a look. That little slip-up likely saved your life, Roger. It was pure arrogance on Schumacher's part."

"Well, I certainly am grateful to all of you."

"Due compensation will show up on your bar tab," Hamish chuckled. "Now that it's over, is there anything else you can tell us?"

"I don't know the details," Stedman replied, "but I'm certain Schumacher and company are busily planning something significant, and they don't have very much time to pull it off."

"Staff Sergeant Murray, you will place the Camp on highest alert, without raising any suspicion. Can the VG's manage that?"

"I'll see to it, Sir."

21September 1943
Camp 30 Haus IV

"Herr Kapitän, you wished to see me?"

"Yes, come in Herr Kaleu! Wilhelm, I've asked Oberstleutnant Werner Eberhart to sit in with us," Schumacher noted pleasantly.

"Yes, of course, Sir. A pleasure, Oberstleutnant!" Klein replied.

"Please, Wilhelm, take that chair. As you know, we have recently had a breach in our security."

"Yes, Sir. The defection of Major Brückner," Klein stated.

"Yes, that's right. We must now be doubly careful of what we say and to whom. We cannot afford for any of this to get out."

"I understand, Sir."

As an aside, Schumacher added, "Wilhelm and I are old comrades-in-arms from our training days, Werner. Sadly, we haven't seen much of one another since we chatted briefly on the train." He then continued, "Very well. We will proceed informally, without titles. Wilhelm, my sources inform me that you have a plan for an escape. If it is a good one, and if I approve it, then I will have to tell you of the importance of our failed attempt at tunnelling. But first, proceed with your plan."

"Thank you, Sir..."

"Frederick," Schumacher interjected, fiddling with the zipper of his oilskin tobacco pouch.

"Frederick," Klein responded. "I hope you do not think it is idiotic, however, I believe it can work, gentlemen."

"Carry on, Wilhelm." Schumacher had a high regard for the young commander, whose clear-eyed, unemotional approach to emergency procedure simulations had won him Second Overall in Class standing, second only to himself. Schumacher knew that Klein's well-merited promotion to Korvettenkapitän had been short-circuited by bureaucratic bungling, as a cover for the Admiralty's hostility to his suffer-no-fools-gladly attitude and running conflicts with decisions handed down by senior staff.

"Thank you for your confidence," Klein replied.

"I haven't heard your proposal as yet, remember?" cautioned Schumacher with a slight smile. He took a drag from his pipe, letting the smoke swirl out his nose.

"Of course, I realize that, gentlemen. My plan, or scheme if you will, is to build a bosun's chair, a small trolley car, then climb the hydro pole, place the device on the main electrical cable feeding the Camp. Then, while hanging onto the trolley, simply roll out of the Camp." Klein searched their faces for reactions.

Schumacher glanced at Eberhart and then looked back at the Kapitänleutnant. "I see. Thank you, Wilhelm, that will be all," he concluded non-committally. "Dismiss."

Wilhelm Klein rose, saluted, and walked toward the door. He turned, adding, "Thank you for your time, gentlemen...it can work!"

"Wilhelm, wait!" Eberhart interjected. "Please, wait outside for just a moment."

When Klein exited, Eberhart turned to Schumacher. "Frederick, I know it sounds hare-brained, but, as the Canadians say, so what? It will cost us next to nothing in either time or labour to pull off. It can be carried out within days, not months. This is a solo act; there is only one man involved, very different from fifty or more tunnel workers and supervisors. Moreover, if he is caught, it won't in the least affect our own projects! At worst, the Kapitänleutnant will do the usual twenty-eight days in solitary. The way I see it, this is a no-skin-off-our-nose proposition. The only way we can lose is if we don't try it, Frederick. What's more, it just might stand a chance.

Schumacher shifted in his chair. "Werner, you've made a good case. Perhaps it is worth a try. His spoken English was excellent at Neustadt. The fellow was educated in England. Ask Klein to come back in, please. That is, if he hasn't stomped off!"

Klein re-entered, looking apprehensively from Schumacher to Eberhart. "Yes, Herr Kapitän, Oberstleutnant?"

"Not so damn formal, Wilhelm. I was too hasty in my decision-making, as Werner has taken great pains to point out," Schumacher observed

expansively. "We have decided to authorize your plan. Operation *Highwire*; how does that sound? Now," he continued, "Werner and I need to fill you in on some highly confidential information which you may not share with anyone. *Ehrenwort*?"

"Of course, *Ehrenwort*."

"The tunnel, Operation *Kartoffel*..."

"*Kartoffel*, potato, Frederick?"

"Yes. You see, thanks to Karl Semmler's efforts, the humble potato became a symbol of our pride and self-reliance. Then, the very ground from which it was harvested provided the clue to a puzzle; namely, how to escape from the Camp to a point on the St. Lawrence River where a submarine could rendezvous and return us to the Fatherland."

"Is that what the tunnel was about, Sir?"

"Yes, Wilhelm. Briefly, through coded messages exchanged by some of the men with their relatives in Germany, a U-boat was scheduled to meet a number of men, including me, and return us to the Reich for active duty. That is, until the tunnel regrettably caved in."

"I see."

"The timing was disastrous. There is no hope of mounting another breakout by a tunnel. Worse, there isn't enough time to send a written message to Germany to cancel the rendezvous. So, yours truly would have had, as the Canadians say, egg on his face with the Admiralty. Not an enviable situation, you'll agree. Timing is everything now, and this is where your plan comes into play. Wilhelm, we need you to escape and get to the pick-up location in New Brunswick with all speed. There, you will advise the U-boat commander that we will not be arriving, and will ship out with him directly."

"That is perfect! Frederick, I know that my plan will work. I am fully confident that I can make it there in record time."

"Good. You are authorized to get started on your trolley system immediately; you'll leave in three days. Please give Werner a list of all the matériel that you will require today. The theatrical group will likely have at hand, or be able to fabricate, any unusual items called for."

"Thank you, Frederick. I won't let you down. *Ehrenwort*."

"Werner, make sure that the theatrical boys have his clothes ready for this Friday, and notify the forgery group. He'll need ID etcetera. That reminds me; Semmler has the connection for obtaining bona fide

Canadian currency. I don't want Wilhelm taking any chances of being picked up by the Mounties over a hamburger and French fries, in some wretched greasy spoon."

Eberhart smiled. "Curious, isn't it Frederick, how we've all become so Canadian in our speech, in a year or so. I'll get right on it, Herr Kapitän!" Saluting, he turned and walked out the door with Klein.

'This had better work, Gretta,' Schumacher reflected, 'or your Frederick will be retired on the pension of an *Oberfähnrich zur See*, Sub-Lieutenant, that is, if I'm not shot by the Grand Admiral himself.'

24 September 1943

Camp 30 Haus IV

"Excuse me, Frederick; Operation *Highwire* is on standby."

Setting down *Die Brücke*, the Camp's newspaper, Schumacher quickly removed his eyeglasses. "Really? Outstanding, Werner! When does he go?"

"Within the hour."

"Is everything ready? Do we need to review the plan again?" queried Schumacher uneasily. "Werner, this time we can't fail. I cannot let down the Grand Admiral. That is final."

"You...we, won't, Sir. The plan...?"

"I'm delighted that you are so confident, Werner. Think about it; the Kriegsmarine's Admiral Dönitz, sending a U-boat all the way to Canada to rescue...us!"

"Frederick, the plan!" Eberhart insisted doggedly.

"Yes, the plan. Forgive me; I am so anxious to see that this scheme works. It's extremely dangerous and Herr Kaleu Wilhelm Klein is a very brave soldier to attempt it. Now, lay it out for me again."

"Sir, the theatrical boys have done a marvellous job of constructing the bo'sun chair's pulley system."

"How does it work?" asked Schumacher.

"The pulley is carved from hardwood, designed to fit over all three electrical cables, the power lines coming into the Camp. They took rollers from the Haus windows, being careful to leave one roller in each window so that they would still open and close. They then fastened the

rollers to the pulley system and, for good measure, carved out a handle at the bottom of the pulley. A beautiful piece of handwork, if I do say so myself, Sir."

Schumacher furtively retrieved his glasses from within the folds of the newspaper. "Excellent! *Ach so, das Lager!*"

Unrolling a map of the Camp, Werner began to review the *Highwire* escape stage. "Here's the tower, Alpha, with one guard. The next one, Beta, is 100 metres away, over here, and out of that guard's line of sight: we have checked the calculations and we're certain of that. However, as luck would have it, the power line selected is very close to Alpha..."

"You said this would work!" Schumacher interrupted impatiently. "It sounds like, what do they call it, a crap shot."

"Shoot, Sir. This in effect, can and will work in our favour. The Alpha guard can only see the blind spot from where Klein will be approaching by looking directly down. We will create a diversion over here, on this side of the open field. The guard naturally will look over there and that's when Klein will make his move to the hydro pole."

"I've given my go ahead, with mis-givings and reservations, and I repeat, this is risky, very risky. Nevertheless, it just might work!" replied Schumacher pensively. "Somewhat like slipping underneath a destroyer and hiding out in her ASDIC's blind spot."

"Sir? Oh, in a U-boat! Yes, I sup-pose," Eberhart offered. "Fifteen hun-dred hour roll call is done so we won't have to worry about another headcount until 2215h..."

"That should be more than suffi-cient time for Klein to scarper," Schumacher surmised.

"Sir?"

"An English expression I picked up at Grizedale Hall from the 'screws', the

One of many guardhouses at Camp 30
Bowmanville Archives /
DND - National Archives of Canada

guards," Schumacher replied chuckling, and then growled, "Put the word out. Thirty minutes, counting, now!"

"Is everything ready, Werner?" asked Schumacher quietly.

"It is, Sir."

"Very good. Give the signal!"

Eberhart removed his cap.

On cue, Ensign Eckert yelled at the referee, "Foul, are you blind? That was a foul!"

PoW Officers stand in front of one of their Haus' – Camp 30
Volkmar König

Instantly, two opposing players attacked one another, throwing punches wildly, then four, and four more, joined in. Within seconds, the soccer game had erupted into a fully-fledged brawl. Fists flew as bodies writhed in combat on the ground.

"Stop that! Stop that fighting!" yelled a guard as he ran toward the largest pile of bodies.

Another guard shouted from the Alpha tower, "Break it up, or I'll fire!" None of the combatants paid attention.

Ensign Eckert watched Oberstleutnant Eberhart closely. As Eberhart replaced his cap on his head, Eckert bellowed at the top of his lungs, "Come on, Navy!"

Upon Eckert's rallying cry, with a small suitcase strapped to his belt, Kapitänleutnant Klein released his grip from the pole to which he had clung and slid down the power wires, dangling precariously from his handmade pulley. Just as he reached the fence, something grabbed his leg.and he came to a jarring halt.

'What the hell is it? Have the guards seen me? Am I hooked on something they put up to snag me?' With these thoughts racing through his mind, Klein looked down. The loop of his shoelace was tangled in the barbed wire. He attempted desperately to free his leg, but it wouldn't budge. 'Christ, now what?' Struggling to free himself, he began to tire. 'They'll shoot me, like a duck in a shooting gallery.' He realised that his only hope was to reach down as far as possible with one hand and undo the knot in the shoelace.

Klein glanced at the mêlée below. It was a display of go-for-broke unarmed combat, the likes of which would have made the cadet academy's drill instructors wince. The guards on the ground were receiving a thrashing while the lone guard in tower Alpha stood staring at the brouhaha, mere metres away from Klein. Reaching down, Klein stretched out his left hand but was unable to grasp the lace.

'I'm not going to make it,' he thought. Considering the alternative of plunging onto the barbed wire fence, he knew that he had to make one more try. Schumacher and Eberhart watched in grim silence. The tide of battle had turned. The guards were now gaining the upper hand and the fighters were growing exhausted. Klein knew that he had only seconds before the mayhem ended and he would be spotted.

Taking a deep breath, he reached down, cocking his leg upward. With a lunge, he tore at the shoestring, releasing the bow. With a convulsive jerk, he lurched forward. Gathering speed, the pole on the outside of the fence swiftly loomed closer. Releasing his grip at the precise point that he had calculated, re-calculated, and memorized thoroughly, Klein dropped to the ground, a dead weight. With no time to check for sprains or worse, he grabbed his bag and darted into the cornfield.

"He made it, Sir!" exclaimed Eberhart.

"Yes! Yes! Indeed he did! Now for the hard part," Schumacher commented as he turned to watch some of his men help the guards to their feet.

"Sir?"

"Making it all the way to the east coast of Canada and finding the U-boat."

Finally, Success

North Bowmanville

24 September 1943

"Honey, aren't the leaves spectacular? Look at that stand of sugar maples. Magnificent! If only your Dad's old camera could take colour photographs!"

"Uh huh, sure is!" Glen observed, distractedly.

"What is?" Brenda queried.

"Beautiful! Hey, what do we have here?" Glen interrupted noticing a male hitchhiker trudging along the shoulder. They had been leisurely driving westward for some three miles along rural Concession Street on their way to visit their son, Ryan, in Toronto.

"Glen Copithorn, surely you're not thinking about stopping to give this fellow a lift! Not after all the warnings on the radio and in the news-papers about Nazi spies, or escaped PoWs on the loose?"

"He doesn't look like a bad guy, now does he, Bren? Probably some kind of travelling salesman. The guy's likely in some sort of trouble: his generator's on the fritz, the rad's blown, or he's run out of gas. Hang on; this'll just take a sec." Slowing down, Glen steered the 1937 Oldsmobile onto the gravel shoulder and drew up close to the man walking with his thumb held high in the air. "Say, can we give you a lift somewhere?"

"Oh, yes, thank you. I'm having a terrible day!" the hitchhiker replied, shaking his head in dismay.

"Hop in the back!"

"What's the trouble?" Brenda asked.

"My auto broke down back there."

"Huh, I didn't see one," Glen observed.

"It's a long way back; I've been walking for over an hour."

"Oh you poor man! Here, have some cookies. I'm taking them to my son. He only eats well when his mother visits," Brenda laughed.

"Thank you very much, madam."

"Brenda is my name, and this is my husband Glen."

"My name is Hans, Hans Vanderburg."

"Where can we drop you Hans, a gas station?" asked Glen edging the Oldsmobile back onto Concession Street.

"No. No thank you, I'm going into Toronto, back to my hotel."

"Well, what about your car?" asked Brenda.

"I locked it, so it will be fine for tonight. My partner will drive me out in the morning and we'll have a wrecker pull it back," replied Klein.

"You mean, 'towed back by a tow truck'? Whereabouts is your hotel?"

"Yes, sorry, towed...by a tow truck. The Royal York, Glen."

Glen and Brenda glanced at each other. "That's a pretty fancy establishment, Hans," remarked Brenda.

"Yes, I'm here on business from Montreal. It was the only hotel name I could remember when I was...booking it," replied Klein.

"Well, Hans, you're in luck. We're going to Toronto to see our son, Ryan. He's staying in a rooming house near the University of Toronto. It's kind of a dump, if you ask me, but he says he loves it, eh Bren? Kids! Most weekends we bring him grub and Bren cooks a good Sunday dinner."

Klein nodded and sat in silence for the remainder of the long drive. As they rounded the corner of Yonge Street onto Front, within two blocks of the Royal York Hotel, he spoke up. "This will be close enough, thank you. I can walk."

"Nonsense, we'll drop you right at the door," Glen stated firmly.

"No, no, this is very good. I can use the exercise," Klein insisted, smiling.

"Alright, if you're sure. You've walked a heck of a long way already, but whatever you wish. Here you go, Hans," replied Glen as he pulled up to the curb under the watchful gaze of a bicycle-mounted policeman.

Klein stepped out, thanked them graciously, and closed the car's rear door. When the traffic light turned green, Klein craned his head to the right to ensure that the Copithorn's car was out of sight, and then stepped off the sidewalk directly into the path of a horse-drawn milk wagon rounding the corner.

"Hey, are you some kind of idiot?" the driver shouted. Klein stepped back onto the curb and waved the cart past. The mounted policeman wheeled up, dismounted, leaned the left handle grip against the lamp-post, and reached into his breast pocket. "Are you alright, Sir?"

"Yes, I am fine, thank you, officer, Sir."

Undeterred, the policeman retrieved his whistle on its white lanyard and blew one short sharp blast, whereupon the milk cart sped up. "Stop! Stop I say!" The cart continued westward, rocking on its springs while the bicycle slowly slid backward and clattered onto the sidewalk.

"Stay right here, sir. I'm charging that gentleman with a range of offences: failure to yield to a pedestrian, failure to obey an officer of the law and maybe a lot more! I'll need to take down your statement," he shouted to Klein as he scrambled to resurrect and remount his bike, preparing to give hot pursuit.

'Get out of here, now, Willy!' Klein reflected grimly. The next minute passed agonizingly slowly until, on the green light, Klein bowed his head and struck out across Front Street, then slowed to a medium pace to avoid drawing attention, and continued on to the entrance of Union Station.

He walked into the cathedral-like marble grand hall and looked up at the ornate brass clock resting on its pedestal. 'Damn, 1750h! It must be close to closing time.' The small muscles in his face and neck contracted spasmodically, pulling down the corners of his mouth into a grimace. 'Breath, now again.... good.' "Excuse me, madam, are you open?"

"Closing in ten minutes." The ticket agent, visibly aggravated by this 'square' male who interrupted her reading of *Screen Romances*, looked back down at the page, cracking her chewing gum, and then with exquisite timing, set down the magazine deliberately. In authentic Central Ontario nasal, she inquired, "Can I help you?" as she tugged at her right earring.

"I'd like a ticket to Montreal, please."

"One way, or return?" inquired Miss Monotone.

"Return, please."

"Returning...?"

"Sorry..."

Drawing a deep breath, she leaned far forward in her booth, exposing her ample cleavage. "When...will...you...be... returning?"

"Is that important?" asked Klein, blushing. 'It has been a long time. A very long time,' Klein recollected fleetingly.

"Not to me, sweetie, but I have to ask you see, 'cause there's a price increase on, let me see. Yeah, thought so...November First. That will affect the price of the round trip." Her declaration was punctuated with a.22 calibre chewing gum pistol shot.

"Oh I see. Well, I'm returning on the twenty-eighth."

"September, right? Thank you, that makes life a lot easier. The next train to Montreal leaves tomorrow at 10:13 a.m., E.D.S.T. That's Eastern...Daylight...Saving...Time. Know what?" she posed with an air of intimacy, "You should get here early 'cause there's usually a fair number of soldiers heading to the East coast on that one. It'll be crowded up to the eyeballs.

"I hope you won't take this personally, but you have a nice accent, like that actor, oh, the dangerous-looking foreign guy. Some girls like that dangerous look. He always plays a creepy Gestapo officer. You're taller and don't have a moustache, though. What's his name? I'm losing my marbles. Is it Danish or something?"

"Is what Danish, sorry?"

"Your accent."

The cloying aroma of her cheap perfume reminded Klein of the occasional beery and boisterous nights in town with his classmates while at the U-boat academy. "Oh, no, it's Dutch, thanks." He fished the fare from his billfold, thinking, 'Wonderful, a train full of soldiers'. "Thank you for your help. Any good restaurants around here?" he asked, tucking the tickets into his wallet.

"Sure," she answered tentatively, as though withholding her personal bank account number. "Whatcha looking for?"

"Just a bite."

"That's cute. Okay, go back out to Front. You know where that is, right? Then scoot to your left and walk a long block. Not fancy schmancy, but it's homey!"

"Thank you." Walking out onto Front Street Klein followed her directions until he spotted a small eatery. Entering the front door, he was assailed by the pungent odours of fried onions and cooking grease.

A young waitress wearing a yellow and white uniform with 'Millie' embroidered on the left breast pocket was applying lipstick using a chrome napkin holder as a mirror. "Hi, what'll it be?" she asked, her lips drawn into a crimson bow. "It's up there!" She indicated the menu posted behind her with a slight tilt of her head.

"A hamburger please, with onions."

"It doesn't come regular with onions; that's two cents extra, hon," she replied agreeably. "They're included in the Double Deluxe with the cheese."

"Okay then," he replied, adding, "I'll have the Double Deluxe." He noted that she was chewing gum, but without the voluptuous ticket agent's gratuitous sound effects.

"Sure. Anything to drink?"

"Yes, a coffee please."

"Got that George?" she called through to an invisible cook. "Double D."

"I'm on my break, Millie! Five more minutes!"

"He's so grouchy! It'll be ready in a jif. Cream?" As she bent forward to pour his coffee, Klein noted the similarity between 'Millie' and the ticket agent, notwithstanding the latter's more athletic gum chewing. Although Millie was slender, her uniform barely concealed an ample and youthful body. Her hands were slim, delicate, and her fingernails well manicured, coloured a paler shade than her lips. Klein estimated her age as no more than twenty-five, a year younger than he.

"Do you want to read the paper?"

"Sorry?"

"Newspaper. I have a *Star* under the counter. Would you like to read it?"

"Yes, please." When Klein looked at the front page of the *Toronto Daily Star*, he was fascinated by the absence of blacked-out columns, pictures or articles. 'Good! Well now, what's this?

'Manpower Crisis Looms in Britain

Britain is running out of manpower. "Another 700,000 workers are needed next year, despite the mobilization of some 22,750,000 already," said the Minister of Labour, Ernest Bevin, today. The recruiting of women into the services will virtually stop and they will be diverted into industry. Boys and girls aged sixteen and seventeen will be placed in aircraft factories. Surface coal workers are being sent below, and cotton operatives fifty-five and under will return to work in the mills.

'Incredibly stupid! Wouldn't someone like to know about that back home,' he thought.

"Say, what are you doing in this place on a Saturday night; don't you and your girlfriend have somewhere to go?"

Klein shrugged. "No girlfriend, unfortunately; I am here alone."

"My name is Milena Kona, but my friends call me Millie. What's yours?"

"Hans, Hans Vanderburg."

"Pleased to meet you, Hans. What's that accent you've got?"

"Dutch, I'm originally from Holland. I'm just on my way back to Montreal. And yours?"

"Albanian. My family fled our country in 1939. So far, Italy, Greece, and just this month the Nazis have invaded it. Thank God, we made it to Canada. Wasn't Holland taken over...?"

"Yes, in May 1940. We got out just before the country surrendered."

"I don't know who I hate most. Probably all three, equally," she commented, adding loudly, "except you, George!" laughing.

"I love all Albanians, especially you, Milena darling!" came back a disembodied reply.

"The old lecher. So, Hans, what brings you to Toronto?"

"I was visiting my mother. She hasn't been too well; I'm making arrangements to have her come to Montreal with me so that she can be looked after better," replied Klein.

"That is very sweet of you. I like a man who respects his parents," she commented softly. "And what do you do, besides worrying about your mom?"

"Well, I'm not working at the moment. I tried to sign up for the army but I didn't pass my physical examination, a complication to do with my lungs. I have to report to the enlistment office when I get back to Montreal to see if they have found a desk job for me."

"That would be good for you and for your mom, unless you're sent someplace far away, like Winnipeg."

"Some things you just have to do during these times. Millie, do you know where a YMCA is to be found?"

"More coffee? YMCA, whatever for?"

"Yes, please. I was to return to Montreal today by train but I was late, so now I have to rest here overnight and catch it at 00...at ten o'clock tomorrow morning."

"Then why can't you stay at your mother's house, Hans?"

'Think carefully, Willy.' "You see, there isn't one anymore, because...she has been in the hospital for such a long time and lost everything...including her small apartment."

"Oh, I can believe that! Thank heavens my landlord's a sweetie!" she exclaimed, clasping her hands to her breast. "His wife's another story. If you can wait thirty-five minutes, I get off at eight. Why don't you come to my place? You can sleep on the couch."

Her words, her closeness, and the subtle scent of her cologne were making Klein's head spin. "Oh! Oh, no, I couldn't do that, Millie," he uttered shyly.

"Of course you can! When I look at what you're going through for your mother, it's the least I can do. I have a cozy apartment over on Shuter Street. It's a fair hike up Yonge. We could take the 'red rocket', but the weather is so nice."

"This is so kind of you! I'm forever indebted to you, Millie! How much does my meal cost?"

"Forever is a mighty long time, Hans," she replied, coyly pressing the blunt end of her pencil to her lower lip. "Don't worry, it's on the house; George won't mind...will you, George!"

"I can't hear you, Millie, what?"

"I said don't worry, George, it's only a mouse!" she shouted, giggling.

"What, that little beady-eyed bugger again? Where is he?"

"Likely safe in the cellar by now! Good night, I'm leaving.... early!"

"Sure, sure, so what else is new?" he muttered. "Six tomorrow morning, Millie, and don't be late! No excuses!"

"Don't get your shorts in a knot," she muttered. "Okay, okay, I'll be here you old goat!"

Strolling up Yonge Street, Hans and Mila stopped to admire the department stores' large display windows before crossing Yonge at Shuter. "This is beautiful. So many things!"

"Pretty snazzy, isn't it?" she agreed. "I don't know anyone who can afford this stuff. You should see the displays at Christmastime, Hans, with Santa and his elves actually skating on a rink, the reindeer bobbing up and down, and all the fantastic toys! Hard to believe there's a war on!"

"Millie, what is this 'red rocket' you mentioned, please?"

"That is!" she announced, pointing, as a sleek red and yellow trolley

car clanged its arrival at the intersection. "Pretty nifty, eh? No one in Toronto calls them anything but, as far as I know. Okay, light's green. Let's go, mister!" she exclaimed, taking his arm.

As they walked along Shuter Street, Klein silently prayed they would not encounter the angry policeman. "My, that is a big hospital!" he remarked.

"Good one, too, St. Mike's. Here we are, up these steps. That was fast! It seems a lot closer when you have someone to talk with." Millie took her passkey from her purse and unlocked the front door. As they walked across the hall, they heard the sound of creaking floorboards and glanced up at the landing.

"Evening, Mrs. Delaney. It's just my brother visiting from Vancouver. Have a nice evening."

"She's the landlord's wife...has to know everybody's comings and goings, but she's harmless," Millie whispered outside her apartment door. "Welcome to my inner sanctum. Come in and make yourself at home. Kitchen's on your left; there's a beer in the fridge, opener in the drawer, far right and glasses over the sink. Help yourself. I'll be right back after I change out of this uniform."

Klein sat on the three-seater chesterfield, looked around the neatly kept apartment, and then peered out the window. There were very few people in the street. 'Wonder why? Are they expecting an air raid?'

"Hi there!" Millie stood at the entrance to the living room in a pink and white flowered kimono.

Klein half rose. "You, you look... charming!" he blurted. Her medium-blonde hair, pulled back severely and rolled into a bun at the nape of her neck just moments before, now caressed the white skin of her shoulders.

"Why thank you, Hans. Can I get you something? Another beer, cheese and crackers, a sandwich? I haven't bought groceries for two weeks. Come, let's have a look at Mother Hubbard's cupboard," she purred, holding out her hand invitingly.

As they walked into the tiny kitchen, Klein noted that the material of her robe made a whispering sound as it rubbed across her thighs. "An apple would be fine. Just a slice or two..."

"And some crackers and a few chunks of this old cheddar. How does that sound? Don't go away, I'll make up a plate and we can have a little feast! Here, try this cheese. It's Canadian...the best in the world! Close your eyes, and open wide!"

Klein was unprepared for the kiss. It was warm, deep, and lingering. Instinctively, he drew back.

"Oh, oh, did I frighten you?" she asked, feigning alarm.

"Oh, no, just a little bit surprised," he responded timidly. "It was lovely, truly! I'd very much like to do it again!"

'My god, her breasts, her mouth, her skin, her scent, she is so incredibly desirable and I am such a scoundrel for what I am thinking!'

"Hold that thought and this plate, and come with me, mister!"

25 September 1943 0833h

Klein awoke with a start, the fire raging uncontrollably in the U-boat's engine room. He opened his eyes and abruptly sat up, disoriented. The sunlight shining in the mirror of the dressing bureau at the foot of the bed reflected directly in his face. Slowly he turned to the right to see a depression in the bedclothes. "Millie!" He looked at his watch: 0833. 'Shit, she's gone to work! What a night! Get going, Dummkopf, or you'll miss the bloody train again!'

He climbed out of bed and went into the bathroom. Fastened to the mirror with a piece of clear tape was a handwritten note:

Hans: Use this razor and shaving cream (they were my dad's, honest!) and help yourself to anything else-not that you seemed to need an invitation (ahem)! Had a delightful night, do come by next time you're in town! Good luck with your mom! P.S. The front door will lock behind you when you close it tightly.

Fondly,

Millie.

Klein smiled as he read. He quickly showered, shaved, and dressed, all in less than ten minutes. His clothes, thrown in a heap on the floor the night before, were now laid out neatly on the seat of the single bedroom chair. His train tickets lay on the bureau and he picked them up, placing them carefully in his shirt pocket. Slipping on his jacket, he went out, closing the apartment door noiselessly. His eyes rose very slowly to the top of the stairs. Mrs. Delaney glared down.

"Must catch the train to Vancouver, Mrs. Delaney!" 'Christ! That's

all I need, for her to call the police.' "Goodbye!" Klein quickly walked out the front door and stood on the top step, confused. 'Which way? I can't remember. There's someone who looks as if he should know.' A well-dressed man had come out of St. Michael's Hospital and was crossing Shuter Street, directly across from the apartment. Klein made a split second assessment and hurried down the steps. "Excuse me, Doctor. Can you please direct me to Union Station?"

For a moment, the man was taken aback. "Certainly, my good man. Simply follow this street, Shuter, west over to Yonge Street and then go south, left. Walk straight down to Front Street and turn right. You can't miss it. It's across the street. Alternately, you can take a streetcar."

"Thank you, Doctor," replied Klein and turned to walk away. 'Streetcar, not the 'red rocket'. That's one, Millie!' he reflected.

"Have I treated you recently in the clinic, young man?" the doctor inquired.

Klein paused, and responded with a smile, "No, I don't believe so, Doctor. Why?"

"I'm curious to know how you knew my profession."

"Just a lucky guess, Doctor," Klein replied deferentially. "May I ask what you treat there?"

"I'm a specialist in the social diseases: gonorrhoea, syphilis, chlamydia, the lot."

"That must be...very interesting," Klein replied politely, glancing anxiously toward Yonge Street.

"Yes, but I see far too many young people like you these days, and every single case preventable," he remarked. "Take care. Good luck, young man."

"I will. Thank you. And a good day to you, Doctor!"

With his eyes averted, Klein strode rapidly past the ticket booth. He kept walking until he reached the schedule callboard, then looked up to find the platform number. Boarding a coach at the rear of the train, Klein noted that men in Canadian Army and Navy uniforms far outnumbered civilians, just as the ample agent had predicted. Kapitänleutnant Klein selected the last remaining seat at the rear of the car. As instructed by Eberhart, he had deliberately chosen to travel by coach rather than in

Finally, Success

First Class, Toronto to Montreal, and had not purchased a fare from Toronto to New Brunswick to avoid drawing unwanted attention. Although Klein was sure that the agent would remember him, a slip up which he regretted, he was pleased at how smoothly things were progressing overall, and at how effortlessly he had blended in. For some reason, he reflected, his encounter with Millie did not cause similar misgivings. Idly, he wondered if the Camp's guards were aware by now that he was missing.

"Tickets, tickets, have your tickets ready please," announced the conductor. "Tickets, sir!"

"Yes, of course," Klein replied handing over the ticket. "Do they serve meals, Sir?"

"Not in this car. You have to go up to the parlour car, three forward. Keep your stub. Tickets, tickets, please."

"Thank you." Following the example of his fellow passengers, Klein attached the stub of his ticket in the clasp of the window shade then made his way forward to the parlour car, through a series of adjoining doors. Entering the diner, he sat down at the nearest empty table.

"Coffee, sir?"

"Yes, thank you. In fact, I would like breakfast; I'm very hungry. How much is it?"

"Twenty-five cents, with coffee," answered the waiter.

"Twenty-five cents," repeated Klein as he reached for his billfold. "A minute... Christ, my wallet!"

"Sir, such godless profanity is unacceptable!" the waiter asserted piously. "Kindly stop now or leave this car immediately!"

"But my wallet, my wallet is gone!" cried Klein as he fumbled through his jacket pockets. "I have a ten cent piece in my trouser pocket, that's all."

"Well, sir, for that I can give you one egg, toast and coffee; no sausages or bacon. I'm sorry."

"That would be fine, thank you very much." Kapitänleutnant Klein ate hurriedly. As he drank his coffee, he looked out the window at the Canadian countryside, wondering where, how and when he had misplaced his billfold. 'Maybe *Herr Doktor* was a phoney, a pickpocket,' he reflected, smiling in spite of himself. Leaving the dime along with an apologetic, 'Sorry. And Thank You' scrawled on the bill, Klein returned to

his coach and lulled by the rhythmic rocking of the train, promptly fell asleep.

"Montreal! Montreal, next stop! Montreal."

Stepping down from the train, Klein moved through the throngs toward the nearest ticket booth. "May I have a ticket to Bathurst, New Brunswick please?"

"*Aller et retour, monsieur*? Round trip, Sir?"

"No, just one way. I'm staying at my sister's for a while."

"*Douze dollars, s'il vous plâit.* That will be twelve dollars please," said the elderly agent.

"*Excuse*, would it be possible to cash in my return ticket to Toronto for a ticket to Bathurst? You see, I've lost my wallet and I won't be able to get any money until I get to my sister's home in Bathurst," pleaded Kapitänleutnant Klein.

"Yes, I suppose so. It works out about the same," he stated with a shrug. "Too bad though. I hope that you find it. Your change, *monsieur.*"

"Thank you very much, *monsieur*. What time does the train leave?"

"Four this afternoon. You have plenty of time."

"Thank you again," Klein said, picking up and pocketing the money. Walking nonchalantly to a bench in the middle of the station hall, he sat down and picked two newspapers, one in French and the other in English. He again noted how wonderful and exciting it was to read about events in the war without the censors' blackouts defacing every page.

Russians Recapture Bastion of Smolensk shouted the headline in *The Gazette*. Klein, absorbed in reading the reports from the fronts, did not hear the first two notices, in both French and English, regarding the loading of the train to Bathurst. Then, "Final call for Bathurst," boomed over the public address system, at last drawing his attention away from the papers.

'Damn!' he thought as he broke into a run for the boarding platform, his suitcase flapping awkwardly from side to side. He could see the conductor hanging out of the last passenger car as the train started to roll down the tracks.

"Hurry up, son!" shouted the conductor as Klein closed in on the accelerating train. "Here, take my hand."

"Thank you very much." Klein pulled himself up using the conductor's arm.

"That was close, young man! You almost missed the train."

"Thanks to you, I didn't," Klein panted. "Here's my ticket."

"Very good. Coach is this way. There are few empty seats. Please make yourself comfortable."

Klein walked down the aisle until he found an unoccupied window seat. Settling in, he curled up in the corner and soon fell asleep once more.

"Sir? Sir!"

Klein awoke with a start.

"Sir, we'll be coming into Bathurst in a couple of hours. Would you like something to eat first? All of the others have already eaten, but you were in such a deep sleep that I didn't want to disturb you."

"I would love something to eat but I have very little money. My wallet was stolen in Montreal," Klein confessed.

"Let me see what I can do," the Porter replied cheerfully. A few minutes later, he returned with a tray full of food. "Here you go sir," he announced, setting the tray down in front of Klein.

"But I have no money. I have no way of paying for this."

The Porter leaned over. "Son, I'll let you in on a little secret. By tomorrow, this food will be day old, meaning that we can't serve it. It will be sold by the pound when we get to Bathurst, where it will likely go to feeding some livestock. I'd much rather see it go to you, sir," he added kindly.

"Well, I can't thank you enough! This is extremely thoughtful of you," replied Klein, genuinely moved.

"My pleasure; you just enjoy, sir. I was down on my luck during the Depression, like so many others. It was the kindness of strangers that I most remember. You know how often it came out of nowhere, unexpected-like? And I vowed to pay it back. Can you use a fiver, sir? Not meaning to offend."

"No, I, I'll be fine. But thank you," Klein stammered, overcome by this humble man's generosity. He looked at the tray in front of him and

shook his head, seeing two large sandwiches, an apple, two oatmeal cookies, and a half pint of milk.

After enjoying the lunch, Klein settled back for a relaxing read of the local papers. Lulled by the gentle swaying of the coach and rhythmic click of the wheels, he drifted off once again. Klein was jolted awake as the Conductor strode through the car announcing, "Bathurst! Next stop, Bathurst!"

"Bathurst coming up. Best get ready. It's a short stop, sir!" the Porter advised.

Klein got out of his seat. "I can't thank you enough. Someday I will make it up to you," he declared.

"No need to, sir. Happy to help; have a nice stay."

Klein stepped down from the train, suitcase in hand. Walking into the station, he looked around for a tourist centre or information booth. 'Aha, over there.'

"Excuse me madam. Would you have a map of the region?"

"Yes, sir. Where are you headed?"

"My sister lives at Maisonette Point, and I'm off to visit her," Klein replied.

"This map should help; it shows an enlargement of this area. We're here." The woman pointed to the map. "This is Chaleur Bay, and here's Maisonette Point, near Caraquet."

"How far is it, please?" inquired Klein.

"Mmm, roughly thirty miles," she replied. "Give or take."

'Fifty kilometres,' he thought. "What's the best route to take?"

"Highway Eight. You can catch it just outside of town. Here," she replied, pointing at the map.

"Thank you very much, madam. I think I've got it."

"Well, take the map; that's what they're here for. It's a long walk, son. Just a jiffy." Reaching under the counter, she produced a small, flat, wax paper-wrapped package. "You might enjoy this along the way," she replied, smiling. "It's maple fudge; my grandmother's recipe from Quebec. It always takes first prize at the local fairs. Here, take it!"

"You are too kind! Thanks very much," said Klein, thinking again how friendly and kind ordinary Canadians were.

Bidding her goodbye, Klein left the station. By now it was getting dark. Hesitating, he decided that it would be best to wait until the next morning and leave at daybreak. Besides, he was a day ahead of schedule and would likely have to wait a full day for the U-boat.

He went back into the terminal and asked for directions to the nearest YMCA where he was given a hot meal and a bed for the night.

26 September 1943

The next morning, Klein got up then went down for breakfast. Afterwards, he started out on the final leg of his journey to Maisonette Point and the point of rendezvous with the U-boat. Walking out into the bright sunshine, he pulled out his map and looked for Highway 8 East. It appeared to start about two kilometres outside of town.

Klein headed out toward the highway. After walking for half an hour, he was assured by the sign reading **Maisonette Point - 32 Miles** that he was, in fact, headed in the right direction. Realizing that he couldn't walk the entire distance, he decided to put out his thumb and try hitchhiking.

Some time later, a truck slowed down, then stopped on the shoulder ahead of him. As the truck backed up, Klein ran ahead to meet it.

"Where you headed, fella?" asked the driver.

"Maisonette Point. Are you going that way?"

"Close by. I can drop you off just a mile or two away. All you'll have to do then is walk straight down the road. It'll take you directly to the Point," the man replied. "Hop in!"

"I'm very grateful," Klein remarked as the truck got underway. "I couldn't help but notice the nets and wooden cages in the back of your truck. Are you a fisherman?"

"That I am, boyo. A lobsterman. Lookin' for a job?" he asked. "Hard slogging, but dependin' on the haul, it can be well worth the effort, money-wise. The American brokers pay top dollar for my catches. Them rich folks in New York, Boston, and the like consider 'em a delicacy. Interested?"

"Oh, you know, I'm just not up to it. But thanks. I received a deferment from the government because of my heart. A murmur. Something's wrong with a...a valve. I can't handle heavy work," Klein stated forlornly.

"Well, that's a shame. I could use a healthy young fella on the boat about now. All the able-bodied lads hereabouts picked up and joined the service. Well, here we are. You go easy now, boyo."

Thanking his benefactor, Klein began walking the final two miles to the coast. After a forty-five minute walk, Klein realized that he had made it to his destination. He had travelled all the way from Camp 30 Bowmanville, Ontario, to the coast of New Brunswick. 'Before long, I'll be back to the war!' he exulted.

CHAPTER 11

CLEVER CANADIANS

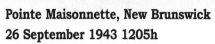

Pointe Maisonnette, New Brunswick
26 September 1943 1205h

Klein's heart raced with excitement as the gravel trail that he had been following now gave way to pebbles and sand. Savouring the first tang of brine on the brisk, south westerly sea air, he breathed, "This is where I belong!"

Painfully, he acknowledged how intensely he missed his command. He remembered the exhilarating, bitter kiss of ocean spray, as he stood on the bridge of his U-boat, conning her through the fierce chop of a North Atlantic squall.

Overhead, in the intensely blue sky, an astonishing variety of seabirds mewed. Soaring, dipping and gliding, they executed sudden, acrobatic plummets to the waves, and then soared again, their beaks brimming with herring.

Puzzled, Klein hesitated. Perhaps he had slipped-up; there was no lighthouse to be seen. Five hundred metres in the distance, he counted two pairs of soldiers patrolling the beach in front of a square, two-storey, white clapboard building. 'This is odd! Why are they here, in the middle of nowhere? There's only one possible explanation, Wilhelm. They not only know about the U-boat, but they're expecting you. Damn it all!'

Using a tall patch of sedge grass for cover, Klein crept forward, pausing every few seconds to reconnoitre the beach and the area surrounding the structure. Deciding that it was too dangerous to draw any closer, he turned eastward and scuttled away from the soldiers. Scouting a secluded stretch of shoreline, he selected an isolated row of sand dunes. There he found a suitably shaped piece of driftwood with which he began digging furiously. Soon he had excavated a shallow foxhole and, satisfied with his handiwork, climbed into his dugout.

Finding the remains of the fudge in his jacket pocket, he settled back to munch on it and to wait for U-536F. As Wilhelm drifted off to sleep, he thought about sweet Mila and he smiled. 'When the war is over...'

Pointe Maisonnette
26 September 1943 1600h

"How long do you think it will be, Commissioner?" asked Robert Brooks. "Sandwich, anyone?"

"Thanks, Rob. I'll have one. It won't be long. Our boys have Kapitänleutnant Klein under close surveillance," replied RCMP Commissioner Ted Reynolds. "He's sound asleep in a trench on the beach, at present."

"Good for him. What's the situation in the Bay of Chaleur, Commander?" Brooks inquired.

"Thanks to you BSO chaps, we know every detail of Dönitz' rescue plan, Operation Kiebitz. Kapitänleutnant Langer's U-536F is in place, here, in Chaleur Bay," he emphasized, pointing to the U-boat's coordinates on a navigational chart. "The Canadian Navy has been tracking the U-536's movements electronically from Langer's point of entry into the Gulf of St. Lawrence. However, we're not ready to show our hand, as yet. I have a flotilla consisting of one destroyer, three corvettes, and five

Bangor minesweepers on his tail. That fellow is not going anywhere," replied Lieutenant Commander Stephen Spence. "With any luck at all, we'll not only bag Klein, but the U-boat, into the bargain."

"Let's hope so. For now, it's a game of nerves; who will blink first," Robert Brooks commented.

"Hurry up and wait," Spence added. "As soon as darkness sets in, Klein will undoubtedly make an attempt to signal the U-boat, or vice-versa," continued Commander Spence. "It is imperative that your men be on high alert, Commissioner."

"The men are dispersed, as directed, along the beachfront. They'll be watching the water all night looking for visuals," Reynolds queried.

"Speaking of submarines, Commander, that was quite the raid carried out on the German battleship, *Tirpitz*!" Brooks stated.

"I didn't hear about it. Where? What happened? That is, if it's not confidential, you two!" Reynolds queries.

"Up in Norway, on September 22," Brooks volunteered. "Can you say anything more, Commander?"

"I don't know a great deal. The Jerries have already admitted that it happened. The 46,000-ton *Tirpitz*, along with her sister-ship raiders, has been a bogeyman, a constant threat to Allied shipping, since she was commissioned in 1941. She just sat there in the fjord, lying in wait. Hadn't ventured out for dog's years. Nonetheless, her very presence eats up our scarce convoy escort resources. Did you know that Prime Minister Churchill referred to *Tirpitz* as 'The Beast'?" That should give you some idea of the importance that he placed upon her destruction.

"The PM's flair for picturesque language was right on the mark again," Brooks added.

"Indeed. *Tirpitz* was attacked at anchor in Altafjord, Norway, by a classified number of Royal Navy midget subs, X-craft," he continued, smiling. "Apparently the charges produced a blast so massive that it lifted *Tirpitz'* stern six feet out of the water."

"That is amazing! And was she sunk?" Reynolds asked.

"Disabled, yes, but to the best of my knowledge, no, not sunk," replied Spence.

"And you're not going to tell me, Robert, are you? Were the crews...?" asked Reynolds.

"Were they what?"

"Were they trained at your facility?"

"That, my friend would be confidential," Brooks stated. "And I'm surprised that you asked, Commissioner!" he added sharply.

"We do need to catch this U-boat though, Ted. It's imperative. Commander Spence and our boys have put a lot of planning into Operation *Pointe Maisonnette*. It's vital. Just the other day twenty U-boats attacked our convoys, ONS-18 and ON-202, with devastating results."

"Which were?" asked Reynolds.

"Tell him, please, Commander."

"We lost 36,000 tons of merchant shipping with three of our escorts sunk."

"And the Germans?" Ted inquired.

"Three U-boats sunk and three badly damaged," Spence replied.

"That hardly seems equal."

"It's not," Robert stated emphatically, "which is why we have to get this U-boat. Right, Commander?"

Spence nodded silently in agreement, and then looked up from his chart. "Someone's at the door."

"I'll get it.

"Major Higgins, come in," Robert Brooks invited.

"Mind if I join the party? It's damn chilly out there!"

Maisonette Point
27 September 1943 1915h

"That's it. Nice and gentle, Fritz. Up these stairs you go," urged the private, jabbing the point of his bayonet into the small of Klein's back.

Klein paused and turned, staring coldly into the face of the Canadian soldier. "That was not called for, Private." He held his gaze for a split second longer then turned again and began to climb the wooden staircase. Initially shaken when taken by surprise, Klein had by now regained his composure. 'So this is a Canadian lighthouse? Not like the ones in the pictures,' he reflected.

When they had reached the top of the lighthouse, the soldier knocked on the door.

"Sir, Private MacKnight. Permission to enter?"

"Come in, Private," Higgins snapped.

Brooks looked from Reynolds, then to Higgins and finally, to Spence, all of whose faces were ashen.

"Major, I found this fellow hiding in a trench, down the beach a ways, eastward," Private MacKnight declared proudly.

"Major Higgins, I thought I said, 'observe'," Reynolds replied stonily.

"So you did, Commissioner. I'll find out what happened, Sir.

"Private, I want to talk with you. Outside!" Major Harry Higgins strode to the door. "Not tomorrow. Now, Private!" They exited; the door slammed shut.

"Kapitänleutnant Wilhelm Klein, I presume?" Brooks began.

Although prepared by Eberhart for such a contingency, Klein's composure wavered briefly. "No, Sir. With respect, but you are mistaken. My name is Captain Hans Vanderburg, formerly with the Royal Canadian Engineers. I am on secondment to Imperial Electric."

"I see. And do tell us, if you would, exactly why a former Captain of the RCE's is found lying asleep in a trench, on this godforsaken beach, at 1900?" Brooks persisted. "Classified war work, is it? Studying the tides I suppose?"

"Actually, Sir. That is quite close to the truth..."

"And that would be?" Reynolds interjected, struggling to keep a straight face.

"I'm developing anti-submarine warfare apparatus for the Royal Canadian Navy," Klein replied in a confidential tone. "I was carrying out a wave motion analysis. Beyond that, I can't say. Sorry."

Brooks, Reynolds, and Spence stood in shocked silence. 'This guy is good, damn good,' thought Robert. "And as the private took you unawares, you panicked and inadvertently left your notepad on the beach. Very well then, Captain Vanderburg. I'm sure that you won't mind emptying your pockets for us.

"I suppose it doesn't matter whether I mind or not," Kapitänleutnant Klein responded composedly.

"Let's see now: some Canadian coins, papers, and English coins.

What are you doing with English coins?" Reynolds asked, examining the contents casually.

Klein stared out the window.

"Ted, a word please? Outside?"

"Yes, of course, Robert."

"What did you notice, Ted?"

"His RCE papers are very, very good typographically, but an obvious forgery. Look at the ink smudge on my index finger. It's faint, but unmistakably it was made of an inferior dye."

"Okay. We cannot let on where he went wrong. He'll take it straight back to Camp 30 and feed it to Schumacher and on to the *Abwehr*. Agreed? And enough game playing?"

"Agreed."

"Kapitänleutnant Klein, who prepared your papers for you?" Robert Brooks continued, offhandedly.

Klein continued to stare out the window in silence.

"Fine, Kapitänleutnant. Do you recognize this, perhaps?" Brooks held up Klein's wallet.

Klein glanced at Brooks, swallowed, and then looked away, in silence. Brooks noticed that the veins in Klein's temple were pulsating. After a lengthy silence, he spoke softly, as though talking aloud to himself, "My wallet, but how...? The girl, Mila, Millie! But she couldn't have been involved. I went into that shitty restaurant purely by chance!"

"Yes, you did, Wilhelm. But you see; my people were following you. From the time you alighted from Copithorns' Oldsmobile, went to the ticket booth at Union Station, and on to the restaurant, you were cooked."

"Even Mila?"

"Even Mila/Millie, old man. Sorry. I can't say how exactly, except when you went into the restaurant, she was already there."

"*Verdammt*! George, in the back! Bloody hell! That was you!" Klein exclaimed.

"Really, Kapitänleutnant Klein, you are making a rather large assumption," Robert replied. "I must say that your three years of education in England has paid off in spades. Your command of the language is, shall I say, impressive. Anything that you wish to contribute?"

"For what purpose? You say that you know who I am, and where I'm from, so, why not take me back? There is nothing further to say."

"Does that mean that you will not cooperate with us, Kapitänleutnant?" asked Reynolds.

"I have nothing to say," Klein confirmed.

"Ted? Commander, may I have a minute with you both?" asked Robert.

"Certainly."

"He's not going to give an inch, much less send false messages to the U-boat," Robert confided. It's not as though he's facing the rope. He knows damn well that the most he will do is twenty-eight days in solitary.

"If only that soldier hadn't brought him in. Until then, we stood a good chance of Klein sending the signal to Langer on his own...."

"And enticing the 536 into shore," added Commander Spence.

"Yes. I'm sure that Harry Higggins is as sore as the devil about that, too. Poor old Private MacKnight. What now?" asked Reynolds.

"Have Klein locked up in a paddy wagon, handcuffed, and sent back to Bathurst tonight, heavily guarded." Brooks ordered, then added as an afterthought, "I think it would be wise to arrange some additional backup with Higgins.

"Not by train, Ted. I don't want to read in the morning paper how 'the plucky Kapitänleutnant dove daringly out of a coach window', like the local hero, Von Werra. Return him to Camp 30 soonest. Oh, and insist that Jack Armstrong assume full responsibility for his transportation and safe arrival at Bowmanville.

"As far as Langer is concerned, it's tonight or never. Do you agree, Commander?"

Maisonette Point
27 September 1943 2200h

Brooks, Spence, and a Royal Canadian Navy signals Ensign stood on the beach, waiting and watching for any sign of U-536F. At 215930hours, Commander Spence broke silence. "Is the message clearly understood, Ensign?"

"Understood, Commander."

"Ready?"

"Ready, Commander."

"Commence signalling...now!"

Pointing a powerful flashlight, the Ensign flashed a series of dots and dashes seaward, to an unseen U-boat.

"Is the U-536F out there, Commander?" Robert asked.

"Oh, yes! She's there, Mr. Brooks."

"You're positive?"

"Positive! Whether or not Langer falls for our bluff is another story."

Camp 30
27 September 1943 2215h

"Do you think that we can pull it off again, Sir?" asked Konrad Eckert anxiously.

"Of course, Ensign!" Korvettenkapitän Schumacher replied. "Why not? Ready, march!" Five abreast, the PoW's marched past the Canadian guard.

"Five, ten, fifteen, twenty... All accounted for, Staff Sergeant."

"Very well, Corporal, have the PoWs dismissed," replied Murray.

PoW 'dummy'
Bowmanville Archives

"Captain, you may dismiss your men."

Inside Haus IV, Schumacher remarked to Ensign Eckert, "You see, Eckert, our dummy 'Klein' performed admirably again. A 'model' submariner, he is," Schumacher laughed.

Maisonette Point Aboard U-536F
27 September 1943 2201h

"Sir! A signal from the shore!" reported the Watch Officer excitedly.

"I see it, Leutnant. What is it saying?" Kapitänleutnant Langer gripped the conning tower's protective railing to steady himself, as the waves washed over the deck.

It says, "Come in. Ready for pick up."

"And the codeword?"

"No, it's missing. The signal was sent twice. What do you make of that, Herr Kaleu?"

"It could be an unintentional error, Leutnant, or, a false signal. Either way, it is troubling."

"What now, Sir?"

"Patience, Leutnant, patience. Signal back: How many of you are there?"

"Signal says, One. He's alone, Sir!"

"Alone? There should be at least twenty of them. What in the name of the devil could have gone wrong? Signal that we'll send in a party."

Maisonette Point Aboard the Corvette HMCS *Chippewa*
27 September 1943 2205h

"Lieutenant, this diffused lighting technology is going to take some getting used to. It's scarcely believable how close we are to that U-boat, yet, apparently they can't see us!" remarked Captain Gilbert. "Even though I was on board the test ship for the evaluation trials in Halifax, I must admit that I find it eerie. How are the men taking it?"

"Frankly, Captain, even with our training exercise, it's spooking them. To walk around on the bridge with lights that are bright enough

to show the time on your watch at midnight, yet, we're invisible to the enemy. It just doesn't make any sense at all to them."

"Midshipman, could you come here, please?"

"Yes, Captain?"

"Midshipman, you're Brant, right?"

" Brant, Sir. Richard."

"Well, Midshipman Brant, explain to the Lieutenant how this diffused lighting works."

"Very well, Sir. Sir, it's a Canadian invention. The concept is that a ship at night appears to be darker than the sky, thus it stands out. Once diffused lighting is turned on, the ship and the sky blend into one and the ship becomes invisible."

"Very well done, Midshipman Brant," Gilbert replied.

"Thank you, Sir."

"And do you believe that this concept actually works, Midshipman Brant?"

"Well to tell you the truth, Sir, I'm not sure, although we do know that there's a German sub out there and we haven't been torpedoed, yet."

Aboard U-536F

"Landing party ready?"

"Aye, Sir."

As four of Langer's men were about to launch a dinghy, the Chief Radio Operator thrust his head out of the conning tower. "Herr Kaleu, I'm picking up a corvette: 1,000 metres, flank speed, closing quickly!"

"All below," Langer shouted. "Close the hatch. Dive!

"Bring her down to twenty metres and then shut down engines!"

"But Sir, shouldn't we be heading further out? Twenty metres is not deep, Sir."

"No, that's what they expect, Leutnant. We'll hug the shoreline for now."

Aboard HMCS *Chippewa*

"They've seen us, they're diving. Ready depth charges. Stand by all quarters."

Maisonette Point The Lighthouse
27 September 1943 2215h

Spence switched on a portable speaker, "So you chaps can follow the action," he explained to Reynolds and Brooks.

"Commander, he's submerged, and holding at twenty metres. Over," a voice reported from an electronic tracking van that was parked outside the lighthouse.

"Send co-ordinates to flotilla and stand by. Corvettes *Chippewa* and *Micmac*, ready to attack at will. Over."

"Roger, Wilco."

"Exactly what I was hoping would not happen. Langer spotted one of our corvettes, *Chippewa*, and has gone under. Damn! Here, try my night vision binoculars," Spence commented.

"Thanks. Now what, Commander?"

"We'll try and force him up to the surface, Commissioner. We want that U-boat. Badly! Very badly!"

For the next two days, Kapitänleutnant Langer and the Canadian Navy played cat and mouse until, with great skill and much good fortune, U-536F was able to break out into the open Atlantic Ocean. Upon arrival at homeport, Langer was astonished to discover his sub tightly encased in a clutter of fisherman's netting, no doubt attributed to his long journey through the New Brunswick coastal waters.

CHAPTER 12

WAR IS HELL

16 November 1943

Camp 30

Colonel Armstrong stepped from behind his desk and greeted the three ranking officers. "Gentlemen, welcome! May I take your coats? Please, be seated. Tea?"

Declining Armstrong's offers, Korvettenkapitän Schumacher, Oberstleutnant Eberhart, and Generalleutnant Schröder stood at attention, expressionless, facing his desk.

"Gentlemen, please! This forced formality is not necessary. Do sit down."

Armstrong's appeal was met with total silence. After an uncomfortable length of time, Captain Schumacher spoke, in English. "Colonel Armstrong, if I recall correctly, the last time we four met resulted in extremely unpleasant consequences. How can you expect that we would be overjoyed to be ordered back?"

"That's true, Captain. I do see your point," Armstrong conceded, "however, that was...."

"Excuse me, Colonel," Schumacher cut in abruptly, "but I must ask now, as then: what matter can possibly be of such importance that it requires the presence of the Generalleutnant, the Oberstleutnant, and me? Please, be good enough to explain."

"Yes, yes, very well. As you say, that was then, Captain. Unfortunate, but we endured. 'That which doesn't kill us makes us stronger', as one of your philosophers put it so pithily."

"'What does not destroy me, makes me stronger'. It was Nietzsche," Schröder observed curtly, in German.

"Ah, yes, of course. Nietzsche," Armstrong replied distractedly, on the verge of making a scathing comment about Nietzsche's rather low opinion of German culture in general and Germany in particular. He stopped short, to avoid an outburst from Schumacher.
"Generalleutnant, gentlemen, my agenda is clear-cut. I would like to know exactly when you are going to put a stop to these foolhardy and

pointless escape attempts? To be frank, I simply don't understand it at all, unless your purpose is to create minor annoyances for me and for the Canadian authorities, in which case, I concede that in one or two instances, you have succeeded. Congratulations. But have they changed the course of the war? Not an iota. Life is wonderful here for you and your men. Why would any of them want to return to war-torn Europe?"

"Colonel, with respect, you are not only an officer, but also a highly-decorated veteran of the Great War. Frankly, Sir, I am shocked and offended that you would even raise this topic for debate," snapped Schröder. "It is a given, Sir!"

"Yes, yes, I understand, Generalleutnant. However, it is also a given that, as commanding officer of this facility, I must point out that such activities are an utter waste of your time and substantial talents. For example, let me read you a sampling of current accounts from one of our local newspapers. Some of them are really quite humorous, even bizarre.

"Grab Nazi Trying To Steal Plane-Second Surrenders At Farm

Alert Guards at ▮▮▮▮▮▮ catch Escapee From Bowmanville Inside Airport Grounds - Two Enemy Fliers Left Prison by Unknown Means

Caught at noon today by guards at the ▮▮▮▮▮▮, as he awaited an opportunity to steal a training plane and make good his escape, Lieut. Frederick Oeser, 23 year-old Nazi officer, was this afternoon returned to the ▮▮▮▮▮▮ war prison camp from which he escaped last night. His fellow escapee, Lieut. Bidward Fibieg, had given himself up volun-tarily earlier in the morning at an ▮▮▮▮▮▮ farm home, and preceded Oeser back to the prison camp.

Caught Behind Furnace

Oeser's daring attempt to steal one of the light training planes on the airport grounds was foiled by the alertness of airport guards who noticed a stranger on the grounds and immediately pursued him. The capture, an air force official said at noon, was finally made behind a furnace in one of the buildings, where the German had endeavoured to hide himself.

Fibieg, the first to be taken into custody, gave himself up voluntarily at the farmhouse of Fred Clemens in East ██████████ Township, and was escorted to the ████████ jail by Sergeant of Detectives ███████ of the city police force and Provincial Constable ██████.

Tried To Steal Suit

Oeser must have gained access to the flying school by climbing over or crawling under the steel fence around the airport, Flight Lieutenant ████████ told the Times-Gazette. The diminutive Nazi, skulked around the grounds, apparently looking for an opportunity to obtain a flying suit and steal a plane.

Alert guards, noticing the stranger, followed him and took him into custody as he hid behind a furnace in one of the ████████ buildings. Names of the guards could not be ascertained prior to press time.

Officials from ████████ arrived at about 12:30 p.m. and immediately took statements from the guards and local attending officers before setting out for the prison camp with their second returned captive of the day."

"Colonel Armstrong, what has been censored? Bowmanville?" demanded Schumacher.

Armstrong glanced at Schumacher and shrugged. "Insert whatever you wish, Captain. May I continue, please?

"Goes to Farm Home

Mrs. ████████, housekeeper for ████████, told the ████████ that Lieut. Fibieg called at her door at about 10:00 this morning and told her he was an escaped German prisoner. He asked her to notify the prison camp in Bowmanville. When asked why he did not go to the police station, he replied that he was too tired to continue.

Mrs. ███████ said she then went inside and asked Mr. ███ ██████ advice. He instructed her to telephone ████████ police and the officers arrived shortly afterwards. While they were waiting for the police, ████████ invited the Nazi flier in the house. Mrs. █████████ said he was shy at first, but he was extremely grateful when offered a roast pork sandwich and a cup of tea.

Slept in ditch

Mrs. █████████ said the German's wet and muddy appearance indicated he had likely slept in a ditch. He wore a blue cap, and a brown civilian overcoat over a suit of blue dungarees.

"He told ██████████ that he liked Canada and didn't want to return to Germany," the housekeeper said. "He had the bearing and manners of a gentleman," she added.

When the police arrived, they allowed the Nazi to finish his sandwich before taking him to the police station, according to Mrs. ██████████.

Officials at the █████████ camp did not reveal how the two men escaped other than intimating that it was by ingenious means. Their short-lived term of freedom began at about 10:15 last night.

Second Escape

It was the second time that Oeser, a diminutive Austrian Nazi, has made a break for liberty within three months. He escaped from the █████████ camp in a laundry truck on 30 December, but was captured in Oshawa twenty minutes later.

Oeser is described as 5 feet 4 and one-half inches tall. He is dark, with Grecian features and his hair is cropped short. He bears the scar of a bullet wound on his left shoulder.

Fiedig is described as 5 feet 10 inches tall and weighing

160 pounds. He is ruddy complexioned and is believed to have a scar on his left cheek.

Both men speak English with pronounced accents.

On his previous attempt to escape, Oeser jumped into the back of a laundry truck as it was leaving the prison camp on its return trip to Oshawa. He remained hidden during the short trip, but jumped out when the driver, ██████████ of Oshawa, guided the truck into the laundry parking lot.

Ranstead was suspicious when he saw a pair of light blue prison trousers beneath Oeser's overcoat as the man walked away. He grabbed Oeser who submitted without a struggle."

"Colonel, I must object strenuously!" Oberstleutnant Eberhart interrupted. "No member of the Luftwaffe would ever turn himself in like that. This is a work of fiction, a fabrication, a bundle of outright lies. It categorically did not happen!"

"Very well, Oberstleutnant. If it didn't happen, you needn't get so agitated.

"Just examine the evidence, gentlemen: airplanes, laundry bags, fertilizer wagons, and even an empty piano box. Pathetic. Saint Peter on a bicycle! Tell me, please! I have to wonder, exactly what in the name of all that's holy are your men thinking?" Jack shouted in frustration.

"I don't see what you find so humorous about soldiers doing their sworn duty, Colonel," retorted Schröder. "Furthermore, Sir, I not only find your tone and choice of language offensive and personally demeaning, but, as a practicing Roman Catholic, extremely distasteful."

"Quite so. My sincerest apologies, General," Armstrong conceded. "I just find their methods comical. However, I must admit that the sled and mannequin were most original, even ingenious. Of course, none of you had a hand in those exploits," he added, scathingly. "Speaking of which, how is Herr Klein enjoying his twenty-eight days in solitary confinement following his outing to New Brunswick?"

"Kapitänleutnant Klein is well, Colonel," Schumacher stated icily.

"Really, and you know of this? At first hand, I suppose?" countered Armstrong.

"Permit me to say that one or two of your guards are not models of

discretion," Schumacher replied, smiling briefly.

"Now, was there anything of importance, or did you just invite us in to enjoy a laugh at our expense?" demanded Schröder scornfully.

"No disrespect intended, gentlemen. I simply wanted to remind you that these efforts to escape are ridiculous. The war will soon be over, so why don't you all just sit back and relax?"

"Thank you, Colonel, for this delightful conversation. Good day," stated Eberhart, as the three Germans saluted and turned to walk out the door.

"'Not models of discretion', eh? Get me Staff Sergeant Murray!" bellowed Armstrong.

Camp 30 Haus IV
28 March 1944

"Werner, I have a situation to discuss with you," said Schumacher. "What's that, Sir?" asked Eberhart.

"I want to read you a transcript of a report received via our short wave radio. It's direct from Berlin.

```
Allied PoWs Escape from Prison Camp.
```

```
Just after dusk on 24 March, seventy-nine Allied Airmen
escaped from a Stalag, south east of Berlin. It is
believed that the airmen had been digging the 120-metre
tunnel for over two years when finally they made good
their escape. A massive search is underway for the miss-
ing airmen.
```

"Werner, if Allied PoWs can successfully tunnel out, surely to heavens we can, too."

"Two years, Sir. But do you think the war...?"

"If you're not prepared to take this on, Werner, I'll find someone who is!"

"Absolutely, Sir! When do we start?"

"Right away. I'll expect a report with your recommendations on Friday. And keep that little engineer, what's his name, out of it, for the time being. The Camp is crawling with engineering and science types. I want fresh ideas. A clean slate."

"Do you mean, this is my project, Frederick?"

"It is indeed, Werner. Now get to work on your proposal."

"Yes, Sir! I look forward to it."

31 May 1944

Camp 30 The pathway

"Werner, come, walk along with me."

"Sure. Something is bothering you, Frederick?"

Schumacher stopped. "It's over," he stated. "All over."

"What's that, Sir?" asked Eberhart.

"The tunnel. Stop the tunnel!" Schumacher insisted.

"Stop it? But Frederick, we're making such good progress. The team tells me that they will be finished in another month, six weeks at the most," pleaded Eberhart.

"I don't care. It's finished. No one is to enter it again. On my orders."

"What happened, Frederick?"

"Do you remember our conversation when I asked you to take it on...the tunnel that is?"

"Yes, of course."

"Well, I have just learned from reliable sources that fifty of the seventy-nine Allied PoWs who escaped from *Stalag Luft III* were executed in cold blood by the Gestapo, on direct orders from Hitler himself," said Schumacher. "Many of those lads were Canadians."

"Frederick, I'm shocked!" replied Eberhart. "That's hard to believe!"

"I know, but it's a fact. I'm afraid *Der Führer* has lost his grip. Post-Dieppe was bad enough, and heaven knows we paid for that imbroglio. But this, Werner! This is a monstrous crime against mankind, a blow against all military men: you, me, our comrades here, our sons, and brothers. Consider the way in which the Canadians have treated us. If we escape, like Klein and the others, we are given twenty-eight days in solitary confinement and that's it! But this, this is insanity. Werner, there will be no more escape attempts from Camp 30. That is my final decision."

A work gang on work detail
Bowmanville Museum / DND - National Archives of Canada

"Yes, Sir, I'll see that all work stops immediately. In a sense, Colonel Armstrong has won, hasn't he, Frederick?"

"Perhaps he'll see it that way, when I tell him. Frankly, I don't think so. What's more, I don't give a damn.

"We fought fairly and honourably, but who knows that? Instead, we're denounced and vilified in the press as Nazis. It was the great British statesman, Edmund Burke, who wrote, 'The only thing necessary for the triumph of evil, is for good men to do nothing'. Well this, Werner, is our way to do something, and to say, 'Thank you, Canada.' The Colonel is free to take from it anything he wishes. You know, Werner, despite his bluster, he's not a bad sort of fellow; quite the opposite, in fact. Lord knows he must be under intensive pressure from his superiors. I think we three intimidate him, don't you? As the American General Sherman rightly said, 'War is hell!'"

"I'm really thankful that you made this decision, Frederick," Eberhart affirmed quietly.

"Well, get on with it then, Werner. I want the operation completely shut down within the hour!"

6 June 1944 Haus IV

"Get up, Helmut! It's already half past two! Roll call at 1500!" Ensign Eckert shook his friend's shoulder vigorously for the fourth time since noon.

A low moan emanated from beneath the heaped-up blankets. "Please, just leave me here to die. I don't feel very well."

"What do you mean you don't feel very well?" Eckert scolded. "Are you hung over, chum?"

"No! I'm sick to my stomach. I have terrible cramps. Get out of the way! I'm going to be sick!" Helmut mumbled. Holding his hand over his mouth, he stumbled toward the washroom.

"What the hell has gotten into that man?" Eckert muttered.

6 June 1944 Colonel Armstrong's Office

"Colonel Armstrong! Staff Sergeant Murray is on his way here to see you. He says it's urgent," Muriel Burns called through the half-open door.

"Send him in directly, Muriel," sighed Armstrong. Moments later, he heard Murray announce himself.

"Come right in, Bob! My goodness, man, you look flustered! Have a seat. What is it?"

"Begging your pardon for bursting in on you, Colonel. Sir, it's the PoWs! Only half of them showed up for roll call this morning," Murray announced breathlessly.

"What? Oh, I see." Armstrong removed his reading glasses, and looked at Murray with a direct stare. "Let it be, Bob. That is all."

Robert Murray hesitated, and swallowed. 'Duty before honour.' He pressed on. "Colonel, no offence Sir. But, 'let it be', Sir? Are you saying, Sir, no roll call? None at all, Sir?" queried Sergeant Murray in disbelief.

"That is exactly what I said. Do you not see what has happened, Staff? The PoWs have obviously learned of the Allied invasion of France. They must be devastated. We'll give them the day off, in consideration of...something or other. Don't fret, we'll resume roll call, as usual, tomorrow morning, Staff! Dismiss!" With a benevolent smile, Armstrong replaced his horn-rimmed eyeglasses, and paused, waiting expectantly for Murray to leave.

"Miss Burns, did you find the May payroll vouchers, yet?"

"They're in the blue folder. Look in your in-basket, Colonel!"

"Ah, yes!"

"Yes, Sir!" Staff Sergeant Murray saluted and retreated. 'Cancel roll call! Because of a raid? It must have been one jim-dandy of an operation, that's for sure!' Murray clucked, shaking his head in bewilderment at this shocking suspension of established procedure.

D Day 6 June 1944 Haus IV

"How is he, Konrad?" asked Schumacher. "Has he a fever?" Eckert sensed that the Captain's tone reflected genuine concern for the welfare of Chief Petty officer Helmut Bauer, of U-96F.

"Not well, Sir: a fever and terrible cramps, besides. Poor Bauer! He hasn't left the head since, I'd say, close to 1400," Eckert replied.

"Sounds very much like food poisoning to me. Scores of men are under the weather. You saw it for yourself, Konrad. Barely half the lads were able to show up for this morning's roll call."

"Is there anything that we can do, Sir?"

"I'm notifying the Camp doctor. By the way, do you know if he had the potato salad at dinner last night?" Schumacher inquired.

"Yes, as a matter of fact, he did, Sir. I gave it a pass myself, as I'm not on the best of terms with mayonnaise. He brought a plate back with him to the Haus, too. I saw Bauer gorging himself on it around 2100."

"Oh my, the poor man. That confirms it."

"Sir?"

"Of the twenty cases I've investigated so far, everyone of them ate the potato salad. Thank you, Ensign. I'm off to the infirmary. Stay well!"

20 July 1944 Haus IV

"Frederick!"

"Yes, Werner?" asked Schumacher, absently.

"We've heard from Berlin on our short wave receiver! There has been an attempt on the life of *Der Führer* at the Wolf's Lair, Rastenburg!" exclaimed Eberhart.

"What? Do you have any more information? Was it the Russians? Is he alive?"

"He must be! The report said that he will address the German people this evening."

"Thank you, Werner, and please, do keep me informed of any new details. I must let Generalleutnant Schröder know of this immediately," replied Schumacher, already on his way.

Eberhart anxiously awaited Schumacher's return. "Well, Frederick, what did the Generalleutnant say?" he inquired eagerly.

"Not at all what I expected, Werner. Effective tomorrow morning, when the guards enter Camp, our colour party will greet them presenting the ceremonial Nazi salute."

"Pardon, Frederick? But we've never used that salute. Not once, in all the time that we've been here! Surely, the Generalleutnant is aware of the furor that this gesture will create, no?" countered Eberhart.

"First, he is fully aware. Furthermore, he is fully prepared to be held personally accountable to the Canadian authorities. Third, he will not back down; the Generalleutnant's specific words, 'It will be done out of respect for our *Führer*', are crystal clear."

"He has also ordered that all journals, magazines, gramophone records - in fact, anything at all that is non-Germanic in origin be collected and brought to the fire pit tonight at 2000h to be destroyed. Please see that Generalleutnant Schröder's orders are carried out forthwith, Oberstleutnant."

"Yes, Herr Kapitän. I will see to it!"

21 October 1944

Camp 30 The Red Ox

"Frederick, have you heard about Admiral Dönitz' latest 'super weapon'?"

"I don't believe so, Werner," Schumacher replied, wincing at Eberhart's choice of words. "Rocket-propelled submarines?"

"No, not quite."

"Then please, tell me."

"I have heard a report that he has successfully commissioned the U-482, dubbed the *Schnorkel-Boot*," Eberhart enthused.

"Oh, yes. That. We were experimenting with that back in 1940. Is it finally operational?"

"Yes! The U-482 has just returned from a 4,300 km voyage, ninety percent of which was under water."

"Outstanding!" replied Schumacher. "How did the *Schnorkel* perform? A moment, Werner.

"Generalleutnant! Won't you join us?" Schumacher called to Schröder, who had just entered the Ox. "Werner was just telling me about one of Admiral Dönitz' latest accomplishments. Are you interested?"

"Certainly. Carry on, Werner," Schröder commented. He drew up a chair and sat down.

"Very well! Well, Albrecht, the *Schnorkel* is a long tube that extends up to the surface and draws air into the U-boat. There is a valve or safety flap built into the intake to prevent water from flowing back inside. However, it also cuts off the air while it is closed. When it is re-opened and air is allowed back in, it unfortunately causes earaches for the crew. All-in-all, though, I'd say that's not a high price to pay for being able to run submerged for such long distances."

"I only wish that I might one day have the opportunity to command one. However, that doesn't appear likely, given the news out of Germany," Schumacher remarked.

"I know what you mean, Frederick," Schröder agreed. "By the way, an unofficial report from Berlin says that Field Marshal Erwin Rommel took cyanide, on orders from *Der Führer*. The Field Marshal's alleged involvement in the July twentieth assassination plot sealed his fate. The inside story is that Rommel chose to take his own life in order to spare his family the humiliation of a public trial."

"I wondered about that all along. The official line was that he had been severely injured in a Spitfire strafing attack in France on 17 July, and succumbed 14 October, quote, 'due to wounds'," Schumacher pointed out. "The Field Marshal was accorded a state funeral with full military honours on 18 October."

"I just hope and pray that the official version is true. He was one of Germany's greatest commanders," Schröder stated sombrely.

"Another beer, gentlemen?" The waiter, a corporal, stood at a discrete distance, knowing better than to eavesdrop on officers' conversations.

"Three Kings, thank you, son.

"On me," Schröder offered. "Please rise, gentlemen. 'The Field Marshal'."

Konrad Eckert waited until the three commanders were seated before he approached their table. "Sir, may I interrupt you?"

"You already have Eckert. What is it?" Schumacher answered, looking up.

"Sir, we have a new officer in the Camp. He says that he very much wants to see you. Immediately, Sir!"

"Well, what can be so important that he would drag me away from The Red Ox, eh?" Schumacher turned, then lowered his glass of beer, exclaiming, "What the hell? Langer, is that you?"

Kapitänleutnant Langer stood in the middle of the room, hands on his hips. "So, where were you?"

"What do you mean, where was I?" Schumacher demanded.

"Maisonette Point! I brought my boat, U-536F, all the way from Germany to pick you up and you weren't there, Frederick!"

"That was you, my old friend? My apologies, I forget myself. Alric Langer, this is Generalleutnant Albrecht Schröder and Oberstleutnant Werner Eberhart. Come, sit down and I'll order you a beer.

"Waiter, another 'King' here. Thank you.

"You know, Alric, I tried to notify Germany that I couldn't get out," he continued. "Did you not receive my message?"

"The only message I got was one hell of a dose of depth charges from

a Canadian destroyer when I tried to pick you up!" Langer exclaimed.

"I'm so sorry, Alric. You know, this really wasn't necessary. You didn't have to come all this way to explain yourself!"

"Frederick always had a strange sense of humour at the Academy, gentlemen," Langer laughed. "I'm glad to see that your promotion hasn't improved it much! Now, tell me about the Camp."

30 October 1944

Camp 30 The Mess Hall

"Herr Kapitän, may I have a word with you?"

"What is it this time, Konrad?" asked Schumacher.

"I have a proposal, Sir. May I tell you?"

"So long as it has nothing to do with any new, hare-brained escape scheme!' Schumacher replied, looking up at him warily.

"No, Sir. Nothing like that, I swear."

"Very well. Take a chair. May the Oberstleutnant listen in?"

"Thank you," Ensign Eckert replied, taking up Schumacher's offer. "But of course, Oberstleutnant. As our senior officers, your approval is essential."

"So, tell us your grand idea, Ensign."

"Well, I've been talking with some of the men and with respect, Sirs, there seems to be a consensus that we need something to pep up our spirits."

"I see," replied Schumacher. "Oberstleutnant?"

"What do you have in mind, Ensign?" inquired Eberhart. "A Hallowe'en dress-up party, perhaps?" he replied, glancing sideways at Schumacher.

"I suppose some of the Haus' are making plans for that. But no, Sir. This is much bigger in scope. I'm thinking more of an inter-service athletic competition." Eckert sat back, awaiting their reaction.

"A sports competition. Really! You have our attention, Ensign. Right, Oberstleutnant?" replied Schumacher, looking intently at Konrad. "Carry on, son."

Eckert proceeded to describe a tri-service house league in which the

Kriegsmarine, Luftwaffe and Wehrmacht, would conduct intramural trials to select their top performers. The finalists from each division would then compete in an All-Camp Tournament to decide the winners.

"A Camp 30 Olympic competition?" asked Eberhart.

"Yes, but friendlier, Oberstleutnant. The men whom I've spoken with want it to be competitive, but enjoyable, not life-or-death serious."

"What events are you considering, Ensign?"

When Ensign Eckert had finished, Schumacher and Eberhart agreed to take his proposal to General Schröder for consideration.

The following day, Schumacher indicated that the General had received the proposal favourably, with a few reservations: Schröder had insisted that a Tournament Committee be formed to take charge of all aspects and that the proposal be presented in writing. "...and not more than one page in length, Eckert. The Generalleutnant wants it in to him by 0900 tomorrow. Can you manage that?"

"Absolutely! No problem, Herr Kapitän!" Eckert replied cheerfully, but thinking desperately, 'Who can I rope into writing this in less than twenty-four hours. I know, Von Heiden! Educated, but no, bone-lazy. Got it, Klaus Keppler! He was a prof at some university or other. Chances are, he can put two sentences together.'

"Very well," Eberhart continued. "And remember, 0900, sharp. You know how the Generalleutnant is about promptness. Good luck, Ensign."

"Thank you, Sir!" 'Why didn't I keep my big mouth shut! Well, it's too late for regrets,' he reflected, walking slowly back to his residence. 'Now, a committee: Keppler, Secretary Treasurer. Löwen, and Faber; that takes care of the army. Semmler, Wolf, air force. And then navy: me as Chairman, plus one other unsuspecting... Oberleutnant Gerhard Hoffman!' "Got a minute, Sir?"

31 October 1944 1045h

The Mess Hall

Konrad Eckert strode through doorway, smiling broadly. "Gentlemen! We have a tournament! The Generalleutnant was simply ecstatic! And, hold on to your hats; he is prepared to ask Colonel Armstrong to pick up all the costs for equipment rental, printing, uniforms and incidentals."

"Incidentals? Like what?" asked Peter Faber, grinning slyly. "Big-breasted cheerleaders, maybe?"

"In your dreams, Faber!' laughed von Heiden.

"What are cheerleaders?" asked Kurt innocently.

"Don't you ever look at the sports pages in the newspapers, Löwen? Canadian and American football teams have squads of good-looking girls who prance around and do acrobatics just to get the fans going!"

"Going? But they're already there...at the game."

"Forget it!" Peter commented, shaking his head in disgust.

"Refreshments!" Eckert interjected. "The usual. Light fare: juices, cookies, sandwiches, but brought in from a local caterer. And get this! General Schröder will try for a formal awards dinner on the final night! Won't that be something?"

"Let's hear it for Konrad!" shouted Wolf. "Hurray! Come on, men, hurray!"

"Thank you, thank you. We have our work cut out for us. The timing is very tight. I promised the General that we would be ready for the big show by December 1st to avoid running into Christmas festivities. That means that all of the preliminaries will have to be finished by the beginning of, or at the outside, the middle of the final week in November. Can we do it? What do you think, Oberstleutnant Hoffman?"

PoWs with their puppets
Volkmar König

"Well, first of all, thank you for the promotion, Ensign," he replied, warmly. "However, it is still 'Oberleutnant'. Insofar as the tournament preparations, no problem! And to make things flow more smoothly, I suggest from now on that it's first names only. So, I'm Gerhard. Alright?"

"Excellent! Klaus! Please pin up the organizational chart and let's get down to work," proclaimed Ensign Eckert. "We'll begin with your assignments, and then break for lunch. Oh, yes; I am to remind you to come out to the auditorium tonight at 2000h to attend the puppet show. Some of the Luftwaffe PoWs have done a fantastic job of putting together a skit that I know you'll enjoy. It's hilarious; I was at a rehearsal yesterday. Hope to see you there. Klaus, carry on."

Friday 1 December 1944 1530h
The Gymnasium

As Konrad Eckert was walking to take his place at the end of the pool, General Schröder stepped forward and intercepted him.
"Congratulations, Ensign Eckert! This has been a resounding success! Marvellous!"

"Why thank you, Generalleutnant. Your support has made it so, Sir!"

"Naturally, I was hoping to see the army team fare better than it has," confided Schröder. "Frankly, we have been somewhat 'wanting', ahem, in the coaching department. Third place overall, and one event to go," he remarked, shaking his head in disapproval. "You're competing in this race, I see." Schröder continued to grasp Eckert's right hand, as though attempting to anchor him to the spot.

"Yes, the 400 metre breaststroke. If you'll excuse me, Generalleutnant, the starter is waiting to get the race underway," Eckert remarked, courteously.

"I wish you luck, Ensign. The Korvettenkapitän tells me that you nearly drowned during your ordeal in the water. Is that so?"

"That's true, Sir. I suppose you might say I've come a long way in the past two years, or thereabouts." Eckert looked at the crowd, vainly searching for Schumacher. The spectators were unusually subdued. Every eye was fixed upon him.

"Well, as I said before, Ensign, good luck. By the way, you will likely be the first to hear this: I've made certain...arrangements with Colonel Armstrong. I will be selecting the athlete who through selflessness and self-sacrifice has best demonstrated our nation's ideals of sportsmanship, courage, and dedication to the greater ideals of the Fatherland. I can assure you that the prize will be well worth it. I should add that the winner might well turn out not to be the most highly decorated competitor."

"Generalleutnant!" Eckert saluted, turned away, and walked quickly to take his place. The Wehrmacht supporters in the crowd began a rhythmic chant: "Army! Army! Army!" which grew louder until it rose to a deafening roar.

"What was that all about, Konrad?" asked Wolfgang, standing on his right.

"I think I was just offered a bribe, Wolf," Eckert muttered under his breath. "To lose."

"Hmm. Well, good luck, win or lose!"

"Thanks. You too, Wolfie," Konrad replied, glancing past von Heiden to see Kurt Löwen waiting, flexing his shoulder muscles. Konrad flashed Kurt a quick smile just as the starter called, "Ready. On your marks...!" At the pistol shot, Eckert launched himself into the water with a fierce determination fuelled by pride and anger.

As he made the inverted turn to begin the home lap, Konrad concentrated on increasing his stroke rate, unaware of Wolf's or Kurt's positions. His muscle fibres were screaming. He was in over his depth; he knew the four hundred was not his event. He was a sprinter, not a marathon man. 'Shut the hell up, and swim!' A familiar voice intruded. "Keep swimming, son. Don't give up!"

'I'm trying, Herr Kapitän!' Grimly, he struggled to focus on completing the course. 'Just finish. No disgrace.' Gathering all of his reserves, he attacked the water furiously, determined to show Schröder that he could not be bought. His right hand contacted the cold, hard tile. He had made it. Thank the Lord and Captain Schumacher, at least he had finished. 'No disgrace in that.'

"Navy! Navy! Navy! Eckert! Eckert! Konrad the Cat's our man!"

Konrad looked up at the scoreboard and shook his head in disbelief. Not only had he won, he had beaten the second place finisher, Kurt Löwen, by almost a half second.

Together, the three friends walked to the reviewing stand in the Gymnasium to accept their medals from Schumacher, Eberhart, and Schröder.

Friday 1 December 1944 1825h
The Mess Hall

Resplendent in his neatly-pressed dress uniform, Konrad Eckert rose and stepped up to the podium. "Generalleutnant, Herr Kapitän, Oberstleutnant, Gentlemen. I know how anxious you are to hear the outcome of our competition. I am pleased to announce the final standings. In Third Place overall, with 50 points, Army!" This was greeted with scattered clapping and murmurings of displeasure. "Wait, please. Thank you. In Second Place with 59 points, Air Force! And, in First Place, with 67 points, Navy!" The proclamation was hailed with a rising tide of applause and cheers in the navy and air force sections while the Wehrmacht contingent stood, quietly disconsolate. "Congratulations once again to the teams and to every medal winner. A sincere thank you from the Committee to all for your spirited participation!" Ensign Eckert sat down, exhausted from the day's events.

The room erupted with wild cheers and applause as the navy and air force men stood up, hugging their comrades, hoisting their wine glasses and steins, while shouting raucous toasts to their teams and individual heroes.

At length, Captain Schumacher arose and stood silently, waiting expectantly for a semblance of order. Some thirty seconds later, he addressed the now hushed assembly. "Well done, Ensign Eckert. Gentlemen, Generalleutnant Schröder has a special award to present. Generalleutnant Schröder."

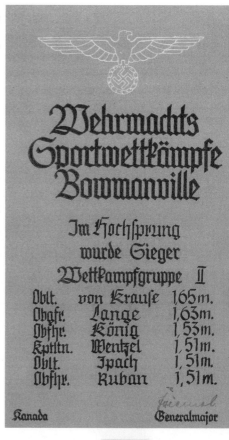

Konrad stared straight ahead, sipping his beer. He could feel Schröder's eyes drilling into the side of his skull.

The General began with the usual pleasantries, then went on to praise the Committee at length, lauding the participants for upholding the ideals of the Fatherland. He then launched into a rambling five-minute sermon on the value of excellence in athletics as a worthy national ambition. Eckert was nodding off when Wolf jolted him with a well-placed elbow in the ribs.

With a gracious acknowledgement to Colonel Armstrong for his generous and invaluable support, the General seemed about to sit down, when he suddenly changed gears. Eckert tuned him out, struggling not to slump in his chair. The meal and the wine, combined with the fatigue had made him heavy-headed and woozy. His eyelids began to flutter. He drifted off again, dreaming that Wolfgang von Heiden was calling him to get out of bed and play football.

"Ensign Konrad Eckert!"

Wolf was elbowing Eckert. "Get up! Get up, Cat! You won!"

Dumfounded and dazed, Konrad shouted loudly, "You got the field goal! Like hell I did!"

The entire room burst into raucous laughter.

"Like hell you did!" Kurt Löwen whispered from the other side.

"Wake him up, Wolf, for God's sake!" he urged, half laughing.

"Come up here, Ensign Eckert," Schröder commanded, smiling broadly.

"Gentlemen, it is with great pleasure that I present the individual who, over the past three weeks, has given of himself selflessly and tirelessly to the betterment of life for us all, here at Camp 30. He is not only a gifted and, I might say, persuasive leader of men, but he is also an outstanding competitor in his own right and a three time gold medallist in these competitions. Presenting, Konrad Eckert!" Embarrassed, Konrad allowed General Schröder to take his right hand to raise it in a victory salute, while flashbulbs popped.

When the pandemonium had finally died down, Schröder quipped in an aside to Schumacher, "I think I made the right choice, wouldn't you agree, Frederick?

"Now, for your prize, young man," Schröder continued. "Here, open this envelope."

Konrad fumbled in an attempt to tear it open. His hands trembling, he unfolded a sheet of stationery.

"Can you read it, or shall I?" offered General Schröder. "Allow me.

"Dear Winner,

You and a companion of your choosing are hereby commanded to appear, in person, at the Royal York Hotel, in
the City of Toronto, Ontario, on Saturday, 2 December 1944,
at 1200h.

Lieutenant Colonel Armstrong will make all transportation
arrangements and will provide you with suitable civilian
clothing prior to your departure.

Upon your arrival in our lobby, I will meet you to conduct
your orientation tour. I encourage you to enjoy all of
our establishment's amenities, including a luxury guest
suite with room service, to make full use of our cocktail
lounges, and to take all meals in our fine dining room,
gratis.

Prior to your departure at 2000 h, Sunday, 3 December, you
are invited to partake of all privileges that this first
class establishment has to offer to its valued patrons.

Wishing you a most enjoyable stay, I am,

Yours truly,

R. D. Cowan, General Manager.

P.S. Enclosed are complimentary tickets for dinner for two
on Saturday evening dinner in The Imperial Room, to be
followed by an evening of musical entertainment with the
famous Charlie Barnet and His Orchestra.

"Well, Konrad, what do you say?" asked Schröder.

"I, I'm speechless, for once," Konrad mumbled, in stunned disbelief. "Now, who will be your partner?" Schröder queried.

Konrad blinked as he surveyed the assembled faces. The room wait-
ed for his decision in silence. "I'd like to take you all! My Committee, of course. Helmut, my best friend; Wolfie, Karl, Kurt, Klaus, Peter, Gerhard..." He paused. "But, I have to choose just one, is that correct, Generalleutnant?"

Schröder nodded affirmatively.

"There is one person to whom I am forever in debt; he not only saved my life, he has been my compass, my mentor, my role model and, my inspiration. I never dreamt that I could ever repay this gentleman for his many kindnesses, support, friendship, and the understanding, shown to me, a lowly Ensign on U-96F. Generalleutnant, that person is Korvettenkapitan Schumacher. I would be honoured to have you join me, if you would. And, you can have the lower bunk, Sir!" Eckert added.

"It's a deal, Konrad!" Schumacher replied, coming forward. "Thank you. I'm truly honoured."

"Yes, Oberstleutnant" interjected Schröder. "Did I forget something?"

"I'm afraid so," Eberhart stated solemnly. "You neglected to mention the one condition under which the Colonel will give his permission!"

The PoWs looked at one another, murmuring with annoyance among themselves.

"*Ehrenwort*, Gentlemen?" Eberhart proposed.

"*Ehrenwort!*" the crowd roared in response.

"I'll report your response to Colonel Armstrong," Eberhart remarked jovially.

"Your driver will be here to pick you up tomorrow morning at 1030 hours," Eberhart announced. "Best get some rest, Gentlemen."

Konrad, Schumacher, Schröder and Eberhart stood to one side, deep in conversation, as Klaus Keppler stepped up to the podium.

"As Konrad seems to be rendered speechless, for once, I'll wrap things up. This concludes the official part of the program. Army! Next year!" he shouted, "that is, if we're still here, God forbid! Enjoy the remainder of the evening, Gentlemen!"

CHAPTER 14
COMING HOME

8 May 1945 1100h
Camp 30 Office of Colonel Armstrong

"Good morning, gentlemen! Muriel Burns' radiant smile was received with glacial indifference. "The Colonel is expecting you!" she persisted. Gently tapping on Jack Armstrong's partially open door, she announced, "Colonel Armstrong, your guests are here. I'll bring the refreshments in a jiffy."

"Come in gentlemen!" Armstrong rose, greeting the triumvirate genially. "Generalleutnant, Oberstleutnant, Captain, welcome! Please, sit down. Ruddy warm out there, for early May! Hope you don't mind this infernal fan. If the noise bothers you, I'll switch it off. Thank you, Muriel. Please, help yourselves to tea and cookies. Muriel's very own."

The three officers sat impassively.

Armstrong cleared his throat, then continued tentatively "Ahem. Gentlemen, as you, as you already, as you know, yesterday on 7 May at 1445 hours, in Reims, France, the German Chief of Staff, Colonel General Alfred Jodl, signed the papers of Unconditional Surrender of all German Armed Forces. General Jodl said, and I quote, 'With this signature, the German people and German armed forces are, for better or worse, delivered into the victors' hands'". Armstrong folded his glasses, seeking to gauge his visitors' reaction to this, the final act. Observing none, he replaced his spectacles and continued.

"By this order, I am directed to officially inform you that your status as Prisoners of War will continue to be in effect until such time as you have been processed for release in London, England." Armstrong paused, and looked up. "Questions regarding anything up to this point? Very well. Effective two days from now, you will be put aboard trains and sent to a holding area in Halifax, from whence you will sail to England. When you arrive, you will be taken to the 'Generals' Prison' for debriefing and political, uh, assessment. Do you have any questions?"

The three officers sat wordlessly. Jack Armstrong paused, then con-

tinued, "Is there something you wish to say after all these years here, at Camp 30, Bowmanville?"

Generalleutnant Schröder answered, "Will that be all, Colonel?"

"Yes, that is all." Armstrong rose and saluted as the men stood up, returned his salute and silently filed out of his office for the last time. He turned to the window, watching until they disappeared from view.

"Are you alright, Jack?"

"What? Oh, yes, sure, Muriel," he smiled, shrugging.

"You'll miss them."

"More than they'll miss me."

"Don't count on that. Here, have a cup. It'll do you good."

"Thanks, but only if you sit down and join me, Mur."

"I thought you'd never ask," she answered gently.

The Mess Hall That Afternoon

"Men, knowing how anxious we all are to get home to our loved ones, I have called you here to update you on our official status," began Schumacher. "I had a speech prepared, but, oh, to hell with it! We're going home! We leave in two days," he shouted, smiling broadly. A rumble of approval swept the packed Mess Hall, until it reached a deafening roar.

Oberstleutnant Eberhart stood up, his hands raised. "Gentlemen! Gentlemen! Quiet! Herr Kapitän has not finished. Thank you."

"We will be departing Bowmanville by train to Halifax within the next two days. As soon as the schedules are available from Colonel Armstrong, they will be posted. From Halifax, we ship out to England where you will be decommissioned by the British military. Then, at last, you will be sent to Germany, where you will be sent home, to be repatriated with your families." This announcement was acknowledged with even more whoops, cheers and whistles. A few sat in silence, dazed, unable to fathom the reality of Schumacher's message.

"Gentlemen!"

"As your Camp spokesman, and under the authority given me by our senior officer, Generalleutnant Albrecht Schröder, I hereby release you from your military obligations. You will, of course, be subject to all laws and statutes of this Province of Ontario, while here, or of jurisdictions elsewhere, and at all times, you will be subject to the laws of the Dominion of Canada, and govern yourselves accordingly," Schumacher stated dispassionately, as though citing the Code of Conduct to raw recruits. "Thank you for your excellent co-operation and your comradeship over these past years. It has been quite a journey. In this very room, you demonstrated the courage of your convictions and acquitted yourselves honourably, under, shall I say, trying circumstances. Your professionalism and conduct as German servicemen and officers have meant, and will always mean, a great deal to me. But, as I said, no speeches. God bless you all. You are dismissed."

As Schumacher stepped down from the makeshift platform, he was besieged by scores of well-wishers, seeking to shake his hand.

"Herr Kapitän!"

"Konrad, my friend! You no longer need to salute me and certainly don't have to address me as 'Herr Kapitän,' or even 'Sir', for that matter. I am just another civilian now, as are you," Schumacher commented affably.

"Yes, Sir, I understand. With respect, if you don't mind, I will always call you, 'Sir.' Sir?"

"Very well, Eckert. What is it?"

"Sir, would it be all right with you if we had a celebration party tonight, here in the Mess? That is, for all of the men?" asked Eckert.

"As far as I know, you are free to do as you wish, within reason, that is. There's no sense in stirring up trouble now, is there Eckert? I don't think that the Commandant will have a problem with that. I'll see that he's brought on board. You and the others enjoy yourselves, and hoist a few for me!"

"Oh, Sir. I forgot to mention. You, the Oberstleutnant, and the Generalleutnant are our honoured guests." Eckert stepped onto a table and whistled shrilly. "Listen up! There will be a celebration party here, in the Mess tonight, starting at 2000hours! Dieter, be sure to bring all of the reserves from the stills!"

2023h Camp 30 Mess Hall

"Kurt, bring me a brew when you come back," yelled Konrad Eckert.

"I can't hear you! The music!" Löwen shouted, cupping his ear. "Accordions!" he muttered, shaking his head in mock disgust.

"Beer!"

"Ya, okay, Eckert! Anyone else! Peter, Wolfie, Karl, Klaus, Gerhard, the rest of you reprobates?"

"Yes, dammit," they yelled back in unison. "Giff me a viskey and don't be stingy, baby!" Peter shouted, perfectly mimicking a line from a recent screening that had been a smash success with the boys.

"Where in the name of ...did all this food come from?" exclaimed Wolf. Did you grow it, Karl?"

"No, it's from Armstrong." The orchestra struck up *We'll Meet Again.* "Oh, my God, look at Klein!" Karl shouted in disbelief. The entire room was on its feet, cheering and applauding wildly as Wilhelm Klein whirled around the makeshift dance floor, winking salaciously, and clutching the dummy in its erogenous zones, had it been a human female. The Theatrical group had given 'her' curly black bangs, eyelashes, and red cheeks, with voluptuous, pouty lips.

The PoW Orchestra
Volkmar König

The band then launched into a lively tango. Klein and 'partner' gamely tried following the music, then, suddenly, lunged for the table of honour, where 'she' flung 'her' arms around Schumacher's shoulders.

Klein, straight faced, gave a contemptuous toss of his head as they continued on, dipping and swirling, until, while executing a *giro*, 'her' left leg fell off. The amputated limb was quickly appropriated by some of the rowdier elements, for purposes unknown. As a finale, Wilhelm tossed 'her' into the air with abandon, then twirled, and caught her, gracefully. The applause was deafening as Klein and 'Klein' solemnly took their bows. Brian Steers bobbed and weaved his way through the crowd, taking photographs.

Kurt elbowed Klaus. "Look at the old man! I think he's going to have a heart attack!" he gasped. "I hope Brian gets a shot of that!"

"He deserves a good laugh, alright," Klaus shouted back. "He's been a fantastic liaison officer, and I'm not that easily impressed, as you might recall from our first conversation in North Africa," he added, his speech slurring.

"Lady and Gentlemen! Your attention! Quiet!" Eckert shouted. The band stopped playing. A hush fell over the hall. "Get on with it Eckert! The fun's just begun!" someone yelled. "Ya, Konrad! The Herr Kapitän said 'no speeches!'"

Right! I promise to be brief!"

"Ya, that's what all you sailors say to the girls!"

"You ought to know, fly girl!" Eckert countered good-naturedly. "Listen, fellows, I just wanted to take a moment to pay tribute to, and to thank, some very important people who've made our stay here much better than bearable!"

He turned to the orchestra. "Gentlemen, if you please!" As the musicians began to play *Auld Lang Syne*, a group of Theatrical Club members entered, wearing the costumes of fairies and wood nymphs, left over from the production of *A Midsummer Night's Dream*. Holding aloft a huge papier-mâché potato, they led a tableau consisting of three actors portraying Oberstleutnant Eberhart, Korvettenkapitän Schumacher, and Generalleutnant Schröder, all bent over, with immense 'prop' pickaxes on their shoulders. Following in pursuit came more performers, dressed as Colonel Armstrong, Miss Muriel Burns, Corporal Brian Steers, Staff Sergeant Murray, and Jean Bell, Murray's office assistant, all armed with cardboard billy clubs and drawn on a train of wheeled carts, previously used underground in *Kartoffel*. Running behind the rest, an actor resembling Jimmy Blair swung an oversized swagger stick to a resounding chorus of 'boo's'.

"Kurt, who is that playing Colonel Armstrong?" asked Karl.

"I believe it's Eckert's friend, Chief Petty Officer Helmut Bauer. He plays the role well!" replied Kurt with enthusiasm. "Is he here, by the way?"

"Who? Armstrong?" Karl asked. "He's just sitting down at the head table, between Schumacher and Schröder."

The applause was deafening as the parade made its way throughout, snaking around and between the tables and then finally coming to a complete stop in front of the orchestra. Unobtrusively, during the procession, trays, each with a magnum of champagne and long-stemmed glasses, were distributed from the servery to each table.

"Good evening, Colonel! So, you've decided to join us!" remarked Schumacher, raising his voice to be heard over the noise.

"If you'll permit me, Captain," Armstrong replied hesitantly.

"Of course. Here. I can move over and let you sit between me and the Generalleutnant. Will that do?"

"Yes, that's fine, thanks!"

"Generalleutnant, Oberstleutnant," Armstrong leaned behind Schumacher, offering his hand to each officer.

"Good evening, Colonel Armstrong," Schröder replied stiffly, inclining his head in acknowledgement.

"Colonel," Eberhart remarked curtly, half-rising from his chair.

Schumacher leaned over. "They're still smarting from this morning. Give them time," he advised quietly.

"I regret that I was so damn officious and formal, Captain. I should have been more understanding, given your situation," Armstrong stated. "My sincerest apologies."

"There was no easy way for you to handle it, Colonel. Unfortunately, we got off on the wrong foot, as you might say, from the time we entered your office. We were bitter, shell-shocked, and angry beyond words when we first got the news, earlier on. Your announcement was the capper. However, as officers, we all could have done better, Jack. May call you that?"

"Indeed you may. Frederick?" Armstrong confirmed, offering his hand.

"Frederick! And don't you forget it," Schumacher grinned, taking Jack's outstretched hand. "A hell of a party so far! I have no idea how Eckert pulled this off on such short notice, do you?"

"Not a clue, Frederick. He came to my office for my blessing and a cheque at 1400 hours this afternoon, and then took off with Brian Steers. Unless he's been planning this shindig for a while, I don't see how it could be possible to set it up so quickly."

"Knowing Ensign Konrad Eckert, I wouldn't put that past him," Schumacher laughed. "Say, that fellow playing you, Jack, young Helmut Bauer, has real talent. But I must say that I'm not taken with the way that loony fellow, Hartmann, is portraying me!" he chuckled. "Oh, well, all in good fun. Colonel, allow me pour you some of your champagne! *Prost!*

"*Prost*, Frederick! To your good health, gentlemen!" Jack stood up, raising his glass to his two other tablemates.

Prost, Colonel!" replied Eberhart and Schröder, politely.

When, at length, Eckert could be heard above the pandemonium, he invited the characters to be recognized. Joining hands, they bowed in the best theatrical tradition. As the applause died down, Konrad proposed a toast. "Friends, charge your glasses! To Lieutenant Colonel Jack Armstrong, the best Commandant a prisoner of war camp could ever have, and who, I should say, personally footed the entire bill for this *Abschiedsfeie*, oh, what the hell, farewell party! Thank you! Colonel, say a few words, please?"

Embarrassed, Armstrong rose hesitantly, then looked back at Schumacher who gave him a hearty 'thumbs up' sign. Clearing his throat, Jack began to speak.

"Well, I'll never look at a potato again without thinking about you lot!" Armstrong waited for the scattered applause to die down. "I must be honest and tell you that when I received notice of my posting to Camp 30, this old warhorse was less than overjoyed. I was eager to be in the thick of the fray, to contribute whatever meagre talents I might possess to serving the cause. But as the poet said, 'God fulfills himself in many ways'. Gentlemen, it has been an honour to be here with you. My time with you has taught me that service to one's country can be manifest in many ways. And, you have demonstrated the true meaning of the professional soldier's code: to carry on in adversity, with dignity, and unwavering dedication to the preservation of the group's *esprit de corps*.

"On behalf of Robert, Muriel, Jean, Brian, the rest of my staff and especially the VG's, I want to thank you sincerely for your fine co-operation and exemplary military conduct. We all did what we did, as soldiers,

serving our countries with honour, with the best of intentions, and, we came smiling through. May God shine his face on each of you as you return to your homes and loved ones. We can take pride in knowing that our Camp 30 was, and will live on, as a shining example to the post-war world of the promise that, with men and women of good will, international understanding and brotherhood can and will survive and flourish, amidst the most trying of times. And if there is one thing that I have learned from you, it is the true meaning of a soldier's word of honour. I salute, you. *Ehrenwort!*"

The hall roared back in unison, "*Ehrenwort!*"

At the conclusion of the toasts and tributes, Eckert called upon Colonel Armstrong and Generalleutnant Schröder to step forward. "*Freunde*, Friends," Konrad stated simply, motioning the audience to rise. "Please be upstanding for the national anthems of our two great countries." As the orchestra began to play, *Deutschland, Deutschland, über Alles*, the men, both Canadian and German, began singing the words or humming Haydn's old hymn tune, softly, and reverentially. The singing of *God Save The King* was similarly stirring. As the conductor finally lowered his baton, Karl leaned over to his companions to whisper, "That was memorable! I'll bet there isn't a dry eye in the house!"

"And this could well be the last time we ever hear that sung," Klaus replied.

"Hear what?" Wolf asked.

"Our national anthem. But still, cynic that I am, this moment will stay in my heart forever," Klaus affirmed.

"Me too," Wolf replied wiping away a tear.

"Gentleman, Miss Burns and Miss Bell, I hope you will enjoy the rest of the evening. A moment, please." Konrad bent over to confer with Jack. "The Commandant has the final word. He has two special requests. One: he asks that you return the pulley wheels for his bedroom windows, before his wife arrives, Herr Klein! And two: Ulrich and Dieter, before you leave, he wants that secret recipe for Old Camp 30 pear hooch! Carry on, all!"

"Colonel, a word?"

Jack turned to see Generalleutnant Schröder offering him his hand. "Thank you, Colonel. Your words mean a great deal to me."

"Why thank you, General!"

"I must say, Colonel Armstrong, that I was especially moved by your references to honour. It made me think that if we had won the war, we would have lost our souls. Well, good evening, Colonel."

"Jack," Armstrong offered.

"Jack. Albrecht," Schröder smiled.

"*Macht's gut*, Albrecht."

"*Macht's gut*, Jack."

As the evening became more boisterous, and the atmosphere laden with smoke, Karl and the group at his table decided to go outside for a breath of fresh air. Karl looked up at the brilliant night sky, remembering his first view of the stars that night from the opening of his secret tunnel.

"What are you thinking, Karl?" Kurt asked.

"Home, my mother and my father." Karl paused. "You?"

"The same, and my girl, Lisette. What about the rest of you?" Kurt continued.

They nodded in agreement.

"I think I want to come back to Canada, after I settle things with my folks. Get a job, you know, sort myself out," Wolf confided. "Maybe I'll become a professional."

"A professional what? Male companion to the broken-hearted and lonely?" Kurt queried.

"No, a professional footballer! And maybe the other, if there's time!" Wolf replied, laughing.

A couple, male and female, arm in arm, slipped into the shadows. "Who's that with our lovely Miss Jean Bell?" Gerhard whispered. "Look, over there, under the elm tree! Oh, my!"

"Faber!" Kurt hissed. "The old charmer. Couldn't find his ass with both hands and a compass, but he can sure zero in on all targets of opportunity, if they wear a skirt! Let's move along, shall we?"

"Semmler! Is that you, Karl?"

Karl turned to see Schumacher walking toward him. "Yes, it's Karl, Sir. Having a good evening?"

"Oh, yes excellent," Schumacher remarked, lighting his pipe. "Can I steal you away from your chums, for just a moment?"

"Certainly."

"Walk along with me, Karl. You know, I never did thank you proper-

ly for your contributions." Schumacher halted. He coughed, withdrew the stem from his mouth, examined the contents of the bowl, and then resumed smoking. "Drat this pipe. I'd be better off just giving it up!" he grumbled, taking it from his mouth to strike the bowl against the sole of his shoe, creating a shower of flying sparks.

"Sir?"

"*Ireland* and the radio parts, your fantastic garden, a farm really. Your positive attitude had the same effect on everyone whose life you touched. You were always pleasant, upbeat, decent and honourable."

"You're much too kind, Sir."

"Yes, I could have used a man like you on my boat. The Luftwaffe was fortunate indeed to snag you. Karl, the new Germany is going to need men of your calibre: industrious, level headed, clever, and honest! I urge you to consider taking a run at public office, sometime. Sooner, mind, rather than later. Here's my address. Don't hesitate to get in touch, if you should ever feel like pursuing this further. All right? That's all I wanted to say. It has been a pleasure, son!" Schumacher grasped Karl's hand warmly, and then disappeared into the night.

"Sir?" Karl called after Schumacher.

Schumacher's voice drifted back. "Yes, Karl, what is it?"

"I...I just wanted to say thank you, Sir. For everything."

"You're welcome, son. Don't overdo it tonight!"

"I won't. Good night, Sir!" Karl sank down onto the grass. He was trembling; his head was spinning. 'Oh, God!' Drawing up his knees, he buried his head. 'What if I had told him?'

"I have a confession. It's about the 'honest' part that you just mentioned, Herr Kapitän."

"Go on." Schumacher stared impassively into the darkness.

"Sir, I had a tunnel. Actually, Sir, I didn't build it; I stumbled upon it, quite literally by accident. I figure that the boys had dug it. I kept its whereabouts secret, although I knew very well I should have told you about it. I'm terribly sorry, Sir. I have behaved dishonourably.

"I only used it to sneak away from the Camp so that I could visit a girl on the farm, over there. I stopped using it soon after *Kartoffel* got underway, in April, '43. It, well, it felt wrong, Sir. No, worse than that. I was betraying you, the Generalleutnant, the Oberstleutnant, the

Committee, my friends, for entirely selfish ..."

"I'm glad you stopped on your own account, son," Schumacher replied sternly. "You had a duty to tell me about it, nonetheless. Klein, and perhaps many others, might have been able to get out without his having to resort to the high-wire act."

"The truth, Sir? I was terrified of what might happen to me."

"Fear makes cowards of us all, Semmler. I can, however, understand. I would have had you brought up on charges and court-martialled. Your chances of surviving that, my boy, would have been slim to non-existent," Schumacher stated flatly. "However, it is my duty to bring charges against you when we return to the Fatherland," Schumacher cautioned.

"But, Sir!"

"I'm sorry Leutnant, the only promise I will make is that I will not tell the other men. A few hotheads around here still might decide to take matters into their own hands. So, who else knew? On second thought, I won't ask you to betray confidences."

"The girl knew, Sir. But, she had no idea where it was. Captain Jimmy Blair came close on one occasion. He caught me returning from an out trip in the middle of a fairly severe thunderstorm. There I was, Sir, wandering around, soaked like a rat, wearing my flimsy gym uniform with a flimsier excuse. I thought he would give me the third degree right there, and beat it out of me, but he let me off with a warning."

"Make no mistake. It was a grave breach, Karl. However, my opinion of you stands, young man, if only because you had the guts to come forward, now, and not ten years down the road. I will do what I can on your behalf, but I can't guarantee that anything I say about your character will sway the panel. It could smack of favouritism and actually work against you. Good night, Leutnant!"

"Come on, Karl!"

'*Was*?' Karl looked up with a start, blinking. He was sweating despite the chill of the night air.

"We're all going into town, for thick and delicious ice cream sundaes!" Klaus bellowed. "That's where the girls are, my boy!"

"Are you guys crazy? No girls will be out at 2230! And besides, we need permission," Karl shouted.

"Like hell! We're free men. Herr Kapitän said so!" Wolf yelled exuberantly.

"No, it's okay. You go ahead, guys. I feel rotten," Karl replied, half-heartedly. "Too much beer!"

"Too bad! We'll see you tomorrow!" Their voices trailed off into the darkness.

Karl stood up, brushed the seat of his trousers, and then slowly made his way to his quarters.

9 May 1945

Bowmanville Lambs Road at Lake Ontario

"What's the matter, Karl? I've never seen you look so pale," Marlene asked, putting her palm on his forehead.

"I'm okay, " he replied, taking her hand away and kissing it gently. "It was kind of a rough night; we had a little farewell party."

"Farewell party. I see," she murmured, smiling gamely.

"I'm going to come back for you, Marlene. I swear!" Karl threw a stone towards the water, then watched to see if it would skip across the surface. Marlene stared fixedly into the distance, without answering.

"You don't believe me, do you?"

"I don't know Karl. I don't know what to think. My mother and father don't even know that I've been seeing you," she replied sombrely. "It's not that I don't like you, I do. And I love you! But they, well, they're old-fashioned."

"I hear what you're saying. I'm German," he stated flatly. "You think they would have a problem with that."

"I'm fairly sure Momma wouldn't. But my father? I'm not so sure. At the end of the argument, Momma would give in. She always wants what's best for me. As for my father, well, I just don't know. He's a farmer, so he keeps very much to himself. What with working fourteen hours a day, he has little time for world events. You know, he does listen to the CBC newscast faithfully at one o'clock, and sometimes he even surprises Momma with the strength of his views. He's a Scot, so he can be stubborn and opinionated. But at heart, he's a kind and gentle man of high principles. And he takes people as they are, not as someone else dictates. I'm trying to be optimistic," she offered, her lip quivering.

"Oh, Karl, I just don't know," Marlene whispered. "Help me think of a way!" she pleaded, now sobbing.

"I love you and it will all work out. I know it will. I know it will. It has to," Karl whispered reassuringly, as he held her tightly. "It has to."

She looked up. "When?"

"I don't know. These things don't happen quickly. We just heard the news yesterday. It will take time. After a while, I'll come back and meet them," said Karl.

"You are coming back? You have to. Mother is already giving me a hard time. She thinks I'm becoming an old maid. She is constantly trying to fix me up with 'nice young gentlemen' from the church. Ho hum. I keep putting her off, telling her I'm much too young to marry," she added coquettishly.

"Really? I thought you were beyond the mountains!" he replied straight-faced.

"You thought what?" she asked, cocking her head in disbelief.

"Beyond the mountains. Old. What's the matter, did I say something wrong?"

"The expression, buster, is 'over the hill' and I'm not even at the foothills yet!" she giggled, kissing him lightly. "Karl, please tell me here and now. Will it all work out?"

"*Ehrenwort!*"

"I believe you."

10 May 1945 Camp 30

Jack Armstrong looked out at the sea of hundreds of faces. "Gentlemen, as you depart Camp 30, I hope that you will take with you the memory that you were treated fairly and humanely by our guards and officers. We did everything in our power to make your stay in Canada as pleasant and fulfilling as possible, under the circumstances. I wish you all good luck and God speed. "Sergeant Murray!"

"Men! In a moment, you will start boarding your buses in an orderly fashion. The guards will direct each group to the appropriate location. Guards will proceed now."

The loaded buses began to roll away from the gate of Camp 30 on Lambs Road toward Concession Street. Karl, seated by a window on the right side, looked out. He was on edge, vaguely depressed and apprehensive. He could see the Mess Hall where the three-day Battle of Bowmanville had taken place. And behind it, Haus II, where the men had put on so many beautiful concerts and plays. Beside it stood the Gymnasium, where the tournaments had taken place on the courts and in the pool. Wonderful memories began to seep into his subconscious. Something was missing. 'There's Haus IV!' he mused. 'My goodness, I hadn't realised how close the corner of the tunnel room was to the road!' Seeing it from this angle for the first time was a revelation.

Soon they were past the buildings, and Karl found himself looking at the open parade grounds as the bus driver shifted gears and picked up speed. To the left, in the distance, Karl could now see Marlene's farmhouse. Now he knew what was wrong: a part of him wanted to stay. He closed his eyes, remembering how many times he had slipped out of the Camp to meet her. Memories of the wonderful times that they had had in the valley at the back of the property came flooding back.

"Hey, Karl! Karl, isn't that your girlfriend waving from the front porch of that farmhouse," yelled Wolf.

"Ya, hey, it's her!"

"Karl, Karl!

Coming Home

October 1985

Bowmanville, Ontario, Canada

"Karl, Karl, do you hear me? Karl Semmler, for the last time, come in here! You're going to catch your death!"

"Right away. You know what? You're right!"

"Of course I am. And don't forget thin and beautiful, too," she replied, fondly kissing his forehead. "What am I right about, dear?" she queried, placing his jacket around his shoulders.

He stood up. "It's time. "And it's taken far too long, old fool that I am."

"Oh?"

"To call that Grant fellow," he smiled, taking her hand. "I want him here bright and early tomorrow morning, church roof or not. Yes," he smiled, "it's time to build that new veranda out back, Marlene, before I'm beyond the mountains!"

1.   *Describe, briefly, a typical day for you at the Camp. Include, if you would, any of your favourite recreational activities, and pursuits, highlights and annoyances.*

King: I never had a boring day in my three years at Camp 30 or any time for that matter during my internment at any of the Camps. My days were filled with sports, English lessons, rehearsals for plays, recitals, reading newspapers, magazines, and listening to the news, just to mention a few.

2.   *Describe or characterize your interactions, if any, with the guards, beyond 'official occasions', such as roll calls.*

King: We had no interaction with the guards other than to wave at them and say hello, or to say hello to the 'Ferrets' as they walked through the Camp. [Ed.: Ferrets was the nickname given to the two-man team of guards who would walk through the Camp on a regular basis.] Sometimes they would ask us how many rounds we had walked today, that type of thing.

3.   *What were your personal opinions of and/or reactions to the events that are now known as The Battle of Bowmanville? If you would, please tell us how the Veteran Guards, as opposed to the Canadian military reinforcements, conducted themselves vis a vis you and your colleagues, as PoW's, during these events.*

King: I can only recall that we were very excited to be in some action as we were trained soldiers and had been out of the action for too long. I mean that we were young and this was exciting and outside of the daily routines. The Veterans Guards stayed totally out of the action. The

Canadians left that part of the fighting up to the younger men who were brought in from Kingston.

4. *How, i.e., by what means, if at all, did you receive war news, from Germany?*

King: We had built a wireless set out of parts acquired throughout the Camp. We had specialists in this area who knew what to look for and where to find the parts. This radio was able to receive short wave transmission directly from Berlin. My job was to listen to the broadcast each day and record in writing, the summary of highlights from the reports of the OKW. [Ed.: German High Command] For a period of about three months, each day at lunchtime I would read the reports to those who were gathered in the Mess. The receiver was hidden in the arm of a chair in Haus II and never was located.

5. *Did you personally ever take advantage of the Ehrenwort code of conduct to leave the camp? If so, for what purposes(s)? e.g. recreation.*

King: Yes, I would take walks, usually up north of the Camp but always with a group of others and always with a Camp guard. I never did go down to the lake as others did, for some reason; I can't recall why not. I would be out for about four hours in total.

6. *Did you have direct knowledge of or involvement in, the tunnel enterprises? Please describe, if 'Yes'.*

King: I was involved in the Navy tunnel. My job was to remove the dirt and put in the attic. We had to abandon it when it filled with water.

7. *Was Mr. Heyda's break out known to all PoWs? Only those involved in the plan? Did you witness his escape?*

King: It was a very high level operation, only those who needed to know, knew.

8. *Was inter-service fraternization (i.e.: Kriegsmarine & Luftwaffe) encouraged, discouraged, or not an issue of any significance; this is, neither encouraged nor frowned upon?*

King: No, it was never an issue; we hung around with whom we wished. There was no segregation of ranks, although for some reason, the

Midshipmen did stay together in the same Haus. If you wished to be moved to another room or Haus, you would apply for the transfer and if approved, you would swap places with another PoW, all done within German control.

9. *By whom and how was discipline administered amongst the PoWs? e.g. by a panel of officers; by the ranking officer of the appropriate service?)*

King: I don't recall discipline as being an issue. The senior officers were in charge and you did as you were told. If you were addressed by a senior officer you would salute and say, yes Sir or yes Major. They would address you as in my case, König, Midshipman if they didn't know my name, but never by first name. If we addressed a Kapitänleutnant or Korvettenkapitän, it was always as: Herr Kaleu or Herr Kaptän, respectively. {Kapitän pronounced as Kap-tän, German Naval}

10. *What is your overall, lasting impression of the quality of the treatment (just/unjust/ professional/ slip shod), which you as POWs received under the administration of the Canadian authorities?*

King: Oh, all I can say is that we were treated fantastically at Camp 30. When I came home and told people that I was a PoW in a Camp in Canada and that we had an indoor swimming pool and tennis courts, they wouldn't believe me!

11. *What is the single most unpleasant memory of your term there, and why? What is the most enjoyable?*

King: I never had an unpleasant moment at Camp 30. (Perhaps for a short period when I was shot during the Battle of Bowmanville; but even then, it was action!)

MY PERSONAL THOUGHTS AND IMPRESSIONS ABOUT MY LIFE AS A PRISONER OF WAR

By J. B. (Bruno) Petrenko

My 'life' as a PoW began on August 31, 1940 after a kind and helpful British soldier was washing my bleeding face with a piece of cloth, which helped me to regain my consciousness.

The British soldier was John Clancy whom I had found by letter many years after the war. He had found the unconscious pilot hanging upside down in his Messerschmitt 109 fighter plane. Obviously, the heavily damaged plane had crash-landed topsy-turvy on a lawn in Great Britain. My 'good Samaritan' had managed to extract the unconscious pilot, who was bleeding from his head, and place him on a stretcher.

I got some medical attention and some tea and they took me closer to my plane and showed me that far away, we could see the still burning engine of the plane. How wonderful that the engine apparently had broken off from the plane before it started to burn.

Then I thought, 'Would it not be great to find a boat nearby and re-join with my people on the other side of the Channel?'

"No," I was told! "You are now a prisoner of war!" Now, I was deeply shocked! A PoW! How terrible! My life is finished! Tears came streaming down from my eyes; I was embarrassed. But I just could not help stopping the tears. After awhile, a senior officer spoke to me. "Now listen, young man, the war has come to an end for you. You are now a Prisoner of War. We will look after you. And once the war is over, we will let you go back to Germany." (This happened in April 1946.) "After all," he added, "being a prisoner of war is not necessarily the worst choice." Then they took me to a hospital nearby.

During the initial weeks and months of our life in PoW Camps, I found it difficult to accept living under a "timetable". We had to get used to daily roll calls, lights off, and meals at certain times, and possibly unexpected events, escapes and other surprises.

But in-between this daily schedule there was free time for each of us to do whatever you wanted to spend your time on. In many camps and in particular in the Bowmanville Camp, there were many possibilities to learn and study things that could help prepare a POW for finding employment after the war.

Here are some fields in which I spent my time in the Bowmanville Camp:

1. I attended many years of legal courses organized by our German lawyers; intensive teaching and hours of homework. Looking back, it helped me a lot when in later years I became involved in writing and negotiating contracts.

2. Language: (a) Daily at least 2 hours studying the Russian language, I had an affinity for Russia through my Russian Father who had been working in the administration of Krasnodar Russia, when I was born. My hope was that after the war, I wanted to write him in Russian. (b) I was regularly working on an English book to improve my English.

3. Music: I was playing the violin and a regular player in our 'Symphony Orchestra'. We produced wonderful music (Beethoven, Mozart, Brahms, Schubert, Johann Strauss).

4. History, philosophical books, regular studies.

5. Physical activities: regular gym classes, basketball, and swimming in the pool, and playing tennis.

6. Planning on where to live after the war:

I was raised in Rudolstadt Germany, after we had left our home in Russia. After the war I could not go back to Rudolstadt because it belonged to Communist East Germany. So it would be advisable for me to try to settle in West Germany. However, why not try to settle in Canada? Would it not be better for my future children to live in Canada? Is there more peace in Canada as compared with Germany; is Canada a more peaceful country?

My personal thoughts...

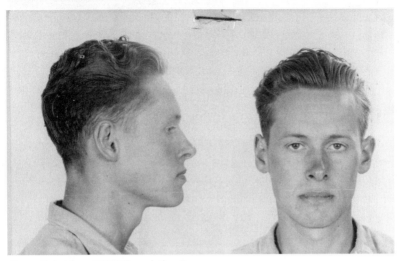

Bruno Petrenko - RCMP Description Form
Bruno Petrenko

That made me reach out for the following plan:

a)   Return to West Germany, try to learn and work in the management of any first class German company that could consider expanding into Canada.

b)   Try to work in Canada for a German company. With God's help it could be possible.

c)   My dear wife Johanna and I settled in Canada, where we could live in peace. We now have two grown children, a daughter-in-law and three grand children.

"Praise be to the Lord."
    April 2003

Camp & photograph No. 210
Red Cross No. 51832

F. 161

ROYAL CANADIAN MOUNTED POLICE

DESCRIPTION FORM

Meys, Ont. June 30th 19 41

1. Name and Aliases   PETRENKO. Jure.   (Lt)

2. Wanted for

3. Nationality or Race   German Air-man

4. Colour   White

5. Age   23

6. Height $25'9\frac{1}{2}"$

7. Weight   144

8. Complexion   Fair

9. Hair, how worn Lt.brown. Military hair-cut

10. Hair on face   Clean shaven

11. Eyes   Brown

12. Nose   Straight thin

13. Mouth   Medium

14. Chin   Slightly receding

15. Teeth   Normal

16. Build   Slight

17. Scars, marks   2 moles on stomach

18. Physical peculiarities

19. Voice, accent, speech   A little English

20. Languages spoken   German English

21. Dress   Air-force (German)

22. Appearance, carriage   Erect

23. Gait

24. Manner   Good

25. Education   High school

26. Occupation   Air-force

27. Criminal occupation and record

28. Habits   Smokes

29. Photograph, if obtainable, date taken   June 1941

30. Remarks

31. Warrant issued and by whom held

Camp 30 -
Under Contruction

Camp 30 under construction.

Bowmanville Archives / DVD - National Archives of Canada

Camp 30 -
Under Contruction

*Bowmanville Archives /
DVD - National Archives
of Canada*

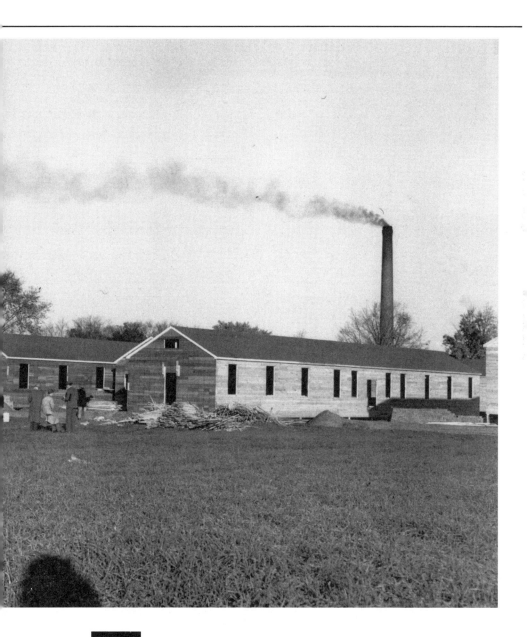

Camp 30 -
Today

Left
Admin Building

Right Upper
*Alan Longfield stands in
front of the Hospital (2003)*

Right Middle
Inside the Admin Building

Lower
*Walkway to the Admin
Building from the mess*

Lynn Philip Hodgson

Camp 30 - Today

The Mess (2003)

The original lighting still stands

Alan Longfield stands in front of the Mess

The open fields of Camp 30

The Hospital

Lynn Philip Hodgson

These drawings appeared on the wall of the 'Roten Ochsen' the 'Officers Mess'

Volkmar Köing

2ud malerei en im "Roten Ochsen" Lager "30"

Camp 30 - Drawings
Made by the PoWs

Lager "30"
Bornsanville
Haus IV SO Ecke

Camp 30 - Drawings
Made by the PoWs

Camp 30
Haus VI and Küche
/Mai '42

Camp 30 - Drawings
Made by the PoWs

Camp 30 - Drawings Made by the PoWs

Camp 30 - Drawings Made by the PoWs

The Camp 30 PoW Orchestra

Marschkapelle des Lager "30" 1943/44   Dirigent: Probst.
Untere Reihe: Francke, Eilers, Granz, Schypeck, Viel, Blome, Dryander, Happel.
Mittl. —"— : Raab, Lersch, Planck v. Bachselten, Viertl, Hendrick, Penndorf, Jörgensen, Hlesche
Obere —"— : Renner, Kloth, Schröder, Heger, Hempel, Ringle, Geyer, Binder, Böttger, Gro

The PoWs Orchestra
Volkmar König

The Camp 30 PoW Orchestra

The PoWs Orchestra
Volkmar König

Tanzorchester des Lager "30"   Winter 1943/44

Hess, Regenauer, Deibl, v. Heider, Kloth, Binder, Poser,
Schrader, Eilers, Stagge, Dr. Rau, Kunst, Sauer, Hoffa, Wieland, Krenn, Kettling,
Raab, Christiansen.

5. Juni 1942

Befehlshaber der Unterseeboote

Lieber König!

Ich danke Ihnen sehr für Ihre Grüße
und freue mich, daß Ihnen das Weihnachts-
geschenk soviel Freude gemacht hat. Im
gleichen Maß, wie Ihr alle an unsere Er-
folge denkt, sind unsere Gedanken bei
Euch und wenn Ihr im Augenblick untätig
sein müßt, so kommt doch die Zeit, wo wir wie-
der alle vereint in der großen U-Bootswaffe
stehen. Für diese kommenden Aufgaben gilt
es sich frisch zu erhalten!

Mit besten Grüßen

Heil Hitler!

Ihr

June 5, 1942

Dear König!

Thank you for your greetings. I am
pleased to hear that the Christmas present
brought you joy. Just as you are following
our successes, our thoughts are with you.
Although you have to be inactive at this
time, there will be a time when we are reunited in our great U-boat force. You have to
keep in shape for these future tasks!
With best wishes
Heil Hitler!

Yours,

Camp 30 PoW's

Oblt. Strasser
Oblt. Haffa
Lt. Renner
Oblt. Kleppmeyer
Oblt. Frohnhöfer

Oblt. Schlicht
Oblt. Blome
Hptm. Krenn
Oblt. Deibl
Oblt. Dültgen

Hptm. Proske
Oblt. Kleppmeyer

Hptm. Kircheis
Hptm. Krieger
Oblt. Bodendiek
Hptm. v. Bergen
Hptm. Schlegel

Camp 30 PoW's

Stage Plays put on by the Camp 30 PoW's

Die Spanische Fliege

POSSE IN DREI AKTEN

Volkmar König

Stage Plays put on
by the Camp 30 PoW's

Volkmar König

Stage Plays put on by the Camp 30 PoW's

Volkmar König

Stage Plays put on by the Camp 30 PoW's

Volkmar König

Stage Plays put on by the Camp 30 PoW's

SCHAUSPIEL VON HANS REHBERG

Volkmar König

Camp 30
History Worth Saving!

Left
Otto Kretschmer's Haus (2002)

Right
Lynn Philip Hodgson stands outside the Hospital fire escape. The famous Mess, which was the site of the Battle of Bowmanville, is in the background (2002).

Rik Davie

Camp 30
History Worth Saving!

Otto Kretschmer

Lynn Philip Hodgson stands in front of the Admin Building (2002) - Rik Davie

Camp 30
History Worth Saving!

Left
U Boat Commanders

Right
A Christmas card
Drawn by one of the PoWs (1942)

Volkmar König

SUBJECT REFERENCES

The Battle of the Atlantic, Time-Life Books.   ISBN n/a

The Battle of Britain, Time-Life Books.   ISBN n/a

Bowmanville Training School, Sandy Bexon, Bill Healey.   ISBN n/a

Camp 30 Ehrenwort, Daniel Hoffman.   ISBN n/a

Camp X The Final Battle, Hodgson, Longfield .   ISBN 0-9687062-3-1

Camp X Silver Dagger, Hodgson, Longfield.   ISBN 0-9687062-7-4

Encyclopaedia of the Third Reich, Dr. Louis L. Snyder, McGraw-Hill Inc. ISBN 1-56924-917-2

Escape From Canada!, Macmillan, John Melady.   ISBN 0-7715-9537-9

How Weapons Work, Christopher Chant.   ISBN 0-8568519-6-5

Inside Camp X, Lynn Philip Hodgson.   ISBN 0-9687062-5-8

The Luftwaffe, Time-Life Books.   ISBN 0-8094-3337-0

Thank You Canada, Eckehart J. Priebe.   ISBN 0-9694392-0-2

The Tools of War, Reader's Digest.   ISBN 0-88850-148-X

U-Boat The Secret Menace, David Mason.   ISBN n/a

U-Boats Against Canada, Michael L. Hadley.   ISBN 0-7735058-4-9

World War Two Through German Eyes, James Lucas.   ISBN n/a

Wolf Pack, David Jordan.   ISBN 1-8622715-8-5

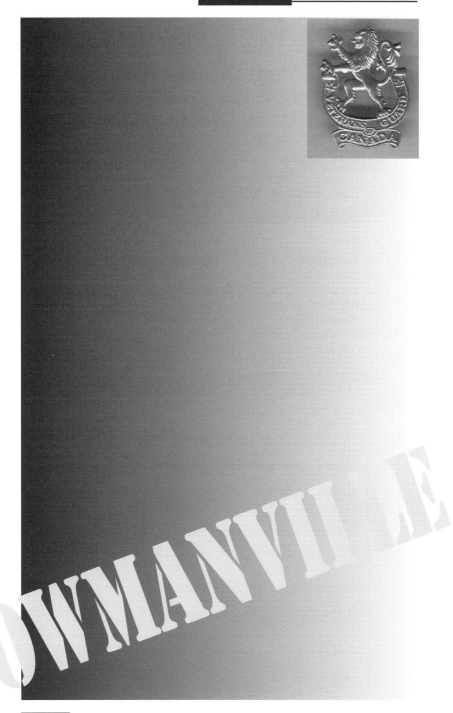

Barbara Kerr

Camp 30 - Bowmanville - Word of Honour is Barbara Kerr's fifth editorial project in the Camp X series. Beginning with the first book, Lynn Phillip Hodgson's best-selling **'Inside – Camp X'** and continuing with the second, Joe Gelleny/Alan Longfield's **'Almost'**, she has worked with Lynn and Alan to assure that this most important part of Canadian history is presented in an accurate, informative and highly readable format. It is her continued wish that these stories earn the courageous but heretofore unknown heroes, the respect and gratitude that they so richly deserve. Barbara can be contacted at barbarakerr@look.ca

Richard Armstrong/Davie:

Rik, a journalist for the Port Perry Star newspaper, specializes in criminal and court coverage. He is an honours graduate in Journalism from Durham College in Oshawa, Ontario.

Rik's somewhat clouded past includes a vast knowledge of, and a love of military history including trivia about clandestine military operations. Rik has written extensively on the use of police service dogs for such publications as Blue Line, a national police magazine, and has written on clandestine police operations for, among others, the Toronto Star. His prime goal in working on Word of Honour' was, "To keep 'em honest."

Rik lives near Port Perry, Ontario with his wife Linda. He is currently working on his first novel.

Lynn Philip Hodgson

Lynn Philip Hodgson has dedicated the past twenty-five years to bringing to light the tales of brave and courageous Canadians who fought in World War II's secret war. Their stories need to be told and he has done this in his best seller, 'Inside Camp-X'.

A businessman for over thirty-five years, Lynn is a proud Canadian, born in Toronto, Ontario. He has dedicated himself to assuring that the next generation will be aware of Canada's contributions to the successful outcome of WW II.

As research consultant in the publication of Joseph Gelleny's book, 'Almost' and as co-author with Alan Longfield for, 'Camp X The Final Battle' and 'Camp X Silver Dagger', and now 'Camp 30 Word of Honour', Lynn continues to work toward this goal. With two daughters, Renee and Karen and two grandsons, Geddy and Alex, Lynn and his wife Marlene of 39 years, live comfortably on Scugog Island in Port Perry.

E-mail Lynn @ info@camp-x.com web site: http://www.camp-x.com

Alan Paul Longfield

Alan Paul Longfield, B. A. (Queen's), M. Ed. (Toronto), has been investigating and documenting the history of Camp-X in collaboration with Lynn Philip Hodgson since 1977, as described in Lynn's best selling book, Inside Camp-X (1999, 2002 Rev.). A former Toronto resident, Alan has lived in Whitby Ontario for twenty-eight years, with his wife, Judi, Member of Parliament for Whitby/Ajax. Their son, Michael, who resides in Toronto, is a documentary film director. Alan retired in 1998 following a thirty-eight year career as an elementary school teacher, science consultant, and principal, with the former North York, (Toronto District School Board).

Camp 30 Word of Honour, is the fourth in a series of Camp-X co-productions with Blake Books Distribution, by Alan and Lynn. Previous partnerships include Camp X The Final Battle (2001), and Camp X Silver Dagger (2002.) The biographical, Almost (2000), the memoirs of a Canadian secret agent, was co-authored by Alan with the subject, Joseph Gelleny. Lynn served as project research consultant.

Alan can be contacted at alongfi@sympatico.ca